Wood 6112

1 2 SEP 2012

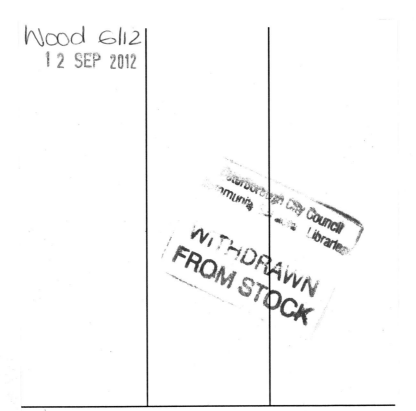

PETERBOROUGH LIBRARIES

24 Hour renewal line ~~08458 505606~~

This book is to be returned on or before the latest date shown above, but may be renewed up to three times if the book is not in demand. Ask at your local library for details.

Please note that charges are made on overdue books

THE THOUSAND EMPERORS

Gary Gibson

THE THOUSAND EMPERORS

TOR

First published 2012 by Tor
an imprint of Pan Macmillan, a division of Macmillan Publishers Limited
Pan Macmillan, 20 New Wharf Road, London N1 9RR
Basingstoke and Oxford
Associated companies throughout the world
www.panmacmillan.com

ISBN 978-0-230-74878-1

1 3 5 7 9 8 6 4 2

A CIP catalogue record for this book is available from
the British Library.

Typeset by Ellipsis Digital Limited, Glasgow
Printed and bound by CPI Group (UK) Ltd, Croydon, CR0 4YY

THE THOUSAND EMPERORS

In brief, then, human history can be split into two parts: the period occurring before the destruction of all life on Earth in the year 2235 C.E., and that following those terrible, final days.

At the time, a network of wormhole connections or 'transfer gates' linked Earth via its moon to its interstellar colonies, though few were aware that secret exploratory missions had uncovered the existence of a second, incomparably vast wormhole network, created by aliens we now call the Founders. Certain Founder artefacts were brought back to Earth with devastating results when one was somehow activated, leading to the sterilization of the Earth within days. If not for the deliberate destruction of the Lunar Gate Array, the same fate might also have been visited upon the colonies. It is this period we now call the Abandonment. The Western Coalition, as it was then known, having recognized that the Earth was doomed, initiated a rapid and successful military takeover of every colony apart from Galileo.

The decades following the Abandonment were hard, lean times, but barely half a century later starships carrying new, retro-engineered transfer gates were already being sent out to reconnect the colonies one to another. It is in this period that the template for the modern political order was laid down.

Although the Western Coalition – by this time, simply the Coalition – had seized political and military control of the colonial governments, the general populations of those worlds had been predominantly drawn from member nations of the former Asian Co-Prosperity Sphere. Coalition–Sphere relations were already deeply antagonistic prior to the Abandonment, and became more so, inevitably flowering into a full-fledged revolt a century after the Coalition's takeover.

The uprising proved to be bitter and protracted, but ended with several worlds finally achieving autonomy from Coalition rule. These worlds – Da Vinci (now Benares), Newton (now New Samarkand), Franklin (now Temur), Galileo (now Novaya Zvezda), Yue Shijie, and Acamar – became known collectively as the Tian Di, and were ruled from Temur by a council of revolutionary leaders numbering nearly a thousand. Although far from being a democracy, this Temur Council provided much-needed stability in the post-revolutionary period.

While the Tian Di and the Coalition co-existed in relative peace over the next several decades, they rapidly diverged both culturally and technologically. The Coalition first renewed and then stepped up its exploration of the Founder Network, despite increasingly alarmed protests from the Temur Council, whose members were afraid of a repeat of the events leading to the Abandonment.

It is undoubted that the Temur Council lacked for effective leadership in the years immediately preceding what we now call the Schism, and the power vacuum following Salomón Lintz's forced resignation as the Council's Chairman offered a clear opportunity for a man as ruthlessly determined as Joseph Cheng. Cheng soon swept to power on the wave of a popular coup, and the promise that he would sever all transfer gates linking to the Coalition to prevent any possible repeat of the Abandonment.

Cheng soon fulfilled his promise and, within days of becoming Permanent Chairman of the Temur Council, the human race was effectively split in two. Those few members of the Temur Council who had openly opposed Cheng's rise to power, including, most prominently, myself and Winchell Antonov, were either imprisoned, forced into exile, or executed on trumped-up charges.

It cannot be denied that the period immediately following the Schism was marked by unprecedented peace throughout the Tian Di. The quality of life for our citizens improved by such leaps and bounds that there was, for a long time, little to no demand throughout the

Tian Di for moves towards more democratic representation. The one real exception, of course, was Benares – a world of limited resources, cruelly under-represented within the Council. It was on Benares that Winchell Antonov, having escaped his imprisonment, founded the Black Lotus organization. Antonov is also credited with giving Cheng's Council the less than flattering sobriquet The Thousand Emperors.

At the time of writing, the Council continues to enjoy privileges unavailable to the wider population, most notably the instantiation lattices that grant them effective immortality through mind-state backups and cloned bodies. It is becoming harder for them to justify this exclusivity, now that the hardship of the post-Abandonment period and the violence of the Schism are little more than history lessons to the majority of the Tian Di's citizens. At the same time, calls for greater public participation in the running of the Tian Di are slowly beginning to grow, even on Temur. There are even calls to reunite with the Coalition which, expectations to the contrary, appears from our limited communications with them to have flourished in the intervening two centuries.

Such calls have long gone unanswered. Cheng has meanwhile begun to retreat more and more from public view, surrounding himself with a circle of trusted advisors known as the Eighty-Five, from whom little is heard bar the occasional official pronouncement.

To this day, there is much concerning Cheng's past that is dangerous to speak of publicly. The Council has worked hard to alter the facts of the past to suit its vision of our future, making it at times extraordinarily difficult to separate truth from fiction.

I write these words with no certainty that they will ever be read. But I am an optimist, even here in my prison, and it remains my hope that I can present to you, the reader – when or wheresoever you might be – some approximation of our true history in the following pages.

Excerpt from *A History of the Tian Di: Volume 1 – From Abandonment to Schism* by Javier Maxwell.

ONE

'Gabion.'

Luc turned to see Marroqui stabbing a finger at him from across the hold, his face dimly visible within his helmet.

'Close your visor, Goddamn it,' said Marroqui, his voice flat and dull in the cramped confines of the hold. 'Depressurization in less than thirty seconds. We're landing.'

Luc reached up and snapped his helmet's visor into place, ignoring the smirking expressions of the armour-suited Sandoz warriors arrayed in crash couches around him. They were crammed in close to each other, bathed in red light.

An alarm sounded at the same moment that the lander carrying them began to jerk with abrupt and sudden violence. Marroqui had warned him about this, explaining that the lander had been programmed with evasive routines designed to reduce the chances of their being shot down by hidden ordnance. Even so, the breath caught in Luc's throat, and he pictured the craft slamming into Aeschere's pockmarked face at a thousand kilometres an hour, scattering their shredded remains far and wide. But the shaking soon subsided, and he finally remembered to exhale, although his hands appeared unwilling to release their death-grip on the armrests of his couch.

The lander lurched gently, and the alarm stopped as suddenly as it had begun. They were down.

A ceiling-mounted readout showed the air pressure in the lander dropping to zero. The rumbling sounds of the craft's internal

4

workings soon faded away, leaving Luc with nothing but the sound of his own half-panicked breath.

Their harnesses parted all at once, sliding into hidden recesses as one wall of the hold dropped down, becoming a ramp leading onto the moon's surface. Thick dust, kicked up by their landing, swirled into the hold as the suited figures surrounding Luc climbed out of their couches, looking like an army of armoured bipedal insects as they moved down the ramp with practised efficiency.

The hydraulics in Luc's suit whined faintly as he followed, stepping onto the dusty floor of a crater about thirty kilometres across. He glanced back in time to see the lander leap upwards before its ramp had time to fully snap back into place, quickly receding to a distant dark spot against Grendel's cloudscape.

Luc hastened to keep up with the Sandoz warriors hustling towards the wall of the crater just a few hundred metres away. All around him he could see dozens of black hemispheres scattered across the crater floor.

Several black spheres thudded into the dust not far from him, dropped from orbit by some unmanned Sandoz scout ship. He saw one crack in half like an egg, disgorging a metal-limbed mechant barely larger than his fist. The machine span in a half-circle until it had acquired its target, then rushed ahead of him in a flurry of fast-moving limbs.

Being this up close and personal with a Sandoz Clan reminded Luc just how little he'd enjoyed the experience on every previous occasion he'd had the privilege. It was like bathing in an ocean of testosterone and barely suppressed rage. He saw the way they looked at him: a mere *Archivist*, for God's sake, some kind of jumped-up librarian from one of SecInt's less glamorous divisions and, worse, a civilian.

It was a common fallacy. He could have pointed out that rather than being a librarian, he was instead a fully accredited investigative agent, and that rather than being some minor part of SecInt, Archives was in fact that organization's primary intelligence-gathering resource. But it would just have been one more opportunity for Marroqui to bitch about having him tag along.

He had to remind himself that the Sandoz Clans looked down on everyone, not just him. Each Clan operated more like a family than anything resembling a traditional military unit, borne as they were out of a strange amalgam of religion, gene-tweaking and asceticism. They all spent their formative years training in the combat temples of Temur's equatorial jungles, and took advantage of instantiation technology otherwise reserved for members of the Temur Council. That, plus their unwavering and very nearly fanatical devotion to Father Cheng, made them close to unstoppable.

Luc's CogNet informed him that sunrise was less than one hundred and eight seconds away. Marroqui was cutting it close.

He stared ahead towards the crater wall, and the monastery entrance set into it. His eyes automatically moved up to regard the crater's rim, already incandescent from the approaching dawn. Grendel rose above Aeschere's horizon to the west, thick bands of methane and hydrogen wrapped around the gas giant's equator, glowing with the reflected heat of the star it orbited at a distance of just a few million kilometres. The sight of it made his skin crawl.

<Mr Gabion,> Marroqui scripted at him, <unless you've ever wondered what being cremated feels like, I wouldn't linger.>

And fuck you too, thought Luc, picking up the pace and racing to catch up with the rest. Grey dust like funeral ashes puffed up with every step.

It had all started with Luc's discovery of an insurgent data-cache in a vault on Jannah, an uninhabitable world of perpetual storms in the Yue Shijie system. Finding it had taken months of careful work, requiring the assembly of a team of specialists with experience in Black Lotus cryptanalysis. Before long a horde of Archivists had descended on the vault, and the information contained therein had led Luc finally to Grendel and Beowulf, two Hot Jupiters in the New Samarkand system.

He remembered running through Archives and almost colliding with Offenbach, the look of confusion on the Senior Archivist's face changing to one of delight once he realized Antonov had finally been cornered.

Within days, Father Cheng had ordered Sandoz forces to Grendel and Beowulf. They found Black Lotus weapons fabricants seeded throughout Grendel's sixteen moons, and machine had fought machine in a terrible war of attrition lasting months. Black Lotus's own fabricants had been unable, however, to produce defensive mechants in sufficient numbers to stand against a nearly endless stream of Sandoz hunter-seekers.

Luc was close enough now to the monastery entrance to see that its airlock had been blasted open, debris from the explosion fanning out across the crater floor. A long time ago, the complex on the far side of that airlock had been nothing more than a research installation. Much later, during the turmoil of revolution, it had been a prison, and finally a Lamasery in the peace that followed. The monks had called it *Wutái Shan*. Following that, it had been abandoned – or so it had been believed, until very recently.

<Sunrise in less than one minute,> Marroqui sent over the CogNet. Luc thought he sounded preternaturally calm, given they were seconds away from being burned alive. <Is the airlock definitely clear?>

<Mosquitoes demolished it,> someone else replied. <Whole upper level is depressurized. Mosquitoes report nothing moving on the next several levels down, either.>

<And below that?>

<Can't confirm, sir. Some 'skeets stopped responding. It might be solar interference with our comms, or they might have run into something unexpected. Can't say otherwise until we get inside and take a look.>

<Fine,> Marroqui replied. <Everyone in, on the double. Sunrise in just over thirty seconds.>

Luc's suit carried him through the blasted airlock with long, loping strides, then down a shadow-filled corridor. A few seconds later incandescent light flared behind him as 55 Cancri finally rose over the crater's lip.

Luc's CogNet displayed the passageway in bright false colours, making the mandalas carved into the walls on either side appear lurid and disturbing. As he made his way further along, he saw that the mandalas alternated with blank-eyed statues set into recesses. Behind him, the corridor grew sufficiently bright that his suit's filters were nearly overwhelmed. The outside temperature had just jumped by several hundred degrees.

Dead bodies loomed out of the dark, frozen in their final death-spasms, mouths open to the vacuum. Luc saw they had died just short of a pressure-field stretching across the passageway. Its soap-bubble surface trembled as he passed through it and into pressurized atmosphere.

He found Marroqui and the rest inside a derelict prayer hall. A golden-skinned Buddha sat cross-legged on a plinth at one end, holographic clouds drifting around its feet. A lotus blossom shimmered and unfolded in the statue's outstretched hand. Dusty prayer wheels still stood in their holders, listless tapestries hanging on the walls. The air appeared to be a standard breathable mix, with no detectable toxins or phages.

Marroqui was the first to retract his visor, soon followed by the rest. Luc breathed in freezing-cold air underlaid by a hint of sulphur. It wasn't hard to imagine the hall as it had been, filled with droning chants and the scent of sandalwood. Marroqui addressed his Clan-members in a Slavic dialect far removed from Luc's native Northam, his CogNet earpiece seamlessly auto-translating everything.

Luc meanwhile called up a three-dimensional map of the entire complex and saw it was composed of nine levels, each portrayed as a flat grey rectangle connected to the rest by cylindrical shafts of varying length. A pair of shafts located at opposite ends of this top level linked it to the next two down, while a second and third pair of shafts laced the middle and bottom three levels together respectively.

Luc dismissed the map once Marroqui had finished speaking to his troops. 'Can the mosquitoes tell us if Antonov is still alive?' he asked the Clan-leader.

Marroqui turned to regard him with undisguised irritation. 'They haven't given us visual confirmation one way or the other, if that's what you mean. Are you sure he's even here?'

'Quite sure,' Luc said stiffly.

Marroqui half-turned to look at his fellow Clan-members with a raised eyebrow and an expression of frank disbelief. Luc heard someone snicker.

'Well, what the mosquitoes *can* tell us is that we hit this complex a lot harder and faster than either Antonov or any of his Black Lotus fighters were clearly expecting,' said Marroqui, turning back to face Luc fully. 'Chances are we stepped over his corpse on the way in here. If you really want to be of help, you should stay behind and see if one of these bodies is his. The rest of us meanwhile can scout out the lower levels, and maybe figure out where those missing mosquitoes went to.'

Luc felt his face colour. *You can stay behind and clear up the litter while we do the real work*, was what Marroqui really meant.

It didn't take a genius to figure out he was desperately unwelcome. His temporary promotion to expedition leader had, he gathered, gone down very badly with Sandoz Command. But without his presence here, SecInt's role in tracking Antonov down would be reduced to not much more than a footnote.

And that would never do.

'Isn't assuming Antonov's already dead something of a dangerous assumption?' asked Luc.

'Haven't you *seen* how badly the 'skeets tore this place up?' Marroqui protested. 'Look – even if he somehow survived the initial assault, he's powerless. All his men are dead, and we've shattered his defences. Whether he's alive or not, you need to stay back here, and let us take care of things from here on in.'

Luc fought to keep his voice steady. 'You weren't at Puerto Isabel. I was there, with another Sandoz Clan. We had Antonov cornered, along with several Black Lotus agents. I made the mistake of listening to someone just like you telling me to step back and let them take care of things.'

Marroqui stared back at him with dagger eyes. 'And your point is?'

'That he *got away*,' said Luc, enunciating the words as if speaking to a recalcitrant child. 'I'm not going to make that mistake a second time.'

'If I'd been in charge of that raid, there wouldn't have been any screw-ups.'

'That's funny, because I'm getting a powerful sense of déjà vu every time you open your mouth,' Luc spat back.

'You're not seriously suggesting Antonov could *escape?*'

'Master Marroqui, I've spent half my damn life trying to find Winchell Antonov, and there's no way he'd wind up here without *some* kind of an exit strategy in place. Right now, my guess is that your missing mosquitoes have something to do with it.'

Marroqui's expression became incredulous. *Exit strategy?* Luc could almost hear him thinking. *Exit to where?* Snoop hunters hid in Aeschere's shadow cone, ready to challenge anything emerging from the moon's surface, while a fat-bellied intercept platform orbited above Grendel's dark side, its deep-range scanners sweeping the whole of 55 Cancri's inner system. And that wasn't even counting the autonomous units scattered throughout the rest of Grendel's moons.

And yet the fact remained that Antonov had managed to evade capture or assassination for nearly two centuries. Luc wanted desperately to be the one who finally caught the Tian Di's greatest fugitive, but the defeats and setbacks he had suffered over the years had taught him the value of caution.

'That's ridiculous,' Marroqui said quietly. 'Of *course* we can't hear from all of the 'skeets; solar storm's fucking our comms up.'

Which was entirely possible, and yet Luc couldn't avoid a nagging doubt that lingered in the pit of his stomach. It might have been safer for all concerned to pull back to the intercept platform and wait the storm out, but Luc felt sure that Antonov, if he *was* still alive, was waiting for just such an opportunity to slip past them. They had to make their move sometime in the next twenty hours, then escape before the storm reached its peak and lashed Grendel and its moons with fiery whips billions of kilometres in length.

It was Luc's call, of course, as expeditionary leader. If he was wrong, he'd pay for it with his career.

'It's going to be most of a day before the storm reaches its peak,' said Luc. 'If we've hit him as hard as you say, then we still have time to figure out why we're having comms problems before we go any further.'

Marroqui stepped up close enough to Luc that their noses were almost touching. 'You're just a bureaucrat,' he said, his voice soft. 'No, less than that: a glorified clerk. I have the safety and the honour of my Clan to consider. *I* say we go ahead and clear this damn place out *now*.'

'If you go against my orders,' Luc replied, 'you're going to find yourself in a shitstorm of trouble.'

'Like I give a damn,' Marroqui snapped, turning back to his soldiers and ordering them to split into separate teams, each to make its way down a different shaft before meeting up again at the reactor room.

Most of the soldiers voiced their affirmatives and made their way back out of the prayer hall, while a few stayed behind. Luc's hands tightened into fists by his sides, the frustration pooling inside him like a hot lava tide.

'How many of our 'skeets are primed with explosives?' Marroqui asked his second-in-command, a pale-skinned woman with a scar on one side of her nose.

'We've used up two, but we still have three left,' the woman replied.

'Fine. Once we've established line-of-sight with those missing 'skeets, let's send those three all the way down to the bottom and have them focus on taking out any automated defences or hunter-killers Antonov might have left waiting for us.'

Marroqui glanced back at Luc. 'You'll wait here, Mr Gabion. Someone has to monitor the uplink with the lander.'

'Your mosquitoes can monitor things just fine without my help. I'm coming with you and your men.'

Marroqui regarded him with distaste. 'You're from Benares, right?'

Luc stared back at him. In that moment, he finally understood the reason for Marroqui's unrelenting hostility. It had nothing to do with the rivalry between the Sandoz and SecInt; it was because he came from Benares.

'I don't know what they taught you in those combat temples they trained you in, Master Marroqui, but coming from Benares doesn't make me a traitor.'

'I never said—'

'So you can either take me down there with you,' Luc continued regardless, 'or take the risk of having to explain to our superiors why you let Antonov escape a *second* time, right on the eve of Reunification. Your choice.'

A muscle in one of Marroqui's cheeks twitched. For a moment Luc thought the Clan-leader might strike him, but instead the other man nodded curtly, his face impassive.

'You follow *every* order I give you while we're down there, instantly, and without question, until the moment the lander comes back to pick us up. Is that clear?'

Luc nodded. 'As crystal.'

'Shit. We've lost another mosquito,' said Marroqui's second in command, waiting by the entrance. 'No, hang on . . . that's another three out of contact, all in just the last minute.'

'What about the rest of the 'skeets?' asked Marroqui.

'They all check out,' she replied.

'We'd better get moving,' said Marroqui, abruptly businesslike. 'Anything out of the ordinary' – and with this, he glanced reflexively towards Luc – 'report it *immediately.*'

*

The entire complex turned out to still be pressurized. By the time they reached one of the shafts, mandalas and statues had given way to rough undecorated surfaces barely visible in the near-lightless gloom. Luc's IR filters showed an open elevator platform dead ahead, ringed by a steel rail. According to the map, the shaft went straight down for almost a kilometre. A faint breeze drifted up from below.

'How come these are working when the power's out?' he asked.

'They run on localized emergency power supplies,' said Marroqui. 'They have to, or there's no way out during a power failure. We shouldn't have to worry about getting down or back up.' He nodded to another woman, with chestnut skin, who had bent down on one knee to examine the interior of a control panel embedded into the wall close by the rail. 'How's it looking, Triskia?'

The woman made some final adjustment and snapped the panel shut before standing once more, her suit's servos whining faintly. 'It checks out, sir. No sabotage. We're good to go.'

Luc tried not to think about the Stygian depths beneath them as he followed Marroqui and four others onto the elevator plat-form. Even so, his heart nearly skipped a beat when the platform began its descent with a sudden, jerking motion.

Halfway to the next level down, updates from the mosquitoes flowed in through Luc's CogNet interface. His maps automatic-ally reconfigured themselves according to their incoming data, displaying rooms and corridors that had clearly not been part of the original complex.

'Any idea what Antonov might have been building down there?' Marroqui asked, referring to the new layout.

'Your guess is as good as mine,' Luc replied.

'Could be weapons caches,' suggested the woman called Triskia. 'Maybe he's still planning on fighting his way past us.'

Marroqui shook his head. 'I don't think so. He'd need bigger fabricants than the ones our mosquitoes have seen so far. If he's still alive, he's down to light weapons, nothing more.'

'Two of the other teams just called in, sir,' said one of Marroqui's men. 'They've reconnoitred at the reactor room, so they should be able to get the power going any—'

As if in answer, rows of lights stretching the length of the shaft blinked into sudden life. Luc squinted, bright phantoms chasing each other across the back of his eyelids. The next time he managed to open them properly, Marroqui and the rest were grinning and chuckling. As far as they were concerned, this was going to be a cakewalk.

The platform slowed, and Luc felt a tightening in his chest. He had the uncanny sense they had passed beyond some undefined point of no return. He glanced down through the metal grille beneath his feet, seeing twin rows of lights racing to meet each other in the shaft's murky depths.

They disembarked into a corridor leading deep inside Aeschere's bowels. Something whirred past Luc, and he jerked around in time to see a mosquito come to a nimble landing on the floor a metre or so from him.

As he watched, translucent plastic wings retracted into the machine's carapace. It turned this way and that, its movements jerky and curiously comical.

'It's one of ours,' he heard Triskia say. 'Why's it—?'

Triskia never got to finish her sentence. Luc watched with horrified anguish as she staggered, blood and bone misting the air as the back of her helmet exploded outwards.

Luc kicked out at the mosquito with one booted foot, sending it crashing into a wall. Marroqui screamed an order, and the air filled with noise and fury as his remaining men opened fire on the machine. By the time it was over, the mosquito lay still, its mirrored carapace blackened and ruined.

Marroqui knelt down beside the dead woman's prone form, swearing under his breath. He passed a finger over her forehead and muttered something that sounded like a prayer. One of the Sandoz's endless rituals, Luc guessed.

'Shig,' said Marroqui, looking back up at one of his men, 'what the hell just happened? *Was* that one of our 'skeets?'

'It was,' Shig replied, his face pale with shock. 'I don't understand why it . . .'

His voice trailed off.

'It doesn't make sense,' said Marroqui, standing back up and looking around. His previous swaggering bravado had all but deserted him now. 'There's no way Antonov could have compromised our comms encryption . . . is there?'

'It might explain why you lost contact with some of your mosquitoes,' said Luc, his voice cracking slightly.

Marroqui's hands twitched spasmodically at his sides. 'Impossible.'

Luc nodded down at Triskia's still form. 'Ask her if she agrees.'

'Ramp up your personal countermeasures,' said Marroqui, his voice edged with steel. 'Fire on *anything* that comes within range.'

'I think,' said Luc, 'this might be a good time to reconsider falling back. We can work out a new strategy—'

Marroqui turned to regard Luc, his nostrils flaring. 'No, Mr Gabion. We're Sandoz. Turning back at this point isn't an option.'

'Even if it means refusing my orders again?'

'Even then,' Marroqui muttered, hoisting his weapon and motioning to his Clan-members to move on.

Luc recalled what little he knew of the Sandoz credo, especially their refusal to surrender. It was going to be the death of them all.

Within the space of a few moments, the shadows and long, bleak reaches of the tunnels beneath Aeschere's surface had become infinitely more menacing. They passed shadowed cells, the walls around them marked with ancient graffiti. Despite the occasional distant buzz of plastic wings, the mosquitoes kept their distance.

Communications with the rest of the Clan, scattered throughout the complex, became increasingly sporadic. At one point they all heard a momentary burst of static from their comms, interspersed with screaming and what sounded like heavy weapons fire. After that, silence.

Marroqui still refused to turn back. They moved rapidly, reaching the fusion plant just a few minutes later. Once there, Luc almost stumbled over the corpse of another of Marroqui's men. The rest lay scattered around, their bodies and the walls surrounding them blackened from plasma fire.

'I still can't raise anyone else,' said a man with freckled skin, looking pale and terrified. Alert symbols drifted on the periphery of Luc's vision as he spoke.

'Is there *any* way we can reboot communications?' asked Marroqui. 'Or maybe reroute them?' His voice had become flat and emotionless, and Luc suspected this was the first time the Clan-leader had ever tasted defeat.

The other man laughed shrilly. 'Sure – standard operative procedure in a scenario like this is to route all our comms through the mosquitoes, but I don't think that's such a good idea.'

'One of us could still head back up top,' suggested one of the others. 'That way we could try and contact the lander by line-of-sight and ask for help.'

Marroqui shook his head wearily. 'It's a good idea, except that you'd have to wait for nightfall, and that isn't due for a few more hours.' He glanced at Luc. 'On the other hand, Mr Gabion, you really might be better off out of this. I could have one of my people escort you back up there and you can wait it out in that prayer room. I can't make any guarantees it's going to be any safer up there, but it might.'

Luc shook his head. 'I have to be there when you find Antonov.'

The Clan-leader's face reddened. 'The situation's changed, can't you see that? We're professionals, we know how to deal with this kind of situation. If you get killed down here, you're dead forever.'

'Doesn't matter,' Luc replied, holding the other man's gaze until Marroqui finally looked away, shaking his head.

'The control room for the entire complex is right below us on the next level down,' said one of the soldiers. 'Before they dropped out of contact, the 'skeets reported Antonov was using it as a command hub.'

'If someone's controlling our mosquitoes, that must mean there's someone still alive down there,' said another.

'Not necessarily,' said Marroqui. 'We can't rule out the possibility they're just running on automatic.'

'Or maybe your mosquitoes were compromised from the moment we walked in here,' Luc suggested.

They all stared at each other.

'Fuck it,' said Marroqui, breaking the silence and stepping over one of the blackened corpses on his way back into the corridor. 'There's only one way to find out.'

They made for another elevator platform, checked it for possible sabotage, and then climbed on board, riding it down in silence before disembarking on the next level down. Luc glanced over at one of Marroqui's squadron, hearing him mutter something repeatedly under his breath that sounded a lot like a prayer.

Marroqui had Luc keep to the rear as they advanced down a high-ceilinged passageway lined with tables and benches. They saw the bodies of more Black Lotus fighters, slumped across tables or curled up on the ground as if they were sleeping. The first wave of mosquitoes had killed them all.

They crowded through a narrow doorway and into the control room. An isometric plan of the entire complex hovered above a dais at the room's centre. All it took was a quick glance to see that it matched the updated version they had received from the mosquitoes.

The bodies of more of Marroqui's men were scattered around the dais, their faces contorted in death. Luc tasted the acid rush of bile as it surged up the back of his throat.

He glanced down, seeing through the steel grid flooring on which they stood that another room lay immediately below this one. Just visible were cryogenic pods of a design he recognized, lined against a wall: emergency medical units, designed for deep-space retrieval; almost tiny spaceships in their own right. Their status lights were dark, indicating they were empty. Clearly, Antonov's men had been slaughtered with such rapid efficiency, they had not even had time to place any of their injured inside the units.

They all heard the faint echo of something scuttling along the corridor beyond the control room entrance. Luc watched as Shig ducked outside for a look.

'Here they come!' Shig yelled, pulling the lower half of his body back around the door frame, then leaning out into the corridor and opening fire. A moment later he made a grunting noise, his feet giving way beneath him as he flopped backwards in the low gravity, red mist staining the air behind him.

Luc twisted around in mindless desperation, searching for another exit. He glanced back down through the thick metal grille and saw a ladder reaching down to the floor of the room below. Dropping to all fours, he peered through the grille. The top of the ladder terminated somewhere on the far side of the control room, hidden behind tall banks of equipment.

He ran past the dais and around the side of a tall steel cabinet in the same moment that Marroqui and his surviving Clan-members opened fire on something behind him. Set into the floor above the ladder was a flat metal hatch, but before he could reach down to pry it open, something picked him up and slammed him against the nearest wall.

He hit the floor a moment later, ears ringing, and felt it lurch beneath him like the deck of a ship caught in a storm. He had just enough time to work out there had been an explosion before the steel panels comprising the floor came apart from one another, sending him tumbling down into the room below, along with the contents of the control room. He just barely managed to scrabble out of the way of the steel cabinet before it landed on him. Someone's torso, still encased in plastic and metal armour, rolled and bounced as it hit the ground, coming to a halt just centimetres from his nose.

When he looked back up at the ceiling of the ruined control

room, he saw several mosquitoes gazing back down at him with insect-like eyes.

Managing to pull himself upright, he stumbled towards dim light spilling through a nearby doorway, squeezed past the dais from the upper floor, which had landed on its side, then ran blindly down a passageway until he stumbled across another elevator platform. He slammed the control panel with his fist and gripped the railing like a man adrift in a storm as it carried him down to the lowest level.

The platform came to a jerky halt at the bottom of the shaft, two rough-walled tunnels angling away from it in different directions. Luc headed down one at random, but didn't get far before more mosquitoes emerged from the gloom, tick-tacking through the still silence towards him. He retreated back the way he'd come and headed down the other tunnel instead, with the uncanny sense that he was being herded in one particular direction – proof, if any were still needed, that Antonov must still be alive.

'I'm here, Antonov!' he shouted, and heard the hysteria creeping into his voice. Grabbing a metal bar from a pile of junk, he wielded it like a weapon, then laughed at the ridiculousness of it. He couldn't possibly defend himself from mosquitoes while armed with nothing more than a chunk of scrap metal, but there was something comforting about the feel of it gripped in his armoured fist nonetheless.

More mosquitoes emerged from the gloom up ahead, but they scuttled backwards at his approach, clearing the way.

'Are you there?' Luc shouted again. 'Show yourself, Goddamn it! Show your fucking face!'

Turning a corner, he found himself at the entrance to a cavern dug out of the rock, a deactivated digging machine at the far end sitting next to a mound of excavated rubble. He swallowed in the dry air, then set his eyes on something that took his breath away.

A transfer gate, embedded into one wall of the cavern.

At first Luc couldn't quite convince himself it was real. A thick metal torus surrounded the mouth of what might otherwise have been nothing more than the entrance to a passageway, leading him to wonder if it had only been tricked up to *look* like the mouth of a transfer gate. Any other conclusion meant accepting the notion that Black Lotus now had access to the kind of technology that permitted the construction of stable, linked wormhole pairs – the same technology that enabled passage between the worlds of the Tian Di.

He stepped up to the gate and saw it consisted of a short cylindrical passageway, no more than a couple of metres in length, a metal walkway suspended over its floor. He gazed into the interior of a room on the far side. The floor of the room was at an angle with respect to the cavern in which he stood, indicating that the gate and its opposite end had not been correctly aligned. Dense metal plating hid the wormhole's horizon, the tori ringing each mouth of the gate shielding a core of highly exotic matter without which the wormhole could not exist. And if all that wasn't evidence enough, he could feel the hairs on his arms and scalp standing up, an epiphenomenon caused by inadequate shielding on the containment fields.

It was real, all right. That room might be located in another part of the complex, or might be light-years away, in some entirely different star system. There was, after all, no limit to how widely separated the two mouths of a wormhole could be.

Luc stepped onto the walkway and felt even Aeschere's minimal gravity drop away once he was halfway across, meaning the far end of the gate was almost certainly on board a spacecraft of some kind. He stepped off the walkway at the far end, drifting through the air until he came to a stop against the wall opposite.

This, then, was Antonov's exit strategy. Luc couldn't help but feel a little awed at the scale of the man's planning.

He heard laboured breathing from behind, and turned to find Winchell Antonov propped against a bulkhead to one side of the gate entrance, one of his hands pressed over a dreadful chest-wound, his skin pale and waxy. His breath came in long, drawn-out gasps, and his thick, dark beard glistened with sweat.

'I'm impressed,' he grunted, fixing his gaze on Luc. 'Really, I am.'

Winchell Antonov: once the Governor of Benares, later the leader of Black Lotus, the single greatest threat the Temur Council had ever faced. In that moment he looked small, despite his nearly six and a half foot frame.

'It's over, Antonov,' Luc heard himself say, his voice ragged. 'It's time to give up.'

Antonov chuckled, then drew his breath in sharply, squeezing his eyes shut and clutching at his wound.

Something click-clacked from nearby. Luc turned to see that several mosquitoes had hopped onto the walkway bridging the wormhole, their tiny needle-like weapons aimed towards him.

'I fear,' grunted Antonov, 'that we find ourselves at a mutual impasse.'

'There's nothing left to fight for,' said Luc. 'Even if you kill me, the Sandoz are going to tear this place apart until they find you.'

Antonov squinted up at him, one corner of his mouth twitching upwards in a grin. 'Aren't you the least bit curious why you're still alive?'

'You want to know what I care about?' asked Luc. 'I'm from Benares. Black Lotus carried out an orbital assault on Tian Di forces stationed there on *your* orders.'

'Ah.' Antonov nodded. 'The Battle of Sunderland, you mean.'

'That decision wiped out half a continent. My parents, my brother and sister – they all died in that attack, along with almost everything I'd ever known. Since then, the only thing I ever really gave a damn about was finding you. You took my life away.'

'Then you might be interested to know that Black Lotus never carried out that assault,' said Antonov, his voice growing weak. 'Father Cheng ordered that attack, and blamed it on us.'

Luc wanted to tear that deathless smirk off Antonov's face with his bare hands. He was the devil made flesh, the Prince of Lies embodied in a man who'd been on the run for longer than Luc had even been alive.

Again, the metallic click of a mosquito manoeuvring on some surface.

He glanced up to see his own face staring back at him from the mirrored carapace of a mosquito clinging to the ceiling overhead with needle-like limbs.

Something stung his neck and he reached up to slap it. A moment later he felt a sudden, numbing coolness spread across his chest, quickly penetrating his skull.

The room reeled about him, his legs giving way beneath him as he collapsed.

Luc opened his eyes to the harsh actinic glare of overhead lights and found himself bound by a length of cord into a chair on the spacecraft's bridge. He had been stripped of his powered suit, and wore only the thin cloth one-piece overall given him by Sandoz technicians prior to boarding the lander. Projections hovered in the air all around him, and when he tried to move, his body obeyed only with extreme sluggishness. Whatever drug he'd been shot full of was clearly still working its magic on him.

Antonov stood by the chair, one hand still clutched to his injured chest as he gazed down at Luc. Even so, Antonov didn't look nearly as weak as he had in the moments before Luc had lost consciousness.

Behind Antonov, Luc could see a single mosquito, balanced on a railing on the opposite side of the bridge, peering back at him with mindless intent.

'What are you doing?' he demanded through lips that were half-numb.

'Quiet now,' Antonov muttered, leaning in towards him. Luc saw for the first time that the Black Lotus leader was clutching something in his free hand that squirmed as if alive. 'This is going to be tricky.'

Antonov lifted his other hand away from his chest wound and winced, then used it to tug Luc's head back against the chair's headrest, holding it there. Luc found himself staring almost straight up at the ceiling of the bridge.

Breathing hard, afraid of whatever it was Antonov was about to do to him, Luc twisted his hands and feet in their restraints to no avail. However, he had the sense that whatever paralytic Antonov had hit him with was slowly starting to wear off.

'Careful now,' Antonov warned, giving him a reproachful glare. 'I can knock you out again if you keep struggling, but you really need to be conscious during this. Otherwise there's a serious risk of brain damage.'

Brain damage? Panic tightened Luc's chest. He could just about see the squirming thing in Antonov's hand from out of the corner of one eye, struggling to escape. It was clearly a mechant of some kind, not unlike a segmented worm in appearance but barely the length of a finger. Its body glittered in the light.

'What the fuck is that?' Luc managed to gasp.

'This,' said Antonov, with apparent pride, 'is a delivery system for the greatest gift I could possibly give you.'

Luc had a sudden intuition of what Antonov might be about to do to him, and tried to twist free. The heavy cord binding him to the chair creaked loudly, but did not give.

Antonov slapped him hard across the face, and Luc grunted with shock.

'I told you,' said Antonov, 'keep still. For your own sake, do not struggle.'

Antonov next stepped behind Luc, wrapping one meaty forearm around his head and rendering him more thoroughly immobile. Luc's nostrils filled with the scent of the other man's unwashed skin, and he wondered how a man so badly injured could still have so much strength.

Something cold squirmed against Luc's upper lip, then jammed itself hard inside his right nostril.

The pain that followed was indescribable. He could hear a sound like chewing, as if something were forcing its way through the gristle and bone of his skull. He screamed, jerking and twisting in his restraints, jaw locked in a rictus grin of terror.

As terrible as it was, the pain faded to a numb ache after another minute. His body spasmed a few times, then became still. Sweat cascaded across Luc's skin, his chest rising and falling with the nervous energy of a hummingbird.

Antonov stepped back in front of him, looking noticeably paler than he had a few moments before. 'I suppose you're wondering just what a transfer gate's doing here,' he said, and let out a weak chuckle. 'That's the understatement of the year, right? Well, now that we're the only ones left alive down here, I don't see any reason not to tell you why.'

Antonov moved to lean against a nearby console, his face very nearly bone-white. 'We're on board a spaceship, as I'm sure you've guessed by now. We kept it in close orbit around 55 Cancri, since the photosphere of a star often proves to be a good hiding place. Once we knew the Sandoz were on their way here, we plotted a course to slingshot this ship towards the outer system, but even that wasn't enough to give us the velocity we needed to get out of range of your intercept missiles. They're chasing us right now, and they'll catch us sooner or later.'

'Where' – Luc swallowed, feeling like he hadn't uttered a word in a thousand years – 'where are you taking this ship?'

'We have other redoubts,' Antonov replied, 'scattered throughout this system and in others. We would have severed the wormhole link once we were all on board except now, it appears, I'm the only one left alive.'

'Then it's over,' Luc managed to croak. 'This isn't how you want it to end, Winchell.'

Antonov shook his head with evident amusement. 'What's the alternative? Surrender myself to you, so Father Cheng can orchestrate my execution on the eve of our glorious Reunification with the Coalition? I'd rather choose my own fate – and with that in mind, you might care to know I've set the ship on a course that will send it plunging back into the heart of the star it so recently orbited.'

Luc stared at him, speechless.

'Now, I don't know just how *au fait* you are with wormhole physics,' Antonov continued, his face twisting up in pain as he spoke, 'but they're surprisingly robust under certain conditions. Once this ship's descended far enough into 55 Cancri's photosphere, the shielding will give way and the transfer gate linking it back to Aeschere will be destroyed. However – and this is the theory – the wormhole *should* maintain coherence just long enough for a great deal of superheated plasma to come rushing into the complex.'

'Why? Why not just . . . surrender?'

'For many reasons, Mr Gabion, but chiefly because Cheng would never let me live, knowing the things that I know.'

Luc shook his head in incomprehension. The inside of his head felt as if it had been hollowed out. 'What things?'

Antonov chuckled. 'You need,' he said, 'to make your way back up to that control room where you left your friends, back on the other side of the transfer gate. There are cryogenic units there – do you understand?'

'No. No, I don't.'

'Oh, but I think you do. Get yourself inside one of those units, and you should have a decent chance of surviving the inferno.'

'But *why?*' Luc demanded. 'Why—'

But before he could say anything further, Antonov reached out to touch the side of his neck with something cold and sharp, and he lost consciousness once more.

Listen to me, Luc. You're still asleep.

Antonov's voice sounded like it came from everywhere and nowhere. Luc found himself afloat in a dreamless void, unable to determine where he was, or how long it had been since he had been knocked out. His limbs felt like a distant memory.

You're going to wake up soon, he heard Antonov continue. *There's a lot you don't understand yet, but you will, given time. But first, you must deliver a message for me.*

What message? Luc tried to say, but he couldn't feel his lips or his tongue.

The answer came a moment later:

After they come and rescue you, I want you to access Archives through your CogNet link. Then open a record with the following reference: Thorne, 51 Alpha, Code Yellow. Do you understand?

No, Luc answered. *I—*

Once you've done that, add the following statement to the text file contained within it: 'I'm calling in my favour.' Five words, Luc. That's all I ask.

I don't understand, Luc shouted into the abyss.

Someone did something a long time ago they shouldn't have, said Antonov, his voice slowly fading. *And now they're going to repay me for keeping it quiet all these years. Remember what I said, Luc: 'I'm calling in my favour.'*

As if a switch had been thrown, Luc had control of his limbs once more, and could feel something hard beneath his back. His eyes flickered open in the same moment he realized his CogNet link was live once more, and he discovered more than four hours had passed since he had first entered the complex in the company of an entire squadron of Sandoz. Night would by now have fallen across the crater, meaning it was safe to go back out onto the surface.

Even more importantly, he was free. The tangled loops of cord that had bound him now floated loose around the chair in which he was still slumped.

Reaching up, he tentatively touched his head, exploring the contours of his skull. There had been something dreamlike about the whole encounter with Antonov, as if it hadn't really happened, but when he touched fingers to his nose he found it crusted with dried blood.

Updates flooded in through his now-active CogNet: he learned that two more Sandoz squadrons had already entered the complex's top level, and were working their way down towards him without meeting any resistance, machine or otherwise.

Luc pulled himself out of the chair, then stopped, seeing Antonov slumped against the railing on the far side of the bridge, head bowed forward. Luc kneeled before him and touched fingers to the rebel leader's wrist. Dead.

Then he glanced towards the main display and felt a chill form around his heart.

<This is Luc Gabion,> he sent via the CogNet. <Can anyone hear me?>

<This is Master Siedzik here,> someone replied. <You're the only one whose vital signs are showing, Mr Gabion. Where are Marroqui and the rest of his Clan?>

<They're all dead,> Luc responded. <I'm the only survivor.>

Siedzik didn't reply for some time, and Luc guessed he was conferring with his superiors on the orbital platform.

<Where exactly are you?> Siedzik sent back. <We can't get a location fix on you.>

That, Luc knew, was because he was no longer beneath the surface of Aeschere, but on board a starship some millions of kilometres distant. The only reason they could converse at all was because the ship's communication network was automatically bouncing his CogNet link back through the connecting gate. But there wasn't the time to try and explain all that to Siedzik, even assuming he'd believe one word of the explanation.

<I'm on the lowest level,> Luc replied after a pause. <Antonov compromised our mosquitoes and set them to attack Marroqui and the rest of his Clan. Antonov's here, but he's dead. I don't know if that means the mosquitoes still down here won't attack you, but I'd urge being *extremely* fucking cautious one way or the other.>

<Stay where you are,> Siedzik commanded. <We'll be with you shortly.>

<No,> Luc sent back. <You need to head back up to the surface. I think Antonov's set some kind of a booby-trap.>

<What kind of—>

<I'll let you know when I find out,> Luc replied, cutting the connection before Siedzik could demand any more details.

He pulled himself into a navigation booth surrounded by interface and astrogation gear. The ship linked into his CogNet just long enough for it to work out he didn't know how to operate the navigational systems, and replaced most of the scrolling data surrounding him with a series of simplified questions and help menus.

It didn't take long for Luc to work out that Antonov had not, in fact, been lying: the ship had already dipped into the turbulent upper reaches of 55 Cancri's photosphere, and the external temperature was already a couple of thousand degrees beyond the craft's design parameters. He had minutes, perhaps only seconds, before it shattered under the strain.

He stood jerkily, skin clammy with sweat, and pushed himself towards the exit from the bridge. It took another couple of minutes of fumbling and swearing in the zero gee before he managed to navigate his way back to the bay containing the transfer gate.

Luc sailed through the gate and back into Aeschere's hollowed-out heart, sidestepping millions of kilometres in the blink of an eye. The little moon's gravity took hold of him as soon as he was through, tugging him down towards the dusty floor of the cavern. Without the benefit of his spacesuit, it was numbingly cold, every breath filling his lungs with icy daggers.

An icon blinked in the corner of one eye: Siedzik.

<Gabion. We've got a fix on you now and we're on our way to your current location,> Siedzik sent as soon as Luc activated the link. <Stay right where you are.>

<Get out,> Luc sent back. <I told you to head for the surface. You need to get out *now*.>

Luc caught a brief flash of Siedzik's visual feed, and saw Siedzik and several more Sandoz warriors making their way towards an elevator platform at the far end of the complex.

<I am *not* of a mind to accept orders from civilians,> Siedzik responded. <So when I tell you—>

<Screw your stupid fucking rules! I said this place might be booby-trapped, and it is. It's going to go up any minute.>

He stumbled back the way he had come, towards the nearest shaft and another elevator platform. His legs were still half-numb from Antonov's paralytic, making it hard to run, and he caught sight of several mosquitoes lying inactive in the dust, their legs neatly folded beneath their tiny bodies.

The air misted white as he panted for breath, the cold sinking deeper and deeper into his flesh. It was almost funny; even if he managed to avoid being engulfed in white-hot plasma, he'd still be running a serious risk of hypothermia.

Reaching the platform, he slammed its control panel with one hand, then collapsed onto all fours, hooking his fingers through the metal grille as he was carried back up. It clanged to a stop a minute later, and Luc ran as best he could, until he was back at the control room where Marroqui and his Clan-members had died.

At the same moment he reached the threshold of the control room, the ground beneath his feet began to tremble, at first gently but then with greater violence. A deep bass murmur rolled up from the depths of the complex.

He was out of time.

Most of the cryogenic pods that hadn't been buried beneath falling debris had clearly suffered massive damage from the explosion that had devastated the control room. Only one appeared to have escaped unscathed – unlike the rest, its control panel still glowed softly in the dust-filled darkness.

Luc headed straight for it, the rumbling all the while growing louder and closer. He tore the lid open and climbed inside, listening to the exhausted rattle of his own breath as he lay back.

The lid clicked back into place above him. An internal light came on, low and red. Icons and menus appeared around him, filling the coffin-like space.

He selected an option marked Critical Emergency, bypassing

everything else. A soft hiss began from somewhere just above his head, and he became drowsy within moments.

The roaring grew in volume. Hammer blows began to rain down on the pod at the same moment that a deep chill spread through his bones.

He tried to take a breath, and then another. On the third try, the breath froze in his lungs, and for the third time that day he sank into bottomless darkness.

TWO

Luc dreamed.

He was six years old again, running through a field beneath a curving transparent dome, the sun dropping towards the peak of Razorback Mountain and dazzling his eyes. His hands brushed against stalks of wheat as he ran, ignoring the field-mechant that kept pace with him, warning of the consequences of trespassing.

Something huge flitted through the sky above the biome's ceiling, moving so fast he barely had time to register its passage. He stopped to stare, seeing the dark silhouettes of Council stinger-drones following in close pursuit. A copse of seaweed bushes beyond the biome's transparent wall stirred beneath a sudden breeze, sending startled lizard-wings spinning upwards from their perches to scatter across the sky.

Light flared on the horizon, a second sun rising to meet the first. He saw the peak of Razorback Mountain melting as the firestorm engulfed it.

The ground beneath Luc's feet shook, and he turned to run back the other way, back to the safety of home.

Luc became aware of bright smears of light that made his eyes hurt. Round, pink blobs that might have been faces hovered indistinctly before him. He took a breath, and realized his lungs were filled with some form of liquid, thick and viscous. Panic seized him until he realized he wasn't drowning. Someone had put him into a recovery tank.

I'm still alive, he realized. The dream was still fresh in his mind. It was an old one, but it had never happened in reality. If he'd really been home on Benares during the Battle of Sunderland, he'd have died along with millions of others.

He could make out just enough of his reflection in the tank's transparent wall to see that something was terribly wrong.

<Antonov. Where . . . ?>

One of the pink blobs came closer, resolving into a sallow-faced man with a close-shaved skull, wearing the uniform of a Temur medician.

<Good. You're responding.>

Luc twisted his head back, seeing bright lights shimmering overhead. <Aeschere. I need to know what—>

<There'll be time for that later,> the medician scripted in reply, then turned to someone behind him. <Put him back under.>

<No, wait—>

Any further protests died on Luc's lips.

There were several more such brief episodes of lucidity, each one slightly longer than the last, including one in which Luc found himself being questioned by a medician who never bothered to give his name. He showed Luc CogNet-mediated video of his extraction from the twisted wreckage of the cryogenic unit that had saved his life, but only just.

He couldn't recognize the raw, burned slab of meat in the video, couldn't connect it to himself. The medician allowed him to see himself through the eyes of lenses dotted around the recovery room. He was submerged in a fluorocarbon-rich gel, his body half-hidden amongst a tangle of sensor leads, his flesh burned and flayed. Shoals of tiny black things like tadpoles swarmed around his legs and lower back with apparent purpose, while his face had been reduced to little more than sheets of exposed muscle laid over the skull beneath.

The medician asked questions that Luc tried to answer, sticking to script-speak since Luc's newly-grown throat and larynx hadn't quite finished healing. He learned the cryo-unit had put most of its energy into protecting his head and brain once the temperature of the plasma began to push it beyond its operational parameters. As a result, many of Luc's organs and muscles had been replaced using fast-track tissue work. Even so, the work was going fast, and it might only be another day or two before they were able to lift him out of the tank.

The medician departed, and Luc soon drifted back into a drug-induced sleep. A new dream came to him, disturbing because it felt more like a memory than anything else. He found himself staring into a convex mirror surrounded by folds of dark cloth, but instead of his own face, he saw that of Winchell Antonov reflected there. Antonov's lips moved in silence, his expression full of bitter anger.

The rapidity with which they healed him was astonishing. Each time the medicians brought him back to consciousness, Luc found the pain was a little less than it had been, until finally it was reduced to not much more than a dull ache.

The Chief Medician had Luc decanted from his tank and moved to a room with an actual bed. His new skin felt ridiculously soft and delicate, as insubstantial as rice-paper origami that might come undone in the slightest breeze. The sensation of soft linens against his body was a wonder in itself.

It wasn't long before he got his first visitors. Eleanor Jaq walked into the room, her lithe form wrapped in a SecInt uniform, long brown hair tucked into a small bun at the back of her head. The last time he'd seen her, she'd told him they were finished, and so her arrival was more than a little unexpected.

She wasn't alone. Her companion was Isaak Lethe, SecInt's

Director of Operations, his brow marked by worry-lines. He took a seat to one side of Luc's bed, the corners of his mouth jerking up in a half-smile as if this were the same as any other debriefing. Eleanor remained standing, her expression carefully neutral.

'Mr Gabion,' said Lethe. 'You're looking a lot better than you did when they first brought you in here.'

'I've had better days,' Luc croaked, his voice scraping like rusted razors. He tried to catch Eleanor's eye, but she glanced away. 'Just how long have I been here?'

'You got back to Temur just a couple of days ago,' Lethe replied. 'Medician Merlino told me how much work they had to do on you.'

'Apparently,' said Luc, 'they had to replace pretty much everything.'

'They also rolled your age back about a half-decade or so. My understanding is that made things easier for them.'

'You were lucky,' said Eleanor, eyes finally settling on him. Her nostrils flared slightly, a sure sign she was still angry at him, despite everything he'd been through. '*Really* lucky.'

'I know you're only just out of the tank, but I need to talk to you about what happened on Aeschere,' said Lethe, his expression becoming apologetic. 'I know you probably don't feel ready for it.'

Luc shook his head. 'It's fine. What do you need to know?'

'Sandoz Command are facing questions over how they managed to lose an entire Clan on what should have been a straightforward operation. And it's not like we can ask Marroqui or any of the rest of them what happened.'

'Why not? They'll be re-instantiated, won't they?'

'Yes, and Karlmann Sandoz has already given the order to prep their clone bodies. Unfortunately, since the explosion that destroyed the complex left no trace of them . . .' Lethe regarded him from beneath shaggy eyebrows.

Meaning, Luc guessed, that their instantiation lattices had also been destroyed. 'So they won't be able to reboot them from the point when they were actually killed,' Luc finished for him. 'I get it.'

'Which makes you our only material witness to what happened down there,' Lethe continued. 'The version of Master Marroqui they're about to shovel into a new body hasn't even heard of you. That means at some point you're going to find yourself standing in front of an investigative committee, possibly several of them. And they're all going to ask difficult questions.'

'And that's why you're here?'

Lethe smiled stiffly. 'Actually, it concerns Antonov. You told a Sandoz investigator he was still alive when you reached the lowest level of the complex.'

Luc shook his head. 'I don't recall speaking to anyone from the Sandoz.'

'They sent one of their own here to interrogate you without getting our clearance first,' Lethe explained. 'You were still only half-conscious at the time. One of the medicians told me it's unlikely you'd recall any of it. I filed a protest and managed to get the details of what you told the investigator. So Antonov – was he still alive?'

Luc nodded. 'He was, yes.'

'You also told him Antonov compromised Marroqui's mosqui-toes.'

'Also correct.'

'*Mostly* correct. It turns out those mosquitoes were still trans-mitting some data back to the orbital platform parked around Grendel.'

Luc sat up with extreme care. 'So you managed to recover at least some data?'

Lethe nodded. 'Enough to prove your version of events. Up to a point.'

Up to a point. 'Go on,' said Luc, sensing Lethe was leading up to something.

'Your CogNet link stopped recording just before you reached the lowest level of the complex, and didn't start again until you contacted Master Siedzik. That means we have *no idea* what happened during the period it wasn't functioning.'

'You think Antonov compromised it in some way?'

Lethe ignored the question. 'Apparently you told this investigator that after your encounter with Antonov, you headed straight for the cryo units, but not before sending a warning to Siedzik. Why?'

'Antonov told me he was going to destroy the complex. He even told me the cryogenic pods were my best bet at staying alive.'

'Let me just be clear on this. Antonov *told* you he was going to trigger a detonation?' asked Lethe.

Luc shook his head. 'It wasn't a bomb or anything like that. Antonov had a transfer gate set up down there on the lowest level, connected to a ship orbiting close to 55 Cancri's photosphere. He set the ship to dive into the sun before knocking me out. When I woke up he was dead, and I checked the readings in one of the navigation booths for just long enough to see he hadn't been lying.'

They both stared at him like he'd started barking profanities.

'Didn't I tell the investigator . . . ?'

'No, you didn't,' said Lethe, looking outraged. 'A *transfer* gate? How the hell could Antonov get his hands on technology like that?'

'I have no idea,' said Luc, 'but I swear to you it's the truth. He was badly wounded, dying.'

Luc stopped, his head throbbing with sudden, unexpected pain. It wasn't hard to guess Lethe didn't believe a word.

'How badly wounded?' asked the Director.

Luc swallowed with some difficulty. Sharp spikes of pain radiated from inside his skull, getting worse with every passing second. 'He had a deep chest wound. At first I thought he was too weak to be any danger. But he fooled me. He managed to dose me, then drag me through to the ship's bridge.'

'Why in Heaven didn't Antonov just kill you?' asked Lethe. He had a look on his face like a man trying to figure out a particularly intractable puzzle, one he was sure contained some central flaw that, once identified, would cause all the rest to fall apart.

'I don't know. By the time I came to, he was dead and the ship was locked into its course. All I could do was get the hell out. I made my way back through the gate and up to the higher levels.'

'And the rest of Antonov's people?' asked Eleanor. 'The Black Lotus insurgents?'

Antonov put something inside my head, Luc wanted to say, but as soon as the thought crossed his mind, sweat burst out all over his newly-minted skin, the pain in his skull doubling.

It felt almost like something was trying to stop him talking about it. He gripped the bed sheets, twisting the soft cotton around his fingers.

'Are you okay?' asked Eleanor, stepping around the side of his bed and placing one hand on his upper arm. The sensation of her fingers against his skin was almost unbearably sensual. She glanced back at Lethe. 'Maybe we shouldn't . . .'

'No,' Luc gasped. 'It'll pass.'

He saw Eleanor and Lethe exchange a look.

'Look,' said Lethe, 'if we go to an investigative committee and try and tell them Antonov had transfer gate technology without any proof, there's going to be hell to pay. There are already questions about how badly you might have been affected by the trauma of what happened to you.'

'You don't believe me,' Luc said hollowly.

Lethe sighed. 'It's not a question of whether *I* believe you or not.'

'Just other people.'

'Even if there really was a transfer gate down there, Aeschere's got a low enough average density that the explosion, or whatever the hell it was, brought the roof down on half the complex. It'd take months, maybe years to dig down far enough before we could even *begin* to verify your story. Come to think of it, it was probably sheer damn luck you didn't wind up buried under half a million tons of rock along with everything else.'

'So you think Antonov was never there, that I hallucinated the whole damn thing. Is that it?'

'No, he was definitely there,' Lethe replied. 'We managed to get visual corroboration of that much, at least, from Black Lotus's own security networks just prior to the raid. It looks like he died there as well. Whether I believe there was a transfer gate or not doesn't really matter, not without hard evidence. With no CogNet data and no proof to the contrary, any committee you wind up in front of is going to dismiss every word that comes out of your mouth.'

Luc opened his mouth to protest, but then realized that if their roles had been reversed, he'd have said exactly the same damn thing. He'd have assumed the story about the transfer gate was a delusion, triggered by the dreadful trauma of having half his body burned away.

But it *had* been real. He could feel it, deep in his bones. The proof was in his skull, put there by Antonov. All he had to do was tell them, but even the thought of doing so filled his head with a furious ache.

'I was pretty torn up, right?' Luc managed to blurt. 'When they pulled me out of that cryo unit, they must have scanned me pretty thoroughly, inside and out.'

Lethe frowned, then gestured at something behind him. A mechant drifted forward until it hovered just centimetres above the bed, its sensors directed at Luc.

The ache grew worse. It took all Luc's strength just to force the next words out.

'Listen to me,' he gasped. 'In my head. Antonov put—'

The pain escalated beyond all endurance. His body snapped rigid as something tore at the inside of his head. He was vaguely aware through the haze of agony that two human orderlies had come rushing into the room.

The mechant reached out and did something to his arm where it lay on top of the sheets. Everything began to recede, as if he were seeing the hospital room and its occupants from down the far end of a long, dark tunnel. The pain wasn't any less, but he found he no longer cared about it.

He experienced a kind of fugue, and the next thing he knew lights were slipping by overhead as he was taken somewhere else. Then there were more mechants, and other, unfamiliar faces, and finally another room where he was given into the care of a machine that pressed in close all around him.

Whatever they'd pumped into his veins, it felt good.

He came to, and saw Eleanor standing by a window, staring out across the rooftops of Ulugh Beg. Night had fallen. There was no sign of Lethe.

'What . . .'

She turned and blinked red-rimmed eyes at him, almost as if she'd forgotten he was there.

'. . . the fuck?' he finished, his voice a harsh croak.

She came over to him. 'You had some kind of seizure. They're still not sure what happened.'

He managed to push himself upright in the bed, and saw he was back in the same room as before. 'Well, that's less than reassuring.'

'They ran a bunch of scans on you to see what triggered it, but they didn't find anything.'

Luc stared at her in disbelief. 'What kind of scans?'

'I don't know,' she said. 'You'd have to ask one of the mechants.' She nodded towards one that hovered inconspicuously by the door.

Luc did. 'Deep tissue and tomographic scans were carried out,' it replied, drifting closer. 'No lesions or other possible causes of a cerebral seizure were found.'

'What about Merlino, the medician?' Luc asked, turning back to Eleanor. 'What exactly did he say?'

'He said they can't be sure of anything until they carry out further tests. He didn't exactly say it, but from what I can tell they don't have the faintest idea just what happened to you.'

'But the scans must have found *something*,' Luc demanded, turning his attention back to the mechant.

'Nothing of note was found,' the machine replied, its voice soft and neutral.

He turned back to Eleanor. 'No,' he said. 'That's not possible.'

She stared at him uncomprehendingly. 'Luc . . . what else *should* there be?'

'Antonov put something inside my skull,' he replied, then halted in amazement. The last time he'd tried to say those same exact words, he had been subjected to more pain than he thought was possible. It didn't make sense.

He told her everything he remembered about his encounter with Antonov, leaving nothing out this time, and she listened with one hand over her mouth. It felt like cauterizing a wound. Once he'd finished, she called the mechant back over and asked it more questions of her own.

In response, it displayed projections of the interior of his skull. Beyond some minor lesions that might have triggered a *grand mal* fit, nothing untoward or unexpected had been found.

Luc listened in grim silence, and began to wonder if perhaps he really *had* imagined the whole thing.

'If you think I'm crazy,' he said after she had sent the mechant away, 'try and keep it to yourself, will you?'

She regarded him with something like pity. 'You mean, no crazier than you were before?'

He sighed. 'What happened to Lethe?'

'I told him I'd stay with you and let him know once you came to.'

'Sorry,' he said.

'For what?'

He shrugged. 'For scaring you like that.'

She nodded, reaching out to brush her fingers across the new fuzz of hair growing on his scalp. 'You scared us both pretty badly.'

He squinted at her. 'But do you believe me?'

She hesitated. 'I don't know,' she said truthfully. 'You saw those scans. Do *you* believe what happened was real?'

'I don't know any more. Still . . . I'm glad you came.'

'Why? You thought I wouldn't?'

He laughed softly. 'After that argument we had?'

'Luc, it wasn't because my feelings for you had changed. You know that. But you were taking unnecessary risks, walking into a Black Lotus stronghold.'

'Yeah, but in the company of an entire squadron of—'

'Stop.' She pulled her hand back. 'I saw you, when they brought you back from Grendel. I couldn't even recognize you.' A brittle edge crept into her voice. 'Sandoz warriors can be re-instantiated, but you can't, Luc. There's only ever going to be one of you. That's why I didn't want you to go.'

But I didn't have a choice, he remembered saying to her just a few days before, and that was all it had taken for things between them to start unravelling.

'I'll be honest with you,' said Eleanor, breaking what had become an awkward silence, 'Lethe thinks he might have to discount your evidence concerning what happened on Aeschere. He's not sure an investigation would accept your story about a transfer gate without solid proof.'

'Then what am I supposed to tell people?' he asked. 'Maybe I can't prove it, El, but you've got to believe me when I tell you that the transfer gate was real. All of it was real.'

She sighed and sank down onto the edge of the bed, spreading her long fingers on the blankets. 'Let's say it's all real, then. Remember what Lethe asked you – why didn't Antonov just kill you?'

'I don't know,' Luc replied truthfully, then remembered what Antonov had said: *Access Archives, then open a record with the following reference – Thorne, 51 Alpha, Code Yellow. 'I'm calling in my favour.'*

It occurred to him that there was a way to prove his story was true. But if he really *had* imagined it all . . .

'There must have been *some* reason,' she insisted.

'If I could give you an answer that made any sense, I would.'

If that record really did exist, he'd find it in his own time. He decided not to say anything until he was sure one way or the other.

Eleanor shook her head and stood. 'I need to go. Lethe says the Temur Council are snapping at Karlmann Sandoz's heels, wanting to know how things could have gone so badly wrong. As you can imagine, Lethe's pretty happy about that.'

'Why?'

'Because Aeschere was a fucking *disaster* for the Sandoz. And that's good for SecInt.'

'Technically, I was in charge of that expedition,' Luc reminded her. 'They could blame me too.'

She shook her head. 'The comms records they managed to retrieve show that Master Marroqui went out of his way to countermand your orders every step of the way. He kept pushing to go deeper into the complex when you said it might be safer to pull back until you knew what had happened to those mosquitoes.'

'So I guess we're in the clear.'

Eleanor regarded him with pity. 'I don't understand you. Lethe only put you in nominal charge of that expedition so the Sandoz wouldn't grab all the glory. He didn't care about the danger he was putting you in. And yet you jumped at the chance like a puppy that doesn't know it's about to be drowned.'

Luc bristled. 'I knew the risks going in. It was still something I had to do.'

If you aren't there, Lethe had said, *no one's going to remember all the work you did finding Antonov.*

'And that's why I said what I said to you before. You don't even care when you're being used.'

'I was using Lethe just as much as he was using me.'

'Did *nothing* I say get through to you?' she shot back. 'You're filled with survivor guilt. You *wanted* to get killed on that damn mission, just so you could feel better about not dying along with the rest of your family.'

He stared at her, shocked at what she had said. She reached up to pat the bun at the back of her head as if she wasn't quite sure what to do with her hands, her expression flustered and her chest rising and falling from barely suppressed emotion.

'I'm going to retire,' he said abruptly.

Her eyes widened.

'From active service, at least,' he continued. 'I'm serious. With Antonov gone, there's no reason not to let other people deal with whatever's left of Black Lotus.'

'You never said anything about this before.'

'Because I didn't know just what was going to happen on Aeschere. I couldn't discount the possibility I was wrong, that Antonov wouldn't be there.' He looked at her and smiled. 'But he was.'

'Then . . . you're serious? No more risking your neck?'

'I'll stay on in Archives, but if I do any more field-work, I'll stick to the kind of low-risk background investigations you and me used to do. But nothing like Aeschere,' he added, shaking his head. 'That was more than enough for this lifetime.'

Eleanor looked almost dizzy with relief. 'I can hardly believe you're saying this. You were always so' – she searched for the right word – 'driven.'

Monomaniacal, he remembered her screaming at him once. *Obsessed.* He couldn't really deny the charge.

'All I'm saying,' he said, reaching out for her hand, 'is that things are going to be different from now on.'

He half expected her to pull away from him, but instead she laced her fingers through his. Luc felt like a weight had been lifted from his chest.

'There was another reason Lethe came here,' she said. 'You've been invited to the White Palace for a ceremony.'

'Ceremony?'

'They want to make you a Master of Archives, Luc.'

He blinked at her in confusion and surprise. 'Seriously?'

'Director Lethe thought you might like to hear it coming from me. Assuming you'll actually accept a promotion this time.'

Well, I'll be damned, thought Luc. 'The last time they tried to give me a promotion was different. They wanted to boot me up to the Security Division.'

'But this time,' she said, her mouth softening into a smile, 'you get to stay where you want to be.'

It took time for Luc to learn how to control his freshly grafted muscles, but progress was fast. Further treatments sped up the reconnection of nervous tissues, and simple tasks that at first represented an enormous struggle rapidly became smooth and natural. Even the food Luc ate tasted different. After just a couple of days his skin had lost much of its patchwork appearance, and the next time he looked in a mirror, he saw someone who appeared to have suffered nothing more than mild sunburn. He touched his new face, marvelling at the wonder of it all.

On the day his treatments came to an end, he made his way along a series of narrow paths that sliced through a small court-yard at the centre of the hospital grounds. The courtyard was filled with small patches of greenery interspersed with koi ponds, their waters glittering under a noon sun. At first a mechant trailed after him, but he shooed it away.

He sat on a concrete bench and took a small case from out of a jacket pocket, opening it and extracting a new Archives CogNet earpiece. He fitted it carefully to the lobe of one ear. During his therapy, he'd been forced to rely on a general-purpose piece rather than the secure model normally used by Archives staff.

He activated it, immediately sensing the pulse of humanity in the streets beyond the hospital's perimeter, and soon found himself deluged with data-ghosted messages from colleagues and well-wishers in Archives, including Offenbach and Hetaera. There were so many that their animated images jostled for space around him, some appearing to hover above the nearby koi ponds. He listened to a few before dismissing them all. He'd have plenty of opportunity to go through them all later.

And besides, what he had in mind might be better done without witnesses.

Linking into Archives for the first time since his return from Aeschere, he ran a search for any files with the reference Thorne, 51 Alpha, Code Yellow – and stared numbly at the fish circling in the pond before him when the search returned an immediate hit.

It was real.

The file in question contained a report detailing an incident on Thorne more than 125 years before. Out of all the worlds of the Tian Di, Thorne was both the least hospitable and the most recently colonized, a scrap of rock with a few bare lichens to its name orbiting on the outer edge of a red dwarf star's habitable zone. It was a far from suitable candidate for terraforming, but a penal colony had been set up there following the Schism, and later a series of biological research stations had also been established there. That community of scientists, along with those unlucky enough to be sent there to live out their sentences, huddled in shielded biomes or in deep sheltered caves.

The report detailed the accidental deaths of hundreds of prisoners following a containment breach in a biotech station, but any more specific details had been flagged as restricted. The only name he even vaguely recognized amongst those attached to the incident was that of Zelia de Almeida – a minor member of the Temur Council who had, at the time, been Thorne's Director of Policy.

The report also mentioned that de Almeida had been removed from her post following the incident, while an investigation blamed the whole incident on criminal negligence. There was nothing to connect any of it with Winchell Antonov; nothing to explain why he had asked Luc – in a *dream*, of all things – to come looking for this particular file.

Or maybe he'd come across the file in the past and forgotten about it, until he had incorporated it into a trauma-induced fantasy about secret transfer gates.

He stared hard at the report, visible only to him where it hovered in the air. *You have a choice*, he told himself. *You can either decide the dream was just that, or you can act like it meant something real.*

Luc stared past the report and at the upwards-thrusting skyline of Ulugh Beg, feeling as if he were balanced on the edge of a precipice. He had requested, and been granted, further scans, but there was nothing inside his skull that shouldn't have been there. If there ever had been, it was long gone.

He reached out, meaning to dismiss the record. Instead he opened it for editing, adding in five words: *I'm calling in my favour.*

He saved and dismissed it, feeling like a fool. With any luck, he'd never have to think about it ever again.

Luc found himself back home within another few days, staring around his apartment like he'd never seen it before. It might as well have been a million years since he'd last stood upon its threshold.

He ordered the blinds to open. They parted to reveal the city spread out before him, the fat spindle of the White Palace dominating the evening skies where it floated above Chandrakant Lu Park. The Palace itself was constructed from a series of stacked tiers, with a number of biomes arranged around its upper surface, each filled with the native flora and fauna of any one of a dozen worlds. The whole thing hovered above the park on enormous AG pods. Few people outside of the Temur Council were granted the opportunity to visit the White Palace, and fewer still got to pass through the private transfer gates in its upper levels that led to Vanaheim, an entire world reserved for the sole use of the Council.

Further out from Chandrakant Lu, bridges like spun diamond straddled Pioneer Gorge and the small, cramped buildings from the original, pre-terraforming settlement that had once been located there. People came from all corners of the Tian Di just to see a view like this.

Even though Reunification was still a few weeks away, holographic images of dragons and other mythical beasts were already being projected into the void of air surrounding the White Palace, along with images of the orbiting Coalition contact-ship that carried aboard it a transfer gate linking back to the Coalition world of Darwin. The park beneath was already a hive of activity as final preparations for the gate's ceremonial opening were carried out.

The world had changed while he'd been looking the other way. Antonov was dead, and two centuries of enforced isolationism were coming to an end with the official sanctioning of this single, tentative but nonetheless permanent wormhole link with the Coalition.

Of all the times he wanted Eleanor with him, this was it. But this close to Reunification, everyone in SecInt was working over-time, including her. So Luc had his apartment form a chair facing towards the Palace, and collapsed into it, staring out into the early evening sky and wondering if the rest of his life was going to feel as much of an anti-climax as he was beginning to suspect it might.

Stop being so morose, he chided himself, and asked the house mechant to bring him a glass of warm kavamilch, sipping at it until he drifted off into an exhausted sleep.

He came awake sometime in the early morning, and realized he wasn't alone.

'You look surprisingly well for a man who's been burned alive,' said a voice from behind him.

The house had dimmed the lights some time after he had fallen asleep. He brought them back up, twisting round in his seat to see a man with short-cropped hair standing facing him in the middle of the room, his face maddeningly familiar.

Luc stared at him. 'Who . . .'

'I'm disappointed,' said the man. 'You don't recognize me. Bailey Cripps.'

'Bailey . . .'

'I'm here on behalf of the Eighty-Five, Mr Gabion.'

The Eighty-Five. Father Cheng's inner circle within the Temur

Council, all of whom had been by his side since the days of the Schism.

Luc squinted. He could just about see the hair-thin line of rainbow interference surrounding Cripps like a halo that indicated he was talking to a data-ghost – nothing more than a projection, but an unauthorized intrusion for all that. Anger began to overwhelm his initial feelings of shock.

Luc stood, flustered, and turned to face him. 'Of course I recognize you. You chair the Council's Defence Subcommittee. But I have a right to privacy, even from—'

'Sit back down,' Cripps ordered him. 'I'm here to ask you some questions, Mr Gabion. *Necessary* questions.'

Luc held his ground and remained upright. 'If you wanted to talk to me, you could have just arranged an interview through SecInt.'

'That isn't possible,' Cripps replied. 'This meeting has to be strictly off the record.'

'Why?'

Cripps' eyes narrowed. 'I think you're forgetting your place, Archivist. I came here to ask *you* questions, not the other way around.'

'How do I know you really are who you say you are? I could be speaking to anyone behind that data-ghost.'

Cripps nodded as if satisfied. 'An excellent point. Feel free to check.'

Luc asked his house to trace the source of the projection, and soon learned that it originated from somewhere deep inside the White Palace itself. Further, the signal had been processed via a channel used exclusively by high-ranking members of the Council's vast bureaucracy.

The chair reformed around Luc as he sat back down, facing Cripps. 'Okay. You check out. So what exactly is it that's so damned important you'd come into my house uninvited?'

'I want you to tell me,' said Cripps, 'whether you think the Thousand Emperors should be in power.'

Luc felt his face grow red. 'You mean the Temur Council, don't you?'

Cripps raised an eyebrow. 'Does the name bother you?'

'It's a highly pejorative term, used in Black Lotus propaganda.'

'You still haven't answered the question,' Cripps replied, his eyes hard. 'There are people, and not just Black Lotus supporters, who claim the Council has been running affairs throughout the Tian Di for much too long. Is that a view you agree with?'

Luc felt his stomach curl into a tight knot. 'Have there been questions over my loyalty, Mr Cripps?'

'You come from Benares, I understand.' The way he said it, it sounded more like an accusation than a polite enquiry.

'I think,' Luc replied, struggling for calm, 'that what I did on Aeschere proves where my loyalties lie.'

Cripps gave him a humourless smile. 'That doesn't answer my question,' he said. 'That whole mess left more than a dozen Sandoz dead, their supposedly secure network compromised. Then there's you, the sole survivor, with your miraculous escape and no clear explanation for just what happened to you while you were down in that complex. Given your background, it's inevitable that people are going to start wondering if perhaps you were in league with Antonov in some way.'

'If you want to ask me any more questions,' Luc replied, his fingers gripping his knees, 'you can do it in the presence of Director Lethe of Security and Intelligence.'

'Let's leave SecInt out of it and think of this as just being between friends. Haven't you ever thought maybe the Council's been in power too long? It's been more than two centuries, now. Don't you feel it's time for some new kind of government to be put in their place?'

'What I *think*, Mr Cripps, is that you're testing me for some reason I don't understand. I lost my family to Black Lotus when I was very young, so you're out of your mind if you think I'm an agent for them. Go read my SecInt file. The word "exemplary" gets used a lot.'

'That file also tells me the majority of people in the part of Benares you came from had sympathies for Black Lotus. When you came to Temur as a refugee, you lived in a part of Ulugh Beg with a strong Black Lotus presence.'

'Black Lotus murdered a couple of million Benareans in a sustained assault that devastated half a continent. Believe me, Mr Cripps, I've got more reason than most to hate Winchell Antonov. Besides, everyone in SecInt gets psych-profiled to find out where their loyalties lie. So why are you *really* here?'

There was a reptilian quality to Cripps' gaze, something in the way the skin wrinkled around the corners of his eyes that made Luc think of a predator half-submerged in some watering-hole beneath a baking sun.

'Two reasons,' Cripps responded. 'For one, a couple of years ago you were given the chance at a promotion to SecInt's security division, but you didn't take it. Why?'

'Because it would have taken me out of the Archives division, and away from my intelligence work,' Luc replied immediately. 'The job was mostly bureaucratic. If I'd accepted it, I might never have tracked Antonov down. I told Director Lethe that at the time, and he had no problem with my reasoning.'

'Except that promotion would also have given you the authority to influence Archives' lines of investigation,' Cripps countered. 'That could have made a lot of difference – maybe enough so that we wouldn't be forced to re-instantiate an entire Sandoz Clan.'

'You said there was a second point?' Luc snapped, barely able to contain himself any longer.

'I don't think you have any more love for the Temur Council and Father Cheng than Winchell Antonov ever did,' Cripps replied, a glint in his eyes. He nodded past Luc, towards the White Palace hovering in the air beyond the window. 'Who's to say you aren't a sleeper agent, placed deep inside Archives, and who's to say Antonov's death wasn't faked in some way? No body was recovered, and all we have is your unlikely testimony, delivered to a

Sandoz investigator, which can't possibly be corroborated since no CogNet records of your encounter with Antonov exists!'

'With all due respect, sir,' Luc spat back, 'you don't know shit.'

Cripps' shoulders jerked briefly in a laugh. 'Things are going to be very different from now on, Mr Gabion. I'm going to be keeping a *very* close eye on you. Remember that, when you start your investigation.'

Luc stared at him, baffled. 'My *what*?'

'We'll meet again shortly. Just remember, in the coming days, that you are as much a suspect as anyone else.'

'Suspect in *what*?' Luc shook his head in befuddlement. 'I have no idea what you're talking ab—'

Cripps' data-ghost vanished while he was still mid-sentence, leaving him staring at an empty room.

An investigation, Cripps had said. What kind of investigation?

He pushed both hands across his head, wondering if he hadn't just imagined the whole thing. After everything he'd been through, he couldn't even be sure how much he could trust his own senses. Maybe he was losing his mind. Maybe it was really that simple.

'House,' he asked, 'was anyone else just here?'

'Senator Bailey Cripps, by remote data-presence,' the house replied.

He closed his eyes in silent relief and sank back into the chair, but soon found himself staring back out at the Palace, feeling nothing but a premonitory chill.

The next morning a mechant guided Luc from the metro station at the edge of the park and along a pathway that skirted the bronzed statue of Chandrakant Lu. The White Palace's architect had been depicted with one hand reaching upwards, as if to catch the vast edifice floating half a kilometre above the city. He saw innumerable fliers arriving to decant yet more people to join the hundreds already milling about, a considerable number of whom wore the formal work clothes of Council bureaucrats, while the rest sported the uniforms of either SecInt or Sandoz.

Mechants, most of them conspicuously armed and bearing Sandoz markings, darted through the air, almost outnumbering the crowds. Their carapaces glittered under the bright arc lights that substituted for sunlight beneath the Palace's vast bulk.

The mechant guided him towards an open plaza near the park's centre. He felt a rush of pleasure when he sighted Eleanor standing amidst a gaggle of several other SecInt agents. The agents were gathered around an olive-skinned man wearing a long formal jacket; Luc immediately recognized him as Mehmood Garda, Director of Policy for Benares, and himself a member of the Eighty-Five.

The crowds moved and shifted, and a moment later Luc also caught sight of Vincent Hetaera, his immediate superior in Archives, engaged in what looked like an in-depth discussion with several of his junior research staff.

'Mr Gabion!' Garda exclaimed as Luc approached, stepping forward to clap him on the shoulder and pump his hand at the same time. 'Congratulations on your success at Aeschere. I believe we all owe you a debt of gratitude.'

His voice boomed over even the noise of the crowded plaza. Several security-mechants clearly tasked with guarding Director Garda aimed their machine-gaze at Luc.

'I appreciate that.' Luc almost had to shout the words over the cacophony. He'd heard rumours Garda had participated in the torture and execution of Black Lotus agents, particularly when those agents had been female.

Garda lifted his chin towards the Palace. 'You must be full of anticipation. This is the first time you've been invited into the Palace?'

'It is,' Luc shouted back. 'To be honest, I think I'll be glad just to get this over with,' he added.

Garda drew himself up to his full six-foot-plus height, this time placing both hands on Luc's shoulders and clapping one of them hard. 'Well,' he said, 'I can't think of anyone who could possibly deserve what's coming to you any more than you do.'

Luc caught sight of Eleanor from out of the corner of his eye. 'It's certainly an honour,' he replied.

'And after this?' asked Garda. 'Black Lotus aren't finished just because Antonov is dead. Are you going to help us wipe the rest of them out?'

'I think that remains to be—'

To Luc's considerable relief, one of Garda's entourage approached, whispering in the Director's ear.

'I look forward to seeing you receive your honours in the Palace,' said Garda, briefly turning back to Luc, but it was clear his mind was already somewhere else. 'Affairs of state, I'm afraid.'

Luc nodded, and watched the Director step away and greet someone else.

'Feel like washing your hands?' asked Eleanor, moving up next to him.

Luc suppressed a grimace. 'I guess I should have expected him to be here.'

'You had a look on your face like you'd just drunk your own piss. To be honest, I think he noticed.'

'If he did, I don't think it bothered him a great deal.'

'First Lethe, now Garda. Just when you thought you'd be able to relax a little.'

Luc shook his head wearily. 'Fuck assholes like Garda. There'll always be people like him.' He reached out and took her hand. 'I need to see you. Soon.'

She nodded. 'Look, I'm sorry about last night, it's just—'

'It's okay,' he said, stopping her. 'I seem to be about the only person in all of SecInt who isn't on active duty right now.' He shrugged. 'And maybe it's not such a bad thing that you weren't there.'

'Why not?'

He hesitated, wondering how she'd react to what he was about to tell her.

They had become lovers the year before, on a joint trip to Yue Shijie in the 94 Aquarii system to try and track down one of Black Lotus's many sources of funding.

Like Aeschere, Yue Shijie orbited a gas giant, but unlike that desolate moon, Yue Shijie was well within its system's habitable zone, and large enough to support a habitable biosphere. He remembered standing with Eleanor on the balcony of a ziggurat-like building that, like much of the rest of that world's capital city, rose out of dense jungle stretching to the horizon in all directions. He remembered looking up to see the gas giant's streaked atmosphere, marked here and there by outpourings from Helium 3 factories ploughing through its upper reaches.

They had been stuck there for the better part of a month, chasing after lines of enquiry that led nowhere. Demonstrations and riots stirred up by Black Lotus had made the city streets too dangerous to venture onto. Boredom and alcohol had combined with inevitable effect.

He recalled in vivid detail the curve of her small, high breasts beneath the thin blouse she wore that evening, the curve of her spine when she leaned against the railing beside him. Falling into bed had seemed the obvious thing to do on such a long and lonely night, but neither of them had anticipated how quickly and how deeply their feelings for each other would develop. He wanted to keep her at a safe distance from anything that involved Cripps, yet at the same time, he knew there was no one he could trust more than Eleanor.

'I had a visitor yesterday evening,' he told her. 'Bailey Cripps. He spent the whole time quizzing me about my loyalties.'

Her eyes became round and she stepped back a little. '*Bailey Cripps?* Visited you where, here?'

'He turned up in my home.'

She had a look in her eyes like she wasn't quite sure she could believe him.

'Listen, I swear on Cheng's teeth he was there,' Luc insisted.

'He doesn't strike me as the type to make impromptu house calls.'

'There was nothing impromptu about it. He data-ghosted into my apartment without any warning. I guess Council privileges extend to home security overrides.'

'He questioned your *loyalties*?' Her eyes darted to the side and then back again, and he guessed what she was about to ask. 'Are you sure it was really him?'

'I checked. It was him, all right. He seemed to think I couldn't be trusted because I'm from Benares. He also mentioned something about an investigation, but I have no idea what investigation he was talking about.'

Her expression became more alarmed. 'Investigation? Into what? Aeschere?'

'No, he seemed to mean something else, but he didn't seem interested in telling me precisely what.'

'We need to tell someone about this.'

He shook his head. 'No.'

She shook her head in disbelief. 'For God's sake, why not?'

'This is Bailey Cripps we're talking about. There has to be a reason he approached me directly, instead of going through Lethe or Hetaera. If I tell them or anyone else, I might not get to find out what that reason is.'

She sighed, tilting her head back to stare up at the Palace's illuminated underside. 'I don't like this,' she said, bringing her gaze back down. 'You should tell *someone*.'

'I'm telling *you*, aren't I?'

She shook her head in exasperation. 'Don't you think you've been through enough already?'

'Look, maybe Cripps came to me in the way he did because he knows something about Black Lotus. Besides . . . he's one of the Eighty-Five. What they want, they get.'

'There are some members of the Council,' she said, speaking to him as if he were dim-witted, 'you don't want to get tangled up with.' Her eyes slid to one side, and he followed the direction of her gaze until he alighted on Garda, still working the crowd.

'I just want to find out what Cripps wants. *Then* I'll go talk to Lethe.'

He could sense the anger brewing behind her thinned lips. 'Is that a promise?'

He nodded. 'Yes.'

'Good,' she replied, 'because this is starting to feel like Aeschere all over again.'

Garda mounted a stage set up at the centre of the plaza and began to speak, while mechants from half a dozen different news agencies buzzed through the air, jostling for the best vantage point.

Luc's attention soon drifted back to the Palace floating overhead. Something about the sight of all those millions of tons of metal floating unsupported in the air always felt like a test of one's faith in technology. He wondered, not for the first time, just how many seconds he'd have left to live should the AG pods holding it in place suddenly fail to function.

Glancing at Eleanor beside him, he saw she had an expression like she'd swallowed something nasty. She hadn't taken the news about Cripps well. But during his recovery, left with little to do but think, it had come to Luc that so much of his life had been devoted to finding Antonov that there hadn't been room left for much else. He'd sometimes wondered what kind of life he might have led if the Battle of Sunderland hadn't brought everything to a crashing halt at such a young age.

Maybe now was the time to find out. And as much as he hated to admit it even to himself, Cripps' vague allusion to an unspecified investigation had awoken within him a sense of purpose he had not felt since his departure for Aeschere.

Garda's speech finally came to an end, and Luc realized he hadn't taken in a single word. Two massive doors in the Palace's underside, positioned directly above the plaza, slowly swung apart on cue. All around the park, fliers thrummed into life while low, sonorous music flowed out of hidden speakers.

The interior of a docking bay became visible beyond the doors. Dozens of mechants rose towards it, as if the Palace were in actuality a moon, the mechants drawn upwards by the tug of its gravity.

'This is it,' said Eleanor, taking his arm and flashing him a smile that looked only half-genuine.

A mechant approached and asked them to follow it. They trailed after it towards a sleek-looking craft onto which at least a dozen other people were already filing.

They boarded and took their seats, Eleanor taking his hand and holding it tightly.

'Nervous?' she asked.

'A little,' he admitted. He wondered if Cripps would be present during the ceremony. He leaned back, half-listening to the people chattering around them as the flier waited for clearance. Most of them were ordinary citizens, on their way to be granted privileges and rewards for services rendered. It was all part of the Temur Council's unceasing public relations campaign designed to remind people how good life was under Father Cheng.

The upper part of the hull was transparent, and Luc watched as other fliers scattered around the plaza took off, one after the other, rising straight up and disappearing into the blaze of the docking bay's lights. Then, finally, they were on their way, landing inside the Palace after a trip that lasted barely a minute.

Once they disembarked, more mechants, decorated in the gold and blue livery of the Temur Council, took care of guiding the flier's passengers towards an auditorium located on the Palace's lowest tier. One of the mechants flew towards Luc and Eleanor, coming to a halt immediately before them and bringing them to a startled halt.

'Mr Gabion,' said the mechant in a smooth contralto. 'If you would follow me, please.'

Luc saw the curious glances of the other passengers as they

passed by. He felt strangely embarrassed, as if he'd been caught gatecrashing.

'Why?'

'It concerns a matter of the utmost seriousness,' the mechant informed him. 'One that requires your absolute discretion.'

'Required by whom?' asked Eleanor.

'I am not at liberty to say, but the request comes from within the Temur Council.'

'Then we'll both come,' said Eleanor.

The mechant's AG fields buzzed quietly for a moment before it answered. 'I'm afraid this is a matter for Mr Gabion only, Miss Jaq. Director Lethe has been informed of your necessary absence from the ceremony. Mr Gabion, please follow me.'

Eleanor opened and closed her mouth, then stared at Luc with a concerned expression.

'I don't like it,' she finally said in a low voice. 'Why now, of all times?'

'I'll be fine,' he said, reaching out to squeeze her arm.

She tried to force a smile, but the strain was clear on her face.

He nodded to the mechant and it led the way, gliding towards an AG platform at the far end of the bay. The platform began to accelerate upwards as soon as he stepped onto it, the mechant rising at the same rate in order to keep even with him. He glanced down once to see Eleanor looking back up at him, and tried to ignore the deep unease lurking at the back of his thoughts.

The platform kept rising, and Luc realized with a shock it was going all the way to the top, to the Hall of Gates. He made a point of not stepping too close to the edge of the platform. Its AG fields would prevent him from falling off, but he had little desire to see just how far he had risen.

'The matter for which your presence has been requested rates a C category under the Security review of 285 P.A.,' said the mechant, turning towards him as the platform began to decelerate. 'You may not disclose the nature, location or any other pertinent aspect of your final destination to anyone with a less than

C-category security rating, under penalty of the permanent loss of all granted privileges, and possible detention or permanent discorporation at the pleasure of a court assembled from select members of the Temur Council. The same penalties also apply to anyone with whom you share this information, and anyone amongst their immediate family, social or work groups suspected of coming into possession of this information.'

Luc nodded dumbly, thinking: a C-level security rating. There weren't many that were higher.

'Please acknowledge, before we reach our destination, that you understand and accept these terms,' the mechant finished.

'I don't have the rank for that level of security rating,' said Luc. 'I'm not sure I've even met anyone who does.' *Outside of members of the Council, anyway.*

'You have been granted a temporary C-rating security clearance,' the mechant replied. 'Do you agree to the stated terms?'

Luc stared at the machine. 'I do.'

The platform passed through a circular opening in the atrium's ceiling before finally coming to a halt at the centre of a low-ceilinged circular hall. Luc saw more than a dozen transfer gates spaced equidistant from each other set into the walls: private transfer gates, each one leading to a major Tian Di colony and reserved for the sole use of members of the Temur Council. One other gate led to Vanaheim.

The mechant moved towards the Vanaheim gate. Luc hesitated once he realized where it was leading him.

'I just want to be clear on this,' he called after the machine. 'I've been requested to travel to Vanaheim?'

'Yes,' the mechant confirmed, pausing briefly before gliding onwards and through the gate. Luc followed, feeling increasingly out of his depth.

He felt some of his weight fall away when he stepped through a pressure-field on the far side of the gate. Vanaheim's gravity was almost a fifth less than that of Temur.

He had never been to Vanaheim before; few outside of the

Temur Council ever had. The air felt dense, almost soupy, and had a curiously honeyed scent to it. He glanced back through the gate to the interior of the White Palace, thinking of his home somewhere on the far side, so very close and yet so very far away. Then he turned around to regard the concourse on which he now found himself, and the greenish-blue sky visible through a curved glass ceiling several metres overhead.

There was no sign of anyone else.

The complex of which the concourse was part stood on raised ground on one slope of a river valley that was home to Liebenau, the single largest settlement on the entire planet. Luc saw a Gothic mansion at the centre of a vast, rolling estate, bordering what appeared to be an ancient Hindu temple; there were other buildings of varying and clashing architectural styles, most drawn from old Earth, although a cluster of grey-and-brown, utilitarian-looking structures were clearly inspired by post-Abandonment biome architecture. A few crystalline towers, not so different from those found on Temur and the capitals of other Tian Di colonies, rose towards the sky like upright spears.

Most of these were the homes of Cheng's inner circle, the Eighty-Five; they all orbited a single, vast complex of ancient-looking buildings, which were in turn surrounded by a high, rectangular wall topped at each corner by pagoda-style roofs. A moat surrounded this wall. Extensive gardens helped to further separate and distinguish the Red Palace – as it was known – from the rest of the settlement. It had been modelled, he vaguely recalled, on a palace built on Earth many centuries before the Abandonment.

The mechant moved ahead of him and towards a single flier parked just beyond an exit. A door in the craft's side swung open as they approached.

'Now we're here,' he called after the mechant, 'would you mind at least giving me some idea what the hell this is about?'

'You are required,' the mechant informed him, coming to a halt next to the flier, 'to assist in the investigation of a murder.'

THREE

His name was Jacob Moreland, and he was a spy.

His mission had begun seventy-four years before, when he had been placed into a one-man craft launched from a Sandoz platform in orbit around Novaya Zvezda. Along with an armada of identical craft, each carrying a lone passenger, the ship carrying Jacob had accelerated rapidly out of the system, reaching eighty per cent of light-speed within half a year. The star around which Novaya Zvezda itself orbited soon became just one more exquisitely jewel-like point of light amongst countless others.

Jacob slept unawares, his body buffered by impact-gels and cooled by onboard cryogenics.

For a very long time, Jacob Moreland was, by any objective measure, dead. The instantiation lattice within his skull had encoded much of the fleeting data that made up his conscious mind, while more specialized structures did their best to repair the unavoidable damage done to his delicate human tissues by prolonged deep-space flight.

Attrition soon took its toll, as some of the craft accompanying Jacob on his long journey were destroyed by micrometeorite impacts. It had proven necessary to provide each ship with relatively low-grade shielding, since this increased their chances of evading detection by the Coalition's deep-space monitors. That a certain number of craft were likely to be lost had been taken into account during the mission's planning stages. It was an unfortunate, but ultimately necessary, sacrifice.

A few other of the ships suffered fatal systems failures, victims of high-energy particle impacts that interfered with their delicate circuitry. The rest continued on their long flight across the light-years, their onboard computers communicating with each other via encrypted channels, aware within their limited intelligence that, as time progressed, their numbers were steadily dwindling, although not yet below mission-critical levels.

At the apex of their journey, the armada was moving at just a shade over 97 per cent of light-speed. Time-dilation slowed the pace at which the attritions of age and radiation damage wore away at their passengers. The onboard medical systems did their best but, inevitably, there were further casualties: those ships bearing the irretrievably dead automatically shut themselves down and fell behind the rest, to drift between the stars forever.

The years passed, and the ships flew on. They did not begin to decelerate until the last decade of their voyage, finally braking into the 36 Ophiuchi system, deep within Coalition territory.

Automated defences patrolling the outer worlds of 36 Ophiuchi detected a number of the approaching ships, analysing their trajectories and responding by moving hunter-killer mechants into intercept patterns. The craft came under fire from kinetic weapons that sent chunks of asteroid slag curving in towards them along gravity-assist paths.

Attrition once more took its toll as the majority of incoming craft were destroyed, and the survival rate of the spy-ships finally teetered towards mission-critical levels. The computers on board the ships risked data-bursts between each other, readjusting their shared flight plans according to decades-old algorithms: if only a few of them managed to reach their destinations, the project set in motion so very long ago might yet have a chance of succeeding.

The survivors lost themselves amidst the rubble of a dead world, long ago drawn into a belt of debris a billion kilometres beyond 36 Ophiuchi's habitable zone. Only half a dozen of the spy-ships now remained.

Each took it in turn to accelerate towards the inner system, matching courses with cometary bodies and asteroids in order to disguise themselves, drifting sometimes for months before finally manoeuvring into new trajectories that would carry them all the way to Darwin, the system's sole inhabited world.

It wasn't long before Jacob's turn came.

For the first time in several decades, he began to dream, his core body temperature slowly rising as complex cryoprotectant solutions were leached from his bloodstream. His heart began to beat, falteringly at first and then with added strength. Nutrients entered his body via a complex of hollow fibres inserted into his spine, while invisibly tiny microchines worked hard at repairing the inevitable cellular and neural damage sustained during the voyage. Some minimal damage had also been sustained by his instantiation lattice.

Jacob Moreland would live, but some of his memories were gone forever. This much, too, had been anticipated.

Networked autonomous security devices parked in Trojan orbits, balanced between the blue-green world they guarded and the star it orbited, detected the majority of the surviving spy-ships and swiftly destroyed them. Only Jacob's ship escaped, by wrapping itself within a hastily improvised informational cocoon that made it appear to be little more than an unmanned reconnaissance vehicle on a registered mission. It had been lucky, matching the trajectory of a cluster of supply drones, returning from the A-M refineries orbiting just inside 36 Ophiuchi's solar corona.

Jacob Moreland drew breath and gasped, his lungs still filled to capacity with breathable nutrient gels that tasted vaguely of mint and antiseptic. A moment later, he remembered his name.

He became more fully conscious during the final stages of atmospheric re-entry. Fresh data flowered in his mind, generated by the instantiation lattices riddling his cerebral cortex and nearly indistinguishable from his own, entirely natural thoughts.

Plasma cannons, designed to destroy random garbage falling

from the orbital wheel that encircled Darwin, burned his craft as it dropped towards the upper layers of that world's atmosphere. It responded by releasing a burst of chaff that fooled the cannons into thinking their target had been destroyed. The ship then dipped lower into the atmosphere, burning off its ablative surface before dropping towards the cloud level.

Jacob's pulse began to quicken as he remembered not only who, but what, he was. Upon his request, sensors embedded in the craft's skin relayed to him images of the night-time landscape towards which he was falling. He saw deep valleys, ancient mountains rising above shallow seas, and glistening salt-flats that stretched across continents. He saw cities like brilliant kaleidoscopes of light, dense conurbations that reached silver fingers far above the planet's atmosphere, linking into the world-wheel dotted with countless antimatter forges and industrial complexes.

This, then, was Darwin, a world that had become the economic and cultural heart of the Coalition following the Abandonment.

His craft bucked as it passed through the turbulent layers of air at the edge of a high-pressure zone, then dropped towards a ragged and apparently unpopulated coastline, minuscule thrusters slowing the ship's rate of descent in the last moments of its flight. Seconds before the ship finally touched down, Jacob caught sight of green and violet-leaved flora growing amidst spongy-looking trees that bowed under the weight of their broad, finger-like branches.

He staggered out of the blackened shell of his craft in time to see the first fingers of dawn colouring the night sky. He coughed and retched, his lungs and throat still carrying traces of suspension fluids from his long voyage. Cold air whipped against his naked skin. Feeling weak and helpless, he sagged to his knees, pushing both hands deep into gritty soil as a deep and ravenous hunger gripped him.

His instantiation lattice fed data to his conscious mind as he kneeled. He learned that he was the only survivor out of the nearly forty men and women who had been launched from the Tian Di so many years before. Despite the deprivations of his voyage, he found that he could still remember most of their faces and names, having come to know nearly all of them over the course of the year they had spent training for this mission. They had all known how high the risks were. Even so, he was appalled to find he was the only one left.

And if he failed, the mission failed with him.

Staggering back over to the craft, he quickly retrieved a one-piece combat suit, pulling it on before he could freeze to death in the chilly air. He next retrieved a case, then stepped quickly away from the craft as his lattice flashed him an alert.

From a safe distance, he watched as the ship that had carried him so far immolated itself, its hull collapsing into sections that burned with a pungent smell. Flames flickered inside the craft's interior, reaching up past bone-like spurs that would crumble away to nothing within just a few days. In time, the only evidence that there had ever been a craft here capable of travelling between the stars would be unusually high trace amounts of rare minerals in the soil, along with a marginally higher than normal level of background radioactivity. But one would have to look very, very carefully indeed.

Jacob stood watching for over an hour as the ship continued crumbling into gently steaming ashes that filled the night air with a scent like burning grass. Something about it filled him with a curious sense of loss, which was strange, given that he had been placed in suspension prior to being loaded aboard the craft. Nevertheless, on some deep level, a part of him recognized that this had been his home for long decades, and so it felt strange to finally leave it behind.

From this point on, there was only one way left for him to return home to the Tian Di – and doing so would constitute a major part of his mission.

When he felt ready, Jacob reached into a pocket of his combat suit, retrieving a device small enough to nestle almost invisibly in the palm of his hand: a pin-sized transceiver. He activated it, and even though there was no reason to think it might malfunction, he nonetheless felt a palpable sense of relief when it proved fully operational.

His journey across the light-years had all been just a prelude to this, the moment when his mission truly began. His first step would be to make contact with Tian Di agents who had been in place on Darwin since before he had even set out. Once their own transceivers notified them of his arrival, they would find him and aid him in fulfilling his mission.

It might have taken him decades to reach this world, but the return journey would take, quite literally, no time at all.

FOUR

The flier carrying Luc and the mechant that had fetched him from Temur dropped below cloud-level a few hours after it had set out, and he got his first glimpse of a small island situated no more than a couple of kilometres from a coastline of high cliffs dense with reddish-green forest. The island didn't appear to be much more than a stub of grassy rock sticking out of the ocean. Tall waves crashed against its shore, and as the flier dropped down he saw a number of brick and stone buildings clustered close together on its grassy slopes, a few of them topped by gold and silver onion domes that glittered beneath Vanaheim's sun. The flier canted to one side, shuddering slightly as its broad dark wings cut through a strong wind that tore foam from the peaks of the waves.

'*Now* do you mind telling me where the hell we are?' Luc demanded, staring down through the transparent hull.

The mechant had disappeared into a slot in one wall of the cabin as soon as they had boarded. 'We are approaching the residence of Sevgeny Vasili,' it explained from within its nook. 'We will disembark in the next few minutes.'

Sevgeny Vasili. Until now, the mechant had refused to tell him anything beyond that single, cryptic reference to a murder enquiry. It hadn't even been willing to tell him *who* was supposed to be dead.

He reviewed what little he knew of Sevgeny Vasili. Like Cripps and Garda both, Vasili was a long-standing member of the Eighty-Five, and had been since the very earliest days of the Temur Council.

He was also aware that Vasili had been central to the negotiation process with the Coalition that had led directly to the Reunification.

The flier dropped to a silent landing in a walled courtyard on that part of the island facing towards the mainland. Luc saw as he disembarked that several other craft were already parked there. The air tasted cold and clear, and he shivered. His Archives uniform was far from adequate in such chill air.

Whatever was going on, he had the distinct feeling he was the last to arrive.

The mechant emerged once more and led him through a brick arch that exited the courtyard, and then along a shrub-lined path that terminated before a broad, wooden door that swung inwards at their approach. Luc found himself inside a high-ceilinged hall that might easily have passed for a throne-room in some ancient Earthly kingdom. Carved wooden columns reached up to a beamed roof, while a fireplace at the far end looked just about big enough to fit a whole flier within it. The flagstones beneath his feet seemed to have been worn smooth with age, while the air within the hall smelled of damp and mould. The only light came through narrow windows set close to the ceiling.

Much of this Luc noticed only peripherally, his attention being otherwise taken up entirely by the half-dozen men and women clustered together in the best lit part of the hall beneath a leaded window. Not only did he see Bailey Cripps amongst their number, but also Joseph Cheng – the Benevolent Archon himself, Permanent Chairman of the Temur Council, and certainly the most powerful man in all of the Tian Di.

He paused at the gathering before him, almost frozen to the spot.

'Is that him?' spat a man next to Cripps.

Luc stared at the man who had spoken before suddenly real-izing who he was: Victor Begum, one of the two founders of the Sandoz Clans along with old Karlmann Sandoz. He was as muscled and intimidating as Marroqui or any other Clan-leader Luc had ever encountered.

'Easy, Victor,' said one of the two women amongst the group, thick dark hair spilling like a wave across her shoulders. 'You *are* Luc Gabion?' she asked, glancing towards him.

'I . . . yes,' Luc managed to say. 'Yes, I am. I'm not sure why I've been brought here.'

He heard the door swing shut behind him, the sound echoing through the hall with all the finality of an executioner's axe. For some reason, his feet had become unwilling to carry him any further into the room.

'Did the mechant that brought you here tell you nothing?' asked the same woman.

'No, except that there had been a – a murder,' he replied, his voice pinching off slightly.

A small, balding man with round cheeks made a barking sound, his face contorted in anger. He took a step towards the dark-haired woman, who turned to face him, raising one hand as if to ward him off.

<This was a bad idea, Zelia,> the balding man scripted, glaring over at Luc as he did so. <He doesn't belong here.>

Zelia. Luc stared at the woman, remembering the details of the Archival record he had altered back at the hospital. She had to be Zelia de Almeida, formerly Thorne's Director of Policy.

<Ruy, I asked you to avoid using script-speak while Gabion was here,> de Almeida sent.

<Now that I think about it, I'm not so sure you belong here, either, Zelia,> said the man called Ruy, staring furiously at Luc the whole time. <You can expect me to lodge a formal protest as soon as we're finished here.>

It took Luc a moment to understand that he was privy to a conversation he shouldn't even have been aware was taking place; the permission flags surrounding Ruy and de Almeida's words made it entirely clear their conversation was intended to be private, and yet Luc was able to pick up every word.

<Maybe you could explain why *you're* here, Ruy?>, de Almeida sent in response, her eyes fixed on Luc as she scripted. <I don't recall asking you here.>

There was something calculating in her gaze, and Luc felt a flash of guilt that made him look away, as if he had done something wrong.

<I don't need your permission,> Ruy scripted back at her, growing ever more red-faced. <Joe asked me to be here.>

Joe. Luc blinked, realizing with a start Ruy must be referring to Joseph Cheng. It felt strange to hear a man of such enormous power referred to in so avuncular a fashion.

'Mr Gabion is here because Zelia made an excellent case why he should be present, Mr Borges,' said Cheng, opting to speak out loud. 'I hope you're not questioning my judgement in this matter?'

Ruy Borges's face went from red to white in a matter of moments. He turned towards Cheng, first glancing quickly at Luc with the expression of a man who had just trod on something unpleasant.

'My apologies,' Borges said to Cheng. <I shouldn't have spoken out of turn,> he added.

<I'll also ask you to avoid script-speak from now on,> Cheng replied. <Gabion must be allowed to see and hear everything we do or say.>

Borges nodded, suddenly submissive where he had been demanding. <Then may I at least ask *why* he's here?>

De Almeida turned to Luc. 'Mr Borges is curious to know why I had you brought here,' she told him. 'I'm sorry for bringing you here with such little warning, but I'm sure you understand why it was necessary.'

'The victim – was it a member of the Council?'

'It was, yes. A man called Sevgeny Vasili. Are you familiar with the name?'

'Yes.'

'Then I assume you also understand what would happen to you if anyone outside of this room were ever to discover the purpose or details of our meeting here?'

Luc nodded uneasily and swallowed. 'I can make an educated guess.'

'*No one* is allowed on to Vanaheim except for members of the Council and their guests, all of whom are strictly vetted and closely watched at all times. You can understand this presents us with some difficulties when it comes to figuring out who might be responsible for Sevgeny's murder.'

'You mentioned "guests" – are there any on Vanaheim at the moment?'

'Apart from yourself?' asked de Almeida. 'A few, all of whom are being detained until we can be absolutely certain they were not involved in any way. No one apart from yourself is being allowed to pass through the Hall of Gates. Even so, the circumstances of Sevgeny's death mean that we've been forced to some uncomfortable conclusions.'

Luc met her eyes, and had a fleeting mental image of something dark and winged, with outstretched talons, swooping down from out of the sky. 'You think Vasili was killed by another Councillor?'

'No.' Victor Begum stepped forward. 'It's ridiculous to suggest any one of us could have done such a thing to one of our own. It *has* to be someone from outside the Council.'

<Please, Victor,> de Almeida scripted, her tone weary. <We can't make exceptions for ourselves if we're going to work out what happened here.>

Somewhere beyond the high narrow windows, Luc could hear waves crashing on the island's shore. His lungs felt like they had turned to granite in his chest, fear sharpening his senses. He was unpleasantly aware that any one of the men and women before him could order his death, without reprisal or consequences, and at a moment's notice, if he failed to satisfy them.

'Excuse me,' he said.

They all looked over at him.

'*If* I were to hazard a guess,' he said, feeling cool sweat trickle past one eyebrow despite the chill air, 'I'd say your biggest worry is whether you can trust each other since, technically, any one of you could be responsible for Vasili's murder.'

There; he'd said it. He waited, breath catching in his throat, fully expecting to die at any moment for words that sounded wildly heretical even as they emerged from his mouth.

'He's right,' said de Almeida, turning to the rest. 'This is why Father Cheng agreed to my proposal – we need the perspective of someone from outside of the Council, someone who couldn't possibly have an axe to grind with the victim.'

'Yes, all very good,' said Ruy Borges irritably, 'but why *him*?'

Good question, thought Luc, turning his gaze back to de Almeida.

'Luc Gabion has entirely proven his loyalty, and his skill, by almost single-handedly apprehending the criminal Winchell Antonov,' she replied.

'Oh,' said Borges, regarding Luc with new eyes and nodding slowly. '*Him*.'

Cheng clapped his hands together, almost as if he were hosting a dinner party. 'I think it's about time we took a look at the deceased, don't you?'

Luc's feeling of being out of his depth intensified as de Almeida beckoned him through a side-door. The smell of putrefaction, mixed with the scent of smoke, hit Luc as soon as he passed through it. Sevgeny Vasili's death had clearly not been a recent one.

Luc found himself standing inside the entrance to a library filled with two rows of tall bookcases. The shelves of the bookcases were lined with actual physical, bound volumes, and each bookcase rose to well above head height, terminating just beneath a ceiling four or five metres overhead. Reading tables and thickly upholstered furniture on ragged and dusty-looking rugs filled the space between the two rows, while the walls of the library appeared to have been cut from the same unadorned stone as the hall.

A body lay slumped a few metres from a pair of glass-panelled doors at the far end of the library, beyond which lay an outside patio with a view over the rest of the island. Two mechants hovered near the corpse, presumably set there to guard it.

Luc stepped forward, then glanced back to see Zelia de Almeida and the rest of the Councillors gathered by the entrance to the library. De Almeida fluttered one hand towards Vasili's inert form as if to say *go on*.

Luc stepped around the body where it lay sprawled across a patterned rug. Part of Vasili's head, along with much of his torso and almost the entire pelvic region, had been burned to ashes. The rug beneath the body was crisped black.

Luc tried to keep his breathing shallow as he knelt on one knee by Vasili's remains. He glanced toward the patio doors, thinking.

Vasili had hit the floor face-down, but the blackened remains of one arm reached towards the patio. Luc put one hand on the scorched rug near what remained of the head, then leaned down until his cheek almost touched the floor, trying to get a better look at the dead man's face without disturbing the body. One side of the skull had melted, exposing the brain, but the side of the face that had been facing away from the blast that killed him was recognizably that of Sevgeny Vasili. That, at least, removed any doubts about who had been killed.

Luc sat back up and looked towards the patio doors, noting that the glass panels nearest the ground had melted and shattered.

He glanced back down at Vasili, and spotted something he'd missed at first glance. Leaning down again, he saw that a book lay wedged just beneath the body, and by some miracle appeared to be intact. It lay partly open beneath Vasili's chest, and what pages Luc could see had a slight metallic lustre to them, as if they were formed from sheets of some metallic composite instead of paper. That, at least, might explain why the book had survived as well as it had.

He reached down to see if it was possible to carefully tug the book out from under the body without disturbing it too much. As he did so, his fingers brushed the edge of one page, and what happened next took his breath away.

He stumbled into the library, frightened and alone. Beyond the patio, the sun cast long streaks of fire across the evening sky as it sank towards the horizon. He searched frantically for what he needed.

There. He raced towards a shelf and picked out the book, catching sight of the lettering on the spine: A History of the Tian Di, *by Javier Maxwell.*

Stepping towards the glass doors, he peered out to see a flier drop towards the courtyard outside. Fear clutched at his heart, but then he took a deep breath, pressing trembling fingers against the pages, desperate to record one last message . . .

'Winchell,' he muttered under his breath. 'I was wrong, so very wrong. I see that now.'

Luc gasped, and rocked back onto his haunches, pulling his fingers away from the book and pressing them against his chest as if he had been scalded.

Just for a moment, he had *been* Sevgeny Vasili.

'Mr Gabion? Are you all right?'

Luc turned to see Cheng standing halfway between the entrance to the library and the corpse. The rest remained huddled together by the door.

Luc glanced down at Vasili's body, the book still mostly hidden beneath it. From where he stood, Cheng couldn't see it.

'I'm sorry, I guess this is all just a little . . .' Luc shook his head, struggling to regain his composure and unsure what to say. Some instinct prevented him from mentioning anything about the book.

<And this is the man you're hoping will exonerate you, Zelia?> jeered Borges.

'Did you note anything of interest?' Cheng pressed.

Yes. 'If I may speak candidly once more . . . ?'

'You may,' Cheng rumbled, regarding him curiously.

'Forensic investigation isn't exactly my forte,' he explained. 'I'm not sure just how much good I can do you here without the help of someone who might be better qualified.'

Cheng regarded him with mild amusement. 'Zelia showed me the details of your record of service for Security and Intelligence's Archives Division, Mr Gabion. It was all very impressive. As Zelia already pointed out, you managed to track Winchell down essentially single-handed, not even counting several other lesser but nonetheless equally impressive triumphs earlier in your career. Under the circumstances, I think she's entirely right to think you're more than sufficiently qualified to give us an objective opinion regarding what took place here.'

It further occurred to Luc that if Vasili's killer really was a member of the Temur Council, he could well be amongst those standing arrayed behind Father Cheng. And given the power of life or death any one of them had over him – or, indeed, over almost anyone throughout the worlds of the Tian Di – there was a real chance he'd be putting his own life in serious danger if he did mention the book. Nor had he missed Ruy Borges's comment about Zelia's need to be exonerated – but exonerated from what? From suspicion of murdering Vasili, or something completely unrelated?

Whoever turned out to have killed Vasili, the last thing he wanted to do, should the killer prove to be present, was blurt out that he'd found a piece of evidence. For the moment it was best to leave the book where he had found it, tucked out of sight beneath Vasili's corpse. Fortunately, none of those present appeared to have the least interest in getting close enough to the body to see the book wedged beneath it.

'Those mechants,' said Luc, nodding up at the machines floating just overhead. 'Did they belong to Vasili?'

'They did,' said de Almeida, stepping up beside Cheng, one hand covering her mouth and nose. 'They're linked into the security network for the whole island.'

'Any sign of them having been compromised?'

Zelia nodded. 'Someone figured out how to erase the house records going back for some days. The mechants' memories are linked into those records, so any data that might have told us who's responsible for this was also wiped.'

'Why haven't you just gone ahead and re-instantiated Vasili from his backups?' asked Luc. 'Surely you could just *ask* him who did this?'

Zelia's lips tightened. 'All his backups were erased remotely, presumably by whoever was responsible for his murder.'

Luc stared back at her, shocked. 'Would that have been easy to do?' he asked carefully.

'No,' she replied, shaking her head. 'Not easy at all.'

Luc glanced at the Councillors clustered by the entrance. All of them, except for Cheng and Cripps, the latter regarding him with an openly malevolent expression, looked scared. Instantiation technology had kept them all alive for centuries, but when Vasili had died, he had died forever, and none of them wanted to share in his fate.

'Are the backups centrally located?' he asked.

'No, they're widely distributed,' Zelia replied. 'Their locations are a carefully kept secret, for obvious reasons.'

'But *somebody* must know where they're all located.'

Zelia sighed and shook her head again. 'No, I'm afraid not. We programmed AIs to take care of placing them in secure but unknown locations. Nobody has the right to know where anyone else's instantiation backups are located. The only thing I *can* tell you is that as far as I know, they're all located somewhere in this star system, but not necessarily on Vanaheim itself.'

'Whoever did this, then,' said Luc, 'must have had an unprecedented level of access to your security systems.'

'I think,' muttered Cripps, 'that's what I'd call stating the fucking obvious.'

Borges sniggered. 'Any *other* incisive observations you'd like to make, Mr Gabion?'

Luc felt heat rise in his face, but knew the danger of responding directly to such an insult. 'Vasili was running away from something when he died,' he said, turning his attention back towards the corpse and pointing towards the glass doors. 'He was running from someone standing at the entrance to the library. As for the murder weapon, it's pretty obvious it was a plasma beam of some type, set to tight focus.'

<This is ridiculous,> Borges scripted. <Any one of us could have said as much. I—>

Cheng threw a fierce look at Borges, who fell immediately silent.

'Please continue,' said Cheng, turning back to Luc.

'If the weapon used to kill Vasili had been set to wide-focus, or aimed at him while he was standing, it would have shattered the rest of the glass in those doors,' he said, nodding towards the patio. 'The angle of the scorch-marks shows the weapon was aimed downwards. Vasili was already on the ground when he died, although it's anyone's guess whether he fell or was pushed down.' He took a deep breath and let it out slowly. 'Did anyone find a weapon?'

'No, but the radiation levels in here are sky-high,' said the second, unnamed woman in the group. 'We're all going to need immediate cell-regeneration therapy. I can arrange for you to receive medical attention before you return to Temur.'

'An excellent suggestion, Alicia,' said Cheng. 'Is there anything else you can tell us?' he asked Luc.

Luc tried not to think about the deadly radiation already seeping into his bones and muscles. 'Has anything been touched or moved since he was found here?'

Victor Begum spoke up. 'Not a thing. Zelia can vouch for that.'

'Who actually found him?'

'No one,' said Zelia. 'His home security network alerted us, but only once it rebooted itself a little over two days ago.'

Two days ago? 'And that's how long he's been lying here? Two days?'

'Criminal investigations are not our area of expertise,' said the woman named Alicia. 'Given the sensitive nature of things, it took us . . . some time to reach a collective agreement on a way forward.'

Luc stared at her. In other words, they'd spent the past forty-eight hours squabbling about what to do before bringing him here.

'So far I'd say he's making a better initial assessment than your own, Bailey,' said Cheng, with an air of joviality that seemed misplaced given the surroundings. 'Maybe we should give Mr *Gabion* your job?'

Nothing like making a very dangerous enemy, thought Luc, as Cripps' hawk-like glare settled on him once again. The sweat had dried on his skin, coating him in a chill clamminess.

Luc glanced towards the nearest bookshelf, as much to avoid looking at Cripps as anything else. Many of the volumes there had become spotted with ash. He reached out and touched the spine of one, his fingertips black when he studied them.

'Did the house put the blaze out?' he asked.

'Obviously,' snapped Cripps.

<Bailey, I'll have no more interruptions from you,> Cheng scripted.

'How could it do that, if the house's AI systems had been shut down?' asked Luc.

'Only the house's higher cognitive functions were affected,' Zelia explained. 'Something like the sprinkler system wouldn't have been affected by the sabotage.'

'Would the killer have known that?' he asked.

'Why do you ask?' Cripps demanded, his voice taut.

'Maybe whoever did this meant for the library to burn down,' said Luc. 'Maybe they thought that when they disabled the house's systems, that would stop it putting the fire out.' Luc's eyes darted nervously towards Cheng, then away again.

'Why would they want to do that?' asked Cheng.

'If it looked like Vasili had just died of an accident, it might have taken you a lot longer to work out he'd been murdered.'

'This is idle speculation,' Cripps protested.

'But very *interesting* idle speculation,' said Cheng, eyeing Cripps carefully. 'Surely,' he said, turning back to Luc, 'there would be no point to covering up Sevgeny's murder, since we would inevitably have discovered both the sabotage to the house AI and to his instantiation backups?'

'There's no point,' Luc agreed, 'unless the killer was operating under a time restriction. For some reason, he or she wanted to delay the discovery that Sevgeny had been murdered.'

'And why in God's name would they do that?' Cripps protested.

Luc forced himself to meet the man's eyes. 'I don't know,' he said. 'But it's worth thinking about.'

It occurred to Luc that Cheng and his cronies could decide to blame *him* for Vasili's murder, and no one would ever dare challenge it or demand supporting evidence of any kind. The idea squeezed his lungs like a steel vice, making it hard to breathe.

'Before I go any further,' he said, 'I need to know who you think could have done this, whether or not you think you can prove it?'

It was almost comical, the way they regarded each other furtively.

'That's a very nearly endless list,' said Zelia, her voice impatient. 'Enmities can run pretty deep here.'

'Zelia,' said Karlmann Sandoz, a note of warning in his voice. 'He's a stranger here.'

'He needs to know these things if he's to do his job properly,' Zelia snapped.

<Your pet detective's clearly not up to the challenge,> Borges scripted. <Look at him, he's terrified of us. You should dispose of him, Zelia, before he tells everyone he knows about what he's seen here. Perhaps then you could make him into one of your little *projects*.>

<*Enough*.> This again from Cheng.

Luc tried not to think about what would happen if she and the rest of them realized he was entirely aware of everything they were scripting to each other. 'Councilman Begum suggested Vasili might have been killed by someone outside of the Council,' said Luc. 'Is there any way someone could sneak through the Hall of Gates without being detected?'

'To say that would be impossible is not an exaggeration,' de Almeida replied firmly.

'Who's in charge of security?'

'Planetary security is the responsibility of Miss de Almeida,' Cheng informed him.

'Which is why,' Zelia added, 'I'm qualified to know what I'm talking about. Anyone invited to Vanaheim who *isn't* a member of the Council gets assigned their own dedicated mechant, all of which report directly to me – including the one that brought you here.'

'But who else is involved in the security operation?'

'Only me,' Zelia replied, one of her cheek muscles twitching. 'Everything runs on dedicated AI systems coordinated through my lattice.'

'Surely that's a lot of responsibility for just one person?'

'Mr Gabion,' Alicia interjected, 'Vanaheim is our model for the future – the way every world in the Tian Di will be, one day. Maintaining surveillance on a whole world isn't so hard for even just one person, if you have access to Council-approved levels of technology, and the systems Zelia controls are sufficiently transparent they only rarely require direct or even conscious intervention.'

'But it's clearly not infallible,' Luc pointed out.

Alicia's smile faltered slightly, and she glanced towards Father Cheng. 'Perhaps not entirely, no,' she admitted after a moment's hesitation.

'Let's not discount the possibility,' grated Cripps, 'that there's nothing wrong with the surveillance systems whatsoever.'

Luc saw de Almeida's nostrils flare. 'This is why I wanted someone outside of the Council here,' she said, her voice strained. 'We're already descending into making accusations against each other without proof, and this close to Reunification we have better things to do than use Sevgeny's murder as an excuse to settle old grudges. I'll tell you one thing – whoever is responsible for this had a solid working knowledge of the planet-wide security networks. And they spent a *lot* of time in preparation – video loops and false data were fed into this house's memory, making it appear as if everything were normal.'

Luc studied de Almeida's features, seeing the mask-like tightness of her face as she spoke. She surely must have realized her high-level access to Vanaheim's security networks made her a strikingly obvious suspect.

'If I may,' asked Luc, speaking up as de Almeida fell silent, 'did no one notice that Vasili was missing?'

'They had noticed,' said Alicia. 'But Sevgeny had become something of a loner over the past several decades. He was closely involved in preparations for Reunification, so when he failed to turn up for a few meetings, it didn't really seem all that unusual.' She swallowed. 'I know this must seem strange to you, that no one thought to fly out here and see if he was all right, but you must understand that all of us within the Council have lived very, very long lives, and one thing you learn to do over such long periods of time is to leave each other alone. With his mechants, his own security and Zelia's networks to protect him as well as the rest of us, there was no reason to be alarmed . . . until now.'

A short silence fell, finally broken by Father Cheng. 'Is there anything else you would like to ask us, Mr Gabion?'

'Not at the moment, thank you, Father Cheng,' Luc replied. 'But perhaps if I could take a look around, if that's all right by you . . . ?'

'Of course,' said Cheng, nodding. 'But do remember,' he added, 'that I would be far from happy if you were to discuss what you've learned today outside of our present company.'

'Of course,' Luc nodded.

Cheng turned to the rest. 'As badly as I feel for poor Sevgeny,' he said, 'I think we might also consider this a test for our collective wills, so close to our Reunification with the Coalition. One day, when Black Lotus are finally vanquished and our society reaches a state of true social harmony, everyone in the Tian Di will live the way all of us here do.'

He glanced first at Cripps, and then Luc, before continuing. 'Please don't allow me, or anyone else, to unduly influence your opinion when it comes to identifying the responsible party, but I must confess that I find it less than credible that one member of the Temur Council would willingly take the life of another. Despite Zelia's certainty to the contrary, that leads us to an apparent impossibility – that someone from outside our closed ranks perpetuated the crime. At the very least, this implies a serious flaw in our security arrangements – one that must be taken care of immediately.'

Cheng never once glanced towards de Almeida as he made this final remark, but Luc did not fail to notice the way her cheek once again spasmed as the Permanent Chairman of the Temur Council effectively accused her of sleeping on the job.

'We're eventually going to have to tell the rest of the Council what happened to Sevgeny,' said Borges. 'That's going to cause an almighty ruckus.'

'Not to mention we have only a couple of weeks before the official opening of the Darwin–Temur gate,' added Begum.

'That's where you come in, Mr Gabion,' said de Almeida, clearly fighting to maintain her composure. 'Father Cheng has agreed to allow you limited access to Vanaheim's resources, under my custodianship, until we've completed this investigation. We can start immediately.'

'*Your* custodianship?' scoffed Borges, who stepped forward until he was facing Cheng. 'Surely, with so much access to our security networks, Zelia had the most opportunity to kill Sevgeny!'

'That assumes,' Zelia spat back, 'you can identify a motive on my part. I'm sure when it comes to *motives*, Ruy, nobody here would lack for recognizing a serious fucking desire on *your* part to see Sevgeny dead.'

<How dare you?>

<I will not warn you again,> Cheng scripted, and the flow of words fell away.

'Without wanting to distract you from your purpose here, Mr Gabion,' said Cheng, 'I understand you're something of an expert on Black Lotus. Perhaps I could ask you for your opinion concerning them?'

'Of course, Father Cheng.'

'How much, if at all, have Black Lotus been harmed by Winchell Antonov's death?'

'There are still too many variables as yet to be able to say in the short-term, Father Cheng,' Luc replied. 'At the very least, Aeschere constitutes a major propaganda coup for us.'

'And in the long-term?'

'In the long-term, I don't think they can really survive without his guidance.'

'Yet Black Lotus retains considerable popular support on both Benares and Acamar. In the days following the announcement of Antonov's demise, fresh atrocities were carried out against Sandoz peacekeeping forces on both worlds. The reports I receive from SecInt tell me that new Black Lotus cells are popping up all across Temur at an increasing rate, some within view of the White Palace itself. What would you say if I were to suggest that they are, in fact, stronger than they have ever been?'

'Father Cheng, this man does not have clearance to be cognisant of the full facts concerning—'

Cheng shot an angry glare at Karlmann Sandoz, who had spoken up. 'I want his answer, Karlmann,' Cheng snapped, interrupting him. 'Do you have an objection?'

Karlmann shook his head and said no more.

'Well, Mr Gabion?' Cheng continued. 'I'm concerned that Antonov's death has done nothing more than turn him into a martyr.'

Luc ran his tongue around his lips. 'The problem lies in the underlying root causes of the dissatisfaction that Black Lotus feeds on,' he said. 'The unrest on Benares, the failure of the artificial ecosystem on Acamar . . . people want someone to blame.'

Luc felt suddenly dizzy, and stepped closer to one of the book-cases in order to support himself. Everything was turning bright, while a tiny point of fire in the centre of his skull slowly expanded outwards.

'Surely the fact that we've enjoyed unprecedented peace for centuries counts for more,' Cheng demanded.

'I . . .'

'Mr Gabion?' Zelia stepped forward and grabbed his arm. 'Are you all right?'

'I'm not sure. I . . .'

The fire expanded to fill the interior of his skull. He lurched, feeling a surge of bile rush up the back of his throat.

Not now. He reached out to the bookcase, trying to steady himself. His hand clutched at several heavy volumes, and they clattered to the floor around him as he sank to his knees.

<It's that damn radiation,> Alicia scripted.

<No, this is too soon,> Zelia replied.

'Gabion?'

He opened his eyes and saw de Almeida kneeling beside him, a look of alarm on her face.

This can't be happening again, he thought. Somewhere inside him, something was seriously wrong.

FIVE

The next few hours passed in a blur. Luc had a vague recollection of being lifted out of the building by the two mechants set to guard Vasili's body. After that there had been a journey by flier, during which he drifted in and out of consciousness.

The next time he really became aware of his surroundings, he found himself looking up at the high ceiling of a circular room that had to be at least thirty metres across. The ceiling was decorated with highly stylized depictions of astronomical symbols and of several Tian Di worlds, all wheeling around a stone pillar at the room's centre. An iron stairway twisted around the pillar like a braid, rising through an aperture in the ceiling to another floor above. Bright sunlight spilled through an open doorway at the far end of the room, through which he could make out bristling reddish-green flora. Steps nearby led down, perhaps to some basement level.

Luc sat up with a groan, supporting himself with one hand, and found he had been placed on a broad, raised slab. A small wheeled trolley, loaded with trays of sharp-looking surgical instruments, had been placed next to him.

The rest of the room was crammed with cabinets of various shapes and sizes, and pieces of mostly unidentifiable equipment and machinery, as well as an industrial-sized fabricant that took up nearly a third of the room. A mechant hovered by the fabricant's control panel, suggesting it was engaged in manufacturing its own replacement components.

The rush of agony that had overwhelmed him back in Vasili's library had now faded to little more than a faint and distant throb. He swung his legs off the slab and the room reeled around him. Catching hold of the edge of the slab, he waited until the worst of the dizziness had passed, then lowered his feet to the ground and stood gently.

He felt too light to be back on Temur. More than likely, he was still on Vanaheim. But wherever he was, the climate was much warmer than it had been on Vasili's island.

Something went *thump* on the far side of the room.

Luc tensed, listening, then heard the same sound again after an interval of maybe twenty seconds. It sounded like someone dropping a sack of grain onto the room's tiled floor.

He moved with caution in the direction the sound had come from, keeping one hand out in case he took another dizzy turn. He stepped past a cabinet at the other side of the room, not far from the exit, and found himself looking at a shaven-headed man standing facing the wall, bent-over as if studying something lying on the floor. His arms hung straight down, knuckles nearly grazing the tiles.

'Hello?' Luc asked uncertainly.

No answer.

The man wore a shapeless and filthy smock that reached down to his bare feet, and stood perfectly still, as if his bones had locked into place and he could no longer stand straight.

'Hello?' Luc asked again. 'Can you tell me where I am?'

No answer. Somehow he hadn't really expected one.

He watched as the bent figure took a sudden step forward, banging his head into the wall with some force.

Despite a burgeoning sense of dread, Luc stepped closer, putting one hand on the man's shoulder and pulling him around. Instead of eyes, grey metal ovals studded with pin-like extensions protruded from between the man's eyelids, while much of his lower jaw had been removed entirely and replaced with some kind of machinery with a steel grille built into the front. His flesh was mottled and twisted where it had been fused to plastic and metal.

A moan emerged from the creature's mouth-grille, full of terrible pain and unfathomable anguish.

Luc stumbled backwards, his heart hammering with shock. The misshapen figure turned away from him once more and resumed ramming its head against the wall.

Luc fled, running through the sunlit exit, desperate to get away from the misshapen creature. But rather than finding himself outside as he had expected, he instead found himself standing at one end of a greenhouse filled with a stunning variety of flora. The air tasted moist and peaty.

He shaded his eyes against the sunlight streaming in through the panes overhead and saw Zelia de Almeida standing further down a narrow path. A mechant hovered by her side, a straw basket incongruously clutched in one of its many manipulators. He watched as de Almeida took a small cutting from the branch of a tree, placing it in the basket.

The tree shivered in response, its lower branches weaving in slow patterns that somehow suggested distress. De Almeida reached out again, grasping hold of a slim branch. It tried to pull away from her, but she had too firm a hold on it. He watched as she snipped the branch off with a small pair of secateurs.

The tree shivered more violently than before, and Zelia murmured something inaudible to the mechant. In that same moment, another faceless monstrosity, identical to the one Luc had just encountered, appeared at the far end of the path, another straw basket clutched in its hand.

Luc watched dry-mouthed as the figure shambled along a connecting path, and out of sight.

'Ah, there you are.'

He looked back at Zelia. She was peeling off a pair of gloves, dropping them into the mechant's basket.

'Where am I?' he asked.

Zelia gestured to the mechant, and it moved down the path away from him. 'I brought you to my home,' she replied, stepping towards him. 'Call me paranoid, but I didn't want to take a chance somebody might have interfered with you.'

She placed one hand on his shoulder and guided him back through to the circular room he had just come from.

'Back up, please,' she said, leading him back over to the raised slab. Her manner was brisk and business-like.

Another thump echoed from across the room, but Zelia showed no sign of even being aware of it.

'What the hell is that thing?' Luc demanded, unable to hide his revulsion.

'What thing?' asked Zelia.

'The man with no eyes.'

She glanced behind her with mild puzzlement, then back at him. 'Ah,' she said, nodding. 'Nothing to worry about. Just an experiment.'

'An experiment,' Luc repeated. 'What *kind* of experiment?'

'One that needn't concern you,' she replied briskly. 'You'll be pleased to know I've already treated us both for radiation damage.'

He gestured back in the direction of the eyeless thing. 'But . . .'

She flashed him an angry look. 'We're not here to discuss my private research,' she snapped. 'I want to find out what happened to you back there at Vasili's. How much do you remember, from when you collapsed?'

'I don't know,' he replied. 'One minute everything was fine, the next . . .' He shrugged. 'I've never experienced anything like it.'

'Are you sure?'

'Well . . . something like it happened to me back on Temur, just after they brought me back from Aeschere.'

She nodded, as if this had been the answer she had been expecting. 'I checked your records as soon as I had the chance, but the medicians attending to you couldn't identify a cause for that first seizure. Is that correct?'

He nodded.

<But before we discuss anything else,> she scripted at him, her gaze unblinking, <tell me if you can understand what I'm saying.>

Luc stared at her, unsure how to respond.

A look of grim satisfaction spread across her face. <Just what I thought. You *did* know what we were all saying to each other back in Vasili's library, didn't you?>

Luc swallowed. <Scripting is fairly common, last thing I heard.>

<Except that was a private conversation, mediated through lattices, and using compression and encryption techniques far beyond anything a mere CogNet unit like the one you own could possibly handle. You shouldn't have had any idea what we were discussing amongst ourselves. Just how much did you overhear?>

Luc felt his shoulders sag. 'Pretty much all of it,' he said out loud.

She stared at him with frightening intensity. 'I could have you killed. Tell me, how did you do it?'

'I don't know. I just . . . picked up everything. It wasn't anything I did, it just happened.'

'I felt sure of it, from the moment you stepped inside that miserable hovel of Sevgeny's.'

'You already said your security networks might have been compromised in some way,' he reminded her. 'Maybe that's got something to do with it?'

'No.' She shook her head. 'That's not it.'

Luc made an exasperated sound. 'Look, I have *no idea* how I could have picked up what you were all scripting to each other. I mean, I realized I wasn't meant to at the time, but how could I have told any of you? I was too . . .' *Too frightened.*

'I believe you,' she said. 'But only because I'm scanning you on a number of levels right now, all of which tell me you're not deliberately obfuscating the truth.'

'Okay then, so how *could* I have picked up everything you were saying?'

She raised both eyebrows. 'That's a question that can't have anything but an interesting answer. For instance, would you care to tell me exactly who put an instantiation lattice inside your skull?'

Luc gaped at her dumbly before answering. 'No one. I don't have any such thing.'

She smiled enigmatically. 'Oh, but you *do*, Mr Gabion. Look.'

Images of the interior of a skull – *his* skull, he guessed – blossomed in the air around them. One showed a lump of pinkish-grey flesh encased in fine silvery lines, while another depicted a messy tangle of pulsing blue light rendered in three dimensions, overlaid with a secondary, more orderly grid of red.

'That,' said Zelia, 'is what an instantiation lattice looks like, in the very early stages of settling into its owner's cortex – *your* cortex, to be precise. I had my house AI remotely analyse the inside of your head as soon as I realized what you had in there. But there are differences between this and any other kind of lattice I've ever seen.'

'Differences?'

'What you've got in there, unless my AIs are sorely mistaken, is more advanced than anything used even by the members of the Council, including myself. It has . . . functions I can't begin to decipher.' She took a deep breath and shook her head, her eyes bright and feral. 'The question, then, is how the hell did it get inside your head?'

Antonov.

Luc's blood ran cold and he knew, in that instant, that everything he remembered from Aeschere was real, and not a hallucination. Antonov had done something to him: booby-trapped him in some way, placed a ticking bomb inside his head for reasons he hadn't bothered to explain beyond a few cryptic statements.

He shuddered to think of what might have happened to him if he'd fallen into the hands of Victor Begum or Karlmann Sandoz following his seizure in the library or – even worse – Cripps. He might well have disappeared into some Sandoz stronghold, never to be seen again.

Not that he was necessarily any safer in de Almeida's hands, he reminded himself. Unlike Cripps or Karlmann Sandoz, she was still an unknown quantity.

'I swear to you, I have no idea,' Luc replied, almost begging.

Zelia glanced towards the projections as he spoke, her lips twisting into a thin line. 'Now you *are* lying, Mr Gabion: it's all there in the flow of blood in your capillaries, and the unconscious reactions of your autonomic nervous system.' She studied him with angry eyes. 'If you lie to me again, I'll know straight away. Think you can get that through your head?'

'Yes,' he replied carefully.

'Good.' Her shoulders relaxed a little. 'Now tell me how this came about.'

'Antonov implanted it inside me. We were on Aeschere hunting for him, when our mosquitoes turned on us, killing all of—'

'Yes, yes,' she snapped, interrupting him. 'I'm already familiar with everything that took place on Aeschere.'

'Not everything that happened is in the official report.'

She frowned. 'What do you mean?'

Luc took a deep breath. 'When I told Director Lethe of SecInt what really happened, he warned me he was going to leave some of the details out of the official report.'

'Why?'

'He was worried that what I told him might give an investigative committee reason to call my sanity into question, especially since I couldn't prove much of what I said happened down there.'

She folded her arms. 'Then I take it back. Start from the beginning, and tell me what *really* happened.'

He told her everything that had taken place after he had found his way to the lowest level of the Aeschere complex, leaving nothing out.

'And when you encountered Antonov on the ship, he was still alive?'

Luc nodded. 'He managed to take me by surprise and knocked me out. When I came to, he was in the process of putting some kind of mechant inside me.' He shuddered at the memory. 'It was tiny, like a metal worm. It crawled in through my nose and dug its way through my skull.'

She arched an eyebrow. 'Delightful.'

'So what happens after I finish telling you all this?' asked Luc miserably. 'Are you going to hand me over to the Sandoz for more questioning?'

'Let's just keep all this between the two of us for now.' She paused, looking thoughtful. 'What happened next?'

Luc remembered terrible pain. 'As soon as he was done, Antonov put me back under. The next time I came to, he was dead. I did what I had to do in order to get out of the complex and save my own life.'

'And then they brought you to Temur, where they found no trace of your instantiation lattice?'

Luc nodded.

Zelia regarded him speculatively, then made a gesture. In response, the floating images around them blurred and shifted, and were replaced by new ones, this time of Luc's body in the hospital's regeneration tank shortly after his return from Aeschere. He winced at the sight of his seared and ruined flesh.

She glanced back to him with an expression that almost bordered on sympathy. 'They had to do a lot of work on you, didn't they?'

'When I had that first seizure, they ran scans on me to see if there were any abnormalities in my skull. But they found nothing. The medicians told me everything looked like it should.'

'I'd agree with you that the worm-like mechant you described must be the means by which Antonov got the lattice inside your head. But if that's the case, it doesn't answer the question of why it showed up on my machines, but not those at the hospital . . .'

Her voice trailed off, and she leaned back against a table, drumming her fingers against its edge. 'Instantiation lattices are just about the single most advanced form of technology in the whole of the Tian Di, apart from the transfer gates. Theoretically, a sophisticated enough lattice *could* fool certain analytical devices into thinking it wasn't there. I can't think of anything else that could possibly make sense. But it also begs the question – why would Antonov want to place such a sophisticated piece of technology inside your head?'

She looked at him as if he might be able to give her an answer.

'If I could tell you the reason,' he said, 'I would.'

She nodded to the images floating around them. 'Whatever Antonov had in mind for you, it wasn't for your benefit. You've already had two serious seizures in a row, and I'd be an idiot not to think that lattice of yours is the reason why. Is there anything else you should be telling me?'

Luc told her about his strange dream-encounter with Antonov.

'But you're saying it wasn't a dream?' asked Zelia, once he'd finished.

'I don't know what it was, but he told me that if I survived, I had to open a specific record in Archives and make a small alteration to it.'

De Almeida nodded, her face neutral. 'Go on.'

Luc shrugged. 'He told me I had to add in a line about calling in a favour, then save and close the file.'

'And did you?'

Luc nodded. 'I wanted to see if it was real. If it didn't exist, then that would have proved the whole damn thing really was just some terrible nightmare.'

'What was the file's reference?'

'Thorne, 51 Alpha, Code Yellow.'

She breathed out through her nose, her mouth making a chewing motion. 'Tell me what you found in the file.'

'It described an incident on Thorne more than a century ago – some kind of illegal biotech research that brought about a number of deaths.' He glanced at her. 'You were the Director in charge of Thorne at the time.'

'You've been looking into me?'

'Not as such, but your name was attached to the file.'

'I remember that investigation all too well,' she said. 'Tell me,

Mr Gabion, have you discussed the details of this file or how you altered it with anyone else?'

'Hell, no.' He laughed nervously, wondering if she had any idea how terrified he really was. Almost certainly, he decided. His palms were clammy with sweat, his heart thudding in his chest. 'If I'd told anyone what I just told you, they'd have locked me up and thrown away the key.'

Zelia nodded and stepped around to the other side of the slab, looking thoughtful. She reached up to brush a strand of hair back from her face. As she did so, Luc noticed her hand was shaking very slightly.

He glanced towards the sunlit door, beyond which lay the greenhouse. 'If the others found out what I've just told you,' he asked her, 'what would happen to me?'

'To you? To be brutally frank, Mr Gabion, dissection would be the first obvious step. Molecular tools would be used to tease your lattice apart, atom by atom, and highly invasive scanning routines would be used to try and decrypt whatever data or auto-suggestive routines Antonov might have implanted inside you. Assuming, that is, he hadn't also booby-trapped the lattice to kill you the instant anyone tried to fool with it in any significant way.' She shrugged. 'To put it even more bluntly, Mr Gabion, I would not expect you to live for very long.'

Luc got halfway to the greenhouse entrance, his shoes slapping loudly against the tiles underfoot.

Something flashed past him in a blur, and the next thing he knew he was looking up at the outline of a mechant, hovering directly between him and the painted ceiling.

Zelia stepped over, gazing down at him with an expression of contempt.

'Promise me,' she said, 'that you won't waste any more of my time with stupid stunts like that.'

'You just told me I'm going to have my brain picked apart,' Luc groaned. 'What the fuck would *you* do?'

'I already told you nothing would happen to you so long as

nobody else found out you were in possession of a lattice.' She gestured towards the mechant, and it drifted back out of the way. 'I keep my word, Mr Gabion.'

'You're serious?' He pushed himself up into a sitting position on unsteady hands, staring up at her with desperate hope. 'You're not going to hand me over to them?'

'I want to know just what Antonov was up to when he gave you that lattice. If I shared what you've told me with Father Cheng or anyone else in the Council, the first thing they would do is take the matter out of my hands. However, I have very good reasons for not wanting that to happen.'

He decided not to ask her what those reasons might be. There was something unsettling about her eyes, about her whole demeanour, the way she carried herself as much as the way she looked at him, as if he were an object rather than a human being.

'So what happens now?' he asked.

'Nothing for the moment, Mr Gabion,' she said, her eyes bright, 'except that you'll finish the job I brought you to Vanaheim to carry out. And if you ever – *ever* – think of telling anyone about our conversation here, believe me when I say there would be consequences.'

'You're not exactly giving me much choice.'

'No, I'm not.' She reached out a hand and he took it, standing up. Her grip was surprisingly strong.

'Now that we're clear on our relationship,' she said, 'I want to know if there's anything else you want to tell me. Any other apparent hallucinations or memories you think might be pertinent.'

'Nothing that really made any sense to me,' he admitted.

The mechant drifted closer to him, instruments unfolding from its belly.

'Tell me anyway,' said Zelia, her eyes slitted like a hungry cat.

Luc stared at the mechant and licked his lips. 'Okay. I had this dream a couple of times where I found myself looking into a mirror – or what I *thought* was a mirror, at first, but turned out to be a mask someone wore over their face. Except instead of seeing my own reflection in the mirror, I saw Antonov's.'

De Almeida stared at him intently. 'You're certain of this?'

Luc shook his head helplessly. 'How can I be certain about *anything*? It was just some crazy nightmare. But it felt . . .'

'What?' she demanded.

'Real. It felt real.'

'I think Antonov planted some of his own memories in your head,' she told him. 'I'm going to be honest with you. Once a lattice is in, it's in for good, and the means by which Antonov placed it inside you strike me as extremely crude compared to how it's usually carried out. The whole process has to be carefully monitored under laboratory conditions from beginning to end, and it can take weeks, even months, for a lattice to properly meld with the surrounding tissues. But what he did to you will almost certainly kill you, probably within weeks, sooner if left unattended.'

Luc nodded dumbly. 'Isn't there some way to, I don't know, reverse the process? And if I've got an instantiation lattice in my head, doesn't that mean you'd be able to create a backup of my mind?'

'A backup couldn't be made at this early a stage of your lattice's growth, no. It simply wouldn't work. And a mature lattice is precisely what will kill you. But in return for your aid in finding Sevgeny's killer, I'll do my best to reverse any damage brought about by your lattice until I can figure out some other, more long-term solution. The whole affair will remain our secret, yours and mine alone.'

She stepped a little closer to him. 'But while you're searching for Vasili's killer, don't make the mistake of thinking you can hold anything back from me. Not anything – is that clear?'

'That's clear,' he said. 'But if I'm going to do what you want me to, I need to be able to speak candidly with you, and without fear of repercussion.'

'Why? Was there something you had on your mind?'

'I need your reassurance first.'

She sighed and waved a hand. 'Fine. Go on.'

'It doesn't take any great skill to work out that some of your fellow Councillors think you're guilty as hell when it comes to Vasili's murder. Based on what I heard back in that library of Vasili's, you're one of the few people around with the necessary access to Vanaheim's security systems and the expertise to be able to carry it off.'

'I can give you my personal reassurance that I did not kill Sevgeny. For one, I have no possible motive – as I believe I already pointed out to Ruy Borges.'

That remains to be seen, thought Luc. 'Nobody got round to telling me what *would* be a good motive. Why would someone want to kill Sevgeny Vasili?'

'A desire to hinder Reunification,' she said immediately.

'There are people in the Council who would go that far?'

Her face coloured slightly. 'The fact of Sevgeny's murder suggests that some might. Sevgeny was the architect of Reunification with the Coalition worlds, but most of his fellow Eighty-Fivers stood against it. Cheng put him in charge of the process of negotiation once he and the Eighty-Five were forced to concede to Reunification, under pressure from the general members of the Council.'

'*Could* that be why one of them might have murdered him? Because they were against Reunification?'

She sighed. 'It can't be ruled out.'

'What about you?' he asked. 'How do you feel about Reunification?'

She glared at him. 'What does my opinion of it matter?'

'I just want to get a sense of where everyone stands,' he said.

Her answer was hesitant, and reminded Luc vividly of just how very, very old people like Zelia de Almeida really were, appearances to the contrary. 'Back in the days before the Schism, I thought completely severing contact with the Coalition was a mistake. It wasn't like they were taking chances with any of the advanced technology they found in the Founder Network, so there was no risk of another Abandonment. Instead they were taking a slow and cautious approach, studying everything they discovered *in situ* and only allowing it back through the transfer gates to their own worlds once they were absolutely sure they properly understood what they had.'

'But people had reason to be scared, didn't they? The human race came very close to extinction because of the things we'd discovered in the Founder Network.'

'Yes,' she admitted. 'But I think reunifying with the Coalition is a good thing, even necessary.'

'Why?'

She stared off into the distance before answering. 'It's my belief that without Reunification, the Tian Di is in serious danger of becoming stagnant. Perhaps dangerously so.'

Luc nodded, thinking. 'Can you think of any other motives Vasili's killer might have had apart from a desire to stop or slow down Reunification?'

She smiled humourlessly. 'That's for you to figure out, Mr Gabion, isn't it?' She stepped away from him, her manner suddenly brisk as she made towards the raised slab he had earlier found himself on.

'Before we go any further,' she told him, 'I need to interrogate your lattice. Hopefully I can counteract its growth process by reconfiguring some of its basic functions.' She indicated the slab. 'Please.'

Luc nodded and walked back over, taking a seat on the edge of the slab. Zelia's mechant followed close behind, reaching out with a steel and plastic proboscis that weaved and twisted in the air before his face.

'What's it doing?' he asked nervously.

'It's allowing me to talk to your lattice,' de Almeida replied, her expression intent, eyes focused on something Luc couldn't see. He felt a slight tingling in his scalp.

'All right,' she said as the mechant retracted its proboscis and moved back. 'I've set up neural blocks that should help retard the lattice. Now you can go home, Mr Gabion. You have your work to return to, and an investigation to carry out.'

'How can I do that from Temur?'

'Remember I have Father Cheng's permission to bring you here as and when necessary. When I need you, I'll call on you. In the meantime, you can return to your work in Archives. Now follow me.'

She led him down the length of the greenhouse and through tall doors at its far end. The sky had darkened, the air outside only slightly cooler than it had been inside de Almeida's laboratory. Pale filaments of nebulae, perhaps only a few light-years away, rose above the horizon.

A flier dropped silently down onto a broad concrete apron close to the greenhouse. Luc glanced back and saw tall, sand-coloured towers surrounding the circular building he had just emerged from, side by side with a tile-roofed mansion. Beyond the buildings, cultivated gardens segmented by gravel paths had been planted with gently rustling trees of the same species as those in the green-house.

'If you really want me to find out who killed Vasili,' he said as they approached the flier, 'I'm going to need to talk to people. And you need to show me just what went wrong with your secur-ity systems.'

'Nothing went wrong with them.'

Luc frowned. 'I don't understand. Cheng said that someone must have compromised—'

She regarded him with wide, angry eyes. 'Unfortunately, Bailey Cripps was quite correct in his assessment when he said there was nothing whatsoever wrong with Vanaheim's security systems. I spent the last few days taking them apart in order to come to that conclusion.'

'But in that case—'

'Whoever did this, Mr Gabion, wants to make me appear to be the guilty party.'

'You think someone's trying to frame you?'

She nodded.

'That could make your case very difficult.'

'That goes without saying. Who exactly do you need to talk to?'

'Everyone.' He shrugged. 'Anyone. Councillors, certainly.'

She sighed. 'I thought you might say something like that. But it could prove difficult.'

'Why?'

'Because you're not a Councillor yourself. None of them *have* to talk to you, unless Father Cheng tells them otherwise.'

'But Cheng agreed to your running this investigation, didn't he? Surely they have to obey him.'

'You'd think so, but to be frank, it took a lot of persuasion to get Father Cheng to agree to letting you come to Vanaheim. None of them really care about Vasili, they only care whether their neck's next on the block. And what Cheng wants most of all is for all of this to go away before the Reunification ceremonies begin.'

Luc reached out, putting one hand on the side of the flier's open hatch. 'I'd like to take another look at Vasili's body.'

She frowned. 'You've already seen it.'

'That was more of a quick glance. Plus, I need to interrogate Vasili's home security system. And take a second look around that island.'

She nodded tiredly and gestured to the flier. 'I'll see what I can do. In the meantime . . .'

Luc nodded and climbed on board.

'One last thing,' he said, turning to look down at her. 'Were you aware that Bailey Cripps came to visit me at my home before I was even brought to Vanaheim?'

Her eyes widened in shock. 'What?'

'He had,' said Luc, 'concerns about my loyalties.'

'What did he say?'

'He said I was just as much a suspect, though he didn't specify what I was a suspect *of*.'

De Almeida stared off to one side, her nostrils flaring in the same way they had on Vasili's island. Then she turned back to him. 'Thank you for sharing that with me, Mr Gabion.'

'I think,' he said, 'that you need my help just as much as I need yours.'

Fire flashed in her eyes. 'And how do you figure that?'

'You brought me into this because you thought I was good at my job. In that case, I can tell you I'm pretty sure the rest of the Council, or at least those I met today, are getting ready to hang you out to dry.' He felt the conviction of his own words as he spoke. 'That's assuming you're telling me the truth, and you really *didn't* kill Vasili. But even if you didn't, the odds are stacked against you. I didn't get the sense you were well liked by any of those others I met – quite the opposite, in fact.'

'You're speaking out of turn, Mr Gabion,' she said, her voice low and dangerous.

'I told you I need to be able to speak candidly. I can't be afraid of speaking to you, and those are the facts as I see them.'

'Any other nuggets of wisdom you'd care to share with me?'

'I think your bringing me to Vanaheim was a move of desperation on your part. You thought if I could work out who really killed Vasili, it would keep the rest of them from turning you into a scapegoat.'

She took a deep breath and closed her eyes for a moment. 'I may have underestimated you, Mr Gabion. I see that now.'

'As for Cripps, my best guess is he came to me because he thought I was in league with you in some way. You told me you'd all left Vasili's body where it was for a couple of days; time enough for you to wonder when they were going to start accusing you of his murder and look for ways to prove yourself innocent. That's why you approached Cheng, seeking his permission to bring me here. And it's obvious Cripps thinks you *are* guilty, because as soon as he got wind of that decision, he decided maybe I was working with you to cover things up.'

She thought about this for a moment. 'You're sure about that?'

Luc shrugged. 'Alternatively, maybe Cripps was trying to throw me off for some other reason.'

'Perhaps *he* did it.'

'Maybe he did,' Luc agreed. 'He certainly acted like a frightened man, and he really doesn't trust you.'

She let out a small laugh. 'The one thing I and Bailey Cripps have in common is that we don't trust anyone. It's an essential trait for a long career in the Temur Council. I'll be in touch, Mr Gabion. I'll do my best to arrange interviews with anyone who might be able to throw some more light on this whole sorry mess.'

Luc watched her turn and stride up the path without another word, then stepped back, the hatch folding back into place.

SIX

When Luc arrived home through the Hall of Gates, it was mid-afternoon in Ulugh Beg. Eleanor came to him later that evening, exploring his new skin with fingers and lips while the setting sun sent shards of orange light slanting through the window of his apartment.

Tell me what happened, she had asked him shortly after appearing at his door, obviously distraught and out of her mind with worry. *Tell me where you disappeared to. When you didn't come back, I really started to think maybe you were gone forever.*

But he knew the risks of telling her too much and getting her involved, and her work in SecInt meant she understood the necessity of keeping secrets. She had not really expected him to answer. Even so, he felt a pang, as if by refusing to answer her questions he was in some strange way betraying her.

He lay back, head propped up on a pillow, Eleanor's own skin limned by the city's myriad lights as she moved above him, hands kneading his flesh. He noticed again the cosmetic alterations she had recently made to her own body: her hips were slightly narrower than they had been, her breasts fractionally and fashionably smaller. She shuddered, skin glistening, then pressed herself down against him, holding him tight as he came inside her. She held perfectly still for a moment, then slid down onto the bed beside him.

*

He lay there for a long time, listening to her sleep. He was still wide awake, despite his exhaustion. Sleep was impossible after everything he'd been through.

Sometime in the early morning, he had the overwhelming sense that someone else was in the room with them.

He lifted his head and saw a hunched figure with its hands pushed deep into pockets, staring out the window with its back to him.

The figure turned and looked at him: Cripps. A rainbow shimmer surrounded his outline.

Luc climbed naked out of the bed and pulled on a night-robe. Eleanor, he saw with relief, hadn't woken. He gestured towards the living room and stepped through. Cripps took the hint, his data-ghost vanishing from the bedroom and reappearing in the living room a moment later.

'There are laws about data-ghost voyeurism,' Luc hissed the moment the door into the bedroom folded itself shut behind him. 'How the *hell* long were you standing there watching us?'

Cripps shrugged. 'A minute, no more. I want to know what you said to Zelia de Almeida, after she took you away from Vasili's.'

Luc dropped into a seat and pushed both hands through his hair, still groggy. 'Or what? You're going to threaten me too?'

'Charming as ever, was she?' Cripps made a gesture, and Luc felt a flush of outrage when the house AI obeyed him, de-opaquing the window and allowing the morning light to come streaking in. Pioneer Gorge's street-markets were already busy far off in the distance. 'I, however, do not need to threaten you,' he continued. 'I need only remind you of your sworn duty to the Temur Council.'

'To the Council,' Luc snapped, 'but not necessarily to you in particular.'

'If you'd prefer, I can arrange to have you taken back to Vanaheim by force, and interrogated there at my pleasure.' Cripps let his gaze drift towards the bedroom door. 'Or perhaps I could have Miss Jaq arrested, and see what she might be able to tell us. Would that be preferable?'

Luc gripped the arms of his chair and reminded himself that the data-ghost had no actual, physical throat for him to take a hold of. 'Does Father Cheng know you're here?'

'Father Cheng trusts me to ensure the safety of both the Council and the citizens it serves,' Cripps replied. 'To that end, I have an open remit to do whatever proves necessary to ensure the Tian Di's survival and safety. Who else do you think I report to, Mr Gabion?'

'All right,' Luc said heavily, 'fine. De Almeida checked me out in her laboratory and found nothing particularly wrong with me. I already knew I had lesions on my brain from Aeschere, which isn't exactly surprising, given the level of trauma I suffered. That's the most probable cause.'

'And what else?'

Luc shrugged. 'She asked me my impressions of the people gathered at Vasili's, and if I had any particular insights. That's about it.'

'Tell me your insights, then.'

'There's really nothing to tell until I have a chance to interview each of the Councillors individually. She said she might be able to arrange that. I also asked to see the inside of Vasili's home a second time.'

Cripps' gaze was unwavering. 'I'm sure you had more to discuss than that.'

'I told her you'd come here once before and asked me a lot of questions.'

'That probably wasn't a very wise thing to do.'

'Why?'

'Well,' Cripps responded, 'Zelia is herself the most obvious suspect in Vasili's murder, is she not?'

'The other day,' Luc reminded him, 'you claimed *I* was a suspect, but there was no way I could possibly have known yet about Vasili's death.'

'That remains to be seen,' said Cripps. 'She brought your name up very soon after the discovery of Vasili's body. Naturally, that aroused my suspicions.'

'And how does that make me a suspect?'

One corner of Cripps' mouth turned up in a smirk. 'Perhaps you didn't pull the trigger on the weapon that killed Vasili, Mr Gabion, but you might have been complicit in his death in some other way.'

'Go on.'

'Sneaking an assassin through the Hall of Gates and transporting them to Vasili's island, as Father Cheng believes, is not something even Zelia, with her high level of access to Vanaheim's security networks, could have done easily. She would have needed accomplices.'

Luc stared at Cripps in shock. 'You think de Almeida recruited me to help her set up Vasili's assassination, then brought me into the investigation to throw you off the scent?' He let out an outraged laugh. 'How long did it take you to come up with that? It's the most—'

'It might have been planned weeks or even months ago,' said Cripps, interrupting. 'Your side trip to Aeschere would have given you excellent cover.'

Luc shook his head, unable to believe what he was hearing. 'And what about you, Mr Cripps? You turn up here twice, unannounced, and making threats – just the kind of thing a guilty man would do to try and cover his own tracks.'

'No, it's the kind of thing a police officer would do, and I'm the closest there is to one on Vanaheim. You can't deny Zelia looks guilty as all hell, particularly since she's perfectly placed to sabotage the same security networks she's been put in charge of.'

Luc was finding it harder and harder to fight back a growing tide of anger. 'I was there when Father Cheng agreed that I could come to Vanaheim and—'

Cripps stepped closer, until Luc could see the dim outline of the window through his data-ghost. 'Let me make myself clear. You collapsed in front of several high-ranking members of the Council, and Zelia was *very* insistent on taking you with her, even though any one of us could have provided you with an equal level of medical attention, and a lot sooner as well. That, Mr Gabion, did not go without remark.'

'For God's sake, I'm just barely out of intensive regeneration therapy!' Luc yelled, briefly forgetting Eleanor was still asleep next door. 'Instead of getting the chance to recover, I got hauled off to play detective without any warning. And if de Almeida wants me back on Vanaheim, I don't have much choice in the matter, and you know that.' *Same as I don't have much choice but to be here listening to you, however I feel about it.*

Cripps nodded. 'Then just do what I tell you, and continue to keep an eye on everything Zelia says and does.' He reached out to touch something Luc couldn't see, his hand blurring as it reached outside of the range of the projector he was using. 'We'll speak again.'

The data-ghost winked out. Luc stared at the empty air where it had been for another minute, all thoughts of sleep vanished.

'Luc?'

He turned to see Eleanor framed in the bedroom door, a look of alarm on her face. 'Luc, what's going on?' she asked. 'I heard you yelling.'

'How much did you hear?'

'Just the last few seconds.' She glanced back through to the bedroom. 'I didn't mean to intrude, I . . .'

'No, it's okay.' He gestured at her to come in. 'It was just work.'

'Archives called you in the middle of the night?'

'And since when did *you* work regular office hours, Miss Jaq?'

She smiled and came to sit beside him, but he could see the strain and worry in her face, and wondered if she'd heard more than she was letting on.

He couldn't help but admire the smooth, taut muscles of her body, carefully optimized to the physical standards required of SecInt agents. She had skills of endurance and prowess that remained unavailable – at least legally – to most citizens of the Tian Di, a necessary advantage in her line of work. And yet, in that moment, she looked almost frail as she reached out and clasped one hand over his.

'There's something going on I don't know about, isn't there?' she said. 'And it's got something to do with Aeschere. Every time I look at you, you're somewhere else.'

He thought of de Almeida, and her revelations about the lattice in his skull. 'I want to tell you, but . . .'

'But you can't,' she finished for him. 'I get it. Though I do think you should talk to Director Lethe.'

Luc shook his head at this, and saw a flash of anger in her eyes. 'Why not?' she asked.

'What I'm involved in is at a higher level even than Lethe.'

'The Temur Council?'

He didn't reply, and her eyes darted towards where Cripps' data-ghost had been standing until just a minute ago.

'You have to be careful when dealing directly with the Temur Council,' she said, her voice soft. 'Very, *very* careful.'

'Believe me,' he said, reaching out to her, 'I know.'

By the next evening the walls of Luc's apartment felt as if they were closing in, and he decided to head into Archives rather than spend any more time on his own.

He could have simply data-ghosted himself there – some of Archives' employees spent their entire careers working remotely, via transfer gate on other Tian Di colonies – but there were certain questions that were best asked face-to-face. That meant a trip to the Pioneer Gorge facility, and to Vincent Hetaera, the Archives Division's Head of Research.

He travelled by overhead tram, watching as the wafer-thin build-ings bordering the north-east quadrant of Chandrakant Lu Park gave way to the classical architecture of the Old Quarter. The tram carried him past the crescent shapes of biomes that preserved the planet's original flora and fauna, then down into the Gorge itself, before leaving him at the entrance to Archives, a vast, truncated pyramid of a building more than two centuries old.

He found Vincent Hetaera standing by the window of his office. 'It's wonderful to see you whole and well,' said Hetaera, stepping over to Luc with a wide grin on his face.

He stopped and regarded him with a shocked expression. 'Oh, I'm sorry,' he said, his tone apologetic.

'What?'

Hetaera's grin grew wide once more. 'I should have addressed you as *Master Archivist* Gabion, shouldn't I?'

'Luc will do just fine. And I'll have the same as you're having,' he said, gesturing to the glass in the other man's hand.

Hetaera glanced down at the glass he held as if he'd forgotten it was there. 'It's just kavamilch,' he said. 'Sure you don't want something stronger?'

'Kavamilch will be fine.'

Hetaera shrugged and picked up a pot, pouring some of the warm brew into a second glass and handing it to Luc.

'I got your request,' said Hetaera as they sat down opposite each other on couches by the window. 'But there might be a problem,' he added with a grimace.

'What kind of problem?'

'The author of the book you're looking for,' Vincent explained. 'Javier Maxwell. He never wrote a book by that name, at least not that we know of.'

'*A History of the Tian Di*?' The book Vasili had taken hold of in the last moments before his death. 'How sure are you about that?'

Hetaera raised an eyebrow. '*Very* sure. Where did you hear about it?'

'I saw a copy,' Luc replied, 'a physical, printed copy, with my own two eyes. Is it possible we just don't have records of it?'

'I *suppose* it's possible, but ever since Father Cheng locked Maxwell away and took control of the Temur Council, his name's had restricted access flags attached to it wherever it turns up in our files. Even with your recent promotion, I doubt you'd be able to get permission to find out if it ever did exist without petitioning Father Cheng himself directly.'

Luc nodded tiredly. He'd come across any number of such restricted access flags during his years of researching Winchell Antonov's endless tangle of connections with terrorist groups scattered far and wide across the Tian Di.

'May I ask,' said Hetaera, 'how you came across this book?'

Luc had been dreading the possibility he might be asked precisely this question. 'It's a confidential source,' he replied carefully.

'Then if the book ever existed, it's more than likely been wiped from the official records.' Hetaera spread his hands. 'If it was a printed book, how old would you say it was?'

'I couldn't begin to guess.'

'Pre-Schism old?' Hetaera hazarded.

Luc shrugged. 'Maybe. I guess it could have been.' He studied Hetaera, wondering just how much he could get away with telling him. 'It was part of someone's personal collection.'

'Well, there you go,' said Vincent. 'We all know how much turbulence the Tian Di went through following the Schism. A lot of things were lost forever back then, and not just books.'

'But I *saw* this book. It *exists.*'

'Yes, but not as far as Archives is concerned, unfortunately.' Vincent gave him an apologetic smile. 'Seems to me that your life hasn't got any less interesting since you got back from Aeschere.'

'Yeah,' said Luc. 'That'd be an understatement.' He'd almost forgotten about the kavamilch in his hand, and swallowed it down. It tasted sweet and warm.

'And what about Archives?' asked Hetaera. 'I know you turned down a promotion to the Security Division before. Now that Antonov's gone, do you think you'll change your mind and move upstairs?'

The corner of Luc's mouth twitched. 'We're on the top floor, Vincent. There *is* no upstairs.'

'You know what I mean.'

Luc sighed. 'To be honest, there's nothing to stop me retiring right now. Never do another damn thing for the rest of my life.'

Hetaera watched him for a moment. 'Sitting around and doing nothing isn't your style.'

'No.' Luc played with his empty glass. 'Staying in Archives feels like the best option. I feel at home here, and now at least I can pick and choose what work I do.' His eyes flicked towards his superior. 'Right now, I've been asked to consult on something on behalf of a member of the Council.'

'Ah.' Hetaera nodded, regarding him shrewdly. 'That would explain the sudden interest in officially non-existent books, so I'll ask no more.' He gestured with his drink. 'There are a thousand jobs in Archives needing investigating, once you're done with this. Tying up the loose ends from Antonov alone could take a lifetime.'

Luc nodded. 'Is Offenbach in the usual place?'

Hetaera laughed. 'Where *else* would he be? Good to have you back, Luc.'

Luc smiled. 'Good to be back, Vincent.'

'There you go,' said Jared Offenbach, leaning forward in his chair. 'Dummy corporations, black market accounts, traceable and currently non-traceable funds, as much as you could want. A lot of it doesn't even go anywhere: it's chaff, designed to lead you far away from where the real money is going. Which is Black Lotus, of course.'

Cascades of colour-coded financial information filled the office of Senior Archives Librarian Offenbach, swarming around both men. The office itself was only dimly visible with the windows opaqued, but Luc could just about make out shelves filled with antique reading devices used to recover legacy data from obsolete hardware.

Luc shifted in his own seat, causing nearby strands of information to ripple in the air as they attempted to maintain their integrity.

He watched Jared pull yet more data from out of deep virtual stacks. Flags indicated that some of the information flowing around them hadn't been accessed, in certain cases, for more than a century, perhaps longer. Offenbach gestured expertly with his fingers, untwining dense braids of data into finer and finer branches, rapidly surrounding himself in a glowing tapestry of light. His nearly hairless pate gleamed under the constant assault of visualized data.

For reasons that remained obscure to Luc, Offenbach preferred to maintain an outward physical appearance considerably more advanced than most. Liver spots dotted his hands, while a hawk-like nose that always made Luc think of a half-opened flick-knife jutted from the centre of his face.

'I'm looking for something very specific,' said Luc, grasping at a set of brightly coloured filaments just within his reach. Tiny clumps of words, names and reference numbers pulsed like jellyfish as his fingers brushed against them. He made a claw of his hand, then flung his fingers wide, causing the clumps to suddenly expand, revealing more details, along with the broad outlines of the financial links that connected the filaments together, almost fractal in their compact density. He performed another deft sleight of hand, and the filaments of data shrank once more.

To one side of the two men floated several dense clusters, rendered in luminous orange and green, representing the financial concerns of more than a dozen Benarean resistance movements. Dark nebulae of restricted or missing data weaved in and out of these brightly glowing clouds, but Luc knew that even this vast quantity of interconnected data represented only one very minor sub-branch of the complete Black Lotus data-set.

'Something specific?' Offenbach spluttered. 'Well, I should *hope* so.'

Luc leaned back. 'The focus I want is on a medium-broad spectrum of interconnectivity, representing whatever relationship existed between Winchell Antonov and Sevgeny Vasili.'

Offenbach blinked a couple of times, clearly choosing his next words carefully. 'I can tell you right now that any such records are likely to be heavily flagged and restricted.'

'That's hardly news to me, Jared.' Luc's work on the Black Lotus data-set had been a constant struggle with restricted-data flags. If Offenbach hadn't been able to help him circumnavigate a number of them in the past, he might never have succeeded in tracking Antonov down. Offenbach was, in many ways, Archives' unsung hero.

Offenbach gave him a look of wry amusement, then reached out, manipulating the data before him with practised ease. The entire set rotated on an invisible axis, bringing clusters representing the relationships between the Temur Council and Sevgeny Vasili into clearer focus. Luc could see that most of the clusters reached back for centuries, all the way to the pre-Schism days. Many of the strands were colour-coded brown and grey, to indicate their special restricted status.

'Strange,' Offenbach muttered.

'What?'

The librarian shook his head. 'Your revised security rating should have gone through now you've been promoted to Master of Archives, but these data-sets simply won't respond to your new rating. They still appear restricted to your eyes, don't they?'

Luc glanced again at the brown-and-grey coded links and nodded. Each member of SecInt, depending on their personal security ratings, saw different things even when looking at the same visualized information. What might appear restricted to Luc might instead show as fully available to Offenbach, and vice versa.

Luc reached out and touched a grey strand, but it vibrated without expanding.

'You're right,' he said, staring at the restricted strands. 'I can't access a lot of these.' He glanced at other, neighbouring strands, which appeared not to be flagged in the same way. 'But I can see others that look like I could access them, if I wanted to.'

Offenbach nodded distractedly. 'But *all* of these should be accessible to you now.' He tapped one finger against the arm of his chair. 'Maybe your new rating is taking time to percolate through the system.'

'That sounds like bullshit even to me, Jared.'

Offenbach sighed and nodded. 'A lot of these threads were capped following Antonov's death. If that much has propagated through the data-sets, then your new rating should have taken effect, unless . . .'

'Unless what?'

Offenbach looked suddenly uncomfortable. 'Usually, when something like this happens, it's because of orders coming from way, *way* up the food chain.'

A member of the Council, in other words. Luc had a mental flash of Cripps, standing in his apartment.

Offenbach raised one magnificently hairy eyebrow. 'You mentioned when you came in that you were asked to help in an investigation of some kind. Would that investigation perhaps be connected to stories I've been hearing about your trip up to the White Palace?'

Luc made a face. 'I see I'm the talk of the town.'

Offenbach let out a half-muffled giggle. 'Yes. So much *intrigue.*'

Despite his outward appearance, Luc sometimes wondered if Offenbach might actually be a good deal younger than himself. He certainly acted like it at times.

'I want to show you something,' said Offenbach, his face lit up with nearly palpable excitement. He sent data-sets flying by with disorienting speed, galaxies of information vanishing into the darkened recesses of his office in rapid order. Finally a single, vast constellation appeared, orbited by dozens of other, smaller clusters.

'What you're looking at here,' said Offenbach, 'is the total data-set for the preparations for Reunification. I don't need to tell you the predictive power of a set like this, do I?'

No you don't, thought Luc, his eyes automatically tracing lines of real and potential influence. 'You don't need to work in Archives to guess a lot of things are going to change following Reunification, Jared.'

'But look here at these subsets. They show regions of un-usually high activity surrounding Sevgeny Vasili over just the last few days, considerably more than might be expected even given his role in making Reunification a success. Clearly *something* is up.'

Luc tried not to show his surprise. 'You were already looking into Vasili?'

Offenbach clapped his hands in excitement, his eyes glittering from across the room. 'Not officially, no. But that level of activity naturally draws our attention and raises flags. Now, as for Vasili's links to Antonov, all we really have to go on is a relatively scant quantity of publicly available data. You know, of course, that they were both on the Committee for Reconstruction following the Abandonment.'

Luc nodded. 'I know that before Antonov turned against the Council, the two men had worked together.'

'In the early days,' Offenbach agreed. 'And later, of course, they became diametrically opposed when Father Cheng took power.'

Luc nodded. 'I'm looking for something deeper than that,' he said.

'I thought you might be,' Offenbach replied. Screeds of text appeared, flickering by at a speed even Luc, despite his experience, found difficult to follow.

For the thousandth time, Luc recalled Vasili's last message to posterity, recorded on the pages of a book the head of Archives couldn't prove existed: *Winchell, I was wrong, so very wrong. I see that now.*

A lifetime of questions were contained within that one simple statement.

'What I can tell you,' said Luc, 'is that there should be a recent connection between the two men, possibly as recently as within the last year.'

Offenbach raised his eyebrows in surprise, suddenly sober. '*That* recent?'

Luc nodded slowly and Offenbach whistled. A moment later the window de-opaqued, letting afternoon light seep in. A thin layer of dust became evident, coating many of the ageing data-readers stacked around them.

'My guess,' said Offenbach, 'is that whoever decided to restrict your access to some parts of the data-sets doesn't want you to find something out.'

'They might stop me from finding those things out,' Luc agreed, 'but clearly that's not a concern for you, since they can't lock everyone out of those data-sets without attracting too much attention. So anything you feel like telling me,' he said, glancing again at the restricted threads, 'is just between us.'

Offenbach's fingers tapped at the arm of his chair. 'All right,' he said, as if coming to a decision, 'then let me ask you a question. Were you aware that no one has seen Sevgeny Vasili for days?'

Luc did his best to keep his face impassive. 'How did you find that out?'

Offenbach gave him a sly look. 'By inference, as well as observation. You know how we work: intelligent filters identify trends and highlight nodes of activity that at first glance might only appear circumstantial or unconnected. Once Reunification gets rolling, there's going to be a massive exchange of cultural and scientific data between us and the Coalition, all mediated by Vasili. And Vasili has been at the heart of the preparations for Reunification for a very, *very* long time.'

'And your point is?'

'Up until several days ago,' Offenbach continued with a note of triumph, 'Vasili was all over Archives like a rash. That exchange of data I mentioned can't take place without Vasili's direct involvement. But now Vasili's vanished from sight, on the cusp of something he's been working towards for longer than most of us here have even been alive. And yet there hasn't been a single adequate word of explanation from anyone in the Council.'

Offenbach shifted in his seat before continuing. 'Now, I know you've been out of the loop since they brought you back from Aeschere, Luc, but you have to understand that unless he pops up again sometime very soon, there is going to be a *major* stink. And then *you* turn up here asking about connections between Vasili and Antonov. I think that's what any self-respecting Master of Archives would call a *significant* correlation.'

Luc sighed and let his shoulders sink in defeat. 'Fine, now that you put it that way, I suppose it's obvious I'm interested in Vasili's . . . recent absence.'

Offenbach leaned towards him, his manner theatrically conspiratorial. 'This isn't official Archives business, is it, Luc?'

'No, it's a commission, from a member of the Temur Council.'

'And of course you can't talk about it. Am I right?'

Luc shook his head ruefully. 'I know you're itching to find out the details, because all your stats indicators are saying something significant is up.'

'Well, *that* much is obvious,' the other man huffed. 'A word of warning for you. Sometimes, when ordinary people get caught up in Council intrigue, their strings get yanked so hard their heads get pulled off.'

First Eleanor, and now Offenbach was taking the trouble to give him essentially the same warning. 'Thank you,' he said, 'for that delightful image.'

'Just an observation.' Offenbach fidgeted for a moment, and Luc sensed he was leading up to something. 'You know, a lot of the data recovered from your trip to Aeschere is still strictly embargoed, despite our department's protests. It leaves us just as handicapped in the fight against Black Lotus as we were before, and I have no idea just how long it's going to be before we can get our hands on that data – assuming the Sandoz ever let us have access to it.'

Luc nodded. Offenbach wanted something in return.

'I think I can do something for you, Jared.'

Offenbach's eyebrows shot up. 'Such as?'

'I still have special access privileges to Sandoz's own archives.' Those privileges had been hard-won on Luc's part, and had fostered what Vincent Hetaera had hoped would become a new era of interagency cooperation. From what Luc had been hearing since his recovery, that era was already proving short-lived.

'You can get hold of the Aeschere data?'

'It's the least I can do,' said Luc. 'Is there anything else you can think of that might be useful to me?'

Offenbach thought for a moment. 'Perhaps. But it's not something that can necessarily be corroborated. You'd just have to take it at face value, I'm afraid.'

'Rumour, then.'

Offenbach moved his head from side to side. 'More than rumour, less than verifiable fact.'

'Listening at doors, in other words.'

Offenbach leaned forward, his voice dropping to a husky half-whisper. 'It's my understanding that over the past several decades, Vasili became isolated not only from Father Cheng, but from the rest of the Eighty-Five. A pariah within Cheng's inner circle, essentially.'

Luc thought about it for a moment. 'That doesn't make sense,' he said.

'Why?'

'If that were the case, Father Cheng would hardly have given him such a prestigious job as preparing the Tian Di for Reunification.'

'But then again,' said Offenbach, 'who amongst his trusted advisors *would* Cheng have given the job to? None of them would have wanted the job. Recall that the Eighty-Five first came into existence as a pressure group within the original Temur Council, agitating for complete separation from the Coalition. And out of all of them, Vasili was easily the most vocal in that regard. Don't you think it's strange that one of the primary architects of the Schism wound up being given the job of rebuilding our links with the Coalition?'

'So giving Vasili that job was a kind of punishment?' asked Luc. *And a very ironic one, if true.* 'That's genuinely fascinating, but I can't see the relevance.'

'Wait,' said Offenbach, still clearly enjoying the moment, 'there's more.'

He waved a hand, and the window behind him opaqued yet again, the room becoming dimmer.

'What,' asked Offenbach, peering from out of the shadows, 'does the name Ariadna Placet mean to you?'

It took Luc a moment to place the name. 'She was Director of Policy for Thorne at some point, wasn't she?' As, he recalled, had been Zelia de Almeida, although Placet had held the post first. 'I seem to remember something about her suffering permanent death while she was there – an accident of some kind.'

'But before that,' Offenbach prompted. 'What is it that links her to Antonov?'

'I'm aware that she was in a relationship with him a long time ago,' Luc replied, wondering just where Offenbach was leading him. 'Starting from not long after the Abandonment. They were both engineers, and sided with the Tian Di Hui resistance fighters when they fought the Coalition occupying forces here on Temur.'

'And?'

Luc sighed. He wished Offenbach would get to the point. 'Their relationship ended long before the Schism. After Cheng took power, she enjoyed a long and fruitful career in the Temur Council until her death.'

Ariadna Placet had been one of the few Council members for whom the instantiation technology had failed. When she had died in a flier accident on Thorne, her backups proved to have been lost or corrupted.

Just like Vasili's, Luc realized with a start.

'What if I told you,' Offenbach continued, 'that there were accusations of foul play regarding her death?'

'There was an inquest, wasn't there?' asked Luc, feeling a rush of adrenalin. 'I don't recall hearing about any such accusations.'

Offenbach grinned. 'Then you might also be interested to know that not very long after her relationship with Antonov ended, Placet became Sevgeny Vasili's lover.'

Luc thought of icebergs grinding together in a half-frozen sea, their vast bulks hidden in shadowy waters. 'Tell me more.'

'Vasili has a reputation for being a very private man,' Offenbach continued. 'Few people outside of the Temur Council knew about the relationship.'

'Who made the accusation of foul play?'

'Vasili did. He never accepted the inquest's findings. He's always insisted the flier Placet was in when she died must have been sabotaged or shot down on purpose, and her backups deliberately vandalized.'

Luc stared at him in amazement. 'Why the hell have I never heard about any of this?'

'Because it's inner circle gossip,' said Offenbach. 'The kind of thing that rarely trickles down from the Eighty-Five to the likes of you and me. From what I gather, Vasili wasn't the kind to keep quiet about his suspicions. He was absolutely convinced Placet had been murdered, along with a couple of other passengers unlucky enough to be on board the flier with her at the time. *That*, I think, is the reason Vasili became so isolated from Cheng and the rest of the Eighty-Five.'

'But if that were true, what would be the motive for murdering her?'

'Assuming all this is true, and Vasili isn't as crazy as the rest of the Council seem to think he is? I have no idea.'

Luc rubbed at his temple. Antonov, Vasili and Placet. 'You've given me even more than you realize, Jared.'

'That's the beautiful thing about data,' said Offenbach. 'Things that only at first appear to be unconnected frequently prove, at a later date, to be intimately intertwined.'

I couldn't have put it better, thought Luc, rising to his feet. 'Thanks, Jared. I'll get that Aeschere data through to you as soon as I can.'

'I can only hope I've been able to help,' replied Offenbach.

Luc headed for the door. 'More than you can possibly imagine,' he said as he departed.

SEVEN

In the three days since Jacob Moreland's ship had crash-landed on Darwin, he had taken to hiding in a deep cave a few kilometres away from where that same craft had quickly set about destroying itself. He sustained himself by sucking brackish moisture from the pocket-like leaves of bushes that grew up the side of the hill below the cave, until it began to rain on the second day, an incessant downpour that continued well into the next evening. He passed the time huddled deep within the cave's recesses, staring out towards the distant flicker of light that betrayed the presence of Coalition mechants still searching the nearby forest and shore.

They were looking for him, of course. His ship had evaded detection on the way down from orbit by disguising itself as random orbital flotsam, but whoever was controlling the mechants must have realized there was a chance at least one of the spy-ships had made it past their defences.

Jacob continued watching through the night until the lights eventually passed into the next valley, and only then allowed himself the luxury of sleep.

He emerged from the cave at dawn on his fourth day on Darwin, by now ravenous with hunger, climbing to the top of a tree and crouching low on a branch in order to peer out across the forest canopy. He could see that the search for him continued to move further and further away from his hiding place: beams of light flickered across the mouth of an estuary several kilometres to the north.

From time to time, as he waited to be rescued by whichever Tian Di sleeper agents picked up his transceiver alert, he would glance up at the impossibly vast bulk of the world-wheel that straddled Darwin's equator. Patterns of light danced around the wheel's inner curve, and up and down the spokes that connected the wheel to the continents and oceans below. From time to time displays of light, not unlike auroras, encircled the wheel like a phantasmagorical wreath, billowing like silk sheets cast into a turbulent wind. Whether it were some strange natural phenomenon, a byproduct of industrial processes, or indeed some form of artistic display, Jacob could not begin to guess.

The search lights finally faded behind a veil of grey rain that tumbled from the sky, blown in from the sea. Jacob returned to his cave and checked the transceiver for what might have been the thousandth time, but there was still no response.

He could not discount the possibility that the agents who had arrived before him might have been uncovered and terminated; but if that were the case, he felt sure their killers would not only have located their transceivers, but used them to track him down the moment he had sent out his distress call. The fact that they had not done so suggested those agents were still out there, somewhere.

Of course, there was always the possibility that if the sleeper agents *had* been captured, they had first managed to destroy their transceivers, or perhaps . . .

No. He pushed his transceiver back into a pocket of his combat suit. It was too easy to get caught up in paranoid fantasies, isolated and alone out here as he was. If he received no response within the next few days, he'd just have to strike out on his own and take his chances.

He set about foraging in the woods close by the cave, and found some wild nuts that proved bitter but edible. He tried a fruit analogous in appearance to berries, small dark clusters the colour of bruised knuckles, but just one was enough to make him violently sick and leave him with a fever that very nearly incapacitated him. He managed to crawl back inside the cave, where it took the microchines infesting his gut several hours to neutralize the berry's poison and calm the fever.

When he next emerged from the cave, pale and shaky, night had fallen once more, and he saw a single light flickering through the line of trees dotting the slope below his cave.

They've found me, he thought with a lurch. Darwin's security forces must have decided to renew their search for him. The chances of him surviving any encounter out here, without backup, against whatever mechants the Coalition were now employing, were vanishingly small.

Jacob waited, silent and still, for several minutes, then came to the conclusion that this was almost certainly a lone individual moving through the woods on foot. He could hear them stumbling through the undergrowth, their flashlight swinging this way and that.

Scrambling into the shelter of a tree's wide, blade-like roots, he waited again.

Before long he saw the figure of a man make its way into a clearing below the cave, nervously clutching a torch in one hand. Jacob studied this individual from amongst deep shadows. The flickering auroras from the world-wheel faintly illuminated the stranger's face, and Jacob saw that the man's hair was grey and unkempt, his eyes pale and watery-looking. His mouth moved as if he were perpetually on the verge of saying something but then changing his mind. He was not young, and the lines on his face and the stiffness of his movements suggested he had not made use of any gerontological treatments presumably available to the Coalition's citizens.

Jacob's lattice searched its databases for a facial match, and found a near-perfect correlation with a sleeper agent named Melvin Kulic who had been sent to Darwin more than a century ago. The match was not quite perfect, however, suggesting this man was instead a descendant of Kulic's, born since his arrival on Darwin.

Jacob felt a bristling of unease. This was not the reception he had been expecting.

'Are you there?' the old man called out, his voice wavering with uncertainty.

A moment later the old man jerked around, flashing the light across the clearing as if he he'd heard something, but Jacob had made no sound.

The light from his torch flickered across the tree behind which Jacob hid. Jacob drew back slightly, momentarily unsure whether or not he should reveal his presence.

That this old man had come looking for him, rather than the agents he had been expecting, implied something had gone badly wrong. His mind churned with possibilities. If he revealed himself, would he be walking into a trap? At the worst he could kill himself, safe in the knowledge that he had prepared instantiation backups prior to his departure from the Tian Di.

That settled it. And, besides, there was nothing to be gained from hiding any longer.

Jacob stepped away from the tree, watching as the old man flashed his light here and there around the clearing. He hadn't seen him yet.

'Listen,' the old man's voice quavered, 'if you're there – and if that damn thing hasn't just gone haywire *telling* me you're here – you'd better think about . . . *Shit!*'

The old man staggered backwards when he finally caught sight of Jacob standing just a few metres away. He stumbled over a root or rock hidden in the undergrowth, and let out a gasp of pain when he landed clumsily.

Jacob stepped forward, reaching out a hand and helping the old man back up onto his feet. At least if it were to prove expedient or necessary to kill this stranger, there would be no possibility of witnesses.

'You're one of them, aren't you?' said the old man, his face a mixture of awe and terror. 'From the Tian Di.' He looked around. 'Where's your ship?'

'You're alone?' asked Jacob.

The old man squinted, and Jacob realized with a start that he had trouble with his eyes.

'Your eyes,' asked Jacob. 'What's wrong with them?'

'My . . .' The old man stared at him in befuddlement. 'Of course,' he replied after a moment. 'You won't know about the Edicts.'

'Edicts?' Jacob grasped at a sliver of memory. 'You mean the Left-Behind – their Church Edicts, is that what you mean?'

The old man nodded. 'The pastors won't stand for any kind of messing around with the body now,' he said. 'Not any more, anyways.'

'Tell me your name,' said Jacob.

'Jonathan Kulic. My father was . . . one of you.'

'Where is he?' Jacob demanded. 'Why didn't he or Bruehl or any of the other agents come here to meet me?'

'I . . .' the old man faltered. 'My father died, years ago.'

'Died? Of what?'

'He . . . he came to believe in the Edicts.'

Jacob stared at him. 'I don't understand. How is that even possible?'

'He didn't have faith in the Edicts at first,' Kulic replied, 'that much he finally told me just before his death. But when he did come to believe in them, he let the microchines in his body – is that what they're called? – die out. After that he grew old so quickly, some in our community believed he had been touched by God, or perhaps punished by him.' Kulic shook his head. 'He never even told my mother where he'd really come from, but he confided in me, on his deathbed.'

Jacob's mind reeled. If Jonathan Kulic was telling the truth, his father – a Tian Di sleeper agent – had gone native, falling for the dictates of an extremist religious group existing on the very fringes of Coalition society. It said much about the moral corruption of the Coalition that such fringe cults were allowed to exist. But then again, groups such as the Left-Behind provided excellent cover for Tian Di agents.

'And the others?' Jacob demanded, stepping closer to Kulic. 'Bruehl? Sillars? What about them?'

Kulic took a step back, looking frightened now. 'Bruehl . . . changed. I don't know as much about Sillars. I told the beacon everything I could.'

The beacon. He meant the transceiver, of course. 'Then why are *you* here?' asked Jacob, stepping forward and grabbing a fistful of the old man's shirt. 'You had nothing to do with any of this; you're not from the Tian Di. Why did you come here?'

Kulic stared back at him with wide and frightened eyes, looking like he was on the verge of tears. 'It's hard to explain.'

Jacob reached behind his back, sliding a thin blade from out of a narrow sleeve situated over his lower spine. He brought it up to where the old man could see its razored edge glinting in the light of the world-wheel, then touched it to the side of Kulic's throat.

'Why didn't you alert the Coalition authorities here that your father had confessed to being a spy?'

'I was too afraid of them,' the old man stammered, 'of what they might do to me. I grew up with stories of the horrible changes they make to you when you join them, of the Fallen in the cities, demons pretending to be human. And, besides, the villages are all I've ever known. He told me – my father, that is – that the Tian Di would wipe Darwin and all the other Coalition worlds free of sin. So when he died, I decided to finish what my father could not.'

Jacob relaxed his grip on the old man. He was nothing more than a weak-willed old fool. In some ways that might make him dangerous, and Jacob knew the safest course would be to terminate him immediately.

Yet the fact remained that his mission so far had gone desperately awry almost before it had started. There was at least a chance Jonathan Kulic might actually be able to help him.

'I need shelter, clothes, and food,' he told the old man. 'I also need a little time to regain my strength. Can you help me?'

The old man reacted with pitiful gratitude, his eyes shining as he sobbed. 'Of course. Of course! You're going back there, aren't you?' he asked. 'Back to Temur, through that new transfer gate.'

Jacob struggled to control himself. His training told him he should reach out and snap Kulic's neck and be done with it; whatever madness had taken over Kulic's father had caused him to share the intimate details of his mission with his son, an act that constituted an appalling breach of protocol.

But then he saw the old man's eyes were again damp with tears. *He's been waiting all his life for this moment*, Jacob realized with a shock – waiting for the day his father's transceiver would activate, and give his life a purpose that had clearly been missing.

Jacob had been lucky to survive the journey across the light-years – and even luckier to have evaded the Coalition's security forces on reaching Darwin. He could almost believe the God of the Left-Behind really had guided this old man to help him, when by all rights he should have been forced to fend for himself.

Jacob reached out slowly and put a hand on Kulic's shoulder, patting it. From here on in, he was going to have to improvise.

'If you ever again mention any of the details of my mission out loud,' Jacob said quietly, 'I will gut you and garland your village with your intestines. Do you understand me?'

The old man's mouth worked. 'I – I'm sorry,' he managed to mumble. 'I didn't mean to speak out of turn.' His eyes darted here and there, almost as if he thought someone might be hiding behind a tree or bush and listening. 'But you could take me home with you,' he added in a hoarse whisper. 'Take me back to Temur, where there are at least real people, and not . . . monsters.'

'Perhaps I could,' Jacob replied with as much fake sincerity as he could muster.

The old man's gratitude was rapidly becoming wearing. Jacob had him wait there in the clearing while he went back to the cave in order to fetch the case he had retrieved from the ship. Then he allowed Kulic to lead him back through the woods to a horse and cart waiting on a dirt path less than a kilometre away. The horse whinnied gently at Jacob's approach, its hoofs pawing nervously at the dirt underfoot.

'Why not use motorized transport?' Jacob asked Kulic, as he climbed into the rear of the cart, which contained nothing but bags of dried hay and a large, tattered carpet with a faded pattern woven into it.

'The Edicts,' Kulic replied, as if that told Jacob everything he needed to know, before taking the reins and coaxing the horse into a gentle trot. They began to move at a steady pace, but Jacob could feel every bump where he sat crouched in the rear.

For the first time since he had stumbled out of his ship and watched it dissolve to nothing, Jacob allowed himself a faint sliver of hope. There was still a chance – small, but real – that he could find the weapon Father Cheng required him to locate, and carry it back to Temur.

Just days from now, and he, Jacob Moreland, would earn his place as one of the greatest heroes of the Tian Di. Millions might die as a result of his actions, but – as all truly good men knew – history was a tapestry necessarily woven from the bodies of the innocent.

EIGHT

At first, Luc thought Cripps had returned when he awoke to find a figure once again lurking in the darkness of his bedroom. But when it stepped closer, he saw instead that it was de Almeida's data-ghost.

He had been dreaming that he was making love to her. He remembered clearly the way her lithe frame had moved above his in a room whose contours were unfamiliar to him. He recalled with astounding clarity the warm scent of her skin and the taste of her lips and tongue, and the urgent thrust of her hips against his own. It had felt so entirely real that upon seeing her data-ghost standing before him, he felt momentarily disoriented, not quite sure if he was awake or not.

'Mr Gabion,' she said, her voice low. 'We need to talk.'

He sat upright amidst the tangled sheets of his bed, irritated and embarrassed, as if she had somehow been privy to his thoughts.

He waved a hand and the window de-opaqued, letting in the pre-dawn light. At least he was alone this time; Eleanor had spent most of the previous evening neck-deep in preparations for a pre-tribunal hearing concerning Aeschere.

'What is it?' he asked, making no attempt to hide his irritation.

'It's Sevgeny Vasili's murderer,' she said. 'They've found him.'

His fatigue drained away. 'Where?'

'Downtown, here in the capital,' she said. 'Dead, unfortunately. Alive would have been better. Do you know Kirov Avenue?'

'Yeah.' Kirov Avenue was in one of the oldest districts of the city, an area heavily populated by Benareans like himself.

'Meet me there,' she said, flashing an address to him before vanishing.

Kirov Avenue was lined by tall apartment buildings that hailed from the days of vat-based architecture, when construction materials had been formed from slabs of fullerene grown in tanks of engineered microbes. There had been a scandal when the buildings had started sagging just a few decades after their construction, causing their once-gleaming facades to slowly melt. The internal skeleton of one fluted tower was clearly visible where the outer cladding had crumbled away. After that, Benareans dislocated by the repercussions of the uprising there had moved in, while everyone else had moved out.

Luc had been one of those Benareans – one of thousands of refugees who had scattered across the Tian Di in the wake of the Battle of Sunderland. It had not, at first, been an easy existence. Orphaned in the wake of the rebellion, he had been given over to the charge of a Benarean family. His adoption had not gone well, and he had only rarely returned to this part of the city since.

He arrived there just over an hour after de Almeida summoned him, stepping out of an Archives flier to find himself confronted by half a dozen armoured Sandoz cars arrayed outside a building whose walls curved gently as they rose towards a peak sufficiently lofty that he couldn't quite make it out.

Several data-ghosts conferred with each other beside one of the Sandoz vehicles, while a few steps away, SecInt mechants kept a small crowd of a dozen or so civilian onlookers at a distance from the building.

Luc decided to keep his own distance until Zelia made her appearance. The data-ghosts, all of which had their backs to him, alternated between studying something on the ground immediately before them and craning their heads back to peer at the upper floors of the adjacent building.

Luc couldn't see just what it was they were all staring at on the ground, but he could make an educated guess. Someone had exited the building the hard way, and at a terminal velocity. As he continued to watch, one of the data-ghosts turned away with a grimace, covering his mouth as if he was about to be sick. This convinced Luc he'd guessed correctly.

Just when he had started to wonder if de Almeida was going to turn up at all, the data-ghost of a small, wiry-looking woman with blond hair and severe eyes stepped away from a mechant she had been addressing and approached him.

'It's me,' the woman muttered, leaning in close. 'Zelia.'

Luc shook his head. 'Why the disguise?'

'It would cause something of a fuss, don't you think, if people were to know there were this many members of the Council standing around Kirov Avenue in the middle of the night?'

'Where?' Luc asked, glancing around. He saw one or two data-ghosts, but none he recognized. . .

'Oh,' he said, feeling stupid. He wondered if Father Cheng himself might be amongst them.

'I want you to take a look at the body.'

'If you've found your killer,' said Luc, 'why do you need me here?'

'Because I think you might know him,' she said, before turning her back on him and suddenly fading from sight.

Luc stepped towards the cluster of vehicles, muttering a curse under his breath.

His name was Reto Falla. He had fallen nearly three quarters of a kilometre from the window of his apartment, landing in a sculpted garden area at the base of the tower, which had long since gone to seed. His legs were grotesquely folded back behind his body, while his torso had ruptured upon impact. The back of his skull had also shattered where it had struck a decorative rock. He had died, Luc noted, with a look of surprise on what was left of his face.

He stepped away as mechants proceeded to hide the body from view inside a temporary, dome-spaced structure. De Almeida's data-ghost-in-disguise beckoned to him to follow her away from the cluster of people, again coming to a halt a short distance away.

'So?' asked de Almeida, 'was I right? You knew him?'

Luc sighed. 'Yes. We both come from the same small settlement on Benares.'

'A settlement that was entirely wiped out during the Battle of Sunderland, I understand.'

'Yes,' Luc admitted, a sudden tension taking hold of him. 'Falla and me and some other kids were on a school trip to a low orbit factory at the time of the attack. All of us became orphans in the exact same moment.'

Luc studied the face of de Almeida's data-ghost, to see if he had evinced so much as a trace of pity. None was apparent.

'But you were already aware, I gather, that he had since become involved with Black Lotus?'

'Sure. He was picked up during a raid some years back, when Black Lotus were just gaining a real foothold here on Temur. That's when I saw him, for the first time since we were kids.'

'When, exactly?'

Luc was sure she already knew the details, but answered anyway. 'They put me in charge of his interrogation, in case knowing me might make him more inclined to be talkative.'

'And did it?'

Luc laughed, glancing back over to where Falla's crumpled form was now hidden inside a brightly coloured dome, shadowy figures moving inside. 'He hardly even remembered me. When I told him we'd grown up in the same place, he just looked at me like I was lying. It had been a long time, after all.'

'Just how deeply involved was he with Black Lotus?'

'He was far from being a high-level operative, if that's what you mean.' He felt a sense of inexplicable sadness that he recognized as just one legacy of the trauma of those years. 'He wasn't much of anything; more of a fantasist, with no real connections. He had some psychological issues, along with a whole roster of dependencies, chemical, neural and otherwise.'

'Curable enough, I would have thought.'

He turned to look at her. 'Some things run too deep, Miss de Almeida. You can't just root them out without fundamentally changing someone's personality.'

'But is he the kind of person Black Lotus would want to recruit?'

'He was certainly disaffected enough, but he never amounted to much. At best, he knew people who knew people, if you follow.'

'So what did you do with him?'

'Nothing. We made him into a paid informant, but we never got anything useful out of him.' He made sure to fix his eyes on de Almeida's. 'And in answer to your next question, there's absolutely no way he'd have been able to pull off anything so sophisticated as a high-level assassination. Not even with a *lot* of help.'

She regarded Luc with a look of amusement. 'It's interesting the way your lives worked out. Him on one side of the fence, you on the other.'

He frowned. 'Reto fell for Black Lotus's bullshit. I didn't.'

'What kind of bullshit?'

'Is there a reason for this line of questioning?'

'Yes,' she replied. 'I want to know the answer.'

'Black Lotus claimed they weren't responsible for the assault on Sunderland that killed a huge number of Benareans, but it's demonstrably not true. As far as Black Lotus were concerned, the Benareans who died as a direct result of their actions were nothing more than collateral damage.'

'That didn't stop a lot of other Benareans joining their ranks afterwards,' said Zelia.

'Then I guess you'd have to ask them for their reasoning,' he replied levelly.

De Almeida again regarded him with a look of amusement that was already becoming as familiar as it was deeply irritating. *The real problem with data-ghosts,* Eleanor had once said, *is that you can't punch them in the face.*

A second data-ghost appeared next to de Almeida's, and spoke to her without acknowledging Luc's presence before vanishing once more.

'Two hundred and thirty-first floor,' said Zelia, turning back to face him. 'That's Falla's apartment. The elevator's out of action past the two-hundredth floor, I'm afraid. You'll have to walk the rest of the way.'

'Or,' he said, 'I could just ghost there.'

She shook her head. 'No. Father Cheng might want you to take a look at physical evidence, and you can't do that if you're only present as a projection. If you start now, I'll see you there in half an hour.'

By the time Luc had ascended in a working car to the two-hundredth floor and climbed up the last thirty-one flights, his skin was slick with sweat and he was breathing hard. It took him longer than half an hour since he also had to negotiate his way past a series of security mechants placed in the stairwells. A final mechant, decorated in the distinctive livery of the Temur Council, led him into a small, derelict-looking apartment.

De Almeida was there in the flesh, although Father Cheng and Bailey Cripps themselves were only present as data-ghosts. Cheng turned to regard him as he entered, and for a moment Luc caught his look of cold contempt, quickly replaced by one of jovial avuncularity.

'Mr Gabion,' said Cheng, his voice booming in the confines of the tiny living-room. 'It appears we've found our killer and saved you a great deal of bother.'

'Take a look at this,' said de Almeida, gesturing to the mechant that had led him inside.

The mechant projected an image of a crude-looking device, blown up until it was nearly a metre across. Luc recognized it as a home-brew CogNet earpiece, a customized unit typically used for circumventing low-grade security networks – part of a thief's arsenal, in other words. Black Lotus often made use of operatives skilled at constructing such devices.

Luc glanced between de Almeida and Cheng. 'All this tells us is that Falla probably made his living as a thief,' he said.

<Zelia,> he heard Cheng script. <You really shouldn't have brought him here.>

<I have your permission to include him in the investigation, Father Cheng. You agreed, remember?> she replied, her expression defiant.

<Yes, but it appears our investigation has come to a pleasingly rapid end. That makes his presence no longer necessary.>

Luc kept his gaze fixed on the projected image, terrified that Cheng and Cripps might realize he could hear their every word.

'Mr Gabion,' said de Almeida, nodding at the projection, 'Father Cheng believes Falla must have used this device to pass through the Hall of Gates.'

'Case closed, really,' said Cripps. 'That thing's crammed with decrypted security data for getting past the White Palace's defences. There's even data proving he was present on Vanaheim at the time of Vasili's murder.'

Luc glanced at de Almeida. Her jaw was clenched, like she was on the verge of going ballistic.

'If you have the actual device here, can I take a closer look?' asked Luc, gesturing to the projection.

Cripps started to say something. 'I don't—'

'Of course,' de Almeida snapped before he could finish. 'Here.' She reached out a hand to the mechant providing the projection, and it dropped the original device into her open palm. It was, as Luc had expected, quite tiny, smaller even than a fingernail.

She passed it to Luc, who studied it closely, ignoring the glare on Cripps' face. When he tried to access it through his own CogNet link, he found to his surprise that it was quite easy. The crude device's temporal archives proved to be not only accessible, but also dated back months. It didn't take him more than a minute to locate data inside the tiny machine that apparently proved the device and its owner had indeed passed through the Hall of Gates.

He shot a furtive glance at de Almeida, and saw her looking back, her jaw clenched beneath angry eyes.

<The data on that thing's been faked,> she sent.

It took Luc a moment to understand she was addressing him directly. He continued to study the device in his palm without replying.

<Our conversation is private,> de Almeida continued, guessing why he was suddenly reluctant to respond. She was looking in the other direction from him now, towards the shattered window. <Neither Cheng nor Cripps will know we're scripting, unless I tell them or you make it obvious. Now tell me if you agree with my conclusion.>

<It *could* have been faked,> Luc sent back, turning the device over in his hands. <That doesn't mean it was.>

The casing had been crudely soldered, as if it had been built in a hurry. In that respect it was entirely unlike similar devices he had encountered in the past, which had been more sophisticated in appearance, often indistinguishable from commercial CogNet units.

'Do we know for a fact that Falla killed himself?'

Luc glanced up. De Almeida had directed her question at Cripps.

<I think it's fairly evident he did precisely that rather than be caught,> Cripps scripted back to her.

<Speak out loud,> de Almeida sent back. <Let Gabion hear you, or switch to open broadcast.>

<I don't think I—>

'If you will, Bailey,' Cheng commented.

Cripps looked like he'd eaten something sour. '*Clearly* Falla killed himself,' he said out loud. 'He must have had a tip-off that SecInt were on their way here.'

Luc stepped across to the shattered window at the room's far end and looked out. The ground was an unpleasantly long way down.

'But a tip-off from who?' asked Luc, stepping back from the window.

'Black Lotus, of course,' Cripps barked. 'He decided to end his life rather than face punishment for his actions.'

'Or possibly, someone connected to Black Lotus made that decision for him,' suggested Cheng. 'It would certainly make it harder to track down whomever was responsible for giving him his orders.'

'It's looking very open and shut to me,' Cripps declared. 'His connections with Black Lotus are extensively documented.'

'Finding that device doesn't prove he killed Vasili, let alone somehow found his way through the Hall of Gates!' de Almeida protested.

'No,' said Cheng, 'but that machine's own internal records strongly suggest he did.'

'Those records,' she said through clenched teeth, 'could have been faked.'

'Oh no, Zelia,' said Cripps, one corner of his mouth curling up. 'On the contrary, I already checked the White Palace's own security records. I found anomalies in them, corresponding to the times and dates inside Falla's crude little toy.'

'But why on Earth would Black Lotus want him to kill Vasili?' she demanded.

Cripps regarded her with a pained expression, as if confronted by an imbecile. '*Surely*, Zelia, that should be clear. This was a tit-for-tat move, a strike against the Council in return for Winchell Antonov's death. As far as I'm concerned, you can stop playing detective now. We'll arrange an immediate inquest and have a decision based on the evidence within the next few days. After that, we can concern ourselves with other questions – such as who might have helped Falla carry out his crime.'

'Wait a minute,' said de Almeida. 'Are you telling me that you think *Vasili* was killed as revenge for our stopping Antonov? He hasn't been at the heart of Council politics for more than a century.

What would be the point? *You*, on the other hand,' she said, practically spitting the words at Cripps, 'would make a far more worthwhile target, especially since you spend so much of your time away from Vanaheim. Why, if Falla found it so easy to pass through the Hall of Gates, would he fly halfway around Vanaheim just to kill a minor and half-forgotten member of the Eighty-Five, when he could have stuck around Liebenau and killed someone a lot more important?'

Cripps shrugged. 'You heard Joe: there'll be an enquiry to figure out the hows and the whys. Right now the most appalling thing about all this is that it's all so easily preventable.' His voice began to rise. 'That means *someone* hasn't been doing their job, *Zelia*. If they had, Sevgeny might still be alive today.'

'If it were to become publicly known that the architect of the Reunification was murdered in his own home,' said Cheng, 'it would be a major propaganda coup for Black Lotus and their supporters, and there are still plenty of those left. I've already made it clear that this is unacceptable. Instead of questioning Bailey's hard work, Zelia, perhaps you should try and find out how it is your vaunted security systems failed to prevent a lone agent, acting with the minimum of support, from entering our sanctuary and killing one of our own like a dog. If it hadn't been for Bailey's swift and decisive action here, Falla might have lived to do much worse things than what he so very clearly did to poor Sevgeny.'

Luc watched de Almeida closely, noting the stricken look on her face. 'I want to see the evidence for myself,' she spat, but Luc could see she was shaken. 'I have that right.'

'You'll see it,' said Cripps, regarding her with a smile. 'I'll be happy to release the complete details of my investigation to you at the appropriate time.' <I'm afraid the evidence still won't reflect well on your security arrangements, Zelia. I'm sorry to have to tell you that.>

<I'm sure you managed to find a way to deal with the pain,> she shot back.

'Mr Gabion.'

Luc started, and realized he was being addressed by Cheng.

'By the looks of things,' said Cheng, 'your investigation has come to an end rather more swiftly than any of us might have hoped. I know it must have been difficult for you to be drawn into all of this at such short notice. You understand,' he added, 'that absolute discretion on your part continues to be both expected and necessary.'

'I understand, Father,' Luc replied. He felt unsure what to do next.

<Take him from here, Zelia,> Cheng scripted. <Then I want to talk with you.>

She glanced at Luc. 'You should go back down,' she muttered, her tone curt. 'Thank you for your help.'

<And wait for me outside,> she added. <We aren't finished here.>

'Father.' Luc nodded to Cheng, and left.

Luc waited on the street by the tower for nearly an hour. It started to rain – a thick, cold end-of-year drizzle that cascaded from the skies, painting the street with wet sheets that darkened the decaying shells of the apartment buildings around him. Police mechants came and went, still guarding Falla's body while SecInt forensics teams carried out their work inside the tent hiding his body.

They eventually started letting the residents of the tower back in not long after forensics wrapped up their work. Shortly after, a SecInt ambulance that had arrived while Luc was inside the building took Falla's remains away.

The police mechants followed the ambulance on its upwards trajectory, and soon the only company Luc had was a couple of civil-engineering mechants tasked with cleaning up whatever blood and tattered flesh hadn't already been washed away. He retreated into a doorway to shelter from the worst of the rain still gusting down from on high, watching the skyline slowly brighten as morning drew nearer.

Zelia appeared from out of the building entrance and came towards him, her expression bleak.

'You look cold,' she said, stepping up beside him and into the comparative shelter of the doorway. Luc could see lines of fatigue around her eyes.

'You look,' he said, 'like you've been given a hard time.'

Anger stiffened her face, and he wondered if he'd crossed a line. But then she nodded distractedly, as if acknowledging the point.

'It doesn't matter what Cheng thinks,' she said in a monotone, staring toward the patch of pavement where Falla's body had been. 'He didn't do it.'

'Falla?' Luc shook his head. 'I don't think so, either.'

She regarded him coolly. 'Explain your reasoning.'

He shrugged. 'I told you. I *knew* Falla. He'd be lucky to outsmart a paper bag. He's no assassin.'

'Not even if his hand had been forced?' de Almeida suggested. 'Desperate people do desperate things, under the right circumstances.'

'Falla had no family after the Battle of Sunderland, and no real friends either – certainly no one who could be used as leverage to force him to do something like that. He was barely any use as an informant, and not much use for anything else.' Luc shook his head. 'Try as I might, I can't picture him as some kind of stealthy killer, finding his way through the White Palace, then flying halfway across Vanaheim in order to slaughter a Councillor in his own home. It just doesn't compute.'

'Not even with Black Lotus's resources to help him?'

'But that's just it,' said Luc. 'Apart from that CogNet piece you produced back up there, I've not seen any evidence of him having access to any such resources. There's no evidence he even had so much as a weapon in his possession.' He let out a sigh. 'The whole thing feels . . .'

'Like a set-up,' she finished for him. 'Frankly, I'm inclined to agree. With that in mind, I want you to take another look at Falla's CogNet piece.'

Luc stared at her. 'You *stole* it?'

She sighed irritably. 'No. It's been taken along with everything else as evidence.'

'Then how can I—'

'I copied its complete contents to my lattice – all the data and hacks Falla supposedly used to pass through the Hall of Gates without being detected.'

Luc looked at her, surprised. 'That could get you into a lot of trouble if Cheng found out,' he said quietly.

'Then let's make sure he doesn't,' she said, a hint of steel in her voice.

'So why don't *you* think Falla did it?' he asked.

'For the same reasons as before. Even though Cripps insists on telling Father Cheng there's some flaw in Vanaheim's security networks, I can assure you there is no such flaw.'

'I remember you said that before, but it's starting to look like—'

'What you don't know,' she said, interrupting him, 'is that every one of the Eighty-Five, Cripps included, has override privileges for those networks.'

Luc ducked his head back in surprise. 'You mean . . .'

'I could never say it in front of Father Cheng or Cripps, but the more time passes, the more convinced I am that it had to be someone from amongst the Eighty-Five who killed Vasili.'

'And the rest of the Council? What about them?'

'I think we'll soon be able to rule pretty much all of them out.' She laughed softly, her expression suddenly bleak. 'Not that I'm crazy enough to say so to Father Cheng's face.'

'If that's the case, then *is* it possible one of them could have used those overrides to sneak Falla through the Hall of Gates, then had him carry out the murder on their behalf?'

She gave a tired shrug. 'Like you said yourself, he's not exactly anyone's first choice for a deadly assassin.'

'But surely having such override privileges defeats the point of even having the security networks?'

'Power has its own privileges, Mr Gabion. Most of the Eighty-Five prefer to keep their movements entirely private, even from the greater part of the Temur Council. Any one of them could have covered their tracks if they were of a mind to frame Falla – or commit murder.'

'So all this time you had your suspicions? Why didn't you say anything before?'

'Because I don't want to make an enemy of the most powerful men and women in the whole of the Tian Di. It might be one of them, or several of them, or for all I know they *all* had a hand in Vasili's murder.' She shrugged. 'It would be tantamount to suicide to accuse them, collectively or individually, without rock-solid, unassailable proof.'

Luc stared at her, scandalized. 'Surely you can't be the only one in the Council who came to this conclusion?'

'If any of them did,' she said, 'they're keeping their mouths shut and waiting to see how things develop.'

Luc licked dry lips and tried to ignore the thumping of his heart. 'They're not the only ones who can override Vanaheim's security,' he pointed out.

She smirked. 'You still haven't ruled me out as a suspect, have you?'

'No,' Luc admitted. 'Even if I wanted to, how could I? The circumstantial evidence against you is still strong.'

'Why,' she asked, 'would I get you to carry out this investigation, if I'd killed Sevgeny myself?'

'To try and make yourself look less guilty,' he replied. He nodded towards the tower. 'The question is, what can I do now? Cheng just said the investigation is over, and . . . I still have this thing squatting inside my skull.'

De Almeida shook her head, keeping her eyes fixed on Luc. 'I told you I'd do what I could to help retard its growth, didn't I? And as for the investigation, it isn't finished until *I* say it is.'

'If Father Cheng doesn't want me on Vanaheim, I'm not sure just what you expect me to do,' Luc protested.

'I run the security networks, remember? I can get you onto Vanaheim without anyone else knowing.'

He stared at her. 'Do you realize what you just said?'

She nodded stiffly. 'Of course I do. And yes, I could easily have delivered Reto Falla to Vanaheim without Cheng or anyone else knowing – but I didn't.' She paused, her gaze flickering across his face. 'Why don't you put your fabulous gut instinct to work and tell me if you really think I had something to do with it?'

Luc sighed. 'No, I don't think you did.'

She arched her head. 'Why not?'

He hesitated, wondering just how much he really did trust his instinct. 'Because you don't act like guilty people usually do,' he explained. 'Now I've got a question for you.'

'Go ahead.'

'I don't get it. Why do you still need me? Surely if you want to carry out some private investigation behind Father Cheng's back, you could do it yourself.'

'Why are you so desperate to get out of this?' she demanded. 'Don't you want me to fix that thing in your head before it kills you?'

He felt like a butterfly squirming as it was pinned to a board. 'Of course I do.'

'There are places that I may ask you to go, and people I may ask you to speak to, that might present me with problems if I tried to do it myself.'

'What people? What places?'

She smiled enigmatically. 'The less you know for now, the better. There'll be a funeral service on Vanaheim for Sevgeny tomorrow, and I want you to be there.'

Luc glanced in the direction of the White Palace, mostly obscured by a tower on the opposite side of the street. 'If Cheng or Cripps found out, they'd have me killed.'

She nodded. 'For now, you'll data-ghost through one of my private channels. That way I can make absolutely sure no one finds out you're there, although you should still be able to communicate with me in secret.'

Luc winced as the street lights became suddenly brighter. He pressed his fingers against his eyes and stared down at the ground.

'Mr Gabion?'

'I . . .'

A high-pitched humming filled his ears. He thought he heard a voice, but far away, and lost in the noise. There was something familiar about it. He staggered slightly as a terrible, throbbing pain consumed his thoughts.

'Gabion? What is it?' demanded de Almeida. 'Another seizure?'

He managed to nod, and she reached up with her other hand, pressing gloved fingers against his scalp. Her touch was softer, more delicate than he'd expected. She was close enough that he could smell her, and for some reason he found himself thinking of Eleanor spread beneath him, her skin painted with perspiration.

'What are you doing?' he mumbled.

'Pulling data from the neural taps I put in your skull the other day,' she said distractedly. 'The growth-rate of your lattice is accelerating.'

Shit. 'Can you do something?' he pleaded, feeling a surge of panic.

'I can only do my best,' she muttered, and after a moment the pain slowly faded once more to a distant numbness. The relief was overwhelming.

'What did you do?'

'I made some temporary adjustments,' she said, taking her hand from his scalp and stepping back. 'Better?'

He nodded.

'Now you have another reason to come back to Vanaheim. While you're there, I can do more to help you.'

'Not if I'm only there as a data-ghost.'

'That's only a temporary measure,' she assured him. 'I'll bring you there in person soon enough.'

Even if you didn't kill Vasili, I can't think of anyone in a better position to do it, he thought.

He glanced up at a faint hum from above, and watched as a flier dropped down from out of the gloom, settling onto the road nearby.

'I'll send a flier for you tomorrow, just before the service,' she said. 'It'll take you to a private office on the White Palace. Once there, you'll be able to data-ghost to Vanaheim.'

'Fine,' said Luc, and watched as de Almeida walked away, her long, dark coat swaying with the movement of her hips as she boarded the flier. His eyes followed the craft as it lifted on AG fields that bowed the rain around its hull before finally speeding upwards and into the sky.

NINE

Luc dreamed he was back on Aeschere, lost in claustrophobic passageways crowded with mandalas and leering statues.

This isn't real, he gasped as Antonov leaned over him, playing with the wriggling worm-like mechant.

Very astute, Antonov replied, grinning down at him. *You've met Zelia by now, haven't you? Be careful of that one.*

Luc struggled to free himself from the chair he had been bound to. *Don't do this to me*, he cried. *I can't go through this again.*

I wish I could stop this, Mr Gabion, said Antonov, shaking his head sadly, *I really do. But this isn't the kind of dream where you can pinch yourself and wake up; you know that already. You're reliving all this because there's a war inside your skull, and I'm winning.*

No. Zelia de Almeida is helping me. She'll undo whatever damage you've done to me.

The neuro-suppressants she put inside you? They only suppress your conscious awareness of a process that can't be stopped. Didn't she tell you that?

She told me she could save me!

Antonov laughed a rich, hearty laugh, leaning back and raising his face to the ceiling. *She's bluffing*, he said, bringing his gaze back down. *Or maybe she thinks she really can retard the lattice's growth, but I seriously doubt it. What I put inside your head is far in advance of the kind of technology even the Temur Council allow themselves. No, my dear boy, she's more interested in saving her own skin than anything else. At best, you're a puzzle to be unlocked, so she can find out what I'm really up to.*

Then why not just tell me why you put this thing inside me, damn it! Luc screamed.

Because we are engaged in a game, Luc – and a very dangerous one, Antonov replied. *And it is never a good idea to show one's hand too soon.*

You're killing me because I found a way to stop you.

Antonov looked confused for a moment. *You think this is about revenge?* He shook his head. *I'm saving your life, and mine as well.*

How in hell do you figure that out?

When you found me, I had no access to my backups, no other way to preserve at least some of my thoughts and memories. What you see before you is all that's left of me.

Luc listened, thunderstruck.

You did a better job than you realized, the dead man continued. *I had cached backups, of course, but SecInt, thanks to its temporary truce with Sandoz, managed to locate nearly all of them – and every last one of them auto-destructed before it could be interrogated.* He clasped one hand to his injured chest. *But this part of me, mere shadow of my former self that it is that now resides inside you, is enough to finish the task ahead.*

He leaned in close to Luc. *Speak to the Ambassador, Luc. With his help, we will both be reborn, and a terrible calamity will be prevented.*

What Ambassador? What—

Luc woke with a start and jerked upright, lungs heavy and aching in his chest. He was back home again.

For all he knew, the dream he had just experienced was at best an elaborate fantasy formed from his own fears and desires – at worst, a sign of incipient madness, triggered by the lattice as it grew in complexity and reach.

But he knew better. Whatever Antonov had done to him, it had been done for a reason. Some part of the dead man, some shadow-aspect, was alive and well inside his skull, drawing out the agony and drip-feeding him whatever tantalizing scraps of information it could use to make him dance to any tune but his own.

Speak to the Ambassador. Luc had no idea which Ambassador Antonov might have been referring to.

Every world of the Tian Di but Vanaheim had embassies, but they meant little in this age of instantaneous travel across the light-years. Mostly, the title 'Ambassador' was an honorary role given to those who'd served the Temur Council with distinction. They could have told Luc he was an Ambassador as his reward for Aeschere, and it wouldn't have meant a damn thing.

He searched the public and secure databases for information on planetary ambassadors currently resident on Temur while he dressed and breakfasted. He vaguely recognized some of the names, but could find no immediately obvious link to Vasili or to de Almeida or anyone else – nothing that might make sense of what the dream-Antonov had said to him.

Glancing in a mirror, he frowned, then stepped closer. His CogNet earpiece had turned dark, an indicator that it had failed in some way and needed to be replaced.

He carefully removed it and looked down at it in the palm of his hand. It was tiny, the kind of thing that was easily lost, but as easily replaced at virtually no cost. The technology was entirely ubiquitous, the kind of thing you grew up around without ever really being aware of how badly you needed it until it was gone.

Except there had been no break in service during his search of several different databases, despite his CogNet earpiece's terminal failure. Antonov's lattice, he realized with a chill, had seamlessly taken over from it without his even noticing.

He stared down at the tiny darkened bead, a mixture of dread and excitement churning inside him.

Then he thought back to his meeting with Offenbach, when he had been unable to bypass the security settings on a number of files. Would his lattice, unwelcome as it was, now enable him to access those same files should he try again?

Luc dropped the darkened bead in the recycling, then headed out.

*

One of de Almeida's mechants guided him to a tiny private cubicle in a walk-in office complex close by Chandrakant Lu Park. He didn't have long to wait before de Almeida's invitation arrived in the form of a tiny point of light that hovered in the air before him.

He reached out. The star-like point puffed into mist the moment his fingertips brushed it, and –

– he was on Vanaheim.

Looking down at his hands, he flexed them, stunned at how perfectly real they looked. He could *feel* a breeze touching his cheek, as if he were really, actually physically present. The haptics alone were on a whole order of sophistication beyond anything he'd ever experienced before while data-ghosting. It had to be because of his lattice.

It was like actually *being* there.

He was sitting on a long stone bench near the middle of an auditorium cut into the side of a hill. The benches formed steps that led down to the foot of the hill, and seated on them at different points around the auditorium were maybe forty or fifty men and women, the majority of whom he did not recognize. Sitting at his side was de Almeida, who glanced towards him out of the corner of her eye, giving him the tiniest nod to let him know she could see him.

The auditorium was large enough that it looked almost empty. Clearly, few amongst the Temur Council had felt inclined to come and pay their respects to their dead compatriot. Most of those present were clustered together near the base of the auditorium, but a few, including de Almeida, sat conspicuously apart from the rest. Mechants sporting a variety of liveries hummed through the air.

Before the steps stood a low, wide platform, and beyond that a sloping grassy plain. Luc could see a meandering river a few kilometres away. Tall columns were arranged haphazardly around the edges of the auditorium, a few bearing broken-limbed statues, as if the auditorium were the remnant of some long dead civilization. Close by a bend in the river stood an imposing-looking ruin, moss growing up its sides, a partly caved-in roof open to the elements.

Luc held his breath, half-convinced someone would see his electronic phantasm despite de Almeida's reassurances.

<You're sure no one can see me?> he asked her.

<No one even knows you're here,> she confirmed.

<What are those ruins?> he scripted, nodding towards the river. They looked old, which made no sense unless Vanaheim had been occupied for far longer than anyone knew.

<Follies,> replied Zelia. <They're not real. Just architectural whims, like this auditorium.> There was a note of disgust in her voice, as if she didn't approve.

He spotted Surendra Finch, Overseer for Temur's security services, and the man to whom Lethe reported directly; Rosabella Dose, who had fired the fatal shot that killed Lewis Finney when Coalition forces stormed the judicial headquarters on Darwin mere months after the Abandonment; Alexander Maksimov, famous for negotiating the surrender of Yue Shijie's transfer gates to the Sandoz; and many less familiar faces that nonetheless had in their own ways influenced the course of the Tian Di over the centuries.

It was intimidating company, to say the least.

He saw Father Cheng stand up from a gathering at the front of the auditorium, and step towards the platform, trailed by several mechants and a small entourage that included Cripps. A projector had been set up on the platform, and as Luc watched, this device unfolded broad panels made of thin metal wafers.

After a moment, the air above the panels shimmered, then darkened to reveal a sprinkling of stars, in defiance of the afternoon light. A grey, cylindrical shape floated in the foreground, occluding many of the stars. The curved surface of a world was clearly visible, revealing that the cylindrical object was in orbit.

As Luc watched, brilliant light flared at the rear of the grey cylinder, and it began to recede from the fixed viewpoint above the planet, dwindling within seconds to a tiny point of slightly flickering light almost indistinguishable from the steady brilliance of the stars. Before very long it had vanished entirely. Luc guessed it was Sevgeny Vasili's coffin.

'Sevgeny would have liked it this way,' said Father Cheng, his voice carrying clear and sharp across the hillside. 'He used to wonder what might lie at the heart of our galaxy; well, in a way, he'll get to find out now. That ship we placed him on board – the last one he'll ever travel on – is a modified version of the same craft that carry the seeds of transfer gates to new worlds. I can't think of a better farewell for a man who worked so hard towards reuniting the two disparate halves of the human race.'

Luc watched with interest as Cheng pointedly cast his gaze around those gathered, and recalled what Offenbach had told him: Vasili had been given the job of Reunification not as a perk, but as a kind of punishment duty.

'We all know how hard Sevgeny worked towards that goal,' Cheng continued. 'He may not have lived to see it fulfilled, but his body, if not his soul, will journey where his heart and his mind often did, to the mystery at the heart of our island universe. God speed, Sevgeny,' he said, glancing towards the dark projection hovering in the air. 'We'll miss you, but you'll always be with us, in spirit at least.'

Cheng stepped down from the platform, and someone new stepped up to say their piece. Luc meanwhile found his attention drawn to a figure that stood alone on the far side of the auditorium, and felt his skin prickle as if he had just been doused in ice-water.

Whoever they were, their face was entirely invisible beneath a mirrored mask. The mask formed part of a suit of cloth and metal that was covered in turn by a loose, flowing coat that billowed gently in the light breeze flowing down the slope of the hill.

The same figure he'd seen in his dreams, with Antonov's angry face reflected in it.

<Who is that?> he demanded, pointing.

De Almeida glanced towards the masked figure, then regarded

him with an expression of amusement before turning her attention back to the man delivering his eulogy on the stage. <That, Mr Gabion, is the Coalition Ambassador, Horst Sachs.>

<I know him,> Luc insisted. <I saw him in my dreams.>

<He certainly fits the description you gave me a few days ago, yes.>

<*Coalition* Ambassador?>

She gave him a sidewise glance full of irritation. <Of course. You know that we've had visitors from Darwin prior to the new transfer gate's official opening. The Ambassador is our most frequent visitor of all. Sevgeny Vasili was scheduled to introduce him to the public during the Reunification ceremonies.>

Luc felt a shiver run through him at the sight of the masked figure. <I'm not sure how people are going to react if he's still wearing that mask. Doesn't he ever take it off?>

<Not to my knowledge, no,> she replied. <People in the Coalition are . . . very different from us, it seems. How different may prove to be a shock for many.>

<Then what I saw really was real,> he replied, feeling dazed.

<Clearly.>

<Then you understand what this means?> he sent back. <Antonov must have had dealings with the Ambassador. Why didn't you tell me he was real before?>

<Because I knew there was a very good chance that he'd be here, and I wanted to see if you genuinely did recognize him.>

'Zelia.'

Luc realized with a start that Ruy Borges had come over to join them. He stiffened with apprehension before remembering Borges could neither see nor hear him.

De Almeida's response was filled with bored exasperation. 'Whatever it is, can't it wait, Ruy?'

'I was just thinking,' said Borges with a lopsided grin, 'of what Javier might say if he was here. He'd have a few words to say about Sevgeny, wouldn't he?'

Javier. He could only be talking about Javier Maxwell.

De Almeida scowled. 'This *really* isn't the time or the place.'

'I almost forget sometimes how much those two men hated each other,' Borges continued, his grin growing wider. 'If it wasn't for Javier being locked up in that prison of his, I'd have thought he was behind Sevgeny's murder.'

'I'm serious, Ruy,' de Almeida growled. 'Go away.'

'Now if *Javier* were the next to be assassinated . . . well, it's not like there's a lack of volunteers when it comes to pulling the trigger.'

De Almeida stared at him with baleful contempt. 'What, exactly, are you saying?'

Borges shrugged. 'Just that if the security systems around that prison of his were to fail and something were to happen to him as a result, well . . . we'd be free of a serious thorn in our side, don't you think?'

Luc saw some heads towards the front of the auditorium had turned away from the latest eulogy, and were keenly watching Borges's confrontation with de Almeida instead.

She stood. 'You're suggesting I killed Vasili, and I should do the same to Javier. Is that it?'

Borges's grin grew wider, his voice slightly louder, easily carrying across the auditorium. 'It's not like everybody doesn't already think you did it. But if something *were* to happen to Javier, then it might help tip the balance in your favour a little.'

De Almeida stared at him with undisguised loathing. 'Am I on trial?' she demanded.

'All I'm saying,' Borges continued, 'is that were you to allow the security on Javier's prison to slip at the right time and place, there are a few people who might be prepared to take care of Javier the way you took care of Sevgeny.'

'Would you be the one who pulled the trigger, Ruy?' A cold smile twitched the corners of her mouth. 'No, of course not. You just like to make speeches and threaten people. And let's be clear on this: the one thing I *don't* control is the security cordon around

Javier's prison. You know that just as well as I do. The Sandoz handle it under Joe's direct supervision.'

Ruy's hands twisted at his sides. 'You know I'm not the only one who wants nothing to do with that *thing* masquerading as a human being,' he spat, stabbing one finger in the direction of the masked Ambassador. 'Joe's hand is being forced when it comes to Reunification. He doesn't say it, at least not to anyone outside of the Eighty-Five – but we all know it. Something's going on that we aren't being told about.'

Zelia's expression became incredulous. 'What the hell does Javier have to do with any of that?'

'Because that's what Javier's always wanted, isn't it?' Borges's voice was rising again, and even the woman delivering her eulogy had paused to listen. 'To expose us to those . . . those monsters in the Coalition.'

Luc glanced towards the Ambassador, wondering how he felt about being described in such terms.

De Almeida waved one hand in dismissal. 'You're a fantasist, Ruy. Show some respect for Sevgeny's memory and sit the hell back down.'

Out of the corner of his eye, Luc saw Cripps moving rapidly up the steps towards them.

'*Somebody* has to say it,' Borges spat. 'Those people in the Coalition have all been changed by the Founder Network. For God's sake, Zelia,' he continued, a pleading tone creeping into his voice now, 'how can we possibly know there's anybody left alive on Darwin who's truly human anymore, even in all of the Coalition? How do we know they weren't compromised, even replaced by whatever it is that's lurking in the Network?'

'Stop this now.'

Borges turned to stare at Cripps, his nostrils flaring. 'No,' he said, shaking his head adamantly. 'There are things that have to be said.'

'This is a difficult enough time as it is,' Cripps growled. 'You're making a scene, Ruy.'

'Everyone knows she—'

'*Ruy.*'

Borges's lips quivered, but he went silent and walked back down the steps without another glance at de Almeida. Luc followed him with his eyes as Borges stalked past the platform, giving Horst Sachs a wide berth as he made towards a group of fliers parked a short walk away.

'Thank you,' de Almeida said to Cripps.

'Don't thank me,' Cripps replied curtly. 'It wasn't for your benefit; he was disrupting the proceedings.'

De Almeida nodded wordlessly as Cripps turned on his heel and headed back down to rejoin Father Cheng, who hadn't so much as turned around throughout the altercation. Luc had little doubt he was nonetheless aware of everything that had just taken place.

<I want to talk to the Ambassador,> Luc said as de Almeida took her seat next to him once more.

She allowed herself a brief sideways glance at him. <I'm already working on making arrangements for precisely that. You might be interested to know Ambassador Sachs was working very closely with Vasili on the run-up to Reunification.>

<He was?>

She nodded, very gently. <They had regular meetings up until just a few days before Sevgeny's body was discovered, as a matter of fact.>

On the stage, the final eulogy came to an end. People were already sharing muttered conversations as they began to move out of the auditorium and towards the parked fliers.

De Almeida stepped away to speak to one or two people, but it was clear from their uneasy expressions that they were disinclined to spend too much time speaking with her.

He glanced towards Ambassador Sachs, who was now in conversation with Cripps. Something about that perfectly reflective mask made his skin crawl. When he followed de Almeida down to the front of the auditorium, he had the uncanny sense the Ambassador was watching him, but with that mask it was impossible to tell exactly where his gaze fell at any moment.

<Gabion.>

He glanced back over at de Almeida. <What?>

<You can rule out the Ambassador as a possible suspect,> she replied, leading his data-ghost across the grasslands towards her flier. <It seems he was at a function held in his honour at the exact same time Vasili was killed.>

<What did Borges mean when he said something was going on? Something that people weren't being told about?>

She sighed. <The honest answer is that I don't know what he meant.>

<I don't believe that.>

<It's true. I . . . > She stopped and looked around. Luc did the same; they were amongst the last to leave, and even if someone had seen her speaking to someone who wasn't there, they might simply have assumed it was a private conversation and left it at that.

'We're free to talk out loud now,' she said, switching away from script-speak. 'No one's going to overhear us.'

<You're sure?>

She glanced around with a furtive expression. 'I never feel comfortable using script-speak, even if I have to.'

Luc activated his data-ghost's audio circuits, but kept the volume dialled down to not much more than a whisper. 'Go on, then.'

'There are rumours,' she explained, 'of secret negotiations between the Coalition and some members of the Eighty-Five. Negotiations that none of the rest of the Council were ever told about.'

'And that's what Borges was referring to just now?'

She nodded helplessly. 'For all I know it's just a rumour and nothing more, but once you put an idea like that in the head of a man like Borges, no matter how tenuous, it becomes dangerous.'

'But what kind of negotiations?'

She shrugged. 'I have no idea, assuming the story is even true.'

'All right, then what about Javier Maxwell? Why would Borges want him dead so badly?'

She scowled. 'It doesn't really have to do with Maxwell at all, it's more to do with what he represents. Borges is scared because Cheng's hand is being forced over Reunification.'

'Forced? How?'

'By the same tide of popular opinion that originally made it possible for him to seize control of the Temur Council – a tide that has now turned the other way, in favour of Reunification.' She kept her voice low as she spoke. 'Even without access to instantiation technology, people throughout the Tian Di are living better and longer lives than at any time since the Abandonment. The days when the colonies had to struggle to survive, when desperately stringent measures were needed – those days are long gone, and everyone in the Tian Di knows it. Now they want the same things we in the Council have – and Father Cheng hasn't given them any adequate reasons why they shouldn't have the same things sooner rather than later.'

'Then why doesn't he just give them to us?'

'Cheng is old. We all are. The mistake was believing that as long as things stayed the same, we'd have stability. Instead, we have stagnation, but Cheng doesn't seem to understand that. He had to be forced into agreeing to Reunification.'

'What forced his hand?'

'There are plenty of indicators showing that without radical social change, the Tian Di might break up. There might even be civil war. The evidence was convincing enough to persuade the majority of Councillors to agitate in favour of Reunification. And for all his power, Cheng can't do anything without the vast majority of us backing him.'

'And Borges?'

'Men like Borges would be more than happy to maintain the current status quo forever, even if the rest of the Tian Di burned. He doesn't want change, and neither, I think, do most of the Eighty-Five.'

'In that case, given Vasili was actively working towards change, surely Borges would make a good suspect for his murder?'

'Our mutual cup overflows with potential suspects, wouldn't you say?' she said.

'That's why I'm going to need full access to Vanaheim's security records, Miss de Almeida.'

She stared at him like she hadn't quite heard him right. 'You're not actually serious, are you?'

'Quite serious. I need access to any and all data relating to the movements of everyone in Vanaheim over, say, the last few days – and preferably the last several weeks. I also need access to the personal records of everyone on the Council.'

She laughed disbelievingly. 'And you really think I would give you that much?'

'If you don't,' he said, 'I don't see how I'd be able to do my job properly. I can't possibly make an accurate assessment regarding Vasili's murder until I first have a good idea of the circumstances and events surrounding his death. Without that context, how can I possibly clearly identify a motive that might give you the identity of his killer? And everything you've just told me makes it clear that there's a lot I still don't know.'

Anger flashed across her face. 'I'll take the idea under consideration,' she replied, her voice clipped. 'But any specific information you need I can get for you immediately, upon request. You don't need direct personal access.'

'Without it, I'm flying blind,' he countered.

And what about Father Cheng? He wanted to ask. *Are we treating him as being above suspicion?*

But he was still too afraid to ask that question.

'Here's what I *can* do,' she said. 'I just sent Ambassador Sachs a request for a confidential interview that you'll conduct.'

'Won't a request like that make him suspicious? What if he tells someone else about it, and Father Cheng finds out you're carrying on your investigation in defiance of his orders?'

'I told the Ambassador it was all part of an overall review of our security measures in the wake of Vasili's murder. As far as he's concerned, you're just someone who works for me, period. He knows nothing of your background, or why you're really here. But it's also a chance to find out why he met with Antonov. In the meantime,' she added, 'I want you to go home and wait there until you hear from me.'

'I understand,' Luc replied wearily, but even before he had finished his reply she had cut the connection. The last of his words echoed dully inside the tiny cubicle, back in Ulugh Beg.

TEN

Over the next few days, Luc dreamed of other faces he had never encountered, and of places he had never visited.

As he woke each morning, he felt sure that Antonov's ghost, lurking within his skull, had whispered secrets that, however hard he tried, could not be recalled. Even when awake, he fell from time to time into a kind of trance, sometimes lasting for several minutes or even longer. He cradled a glass of hot kavamilch one morning, then found once he brought it to his lips that it had turned cold; more than half an hour had passed without his being aware of it.

And then there were the occasional bouts of excruciating pain, each one longer than the last. He barely managed to stop his house from contacting the medical services during one particularly bad episode: just because one hospital's neural scanner had failed to detect his lattice didn't mean another would.

He waited to hear from de Almeida, desperate for her to work her magic on him, but no word came and, as she had left him no way to contact her directly, there was little for him to do but wait.

Eleanor got in touch, but despite his yearning for her company, he avoided her. He didn't know what she might do if he had another seizure while she was around him. Even so, the wounded tone in her voice whenever she left another unanswered message for him tore a hole in his heart.

It took an effort to force himself back out of his apartment. The headaches and fevered dreams of the past few days had left him exhausted, and he found he had little energy for anything more than spending time within the arboretum on the roof of the Archives building, where he could at least enjoy the company of Master Archivists who were now his equals in rank. There, he not only found Offenbach, but also Hogshead, Benet, and even old Kubaszynski, long since retired but on a brief visit from his home on Novaya Zvezda.

He listened to their conversation as it turned to heroic Archivists of old: men such as Gardziola, who had tracked down Samarkandian census records believed destroyed during the Mass Deletions. He heard again the story of Justin Krumrey, who forced the Grey Barons of Da Vinci to relinquish private collections of 21st and 22nd century media, also thought lost forever. He heard tales of Panther Wu, the wrestler-turned-theoretician who first instituted the system of Master Archivists, and whose statue stood wreathed in dark green ivy at the heart of the rooftop gardens amongst which they idled.

He listened to their tales of epic adventure, laughed at their jokes, and returned to his apartment filled with ideas for future research projects and exploratory fieldwork. But when he caught sight of the White Palace floating far above the city, he was reminded that his days might very well be numbered for reasons that remained far from clear. All his plans seemed suddenly worthless, since there was no way to know whether he might live long enough to implement them.

He went to his bed that night filled with a sense of dread that kept him awake through the night, leaving him exhausted and weary by the time morning arrived.

Early the next day, de Almeida finally data-ghosted unannounced into his apartment. Luc had barely slept, his head feeling as if hot pokers were being slowly driven through the bone and tissue.

He felt overwhelmingly, even embarrassingly, grateful at the sight of her. Her data-ghost perched on an invisible seat in his apartment's kitchenette as he made himself some kavamilch, wincing from the pain of his headache.

'I've arranged a time and place for you to meet with Ambassador Sachs,' she began without any preamble, 'but remember that he doesn't know it isn't officially sanctioned.'

'Any news about that inquest Cheng said would be held concerning Reto Falla?' asked Luc.

De Almeida let out a rush of nervous breath. 'I'm sure you'll be far from surprised to learn they've already found Falla guilty of the murder. I asked to see the minutes of the enquiry meeting, but they've been ruled confidential.'

'Even to you?'

'Even to me,' she replied dryly. 'Another enquiry's been commissioned, this time to try and work out how he could have done it. Cripps has been put in charge of that one. I'm pretty sure he's the one who's stopping me seeing those minutes, let alone any of the related evidence.'

Apart from the evidence you managed to steal, Luc thought to himself. 'Any idea why?'

'Apparently I'm under suspicion of negligence,' she replied, her expression darkening. 'It seems they want to carry out a review of the security networks, so they can work out where I . . . where I screwed up.' She almost spat the words out. 'The information on Falla's CogNet piece, did you . . . ?'

'I couldn't find anything that fitted the profile of an active Black Lotus agent.' He shrugged. 'And the data on a CogNet earpiece, particularly a hacked one, isn't hard to fake, as I think you already know. That he even still had it makes no sense.'

'Why?'

'Any assassin with an iota of intelligence or imagination would have dumped or destroyed that earpiece immediately. Instead, there it was, in plain view in his apartment. Everything about it just feels wrong.'

'I came to the same conclusion myself,' she admitted.

'What about the rest of the Council?' he asked, cradling the kavamilch in his hands as he took a seat across from her. 'Surely they have *some* say in the direction of the inquest, or are they just going to accept Father Cheng's decisions without question?'

De Almeida nodded. 'That's precisely it. It doesn't matter what they believe, it's what Cheng believes that matters.'

Luc took a sip of the kavamilch before he continued. He could feel it slowly work its tendrils into his brain, waking him up and clearing his thoughts, even dulling the pain a little.

'I need your help,' he said. 'Whatever it is you did to help me before, it isn't working anymore. The pain's getting worse. And there've been more . . . hallucinations, or dreams, or whatever the hell they are.'

'I told you I'd do what I could,' she said tiredly. 'You'll be back on Vanaheim soon enough.'

'In person this time?'

'You'll have to be, if we're going to get you together with Ambassador Sachs.'

'You need to take a look at me first,' he said. 'I mean it, Miss de Almeida – Zelia. I'm no good to you if—'

'Don't try and pressure me,' she snapped, her eyes hard. 'Do you really think I don't know that?'

Luc bit back a retort. He studied her face, the way her nostrils flared and the tightness of her mouth. She was a lot more scared than she was ever likely to admit.

'They've really got you backed into a corner, haven't they?' he said quietly.

Her nostrils flared again. 'I'm not interested in your unwarranted speculation. I'm only interested in your obedience.'

Luc shook his head and laughed wearily. 'Fuck you.'

Her hands clutched into claws, as if she meant to rip out his eyes. 'I won't abide this . . .'

'Abide what?' He was tired of her threats, her dismissive manner.

Somehow she managed to hold her temper in check. 'You want to test me, don't you? See how far you can push me.'

'Who else do you have that could help you, Zelia? My guess is

Cripps is watching every move you make, which is why you need me to be your errand-boy on Vanaheim. That's how it is, isn't it?'

At that, she got a wild look in her eyes like she might attack him. Luc tensed, briefly forgetting she was only present in the form of a projection, her physical body far away on Vanaheim. After a moment she seemed to remember this herself, and shook her head, looking sad and sorry for herself.

'I know I need your cooperation,' she said, her voice thick, 'as much as you need my help. I suppose it's obvious enough to you that I'm not in the best place just now, politically speaking.'

He thought of all the long years he had worked for Security and Intelligence. He had never pretended bad things didn't happen under the Council's rule, but he'd always believed the long-term stability they'd brought to the Tian Di made them the least of all possible evils.

Or so he'd told himself. After what he'd seen over the past several days, he wasn't so sure what he believed any more.

'Maybe we should get back to why Vasili was killed in the first place,' he said carefully. 'We keep circling around Reunification as a possible motive, given that there's no lack of opposition to it, even now. Can Reunification go ahead without him around?'

She thought for a moment, then nodded. 'That brings me to something I wondered about,' she said. 'If Vasili's death was intended as an act of sabotage against Reunification, it's a stunningly inept one. Why kill him, instead of targeting the transfer gate linking us to the Coalition itself?'

'*Can* that gate be harmed? Is it possible it could come under attack?'

'Not when it's as heavily defended as it is, no. It's secure in orbit, and it's probably going to stay there until the Council finally decides it's safe to bring it down to Temur's surface.'

'Then maybe,' he said, 'we're not looking at sabotage. Maybe the real reason for his murder has nothing to do with Reunification.'

'It's still all speculation until we have something more tangible to lead us in the right direction,' she said, meeting his eyes. 'I want you to get ready to leave for the White Palace this evening. It's risky, but I've arranged your passage through the Hall of Gates.'

His hands gripped the half-empty glass of kavamilch. 'Are you sure it wouldn't be safer for me to just data-ghost there until the heat's off you?'

She shook her head firmly. 'Not with the level of surveillance I'm under following Cheng's inquest, no. Right now it's actually less of a risk to smuggle you there in person.'

He squinted, not sure how much he could believe that. 'If data-ghosting is that dangerous, surely you're taking a severe risk even just by being here in my apartment?'

'And you wonder why I'm tense,' she replied, managing a semblance of a smile. 'I've arranged for you to meet one of my own mechants beneath the White Palace, tonight, ten hours from now. I've prepared a cover story for you. In the event you're challenged on your way into the White Palace, you're there on my behalf to check on some private records.'

'And then?'

'And then my mechant will transport you to Vanaheim.'

You say it like it's going to be easy.

And with that, she was gone, as abruptly as she had appeared. Long goodbyes clearly weren't part of her repertoire.

By the time Luc reached Chandrakant Lu Park later that evening, shadowed by the vast bulk of the White Palace, night had fallen, the trees and paths lit by the soft glow of the park's arc lights. A mechant came towards him as he approached the edge of the park, then guided him towards a flier parked a short walk away. Less than fifteen minutes later he was back inside the Palace, on his way to the Hall of Gates.

He saw no other living souls, only more mechants with liveries indicating whichever department or individual they were assigned to. He could only assume it was some act of technological sleight of hand on de Almeida's part that prevented those other mechants from challenging him.

It hit him then how easy it was to imagine Reto Falla, or someone like him, making his way from his slum apartment and all the way through the transfer gates with the help of some murderous Councillor. If he hadn't already known Falla, he might even have believed it.

Instead of ascending all the way towards the Hall of Gates, however, he was instead guided through a library area – all tasteful lighting, low couches and dedicated mechants – then through a door so low he had to stoop to pass through it, indicating it had been designed with machines rather than humans in mind. He found himself inside a cargo area filled with crates presumably waiting to be shipped to Vanaheim.

The mechant guided him to a small side-room containing only a single heavy-duty plastic crate.

'What the hell is this?' he demanded in a low whisper.

The mechant drifted past him, using its long mechanical arms and whip-like manipulators to lift the lid off the crate. Looking inside, Luc saw it contained only a seat and harness.

'Miss de Almeida considers this the safest way to transport you through the transfer gate,' the mechant replied. 'Do you have an objection?'

'You're fucking kidding me,' he said, staring back at the mechant.

The machine didn't reply, and Luc cursed softly under his breath. Then he heard the murmur of voices from somewhere nearby and quickly climbed inside.

The mechant drifted forward once more and secured the lid on the crate as soon as Luc had fitted himself into the harness. The seat itself was held within a rigid frame that filled the crate's interior.

A dim yellow light came on as the mechant closed the lid over him, and Luc felt a rush of claustrophobia.

A moment later he felt the crate rock, then lift up, swaying slightly. Time passed – at least twenty minutes – and then he found himself under powerful acceleration. It wasn't hard to guess he'd been loaded on board another flier, presumably one on Vanaheim.

No, not just a flier, he realized, as he heard a dull roar build up beyond the confines of the crate; a sub-orbital. For some reason, he was on his way into orbit.

By the time the mechant unsealed the crate once more, he was in free-fall.

ELEVEN

The flier soon docked with a space station, and Luc disembarked into an echoing grey and silver passageway that dwindled into the distance. It had a distinct air of disuse, as if it had been abandoned long ago. He made his way to an observation blister from where he could see the cloud-streaked surface of Vanaheim far below.

It also gave him a view of part of the station's exterior. He could see half a dozen or so transparent domes arranged at different angles along a central hub that, by the looks of it, was at least a couple of kilometres in length. Green shadows filled several of the nearest domes, while those further away looked dark and empty.

Moving away from the blister, he let the same mechant that had sealed him inside the crate guide him further down the passageway. Navigating in zero gee had never been his strong point, and it took a constant effort of will to remind himself that the station's hub was not a bottomless well, and he was not about to go tumbling down its length.

It became rapidly clear the station was badly in need of repair. Access panels had been pulled open, exposing wiring and circuitry, and he saw at least a dozen dog-sized multi-limbed mechants standing still and silent, plugged into juice terminals that were clearly no longer capable of supplying them with power.

'Who does this station belong to?' he asked the mechant, more to distract himself than anything else.

'The *Sequoia* is the property of Councillor Długok cki, Chief Administrator for the Lubjek mining colony in Acamar's outer system,' the mechant replied from up ahead. Its voice echoed slightly in the still air.

He followed the mechant towards a pair of secondary passageways branching out at right angles from the central hub, then followed the machine down the passageway on the right. They passed through a pressure-field, and immediately the air became warmer and denser and more humid, the walls of the passageway thick with moss and vines. After another few metres, Luc found himself drifting up through the floor of one of the domes he had earlier sighted.

The air within the dome was even more humid, filled with wide-leaved palms and trees that pushed against the curved transparent ceiling of the dome. The floor was hidden beneath lush grasses and ferns. Tiny, lemur-like primates with feathery blue fur and broad, fleshy flaps joining their arms to their bodies soared through the warm, soupy air, scattering brightly coloured insects that sported wide translucent wings.

Luc spotted Ambassador Sachs waiting for him at a point where several pathways, nearly hidden beneath the dense flora, converged close to the dome's centre.

'You are Master Archivist Gabion?' asked the Ambassador as Luc came to a halt before him. His face was still hidden behind a mirror mask, and it was more than a little strange for Luc to find himself staring into that mirror, given his dream-memories of Antonov's face reflected in it.

The Ambassador's voice proved to be soft, almost *contralto*. He wore the same long coat as at Vasili's service, while dark gloves concealed his hands. Luc felt a slight prickling on the back of his neck as he wondered if the Ambassador might in fact be some kind of machine, but then noticed pale flesh hidden in the shadows within the Ambassador's hood, where the edge of the mask came into contact with all too human skin.

'Ambassador,' said Luc with a slight bow. 'Councillor de Almeida said you might be able to help in the investigation into Sevgeny Vasili's death.'

The Ambassador dipped his head slightly in acknowledgement. 'Mr Gabion. We are familiar with your recent exploits at Aeschere. We're more than happy to provide whatever assistance we can.'

'I hope you don't mind me asking,' said Luc, 'but why meet here?'

'It's peaceful,' the Ambassador replied. 'And it feels like home, given that many of our lives back in the Coalition are spent far from planetary surfaces. We . . . must confess to some confusion over Miss de Almeida's request. We were under the impression the investigation into Councillor Vasili's murder had recently been closed?'

We? 'Yes, but we're far from clear on how the killer managed to circumvent security and reach Vanaheim,' said Luc, thinking again of the ease with which de Almeida had just done precisely that to bring him here. 'Naturally, we want to reduce the chances of something like this happening ever again.'

The Ambassador nodded. 'We can understand why the Council would want to carry out a review of its own security measures, but don't see how we could possibly be of any help. Surely it's an internal matter for the Council?'

'Miss de Almeida wants to carry out interviews with anyone who met with or spoke with Vasili in the last few days before he died. You *did* say you were willing to help?'

For a second he thought the Ambassador might object. Even with the mask hiding his face, Luc could clearly sense his reluctance.

'Very well, then,' said the Ambassador, with a touch of weariness. 'We wouldn't want to be seen as uncooperative.'

'If I may ask, Ambassador Sachs – why do you wear that mask?'

The Ambassador let out an audible sigh. 'Must we really go over this again?'

Luc hesitated, guessing he'd be far from the first person to have asked that very question. 'Consider it a necessary formality, Ambassador, with my apologies.'

'Very well, then.' Sachs replied, with the tone of one repeating a familiar litany. 'In the Coalition, we believe faces born of nature have little reflection on an individual's true spirit. We don't place limits on ourselves in the way that your own civilization does, and we prefer to be judged by what we do, rather than how we appear. Besides, there are those amongst us who engage in forms of mind and body modification that some within the Tian Di might find . . . intimidating.'

'So do you keep the mask on to avoid frightening people?'

The Ambassador hesitated a moment. 'To avoid *confusing* them would be the more accurate statement. Is this relevant to your investigation?'

No, but it's relevant to me. 'You met with Vasili just shortly before he died?'

'That is a matter of record.'

'Where were you at the time he died?'

'At a function, held in my honour, and attended by Councillors who had participated in the preparations for Reunification. Vasili's absence, it should be said, was noted by all present.'

'And when you last spoke with Vasili, what did you talk about?'

'Nothing out of the ordinary. We had regular meetings to go over whatever details or issues might come about on the run-up to Reunification. He seemed alert but tired that last time.'

'He didn't seem anxious, or worried about anything?'

'If he had,' the Ambassador replied, 'we would have been sure to mention it upon hearing of his death.'

Luc could see he wasn't getting anywhere. 'Vasili was central to Reunification, but would you agree that the Temur Council is far from unified in their support for it?'

'Perhaps not,' the Ambassador replied, with just a hint of evasiveness.

'The fact is,' Luc continued, 'Reunification remains a deeply contentious issue, even now. You've spent a lot of time dealing with members of the Council yourself, so you must have some idea who might have the necessary motivation to want to kill the one man seen as the architect of that entire process.'

'We are far from being experts regarding divisions within the Council,' the Ambassador replied. 'And besides, there are limits to what we can discuss with a non-Council member.'

'I speak for Zelia de Almeida. You can assume that when you're speaking to me, you're also speaking to her.'

'Mr Gabion, we were at Vasili's funeral service – and saw *you* there, as a virtual presence. You had conspired to hide yourself from the eyes of everyone else present, but not from us. You heard Councillor Borges as well as we did: he openly accused her of orchestrating Councillor Vasili's murder. Are you sure it's not *her* your questions should be directed at?'

Luc couldn't hide his shock. 'You saw me there?'

'Indeed we did. It's also our understanding,' the Ambassador continued, 'that Borges is not alone in believing your employer is guilty of perpetrating a murder.'

'That's still to be proven,' Luc countered, wondering how he had so quickly gone from interrogator to the interrogated.

'Then doesn't it seem strange that the person regarded as a primary suspect would herself carry out an investigation into Vasili's death?'

'You knew this when she asked you to meet me here.' He realized he was fast losing control of the situation. 'Why did you agree to this meeting, if you had nothing to say on the matter?'

'On the contrary,' said the Ambassador. 'We agreed to this meeting because we wanted to meet *you*.'

Luc's own astonished face stared back at him from the Ambassador's mask.

'Why?'

'Perhaps, Mr Gabion, you have something to hide. When we saw you there at Vasili's service, we knew immediately that you possessed a lattice unlike any other in the worlds of the Tian Di except, perhaps, our own.'

Luc felt as if time had slowed to a standstill. The sound of his own heart beating seemed to fill the arboretum, like a pulse reverberating through the dense moist air.

'At first,' the Ambassador continued, 'we thought it was Winchell Antonov himself standing there, but when we looked more closely we saw that we were mistaken – at least in part. We later made cautious enquiries and discovered your identity, as well as your involvement in Antonov's downfall.'

Luc's hands had started to tremble at his sides. 'What you're saying doesn't make any sense,' he said. 'Antonov is dead.'

'Is he?' asked the Ambassador. 'And has he communicated with you since he "died"?'

Luc didn't answer, and the Ambassador inclined his head. 'We know that within the Tian Di only members of the Council and Sandoz Clans are permitted the use of instantiation lattices. Your lattice is therefore illegal. We saw Antonov's shade within you when you entered this station,' he continued, 'and I can see that your lattice is new, but growing wildly out of control. Please don't deny this is the truth.'

'At the most there's a – a ghost, an artefact, some remnant of Antonov's conscious mind inside of me,' Luc stammered. 'That, and some random memories.'

'We cannot help but wonder how you came to possess the memories of the man you were sent to capture.'

Luc fought the urge to reach out and rip the Ambassador's mask away, but things had already gone badly wrong enough without compounding them with further errors.

'If we're going to be frank with each other,' said Luc, 'I know you met with Winchell Antonov. That's a dangerous association to have, for a representative of what's still technically an enemy civilization.'

'How do you know we met with him?'

'You said it yourself, Ambassador Sachs. I have some of Antonov's memories, even if they are fragmentary. He seemed to be angry with you for some reason.'

'Why don't you ask him about it yourself, Mr Gabion? It appears the two of you are on far more intimate terms than he and I ever were. Otherwise, the details of that encounter must remain private.'

173

The Ambassador made to turn away, then hesitated. 'Tell Zelia I'm sorry we couldn't help more, but there's nothing useful we could possibly tell her regarding Vasili.'

It appeared their interview was over. Luc watched as the Ambassador turned and stepped along a path leading deeper amongst the moist-leaved ferns crowding the dome; and then he remembered Antonov's words, spoken in a dream: *With the Ambassador's help, we will both be reborn, and a terrible calamity prevented.*

'Antonov told me you could help me!' Luc yelled after him. 'He said you could prevent a calamity, but I don't know what he meant.'

The Ambassador came to a halt but did not turn around. 'He said that?'

'Yes. No, not exactly. It was . . .' Luc swallowed. 'It was in a dream.'

He half expected the Ambassador to laugh.

Instead, the masked figure turned to face him once more. 'In the Coalition, the distinction between dreams and waking are as fluid and meaningless as that which separates life and death. We make equally little distinction between that which you would not regard as objectively real, and what you would consider tangible and solid. The difference, from our perspective, is sufficiently negligible to be meaningless. Like yourself, each one of us speaks with the dead as a matter of course. In fact, the dead could be said to constitute the majority of the Coalition's population.'

'And the calamity? What did he mean by that?'

'Something that is not of your concern,' the Ambassador replied. 'The knowledge would place you in a considerably greater degree of danger than we suspect you are already in.'

'Tell me,' Luc grated, 'or I go to the Council and tell them everything I know, including that you met with Antonov.'

'And if you do,' the Ambassador pointed out, 'they will surely pick your brain apart, neurone by neurone, once they discover that you have a lattice.'

'I'm prepared to take that chance.'

The Ambassador paused for a moment, then said: 'We simply don't believe you, Mr Gabion. You would not, we think, make a good poker player.'

Luc stepped towards him. 'Please, wait. De Almeida – Zelia – told me the lattice in my head is killing me.' He stopped, putting one hand against the mossy branch of a tree reaching over the path. 'I keep seeing and hearing things, and sometimes I don't know which are real and which aren't.'

'Then tell me how you came to acquire the lattice.'

'On Aeschere,' Luc replied miserably. 'Antonov put it inside me while I was out cold.'

'Who else knows of this?'

He couldn't see the use of keeping anything more back. 'Only Zelia,' he replied. 'She's the one who detected it inside me. She told me I can't be backed-up from it before it kills me. Antonov seemed sure you would help me.'

'Is this why Zelia sent you here? To ask for our help?'

'No. This is . . . just me.'

'Yours is a single life,' said the Ambassador, 'measured against countless billions here in the Tian Di and also in the Coalition. As much as you have our sympathy, you must understand that we have greater concerns at the moment. But Antonov would not have done what he did to you without a reason, and whichever of his memories are surfacing in your mind were clearly of importance to him. He's trying to tell you something, and we suspect you're not doing a very good job of listening. Ask yourself, why would he plant a partial copy of himself inside the mind of one of his most dedicated enemies, unless it was for some overwhelming purpose?'

'I know it has something to do with Vasili,' said Luc.

'What makes you think that?'

'I have reason to believe Antonov may have met with him some time not long before his death. He knew who his killer was. Who it was, I don't know, except I'm certain it wasn't Antonov, and I can't believe it was de Almeida, either.' He stared into his own reflection, seeing the haunted look in his eyes. 'But it has to have something to do with Reunification, and I think you know what it is.'

'We truly wish we could help you,' said the Ambassador with what sounded like genuine regret, 'but there are things taking place which you can scarcely comprehend. We suggest, however, that you listen more closely to whatever Antonov is trying to tell you. It may be that he is trying to give you the answers you seek.' The Ambassador paused. 'May we offer a final word of advice?'

'Of course,' said Luc, feeling defeated.

'Zelia de Almeida may value you more for what you carry inside your head than for your investigative skills. You should be careful.'

The Ambassador turned once more and began to walk away, passing beneath the shade of a banyan tree's broad plate-like leaves. When Luc made to follow, a mechant of a type he'd never seen before dropped from out of the greenery overhead, blocking his way.

'Careful of what?' he yelled after the retreating figure. 'Give me a straight answer, damn you!'

'Goodbye, Mr Gabion,' said the Ambassador, before disappearing into the undergrowth. 'We hope you find your answers before it's too late.'

'I have discovered inconsistencies,' said de Almeida, 'in the Ambassador's alibi.'

Mechants moved here and there around her laboratory, specialized models studded with multiple limbs that hovered around Luc's supine form as she gave them barely vocalized orders. The slab he lay on had been adjusted until he was staring straight up at the ceiling. Images of the interior of his skull rippled whenever de Almeida or one of the mechants passed through them, meat and blood furiously splintering before miraculously reforming into dizzyingly complex three-dimensional structures.

'He told me himself he was at a meeting when Vasili died,' Luc replied. He had decided to exercise caution and not tell her everything the Ambassador had said to him.

De Almeida nodded. 'A gathering of members of a coordination committee, tasked with hammering out the details of various trade agreements. Oh, he was there all right – but only in virtual form.'

Luc felt his eyes widen, and turned to regard her. 'He was only there as a data-ghost? He never mentioned that.'

'No, he certainly didn't,' she agreed. 'That means we need to find out where he really was at the time.'

He sat up, mechants bobbing away from him. 'What about your security systems? Can't they tell you?'

She spread a roll of gleaming silver instruments out on a wheeled table next to the slab and selected one, studying it beneath the overhead light. 'Unfortunately, no, they can't. My systems appear to have suffered a curiously well-timed and convenient glitch that I failed to notice until I happened to make specific enquiries regarding the Ambassador.'

'Something like the glitch in Vasili's home security when he died?'

'A thought that had indeed crossed my mind, Mr Gabion.'

She adjusted the stool on which she sat, then leaned in towards him. He saw the curve of her neck just centimetres from his nose, the flesh silky and smooth. She pressed fingertips against his skull, and he noticed she was wearing a scent that made him think of flowers.

She murmured something he didn't catch, and a mechant drifted closer, its multi-tipped blades hovering uncomfortably close to the skin of his neck.

Luc swallowed sour phlegm. 'Is all this really necessary?'

'If you want a shot at retaining your core personality, yes,' she replied, sounding distracted. 'Now stop talking while I get on with this. Ah!' she exclaimed a moment later, 'this *is* interesting.'

Luc felt a pressure against the side of his skull, followed by the sensation of something warm and liquid running down the back of his head. His hands held tightly onto the sides of the slab, muscles locked rigid.

Something whined mechanically and he felt a similar pressure on the other side of his head. Moments later a barbiturate calm flooded his senses and he relaxed.

'Your lattice barely responded to the inhibitors I put in place,' she muttered. 'I've never seen anything like it. It circumvented every countermeasure, and its growth is barely retarded. I'd almost think . . .'

'What?'

'Nothing,' she muttered. 'I'll just have to try something a little different this time. Try and stay still for now.'

Like I'm going to get up and run around.

'You need to put the Ambassador under surveillance,' he said, as de Almeida moved out of direct view. He was finding himself becoming uncomfortably aroused by the smell of her skin, and the visible curve of her breasts beneath the thin tunic she wore.

De Almeida stepped back into view and made a sour face as she tapped at a lit panel on the side of one of the mechants hovering over him. 'That won't be easy,' she said.

'You can't do it?'

'Of course I can do it,' she snapped. 'But I have to be careful to avoid detection. Let's see . . .' she glanced over at one of the hovering projections of the interior of Luc's head. 'You're not sleeping well, are you?'

'Not for some time, no,' he admitted.

She nodded. 'Your brain is struggling to assimilate information coming from two different sources: your own mind, and Antonov's instantiation. I can try and retard the rate of growth again, but unless I can figure out some new strategy . . .'

Luc shuddered inwardly. 'How bad is it?'

'Impossible to say. Remember, this was fast, sloppy work – Antonov was improvising when he did this.'

'So it's not like I'm carrying the whole of his thoughts and memories inside me. He can't . . . take me over, or anything like that?' He had to force the words out.

She laughed. 'Hardly. You can't just dump a copy of someone's mind into a living, breathing human body with pre-existing cognitive structures.'

'But that's what he did, isn't it?'

'True, but the outcome is proving far from beneficial for either party.'

'The Sandoz Clans do it, don't they? And you. You're a Councillor. If you die, you can be reborn in a clone body.'

'Yes, a *clone* body, heavily modified with an *in situ* lattice of its own from the moment of its inception in a growth tank. The clone body must be created from your own DNA as well.'

'And I don't have a clone-body ready to jump into.'

'Precisely. And unless I can find a way to retard this thing's growth, all you have to look forward to, I'm afraid, is madness followed by death.'

Luc stared at her, a sick feeling building inside him. 'Isn't there anyone else in the Council you could talk to in confidence about this? Someone who understands how lattices work?'

'Well, there's Rowena Engberg, and also Cutler Suszynski. They developed the lattice technology together. Engberg still runs the clinic that engineers all of the Council's lattices. Unfortunately, they're both loyal Eighty-Fivers. They'd hand both our heads to Cheng on a plate in a flat instant if we approached them.'

'The Ambassador knew I was there, at Vasili's service. He could see me. He said my lattice is far in advance of anything the Tian Di can make.'

De Almeida nodded distractedly. 'Yes, you told me already.'

'So where the hell could Antonov have got this thing inside me *from*?'

She said nothing, and he guessed she had no more idea than he did.

'I asked you before for access to Vanaheim's global security network. I think maybe it's time you finally gave it to me.'

To Luc's astonishment, she didn't even argue or scoff at the request this time. Instead, she held a hand up towards him, palm out, and after a moment he saw a single bright flash of light, centred on her palm.

Suddenly he was aware of things he had never been aware of until that moment, and yet which felt as if they had always been known to him. The feeling was extraordinary – like stumbling across a part of his mind he had never noticed before.

'Done,' she said. 'You now have *limited* access to Vanaheim's global security, but that access is funnelled through me. I'll be aware of everything you do.'

'Limited in what way?'

'It's restricted to the Ambassador's movements only. You'll be able to see where he goes, and when. Give it a try.'

'How?'

'Picture him. The lattice will pinpoint his location and filter the appropriate A/V data to you.'

Luc closed his eyes and pictured Ambassador Sachs, as he had been on board the *Sequoia*. Within moments he found himself looking at a low, one-storey building spread across a few acres in the centre of a forest clearing.

'I can see a building, but not the Ambassador.'

'You're seeing through the eyes of one of my micro-mechants currently in his vicinity. Just tell it to move in closer.'

He nodded and tried again.

The view jumped as the tiny machine lifted from its perch and swooped in low towards the building. Luc caught sight of a ground-to-orbit flier in the process of dropping onto a landing area to one side of the building, halfway between it and the trees. The sunlight passing through the craft's AG field shimmered with rainbow colours.

The Ambassador emerged from the spacecraft as Luc watched, making his way towards a second flier parked at the other end of the landing area. He still wore his mirror mask and hood, even though he was alone – something which made him seem even more otherworldly than he already did.

'Just how many of these micro-mechants do you have scattered all across Vanaheim?' asked Luc.

'A lot,' de Almeida replied.

The viewpoint shifted again as the tiny mechant buzzed several metres closer. Luc saw the Ambassador board the second flier. It lifted up almost immediately, sending dead leaves spinning into the air as it ascended.

He's in a hurry, thought Luc. Ambassador Sachs must have departed the *Sequoia* only shortly after he himself had. And now he was on his way somewhere else.

'You're telling me the Council seriously don't mind you being able to see every damn thing they're up to like this?' he asked, keeping his eyes closed.

'Apart from the Eighty-Five, you mean?' She laughed dryly. 'The system is set up so they're aware if I'm watching, or can find out easily enough. That way I'm accountable for everything I do.'

So you say, thought Luc. The micro-mechant had lifted its lens to follow the flier as it dwindled into a deepening blue sky.

'So what do you do if you need to know what they're up to, but you don't want them to know?'

'I spy on them regardless.'

Luc opened his eyes and looked up at her. 'And they're seriously all right with that?'

'If I can prove at a later date that it was necessary to do so, of course,' she said, as if it was the most obvious thing in the world. 'Privacy is always respected, but there are times when such things do prove necessary. You can get up now,' she added, standing back.

Luc swayed a little as he stood upright. He reached up to touch the side of his head, and when he brought his hand back down found it speckled with blood.

'Somewhere I can wash up?'

She nodded towards a sink and tap a few metres away. 'Over there.'

Luc ran lukewarm water across his stubbled scalp and down the back of his neck. He glanced up at a mirror over the sink and saw de Almeida putting her roll of instruments away, but started when he realized the exact same hunched figure still stood in the same corner he had seen it days before. He froze, chilled by the sight.

'Zelia,' he said, without taking his eyes off the creature, 'I really want to know just what that thing is.'

De Almeida looked around, confused, then walked across the laboratory until she could see the same pathetic hunched figure.

'I'm sorry,' she said, 'does that bother you?'

Luc turned from the sink to stare at her, appalled beyond belief. 'Doesn't it bother *you*?'

She shrugged. 'He's nothing. A criminal, a malcontent.'

Luc studied her features, entirely free of guilt or empathy. *These are the people you chose to serve,* he reminded himself.

'Just tell me who he is,' he demanded, his voice ragged. 'He's been standing there for . . . for *days*. What the hell could he have done, to deserve winding up like that?'

Her mouth pinched up. 'Damn it, Gabion, these are people who've been sentenced to death. I can make good use of them this way.'

'Make *use* of them?' Luc laughed, but it was a dismal, half-choked sound by the time it emerged from his throat.

'You don't approve?'

'*Look* at him! Doesn't it bother you, to reduce a human being to something like that?'

'Have you ever thought,' she asked, her voice cold, 'about the struggle the Tian Di faced in order to achieve as much as it did, over the centuries? Things like the CogNet, instantiation lattices, data-ghosting, or any of the hundreds of other networked symbiotic technologies that make our lives easier?' She nodded towards the huddled figure. 'This laboratory isn't here just for show. The Council still supports original research into new ways to integrate flesh and machinery.'

'There must be other ways to—'

'Other ways?' she barked. 'It's precisely that lack of insight, that refusal to commit to necessary sacrifices that tells me you could never be a member of the Council yourself. You've seen Ambassador Sachs, haven't you? Whatever's under that mask of his, it's evident the Coalition has become a fully post-human society. We need to understand them and what they've become before their culture overwhelms our own because, let me assure you, their technology is *far* in advance of ours. That, right now, is the central focus of my research.'

She gestured towards the hunched figure. Luc looked on as, very slowly and carefully, it turned on the spot, its feet shuffling and scraping on the bare floor. He watched it lumber towards a curved balustrade set against a far wall, then slowly make its way down some steps and out of sight. Luc found it hard to contain his horror; it was difficult to believe that pathetic, shambling form had once been a person with a name and a history.

'Where is the Ambassador now?'

Luc forced himself to turn back to de Almeida. 'I'm sorry?'

'Ambassador Sachs,' she repeated with obvious impatience. 'You *are* still keeping tabs on him, aren't you?'

Luc switched his attention back to the Ambassador. Instead of a visual feed, this time his lattice supplied a geo-locational tag attached to a virtual map of Vanaheim.

'His flier's headed north-west,' he informed her.

'Fine. Just keep an eye on him. Otherwise, I think we're done here for now.'

'The lattice,' said Luc. 'What's the latest prognosis?'

She bit her lip, clearly mulling over an appropriate response. 'It's hard to be sure. But I'm feeling pretty hopeful I can delay its growth long enough to find some longer-term solution.'

Luc nodded tightly, unwilling to let her see how distressed her words really made him.

A mechant floated down next to her, a tunic jacket gripped in its manipulators. It laid the jacket across her shoulders.

'I'll call on you as soon as I have anything more of value,' she said, stepping towards the spiral staircase that led to the upper floor. 'A flier is waiting outside for you, one I've reserved for your sole use. You'll be pleased to know you won't need to hide inside any more crates in future.'

She quickly ascended the steps, disappearing into a shaft of light slanting down from the next floor up. Luc stepped towards the exit, but then paused, thinking of the eyeless ruin de Almeida had just sent downstairs.

It only took a few moments to descend the steps to the basement level below de Almeida's laboratory.

He pushed open a door at the bottom of the steps, finding himself at one end of a long stone corridor with an arched ceiling. The air tasted damp and slightly mouldy, while junk and what looked like pieces of discarded laboratory equipment were piled untidily in deep alcoves set into the passageway on either side. He could hear the muffled thud of machinery from somewhere up ahead, the slate tiles beneath his feet vibrating faintly in time with the thuds.

The air grew rapidly warmer as he made his way along the passageway. After twenty metres or so it widened to accommodate several steel trestle tables, a few of which were covered over with blood-spattered sheets, almost as if Luc had stumbled across a battlefield hospital.

He came to a stop, seeing two mechants hovering over the naked body of a man that had been laid out on one of the tables. Another eyeless horror – not the same one, he sensed, that de Almeida had just sent down here – stood next to the unconscious man. This creature had needle-tipped machinery in place of fingers; its movements were slow and measured and, as Luc approached, it turned slowly to regard him with its uncanny blank gaze.

Dry-mouthed, Luc forced himself closer to the table. He now saw that the man lying there was being operated on. His skull had been cut open, black pits gaped where his eyes had once been, and much of his lower jaw had been removed. One of the mechants was engaged in manoeuvring a chunk of grey-blue machinery into place where his jawbone had been.

Luc staggered away and threw up in a corner.

He coughed, wiped his mouth, then pressed his forehead against the cool damp stone, breathing harshly. In that moment he heard a sudden, brief burst of static coming from behind him.

He turned to hear a second burst of static issuing from the machinery-clogged throat of the needle-fingered creature. After another moment it appeared to lose interest in him, turning its attention back to its comatose patient. Luc wondered if it had been trying to say something, assuming any kind of human consciousness was still trapped behind that savagely disfigured face.

Luc became aware of a slow, dragging shuffle, echoing from some way further down the corridor. Peering ahead, he saw the very creature he'd come looking for disappear into a shadowed alcove, not far from where the corridor came to an end.

Part of him wanted to turn back, to the world of daylight and air that didn't smell of mould and disinfectant and death. His heart thundered inside his chest at the thought of going any farther. Worse, he had no idea how de Almeida might react if she discovered he had come down here.

But he had to know.

Making his way quickly to the same alcove into which the stooped figure had disappeared, Luc found himself at the entrance to a wide, low-ceilinged room. Instantly he was bathed in a blast of heat emanating from an open furnace at the opposite end of the room from him, the air shimmering violently from the heat. Rubbish was piled up on either side of the furnace door, while several more of de Almeida's eyeless monstrosities worked steadily at shovelling it all into the flames.

He saw the stooped creature he had followed, outlined by the flames dancing in the heart of the furnace. At first he thought it would pick up a shovel and join its companions, but instead, to his unending horror, it climbed in through the open furnace door, burning like a torch as the flames caught at its ragged clothes. Apparently impervious to pain, it continued to move deeper into the furnace before slowly pitching forward.

The roar of the furnace grew incrementally louder for a second or two.

Luc heard a sound like the cry of an animal caught in a trap, then realized it had come from his own throat.

He took several steps backwards and stumbled against the wall of the passageway. His lungs felt like they had turned to ice despite the intensity of the heat.

The next thing he knew, he was back upstairs and halfway through the greenhouse attached to de Almeida's laboratory. He kept going until he was outside, then collapsed against a low wall bordering a garden before again throwing up over some artfully arranged flowers.

As de Almeida had promised, a flier stood waiting for him, a blunt-nosed affair with a more utilitarian appearance than most, meaning it was probably used primarily as a goods vehicle. He staggered towards it as if drunk, climbing on board and barely noticing when it lifted up into clear blue skies.

He closed his eyes, but all he could see was that same stooped figure pitching forward into an inferno.

And maybe one day de Almeida will get tired of trying to help you, and turn you into another one of her monsters.

As he hugged himself, and the flier boosted high into the atmosphere, it came to him that he was going to have to try and save himself, although *how* he might do that remained beyond him. De Almeida was quite possibly psychotic, and the rest of the Council – those same people he'd given a lifetime of service to – were, judging by what he'd seen and heard, even worse.

But that didn't mean he had any choice but to play along for the moment. He thought again of those terrible bright flames, and felt as if strips of gauze had been lifted from his eyes. The world seemed different now, had taken on a new and sinister edge.

Between that – and the long, painful quest to find out what purpose might lie behind Antonov's surgery on him – all he could do was wait.

TWELVE

A couple of hours after rescuing Jacob, Jonathan Kulic guided his horse and cart into a small settlement on the edge of the forest, just as the sky began to redden towards dusk.

Jacob watched the landscape pass by from under the carpet Kulic had thrown over him in the rear of the cart. He kept the case he had recovered from his ship clutched tight against his chest. The settlement that Kulic called home was, to Jacob's eyes, astoundingly primitive. Smoke spiralled upwards from thatched-roof dwellings, while candles and lanterns flickered from inside windows formed from heavy, puddled glass. There were farm animals in pens, and a stable with horses. It was a stark contrast to the spires of one of Darwin's cities, glittering on the far horizon.

Kulic guided his horse and cart into a barn, then led Jacob into his home through an adjoining door. Kulic's residence proved to be a single-storey affair of brick and plaster, with wooden floorboards that creaked with every step.

Jacob's duty was to hide himself in one of these Left-Behind communities, and take advantage of the Coalition's incomprehensible willingness to allow them to continue existing. From his conversation with Kulic throughout their journey from the coast, he had learned that the Left-Behind had become considerably more militant in their beliefs over the decades, having come to reject nearly every form of technology imaginable, up to and including previously accepted technologies such as the internal-combustion engine and electricity. The electric torch Kulic had used to aid him in his search through the deep forest was something he was forced to keep secret from his neighbours.

The only source of heat in Kulic's hovel came from a heavy iron stove, with flames licking behind a narrow grate. Pots and pans hung from steel hooks above a table scattered with the ruins of chopped vegetables. Jacob stood close by the stove, warming his hands before the grate and trying hard not to breathe too deeply, since everything smelled of mould and animal shit. He wondered what the Darwinians, living as they did in their shining silver cities, made of it all when they gazed down at these disease-ridden hovels, clustered together in the mud and filth.

'Once the beacon told me you were here, I spread it about that a cousin might come to visit me from New Jerusalem,' Kulic explained as he closed the latch on the front door. 'That settlement's a long way away from here, a good four or five days' journey on horseback. I thought it'd make as good a story as anything else.'

'It'll do,' said Jacob, his attention still focused on getting warm. 'It's called a transceiver, by the way, not a beacon. Where do you keep it?'

'Downstairs,' Kulic replied, 'in the cellar.'

'I would like to see it, please,' said Jacob, looking around. He hadn't seen any sign of steps or a staircase leading down.

Kulic stepped towards the centre of the room, reaching down to pull a faded, hand-woven rug to one side and revealing a trapdoor with an iron ring set into it. Kulic pulled the trapdoor up with a grunt, revealing a short ladder leading downwards. A foul miasma rose from below, and Jacob covered his mouth, thinking that even the cave in the woods had been better than this.

Kulic climbed down the steps and out of sight. With a sigh, Jacob wrenched himself away from the stove's welcoming heat and followed the old man down.

Farming implements hung from hooks all around the walls of the stone-floored cellar. Kulic lit a gas lantern hanging from a hook in the ceiling then, as Jacob watched, stepped over to a barrel that had been pushed into a corner, a rusted kettle and several dirty-looking rags dumped on top of it.

Kulic brushed all of this junk onto the floor, then lifted the lid from the barrel, which proved to be full of oily-looking water. He took hold of an almost invisibly thin thread hanging over the side of the barrel and pulled on it with extreme care, soon drawing a package wrapped in heavy oilskins up from the barrel's depths before depositing it on the floor. Jacob watched as the old man carefully unwrapped the package to reveal a large wooden box.

'Here,' said Kulic, opening the box and lifting out a fist-sized device, passing it to Jacob with an uncertain grin. Something about his expression made Jacob think of a dog desperate for its master's approval.

He studied the device by the dim light of the ceiling-mounted lantern. In outward appearance it looked like nothing more than a blunt, copper-plated sphere, but in reality it was a compact mass of molecular circuitry impervious to any but the most ruthless scan. It sang with information from the moment his fingers touched it, firing a blizzard of condensed data into his lattice that had the quality of long-held memories.

He looked up at Kulic. 'I see you've been speaking to it, telling it everything that's been happening?'

Kulic nodded, his expression full of awe. 'Yes, just as my father asked me to. I . . . wondered if I was being a fool, talking to a piece of metal, as if it had ears.' He looked at Jacob with hope. 'It worked?'

'Yes.' Jacob nodded.

'My father told me it could communicate with other worlds.'

Then he told you too much, thought Jacob, frowning. The device was indeed built to pick up instantaneous transmissions across space, regardless of distance, although the power consumption required to boost a signal across so many light-years without it dissolving into random noise was quite enormous. Along with news of events back on Temur as well as throughout the Tian Di, Jacob had in just these last moments received adjustments to his mission plan. Although his primary goal remained the same, there was now an added urgency to his purpose in being here.

'The device tells me the Left-Behind split into factions, and that the more rigidly conservative faction became dominant.'

Kulic stared at the device nestled in Jacob's hands with horrified fascination. 'That little thing – it told you all that?'

The Left-Behind had briefly been a powerful force on the surviving colony worlds following the Abandonment, preaching that the artefacts responsible for turning every living thing on Earth to dust had been sent there by God, in order to gather the souls of mankind prior to a final judgement. The religion had eventually been outlawed throughout the Tian Di, but here in the Coalition followers were permitted to exist, so long as they remained far from the provenance of the cities.

'You told the transceiver that Bruehl had begun to believe he was some kind of messiah, destined to lead the Left-Behind through the Founder Network.'

'I still remember him from when I was much younger,' said Kulic, nodding. 'Before he died, my father told me Bruehl was responsible for setting up safe-houses for other Tian Di agents. Bruehl was tasked with penetrating the Coalition's secure military networks, in order to find their weaknesses. But something happened.'

'What?'

Kulic's balding pate glistened under the dim light of the lantern. 'He started telling people God was waiting for us up at the end of time, along with everyone else who'd been rescued when the angels razed Earth; he said that was why the Founder Network had been created, so that all sentient beings could find their way there. This went against the doctrine of the Church's Elders and made them very unhappy.'

'And your father? How did he feel about this?'

'At first he thought Bruehl was insane, but I think my father had a great deal of trouble adjusting to life here. He married because it was expected of him, and it was his duty to fit in. I . . .

realize now that I was nothing more than part of his cover, that he had never really wanted a child.'

'He told you this?'

'No.' Kulic shook his head. 'I worked some of it out for myself, once I knew the truth about him . . .' His voice trailed off.

'Go on,' Jacob prompted.

'I think my father committed suicide, in a way,' Kulic finally said. 'He changed his mind about Bruehl, and began to believe him. I think his new-found religious beliefs were a way to hide the truth from himself, that he no longer wanted to live.'

'Bruehl had quite a few followers, I understand. Your father was only one of them.'

'Yes, Bruehl had a great number of followers after a while. Even I was one. We all followed him when he left for the cities. He said he'd had a vision, that God would guide us through the Founder Network, and the Coalition wouldn't be able to stand in our way.'

'How many of you went with him?'

Kulic shrugged. 'A thousand, perhaps. At that time I had no idea of my father's true identity, and the same went for the other agents like Bruehl. When we left, the Elders condemned us for our actions.' The old man stopped, gazing wistfully into the distance.

'And?'

'And we never even reached the cities. First Bruehl and my father started fighting, and before long the people who'd followed them started to take sides.' Kulic shook his head. 'Folks around here don't like to speak about those days any more, but I was there. A few hundred continued on with Bruehl, while the rest followed my father back home. But not all of us were allowed back in – old scores were being settled, I suppose.'

'And what happened to Bruehl?'

'More people abandoned him and drifted back to their villages over the following days and weeks. As far as I know he managed to lead a few dozen as far as the nearest city, but all I know about what happened after that is rumour and conjecture. From what I heard,' said Kulic, with an uncharacteristic touch of sarcasm, 'they never reached the Founder Network, since God apparently failed to supply them with the necessary authorization to pass through a single transfer gate.'

As if even the Coalition would have wasted one moment listening to the ravings of madmen straggling in from some self-imposed backwater, branches and leaves clinging to their holy beards, thought Jacob. Learning about such things left a sour and unpleasant taste in his belly. He could only imagine that Bruehl and this man's father must have been suffering from some shared psychosis they had somehow kept hidden during their mission training – a psychosis that had achieved full flower once they found themselves surrounded by people even crazier than themselves.

'And Sillars? You haven't said anything about what happened to him. Was he part of all this?'

Kulic shook his head. 'No. Sillars didn't believe like the others did.'

Jacob felt a flush of relief. 'He stayed true to his mission?'

Kulic nodded. 'He argued with Bruehl and my father before we headed for the cities. Bruehl got into a fight with Sillars, and . . .' He licked his lips, eyes darting towards Jacob.

'Go on.'

'My father told me Bruehl killed Sillars. Sillars was afraid Bruehl might compromise their mission and alert the Coalition authorities to their purpose here. I remember one particular night just before we set out, when my father took me to Sillar's house. He had been stabbed, and was losing too much blood for even his microchines to cope. He died that same night. My father claimed it was God's will, and told me I was never to tell anyone what had happened.'

'That's something I was wondering,' said Jacob. 'If they had become so fervent in their beliefs, then why in hell didn't your father or Bruehl ever think to tell anyone else who they really were, where they'd come from?'

'I don't know,' Kulic replied, shaking his head. 'Maybe they were afraid of what might happen to them. But after Sillars' murder, something went out of my father. It's like he chose to pretend it hadn't happened. But when he died, he told me the truth of what he was, and told me someone like you would come one day.'

Jacob stared at the old man with sick disgust. It was nearly unbelievable so much could have gone so badly wrong, but all the evidence was right there, in the transceiver gripped in his own hand. Kulic couldn't have lied to it if he'd wanted to.

'Doesn't anyone from the cities ever come out here?' asked Jacob.

Kulic shivered. 'The people in the cities don't care about us, and I'm glad of it. Sometimes they . . . they watch us, from a distance. But not in human form.'

Jacob stepped closer to him. 'There's something I need to find,' said Jacob. 'It's the reason I was sent here, but it could mean travelling to one of the cities.'

Kulic stared back at him with bright damp eyes. 'I can help you.'

'You don't like it here, do you?' Jacob had been able to feel the old man's hatred for the people he lived amongst, seeping through the words he had spoken to the transceiver, here in the quiet dark beneath his house.

'I despise them all,' said Kulic. 'Ever since I learned of my father's true nature, I realized why I never felt like I belonged. There are fewer and fewer of the Left-Behind each year – most of those houses you saw when we arrived have been boarded up and abandoned for a long, long time. There are scarcely any children born these days.' Kulic swallowed. 'Even so, the cities frighten me. I'm scared that if I went there, they might change me into something that isn't really human.'

Jacob placed his hands on the old man's shoulders, thinking how easy it would be to snap his neck in an instant. Instead he patted him.

'Your father and his colleagues would have maintained a cache of equipment I can use,' said Jacob. 'Do you know of it, and where it's located?'

In truth, he already knew where it was, thanks to the transceiver, but he wanted to test the old man, see if he told the truth. If he lied or acted evasive in any way, he would prove himself useless, and Jacob would be left with no alternative but to dispose of him immediately.

'I know where it is,' said Kulic. 'It's not far from here, buried at the bottom of an abandoned well.'

Just as well you told the truth, thought Jacob, patting Kulic's shoulders one last time before stepping back and letting his hands fall by his side.

'We'll get some sleep and leave in the morning,' said Jacob, and led the way back up the steps.

THIRTEEN

Luc arrived back at his apartment without incident and found several messages waiting for him from Eleanor. This time, instead of ignoring them he sent back an immediate response. He had a sudden desperate urge to see her, to hold her in his arms.

While he waited, he spent a few minutes checking up on Ambassador Sach's movements. De Almeida's networks showed him the Ambassador had most recently paid a visit to the Vanaheim residence of Meinhard Carter, another member of the Council.

When Luc tried to direct one of de Almeida's countless micro-mechants to approach Carter's home, he discovered the precise limits to how far de Almeida's networks could reach, when it got to within only a few metres of a window before its signal faded to static. After that, it dropped permanently out of contact, presumably victim to Carter's own army of personal security devices.

Luc thought again of all that Ambassador Sachs had said to him on board the *Sequoia*, including the revelation that the Ambassador had been able to see him during Vasili's funeral service. Somehow Sachs tied into all of this, and it was clear the Ambassador knew far more than he was letting on.

Even so, he appeared to be doing nothing more than he might be expected to do – taking part in scheduled meetings and paving the way for Reunification, while perhaps also smoothing over the ripples caused by Vasili's sudden disappearance from public view.

Despite the limitations de Almeida had placed on Luc's access to her networks, he found he could nonetheless access a basic summary of Meinhard Carter's role within the Council. It proved, however, to be bafflingly vague. Carter was involved in some kind of research and development, and chaired an advisory body on deep-space exploration. That advisory body included several other Councillors charged with constructing the starships used to carry new transfer gates between old and new colonies. Several of them had worked on Founder research prior to the Schism.

Whatever Carter's current role in the Council might be, the Ambassador had caught him on what was apparently one of his rare visits to Vanaheim. And when Luc tried to find out where Meinhard Carter spent the rest of his time, he found himself blocked at every turn.

It wasn't long before Eleanor appeared to him as a data-ghost.

'I'm not even going to start on the fact you've been ignoring me,' she snapped as he shifted uncomfortably in his chair, 'but I think you should know people have been looking for you. First that whole debacle at the White Palace, then Cripps sneaking into your apartment, and now Lethe's been asking questions ever since you went to talk to Offenbach. I don't care if you're allowed to talk about it or not – were you on Vanaheim?'

He tried and failed to blank from his thoughts the image of a shambling figure climbing into a white-hot furnace.

'I think that's probably not hard to guess,' he admitted.

'That's where you were taken right after we arrived inside the White Palace, isn't it? Where else could you have gone for so long?' She paced before him, looking tense and harried. 'Lethe told me about some raid on a building on Kirov Avenue. He knows you were there, Luc – you were seen. It had something to do with a man named Reto Falla, right?'

Luc nodded.

'Then there's the way you keep disappearing from sight with no way to contact you,' she went on. 'It's clear you're involved in something as big as Aeschere – maybe even bigger, I don't know.'

'I don't understand why you're upset,' he said. 'You know how these things are. It's not like the first time either one of us has been involved in something we can't talk about—'

'Because even then I knew at *some* point we wouldn't have to do it any more!' she shouted, pressing one hand against her head. 'I'm not taking part in any more high-risk fieldwork, and you told me things were going to be different after you'd caught Antonov.' She shook her head. 'But that's not the case, is it?'

'Look, this was a direct request from a member of the Temur Council,' he said, forcing himself to breathe slowly. 'Believe me when I say it's really not something I had any choice in. Why do I have to tell you that, when you know it already?'

'Do you remember what I said to you?' she said, rounding on him. 'That there's only one of you; but that still didn't stop you charging into an unknown situation with a bunch of Sandoz who at least had the advantage of backups.' She shook her head. 'You still don't understand how lucky to be alive you are after all that's happened, do you?'

'So what do you expect me to do?' he said irritably. 'Go marching back up to the Palace and say, "Sorry, I'm quitting because my girlfriend isn't happy"?'

She sank down onto a chair he couldn't see, hands clasped above her knees, head slightly bent forward and eyes closed as if in prayer. 'No. I know you can't do that,' she said quietly. 'It's just that I nearly lost you once before, and I thought I was never going to have to deal with something like that again.'

He pulled himself out of his chair and reached out to put a hand on her shoulder, momentarily forgetting she wasn't physically present. Even so, she leaned towards him, acknowledging the gesture.

'I thought it was all going to be over too,' he said, letting his hand drop back by his side. 'But it's not. Not yet, anyway.'

'There's a rumour going around that Falla was connected with some kind of assassination attempt,' she said, the anger of a moment ago now drained from her voice. 'Lethe made enquiries after you were seen on Kirov Avenue, and got Offenbach to admit you'd been asking questions about Sevgeny Vasili, who no one's seen in days. Everyone at Archives knows there's something big going on, and you're connected with it.'

'Anything else?' he asked.

Her shoulders rose and fell. 'There are rumours about Father Cheng that have everyone worried.'

'What about him?'

'That he might be stepping down as Chairman.'

Luc dropped back into his seat and stared at her in shock. 'What? Where did you hear this?'

She let out a small, bitter laugh. 'With the way you've been running around between here and Vanaheim or wherever the hell they've been sending you, I thought you'd be the one to know something about it.'

'I had no idea. This isn't official?'

'No, it's not official. But the way I hear it, there's a faction in the Council demanding Cheng stand down and let someone else become Chairman.'

'What faction?'

'Luc, if anyone's likely to know about something like that, it's you.'

'This is the first I've heard of any of this, El. Any idea *why* they're calling for Cheng to stand down?'

'Apparently some members of the Council think he's out of touch with Reunification. That things have to change, and that if he can't adapt to the new circumstances then he should go.'

'That sounds like some Black Lotus propaganda I've heard.'

'Well, it's more than that, from what I'm hearing,' she told him, suddenly looking as tired as he felt. 'I've been at SecInt all night – I'm still here, as a matter of fact. They have almost everyone on full general alert, but nobody's explaining why.'

'And you think it must have something to do with Cheng? El, I swear I had no idea.'

'They've got Offenbach running trend analyses to see the possible outcomes of a shift in power.'

'Did you hear all this from Lethe?'

'No, I heard it from another source.' Her eyes darted away from his. 'But when I asked Director Lethe, he admitted he'd already heard something along the same lines. And with everything that's been going on . . . when you wouldn't reply to any of my messages, I started getting seriously worried about what might have happened to you.'

Luc looked at her – straight dark hair falling to her shoulders, face downcast – and wanted desperately to hold her. 'Then come and see me here as soon as you can.'

He winced as a deep throbbing began to spread outwards from the centre of his skull. Icy despair took hold of him: it had to be the lattice, growing once more despite de Almeida's interventions.

'What's wrong?' she asked, looking alarmed.

'Nothing,' he replied thickly, then winced a second time. It was rapidly getting worse.

'Bullshit, it's nothing,' she said. 'I'm coming over now.'

She arrived just forty minutes later. By then Luc had dragged himself into bed and lay in the dark, grunting as wave after wave of pain swamped his thoughts. Fragmented images he could hardly make sense of flitted through his mind's eye. He barely noticed when Eleanor entered his apartment.

He opened his eyes to see her drop her SecInt jacket on the floor before pulling her shirt up over her head, her body silhouetted in the light filtering through the window. She leaned over him, taking his head in her hands. Something about her touch made the pain lessen, become more distant.

He instinctively reached up to touch her breasts as her mouth pressed against his. Within moments she was straddling him, gripping his chest hairs and leaning down to kiss him again.

Somehow, despite the pain, he felt himself become erect, and let her manoeuvre him inside her. By the time he came a few minutes later, hands gripping her thighs, the pain had washed away, like a morning tide receding from a shore.

He told her everything – about Aeschere, the implant, Zelia de Almeida and his encounter with Ambassador Sachs. It was all too much for him to hold in any more. She stroked one hand over his stubbled scalp and listened in silence, her expression far away as he spoke.

For the first time in a long while, as they lay there together in the enclosed darkness of his bedroom, Luc felt content.

'We could go to Director Lethe,' she whispered to him, 'tell him everything you just told me. Things might not be as bad as you think, if we can get you the right kind of help . . .'

'De Almeida wasn't lying to me,' he whispered back. 'Everything she said was true. If anyone else found out about my lattice, I'd be as good as dead, and not even Lethe would be able to help me.'

'How sure are you that this woman can fix you?'

'I'm not at all sure,' he admitted. 'But some chance is better than none. She didn't promise she could do it, only that she could try.'

'But only so long as you do what she wants,' she said, reaching out to touch his forehead. 'You really think it's possible? That there's a part of . . . of Antonov, somewhere inside you?'

'All I know,' he said, gazing at her with pain-filled eyes, 'is that I'm afraid of what I might see every time I go to sleep.'

He woke at dawn, alerted by Vanaheim's security networks that Ambassador Sachs had suddenly dropped out of view. He notified de Almeida as he slid quietly out of bed.

Eleanor sat up and looked at him. 'Do I even need to ask where you're going?'

He shook his head. 'I'm wanted.'

'For God's sake, Luc! You need to talk to Lethe. You can't take this level of risk on your own. You need backup.'

'We've already been over this,' he said irritably.

She shivered. 'There's no reason to think you can trust de Almeida any more than the rest of them.'

He laughed. 'You think I *do*? She's crazy – as a matter of fact, I think they're *all* crazy. Now tell me seriously, what you think you can do to help me that won't just get me killed instead? Because I'm open to any ideas.'

'I swear to God,' she said, 'if that bitch doesn't figure out some way to save your life, I'll hunt her down and put a bullet between her fucking eyes. You can tell her that from me.'

He leaned down and kissed her on the lips. 'Now that's more like the Eleanor I know,' he said, and finished getting dressed.

Luc found himself back outside de Almeida's residence a few hours later, his head heavy with the dull ache of fatigue. He took a moment to work up the courage to walk back inside, afraid as he was of seeing any of her grotesques staring back at him with needle-tipped eyes.

He found her inside, entirely alone, and chewing on a thumb-nail as she studied several projections arranged around her in the air.

'Councillor,' he said, stepping towards her.

'Sachs is still out of sight,' she said, without taking her eyes from the displays. 'I don't know how he's done it. He was on his way back from meeting with Meinhard Carter, and his flier just . . . vanished.'

'You mean it crashed?' asked Luc. 'Are we talking about sabotage of some kind?'

'I don't think so,' she muttered. 'If he'd got into any kind of trouble, his flier should have sent out a distress signal. No, it's more like he's become invisible.'

So what's really got you worried is that someone else can pull off the same tricks as you. Luc stepped up beside her and saw the projections depicted a variety of locations all across Vanaheim.

'So where exactly was the Ambassador before he disappeared?'

She let out a sigh. 'That's a harder question to answer than it should be.'

De Almeida whispered something under her breath, and the projections merged into a single representation of Vanaheim as a spinning globe, more than a metre across. Brightly glowing hoops of navigational data materialized around the globe's circumference.

'Wherever it was,' she said, pointing to one particular location, 'it was somewhere around here, within a thousand-kilometre radius.'

Luc saw a circle appear over one continent and begin to strobe gently, while a dashed line representing the trajectory of Sachs' flier appeared layered over it.

'He was somewhere in this rough area when his locational data went haywire, making it look like he was in a thousand places at once.' She glanced at him for the first time since his arrival. 'Like informational chaff,' she explained. 'That way, it's nearly impossible to figure out whether the craft you're tracking is the true one, since all the rest are just mirages.'

Luc nodded towards the slowly spinning globe. 'Do we know where he was headed to when he disappeared?'

'To another meeting, this time with Hobart Tidman and Hernando Kowallek.' She frowned. 'Which is strange.'

'Strange, how?'

'The two of them have been inactive in Council affairs for a long time. They used to work in artefact recovery.'

'Artefact recovery?'

'They both researched alien technology recovered from the Founder Network back even before the Abandonment,' she explained, her frown deepening. 'They later acted as advisors to Coalition governments before they were cut off by the Schism.'

'And the Ambassador had just come from a meeting with Carter, who heads up an advisory committee on deep space research,' said Luc, feeling a prickle of unease.

'I know what you're thinking,' said de Almeida. 'Believe me, there are *no* Founder artefacts anywhere in the Tian Di. I'd know if there were.'

He looked at her carefully. 'You're absolutely sure of that?'

Her expression became uncertain. 'Let's just stick to the facts we have and not get distracted by speculation. Only one way inside the Founder Network has ever been discovered, and that's still deep inside Coalition territory. As far as Ambassador Sachs is concerned, we need to figure out just how he managed to fool my systems so completely.'

'There was something you said back at Vasili's funeral service, about rumours of secret negotiations with the Coalition. Maybe we *need* to start speculating: what if the rumours are true? And what if Carter, Tidman, Kowallek and the Ambassador are all involved in some capacity? And . . . what about Cheng?'

She looked at him. 'What about Cheng?'

'I just heard a rumour he's been asked to relinquish control over the Council.'

'Where did you hear that?'

She didn't seem angry, just curious. 'Through a contact in SecInt,' he told her. 'Is it true?'

She shook her head as if in sorrow. 'There's some truth to it, yes.'

Luc felt suddenly light-headed. 'Borges was right, wasn't he? Something really *is* going on – something bigger than one Councillor winding up dead.'

De Almeida sighed, all of her usual swagger gone. 'I really don't know, Mr Gabion. If I did, I probably wouldn't need you here. I already told you I'm not always privy to everything that goes on in the Council, particularly where its higher echelons are concerned. Sometimes I have little more than rumours to rely on myself.'

'What I'm beginning to wonder,' Luc continued, 'is whether there's something more to Reunification than is being publicly admitted. What if it's not just about reuniting the human race – what if there's some other reason the Coalition are here?'

Just a few days before, the idea of speaking to a member of the

Temur Council in this way would have been unimaginable to him. So much had changed in such a very short time. Even so, Luc held his breath as he waited for her to reply.

'I think you're on the right path,' she admitted, 'but I don't necessarily know more than you do. But I *want* to know what's going on, because whatever it is, the Eighty-Five are keeping it hidden from the rest of us – from the rest of the Council, I mean. But like I said, you have an advantage since you can still go places I can't.'

'You and the rest of the Council are more powerful than anyone else in history, but you keep telling me you need *me*.' Luc shook his head and laughed, overwhelmed by the ridiculousness of the situation. 'Just how many friends do you have left here on Vanaheim, Zelia?'

She opened her mouth to frame a retort, then instead stepped towards a nearby table, leaning against it and folding her arms over her chest as if hugging herself.

'Not as many as there used to be,' she said quietly. 'Look – what you have to understand is that the one thing still uniting the Council is that we are all survivors. Most of us were alive when Earth died, and we lived through the fighting before and after the Schism. After that, things were in such an appalling mess that we had no choice but to try and hold everything together, and Cheng was key to making that work. We've all shared so much with each other over the centuries that you couldn't possibly understand the loyalty most of us still feel towards the very idea of the Council.'

She gripped the edge of the table, her expression bleak. 'But now everything's about to change with Reunification – and I mean everything. It's possible the Council itself might not survive the transition, let alone Cheng. And as much as I hate to admit it, it's possible our time is past.'

'How could reconnecting with the Coalition cause so much change? They're just people, same as us.'

'Are they? Can you really say that about Ambassador Sachs?'

'I admit the costume he wears is ridiculous, but I'm sure there's an ordinary human being under there.' But even as he spoke, Luc felt the lack of conviction in his words.

'Didn't you hear what I said before, Gabion? The Coalition are vastly more technologically advanced than we are. We could end up swamped by them, and there are those like Borges who'd be prepared to commit violence in order to try and turn back the tide of history.'

Something occurred to Luc as she spoke.

'I have an idea,' he said, gesturing towards the spinning globe. 'According to what I can see here, the Ambassador's flier was in a circumpolar orbit when he was last seen, right?'

She nodded. 'He'd have reached Liebenau in another hour or so if he hadn't vanished.'

Luc looked again at the globe. The Ambassador's flier would have passed over icy wastes stretching for thousands of kilometres. Stepping closer, he saw a chain of white-clad mountains amidst an otherwise featureless void of snow.

There was a brief twinge of pain behind his eyes. Something about those mountains . . .

'What about here?' he asked, fingers brushing through the air where the globe was projected.

'No, there's nothing there, except . . .'

She paused, and turned to look at him, her mouth half-open.

'Wait,' she said. 'There *is* something out there.' She made her hands into fists and pressed them against the sides of her head. 'Stupid,' she muttered to herself, '*stupid.*'

'What are you talking about?'

'There,' she said, stabbing one finger toward the chain of mountains, just a thousand kilometres shy of Vanaheim's north pole. 'That's where Cheng's kept Javier Maxwell locked up all these centuries.'

Luc felt a sudden tightening in his chest. *Javier Maxwell.* The greatest renegade of them all, after Antonov – and the author of the very book Luc had found on Vasili's body. A book that, according to no less an authority than Vincent Hetaera, shouldn't even exist.

'Is it possible . . . ?' he asked.

'That this is where the Ambassador disappeared to? I can't think of any other possibility,' she said.

'Perhaps if I data-ghosted there—'

'No.' She shook her head. 'If Sachs can fool my surveillance networks that easily, he can certainly trick a data-ghost into seeing whatever he wants. This is going to require eyeballs on the ground.'

'What about your armies of micro-mechants? Can't you use them?'

She shook her head. 'Cheng gave the Sandoz sole responsibility for handling security for Maxwell's prison. That means I'm not allowed to have my own surveillance anywhere near it.'

'So unless you plan on going out there yourself,' said Luc, 'you're going to need me to go out there.'

She nodded. 'Unless there's something else out there I don't know about, Maxwell's prison is the only place Ambassador Sachs could have gone.'

'And if we do find him there?'

'Then we have the evidence we need to prove he's been carrying out clandestine meetings, without putting you in any danger. And if we can confront him with that evidence, maybe we'll be able to find out where he really was the night of Sevgeny's murder.'

'But what business could Sachs possibly have with Javier Maxwell?'

'I can imagine a couple of possibilities,' de Almeida replied, 'and if even a few of them turn out to be true, the Council's in far more trouble than I'd realized.' She nodded toward the exit. 'We have no idea just how long he's going to stay at Maxwell's prison, assuming he's even there, and that means you need to leave *now*.'

Within minutes, Luc found himself back on board the same flier de Almeida had used to transport him from Temur. The craft accelerated towards suborbital space, before dropping back down in a long arc that passed over an ocean dotted with ice-floes.

Over the next hour, the floes gradually merged into a feature-less expanse of white that stretched in all directions. After a while the same snow-capped mountains he'd seen in de Almeida's labor-atory rose from around the curve of Vanaheim's horizon, growing larger as the flier carried him towards them.

The mountains continued to expand until the flier finally passed between two of their peaks. Glancing down through the flier's transparent upper hull, Luc saw that the slopes on the near side of the mountains fell away into glaciated valleys and deep ravines that showed evidence of recent volcanic activity; he could see a few small unfrozen lakes here and there, tiny oases whose shores were streaked with patches of scrubby lichen and moss.

The lakes passed out of sight as the flier decelerated, dropping towards a landing on the far side of the mountains near some foothills. The peaks of the mountains were lost in dense cloud.

De Almeida's data-ghost appeared in the cabin next to Luc the moment the AG motors ceased to hum. 'You'll find cold-weather gear in the back,' she told him.

'I thought you said it was too risky for you to data-ghost?'

'I hacked the private account of someone who hasn't data-ghosted in a couple of decades,' she replied. 'It'll be a long while before he notices, if ever.'

'I don't see much of anything,' he said, peering out at his surroundings through the hull's translucent surface. 'Just snow and rocks. Couldn't you get any nearer than this?'

'I didn't want to take the chance of testing the prison's secur-ity perimeter any more than I had to,' she explained. 'This is as close as I can safely get you without risking detection. That means there's still some way for you to go on foot, I'm afraid.'

Luc stared outside. 'Where to, exactly?'

'Look there,' she said, pointing towards the nearest peak. 'The foothills are only six kilometres or so from where you've landed, and that's where you'll find the entrance to Maxwell's prison. There's a transceiver amongst your cold-weather gear – plant it where it tells you to if you can't see any sign of the Ambassador, then come back. If he shows himself, the transceiver will let us know.'

'And the Sandoz guarding this place won't know about it?'

'If you manage to prove that Ambassador Sachs is making some kind of secret deal with Javier Maxwell, no one's going to care one way or the other. I don't think getting there and back should take you more than a couple of hours.'

'And if this doesn't work?'

'Then we'll have to think of something else. There's a storm front closing in on the mountains – don't tarry, because you really don't want to get caught in it.'

'I'd better get going,' he said.

She nodded, the hunger in her eyes reminding him he wasn't the only one fighting for his survival.

'Good luck,' she said, and vanished.

Luc clambered through to the back of the flier, found the cold-weather gear and pulled it on, stepping outside as soon as he was ready. Even with the protection of the gear, a cold deeper than any he had experienced before sucked the heat from the few exposed patches of his face.

He started walking, ice and snow crunching under his heavy boots. Before long it began to sleet, a thick wet slush that stung when it struck any of his exposed skin. He adjusted the sunglasses he'd found amongst the cold-weather gear to cut down the glare from the snow.

Cresting a low hill, he continued down the other side, and when he finally stopped to take a breath and look back the way he'd come, the flier was nothing more than a stark black dot against the horizon. He'd already gone a lot farther than he'd realized. Distances were hard to judge in such a nearly featureless land-scape.

He made his way down the other side of the hill and then up another, and then another, and another. Eventually he came to one that was slightly distinguishable from the rest by virtue of being capped with a lump of half-eroded granite only partly covered in snow. By the time he reached its peak, his legs had gone from aching to half-numb, but when he looked ahead, he could see what appeared to be a hangar cut into the side of a steep ridge several kilometres away.

Coming to a halt, he rested with his hands on his knees, taking a minute to recover his breath before using his sunglasses to zoom in on the cavern. There, he could see a flier parked near the mouth of the hangar.

He ran an analysis and got an immediate positive result. It was the Ambassador's flier, all right – and he hadn't left yet.

Luc had what he needed. Turning back, he saw dark thunder-heads to the north, sweeping in across the snowy wastes, and remembered de Almeida's warning. The wind had already started to pick up, a thin, eerie whine that carved patterns in the ice and snow all around.

And there was something else, just barely audible over the rising howl of the wind. A faint hum, coming closer . . .

He made his way over to the granite stub rising from the peak of the hill and pressed himself into a shadowed indent. As he listened the humming got louder, then started to fade as the source of the sound moved away from him. Luc waited for a good half-minute before cautiously leaning out to take a look around.

He saw a mechant, already at the base of the hill and on its way towards the rock hangar. Breathing a sigh of relief that it hadn't seen him, he made his way back the way he'd come as fast as his tired legs could carry him.

The storm, however, was coming in faster than he had imagined possible. The wind kept rising in pitch until it sounded eerily like the scream of an injured animal. He picked up the pace, very nearly breathless by the time he crested another hill.

<Zelia. Can you hear me? I'm on my way back.>

<Did you see anything?>

<I saw his flier. The Ambassador's still there.>

He transmitted the data he'd recorded and waited a minute until she came back.

<That's good work, Luc. Just what we've been looking f—>
Her voice broke up into static.
<Zelia?>
He waited for her to respond, but all he could hear was the terrible howl of the wind.
<Zelia! For God's sake, please respond.>
Still nothing.

He felt tendrils of panic reach out from his spine and wrap themselves around his chest, gently squeezing his heart. He tried again to contact de Almeida, but again heard only silence. It wasn't outside the bounds of possibility that the storm was causing some kind of signal interference. At least, he hoped that was all it was.

He kept moving, but the storm was coming down fast and it was getting harder to see where he was going. He tried to use the tracking signal from the flier to keep him headed in the right direction, but it failed to respond, as if it wasn't there any more.

Something was very, very wrong. If he couldn't find his way back to the flier before the storm really hit, he was in serious trouble.

He relied on his memory to guide him back the way he had come, but after another ten minutes the light was almost gone. The wind whipped thin skeins of snow into his eyes, half-blinding him. Before long it got to the point where he could hardly make any headway at all against the wind.

'Zelia!' he yelled into the maelstrom. 'Goddammit, Zelia, where the hell are you?'

He wondered if her subterfuge had been discovered, and she had decided to cut him loose rather than admit responsibility for bringing him back to Vanaheim against Father Cheng's wishes. Whatever the reason, if he could get back to the flier he could at least get the hell out of there.

By now, the mountain peaks had disappeared behind flurries of ice and snow raised up by the wind, and he had to fight for each step he took. A part of him wanted to lay down and rest, to be done with it all.

But if he did that, he knew, he'd never get up again. So he pushed on regardless, leaning into the wind, face numb, teeth gritted. The sky had turned almost completely black.

An eternity passed before he stumbled down a steep incline to where he'd left the flier. It wasn't there.

Looking around wildly, he squinted in the freezing dark. Maybe he was in the wrong place.

Again, he tried to pick up the flier's tracking signal, but still got no answer.

He turned, and looked back up the slope of the hill he'd just descended. There had been a rockslide some time in the recent past that had scattered a couple of large, distinctive boulders nearby, and he remembered seeing them when he'd disembarked from the flier. He was definitely in the right place.

The wind wrapped itself around him, as if trying to carry him off. He screamed his fury and frustration into a black and turbulent sky, but the words were lost amid the tumult.

There was still one other option open to him. He could head back the way he'd come, make his way to that rock hangar and see if he could find some way inside Javier Maxwell's prison. It was probably his one chance at staying alive.

He trudged back up the slope he'd just descended, every muscle in his body protesting at the ordeal he was putting them through. His footprints had been almost entirely obscured by the storm. Sometimes the outline of the mountains became briefly visible, allowing him to confirm he was still heading the right way and hadn't got turned around.

It's easy, he told himself. *Just put one foot in front of the other, and repeat. Couldn't be simpler.*

An eternity passed in this way, until his legs felt as stiff and unyielding as frozen rock.

He almost cried with relief when he found his way back to the granite-topped hill, and tried not to think about the many kilometres he still had to go before he reached the hangar. The ridge he was ultimately headed for was, by now, almost entirely invisible amidst the storm.

The night surged around him, howling and tugging at his shoulders like some predator determined to torture him before making its kill.

At some point, he came to the realization he had no idea which direction he was headed in. He turned around, trying to see his tracks in the snow, but the storm had become so vicious they were obscured in seconds.

Picking a direction, he started walking. It became harder and harder to maintain any sense of time. He might have been walking for an hour, or a whole day.

He became aware that he had collapsed to his knees in the snow, but couldn't recall just when he had come to a halt.

Forcing himself upright, he managed a few more feeble steps before feeling his legs give way beneath him once more. He collapsed, tipping forward onto the snow, the breath rattling in his throat.

Lights flickered through the darkened haze around him. To his astonishment, Luc saw that the storm was starting to clear. The stars were revealing themselves, one by one, between drawn-out wisps of snow and cloud.

Some of the stars broke away from the firmament and dipped down towards him, so that he could see they were attached to a dark outline that blocked out part of the sky. But before he could work out what it was, his thoughts had faded into darkness.

FOURTEEN

The journey to the well, the old man told Jacob, was likely to take the better part of a day, and quite possibly longer if the weather turned for the worse. For this reason they left not long after dawn the following morning, with Jacob once again hidden beneath a carpet in the back of Kulic's horse-drawn cart.

At one point, as Kulic guided the cart out of the village, cajoling his horse with whistles and muttered grunts, he drew to a halt by the roadside in order to exchange a few words with a fellow villager. That proved to be the high point of what was otherwise a cold and desperately uncomfortable journey, marked by spine-jarring jolts and bumps that did little to improve Jacob's mood. He hated everything about Darwin he had so far encountered; the early years of his life had been spent in Sandoz combat-temples amidst wild and tropical forests and, despite his training, he had never quite shaken his distaste for the cold and damp.

But what made it all so much worse was that the rag under which he was forced to hide for the first leg of their journey stank of shit and hay, while the only refreshment Kulic had to offer was a sealed clay jug of nearly intolerable home-brewed beer, alongside hard, unleavened bread that Jacob was forced to chew with grim determination before it became even vaguely digestible.

Jacob finally emerged from beneath the blanket an hour out of the village, but soon draped it back over his shoulders when it began to rain, a freezing drizzle that shrouded the hills and forest around them in shades of grey. Kulic had given him some of his father's cast-offs – a rough woollen shirt and a pair of patched cotton trousers, along with a broad dark coat that swept against his ankles. Underneath it all he still wore his one-piece combat suit.

Kulic guided the horses along a dirt path that cut through the woods and ran roughly parallel with the course of a stream intermittently visible through the trees. Before long it became clear they were headed inland, towards a valley beyond which a Coalition city could be seen in all its shining technological splendour.

They stopped late that afternoon so they could both take a leak. When Jacob returned from the woods, he saw Kulic rummaging around in the rear of the cart, as if searching for something. As Jacob watched from amongst the trees, the old man glanced around with a furtive expression.

Jacob waited to see what the old man was up to, and watched as Kulic turned back to the cart, lifting out the case Jacob had earlier retrieved from his ship. Holding it carefully, Kulic turned it this way and that, as if trying to work out how to open it.

Jacob stepped out from his hiding place and quickly slipped up behind the old man without making a sound. Kulic was pressing dirty fingernails against the surface of the case, apparently trying to prise it open.

'What the hell are you doing?' asked Jacob, from directly behind him.

Kulic let out a cry of shock, and span around to regard Jacob with an expression of terror. 'I'm sorry, I . . .' his mouth trembled, the case still gripped in his shaking hands. 'I was just . . . just curious.'

'Curious about what?' said Jacob, coming closer, so the old man was forced up against the side of the cart. Kulic's mouth trembled with fear.

'I . . . I just wanted to know what was inside.'

Jacob stared at him in silence for several long seconds, then reached down to take the case from Kulic's grasp without breaking eye contact.

'It's lucky you have no idea how to open this,' Jacob said quietly. 'It would have killed you even faster than I could. Now get back on that horse and let's be on our way.'

Kulic regarded him in much the same way a rabbit might a snake with its jaws fully extended. He swallowed and slid past Jacob, pulling himself back onto his ageing nag.

Jacob stared at the back of the old man's head, then climbed into the back of the cart. The case was unharmed, of course. It would open only in response to Jacob's unique genetic signature. He kept a hold on the case as Kulic snapped the reins, and they began to move forward once more.

The sky reddened as the evening deepened, and the first stars began to show themselves before they next spoke.

'You asked me to tell you about life in the Tian Di,' Jacob said, calling over to Kulic as the cart juddered and bounced beneath him. 'Why don't you repay the favour, and tell me something more about the people in the cities?'

A minute or so passed before Kulic responded. 'I said they came to visit us from time to time, in disguise.'

'You said,' Jacob commented, 'they didn't appear to be human.'

'They came to us in disguise as animals.'

Jacob smiled to himself. 'Animals?'

'You think I'm naive and foolish,' said Kulic, his tone defensive, 'but I'm not. We know how powerful the people in those cities are, and how lucky we are that they permit us to live our lives the way we choose; we know they can take any form they wish. One of Bruehl's disciples came back with stories of multi-legged things that flew and crawled, of tiny darting machines that spoke with the voices of men.' Kulic's tone had become hushed, full of wonder and fear.

Mechants, in other words, thought Jacob. Or possibly extreme body modifications of a type not permitted within the Tian Di.

'They're not really people any more,' Kulic continued. 'Not in the way that you or I understand them. Villagers tell stories of walking through the woods and encountering beasts – sometimes just deer or birds, except that they have an uncanny intelligence about them that betrays their otherness. Sometimes the beasts are nightmarish things that have little to do with anything in God's Creation, things that glow or fly or crawl on the ground.'

'So why do they come?'

Jacob laughed, the sound harsh and bitter. 'They are spectators come to gawk at the exhibits in a circus,' he said.

The woods had become denser, the path veering off from the river, which had slipped between tall, crag-like rocks so that its passage could now only be distantly heard. 'Did any of your people communicate with them, or them with you?' asked Jacob.

'No.' Kulic shook his head. 'Too many people in the villages are frightened they'd be carried away to the cities, which is silly, of course. There are regulations preventing any interference with our communities. Should any one of us make the free choice to leave the villages and make a new life in the cities, that's another matter, but we can't be forced to make that decision against our will.'

Kulic turned to look back at him. 'If I may ask – is your mission to destroy the Coalition? Is that why you're here?'

'No,' said Jacob, 'that's not my mission.'

Kulic turned back and said nothing, but Jacob could sense the old man's frustration. Here he was, Jacob Moreland, a mysterious stranger from another world, full of answers to questions that must have been stirring through the old man's thoughts ever since his father's deathbed revelations.

Despite himself, Jacob felt a touch of pity for Kulic, and decided there was probably no harm in telling him a little more than was strictly necessary. Besides, he had come to a decision after catching the old man trying to prise his case open.

'However,' said Jacob, 'I *am* here because of the threat of war between the Coalition and the T an Di.'

Kulic stared round at him, suddenly desperately fascinated. 'You mean like what led to the Schism?'

'That wasn't really a war,' Jacob replied. 'It was more of a stand-off. Severing the transfer gates linking our worlds to yours *prevented* an outbreak of war.'

'Then . . . where's the danger?' asked Kulic. 'If all that either side needs to do is shut down the new transfer gate linking Darwin to Temur, then there can't *be* any war.'

'At the same time that Father Cheng has been ordering agents such as myself to Darwin,' Jacob replied, 'the Coalition have been sending their own secret missions to the Tian Di at sub-light speeds. There are offensive machines lurking in the cold outer reaches of our star systems, ready to strike if we do not agree to certain demands on the Coalition's part.' He had received this newest information from the transceiver hidden in Kulic's basement.

Now that he had started, Jacob found it very nearly impossible to stop the flow of words pouring from his mouth. Even though only days had passed from his subjective point of view since he had been first loaded on board the tiny starship that brought him to Darwin, it felt as if it had been much, much longer than that. In truth, it felt as if he had not spoken with another human being for years. He knew this was ridiculous, a kind of delusion. And yet he could not help himself.

'What kind of demands?' Kulic asked in horrified yet fascinated tones. The path took a sharp turn downwards and the old man was forced to duck as they passed beneath low-hanging branches. They were entering the valley now.

'The Temur Council has enemies, even amongst its own people,' Jacob explained, 'that want to bring chaos and anarchy raining down on all of the Tian Di. To prevent this happening, the Council's wisest minds decided to seek out the means to defend themselves. And that means I must . . .'

Stop. You're telling him too much.

Jacob felt abruptly ashamed of himself. 'The details aren't your concern,' he said, quickly changing the subject. 'How long before we reach this well?'

'We're just about there,' said Kulic, leaning forward to mutter in his nag's ear as the road took another sharp turn.

Jacob sat up as they turned into a clearing, at the centre of which stood the ruins of a stone building that surrounded a flag-stoned courtyard on three sides. A decrepit-looking well stood at the courtyard's centre.

The courtyard, like the ruins, had become overgrown with bushes and weeds that pushed through cracks in the flagstones. Jacob walked around for a bit after climbing down from the cart, stretching tired limbs and massaging the muscles in his thighs. Kulic mean-while guided his horse to some long grass, looping the animal's reins around a low branch. Jacob watched as the old man then stepped over to the well, staring down into its inky depths.

Jacob came up beside him. 'What we're looking for is down there?'

'It is,' Kulic replied, reaching down to grab one end of a frayed-looking rope that hung over the lip of the well. He began hauling on it, hand over hand, in much the same way he had retrieved his father's transceiver from the depths of a barrel. He struggled, however, and Jacob ended up doing most of the work, feeling the rope tremble and sway as something heavy connected to its other end swung from side to side in the depths below.

A large bundle, wrapped in more waterproof oilskins and bound up in rope, emerged into the evening light. They heaved it up the rest of the way, manhandling it over the lip of the well and onto the weedy flagstones by their feet.

Jacob glanced back down the well, thinking.

'What is it?' asked Kulic, seeing Jacob's attention was elsewhere.

Jacob bent at the knees, picking up a rock and dropping it into the well. Several seconds passed before he heard a splash.

'It's nothing,' said Jacob, glancing at the sodden rope tightly bound around the oilskin-wrapped bundle. 'Do we have anything that can cut this rope?'

'Just a moment,' said Kulic, returning to his horse and producing a long knife from his saddle-pack. He used it to saw through the ropes, then stepped back so that Jacob could peel away the oilskins, revealing a heavy wooden chest.

Jacob opened the chest, lifting out some of the precious gifts that lay inside; various pieces of modular equipment and, most importantly, a plastic case containing another pin-sized transceiver, which sprang to life as soon as he picked it up.

He nodded with grim satisfaction at the new data the transceiver contained. Clearly, Sillars had been hard at work prior to his murder at the hands of his fellow agents. Indeed, given what the transceiver was telling him, Sillars had more than made up for the failings of his compatriots.

Jacob pulled off the ragged shirt and trousers given him by Kulic, wadding them up and dropping them into the well. Then he placed the miniature transceiver back in its case and pocketed it, before studying the rest of the chest's contents. He discovered several pocket-sized A-M mines, each of which could gouge a crater a mile wide, along with a collection of slim metallic components that, separately, did not appear to have any immediate use but, when snapped together in the right order, comprised a powerful beam-based weapon scarcely less devastating than the mines. It was designed to be broken into parts that would each fit in the pockets and hidden recesses of his combat suit.

He quickly packed the contents of the chest about his person before standing and nodding towards the ruins surrounding the well.

'There's a cellar under this building,' he announced to Kulic.

The old man peered towards the ruins, seeing only weeds, rotted wood and a few bricks outlining the position of the building's foundations. 'How do you know?'

'Sillars left a message when he buried all this,' Jacob explained, unconsciously brushing one hand against the pocket in which he had placed Sillars' transceiver. He then stepped amongst the ruins of the building, pushing past a tangle of sharp-bladed bushes until he came to some half-rotten floorboards, which he stamped on with one foot until one of them cracked, fragments of it dropping into the darkness below.

Jacob pulled on a pair of gloves and began tearing away the clumps of bush and weed around him until more planks were exposed. He could just make out a dim shape in the darkness of the cellar beneath him, hidden under half-rotten rags that had been draped over it.

'Give me a hand,' Jacob grunted, bending down to lift one end of a plank.

Kulic stepped gingerly over, helping to clear away some more of the weeds covering one end of the plank. The plank shattered unexpectedly, the end Jacob was grasping nearly catching him under the chin as it angled upwards. Jacob batted it away, watching it drop into the space below.

They worked like this for several minutes, smashing or lifting planks, although Kulic proved too weak and slow to be of any real practical use. But he worked uncomplainingly, for which Jacob was grateful, until the cellar had been exposed sufficiently that Jacob could drop down into the darkened space below.

'What is that thing down there?' Kulic called down, his voice querulous.

'A flier,' said Jacob, stripping away the rotting sheets covering it.

The machine was a product of Coalition science, easily more advanced than even the starship that had brought him to Darwin. Its hull still gleamed despite its long years buried in dust and filth, and when Jacob reached out to touch its smooth hull with his bare fingertips, it shivered almost as if it were alive.

In a sense, the vehicle *was* alive. According to Sillars' own memories, encoded within his transceiver, the distinction between organic and inorganic technology within the Coalition had by now become entirely academic. The flier could think and feel, after a fashion, and as his fingers brushed its skin, Jacob could sense something very much like loneliness radiating from it after so many long decades of waiting.

Jacob climbed back out of the cellar and dusted himself off with a grimace, before using the last of Kulic's beer to wash the worst of the filth from his hands.

'Step back,' Jacob told him.

Kulic goggled as a low, grating hum began to resonate through the air, more dirt and wood tumbling into the cellar as the hum grew. The flier rose slightly from its resting place, pushing against those few planks that still remained in place. They soon snapped under the strain, tumbling down or spinning away as the flier's AG field took hold of them.

The flier rose into the air above the ruined cellar, shedding yet more dirt, twigs, and bird-shit in the process. Kulic stared up at the craft in stupefaction as it moved towards a patch of clear ground next to the ruins, where it dropped back down and came to a rest.

Kulic turned to gape at Jacob, his eyes shining with undisguised awe. 'And all this time . . . it was just waiting there? I never knew!'

'Sillars never told the others about it – not Bruehl, and not even your father. He didn't trust anyone else with the knowledge.'

'And it was lying here all this time just waiting for you?'

'For someone *like* me, yes,' Jacob explained. 'That was your father's job, as it was Bruehl's and Sillars' – to find ways to exploit and subvert the Coalition's security networks, and make it possible for me to fulfil my duty.' Sillars had transformed the flier into a weapon no less deadly and efficient than any of the devices packed into the case that had so aroused Kulic's curiosity.

Jacob stretched and flexed his fingers inside their gloves until he could feel the bones and muscles pop and stretch. A memory came to him, of long-ago training camps, where he had been forced to crawl through muck and dirt one day, then dart across boulder-strewn craters in near zero gee the next, while mechants armed with live weaponry attempted to gun him down. By the time his training had finished, he had learned dozens of new ways to kill people.

Kulic must have seen something in his expression. His face grew pale, and he started to back away, glancing towards his horse and cart still tied up nearby.

'I'll do anything I can to help you complete your mission,' Kulic stammered, his Adam's apple bouncing up and down as he swallowed. His voice took on a whining tone. 'I helped you out of the woods and hid you. I . . .'

'I know that,' said Jacob, his voice soothing as he stepped closer to the old man. 'And I'm grateful, really I am. But the fact is this mission is much too important to take any risks. Your father would have understood that.'

'Is it because I tried to open that case?' Kulic cried out, still backing away towards the well. 'I didn't mean any harm, I, I was just curious . . .'

Kulic nearly stumbled over a rock hidden amongst the weeds. Jacob glanced towards the well, and Kulic caught the look, glancing over at it himself before turning back to regard Jacob with bottomless terror.

'Oh, Jesus,' Kulic whispered, his breath coming in shaky gasps. His ancient watery eyes stared at Jacob with something almost like longing.

He turned to run, but Jacob lunged forward, grabbing Kulic from behind before he could so much as put one foot in front of the other. Wrapping long, strangler's fingers around the old man's throat, he pulled him close in what was almost a lover's embrace.

'I promise this will be quick,' he whispered, and began to squeeze.

FIFTEEN

Luc.

He opened his eyes to see Winchell Antonov, one hand clasped to his injured shoulder, leaning over him. Antonov's breath came in short, sharp gasps, blood pooling at his feet.

He was back on the bridge of the starship, tied to a chair.

Luc glared dully up at the other man. *I could get really sick of this.*

Antonov laughed. *That's the spirit!* His expression suddenly changed and he grunted with pain, his face shiny and pale. *Tell me, how are you sleeping these days, Luc?*

Badly. If the lattice winds up killing me, then you die too – or didn't you think of that?

But not before you finish what needs finishing. If it wasn't for Zelia, you'd be in Cripps' hands by now, and almost certainly dead. But there are things you need to do that even she can't help you with.

I can't see one reason, Luc spat, *for me to believe one damn word that comes out of your treacherous mouth.*

Really? Antonov's expression was cynical. *And just how grateful have the Temur Council been to you, for all your service in their name? All those years you spent squirrelled away inside Archives, doing everything you could to try and figure where I was or what I might do next – just how much have they rewarded you for all that effort?*

I'm not interested in your fucking propaganda. Just . . . let me wake up, and get the fuck out of my head.

No. You've seen enough of the Council to have an idea of who and what some of them really are, but you're still struggling to accept the truth. They're monsters, even Zelia – and she's one of the better ones.

And you think you were better?

Antonov hacked out a cough before answering, flecks of blood on his lips. *You're closer than almost anyone else ever has been, to finding out things Cheng would rather keep hidden from view forever. Neither he nor his cronies can be sure just what I might have done to you while you were wandering around inside Aeschere. And because of that, every last one of them – particularly those damn Eighty-Fivers – would rather see you dead than take a chance you might know something you shouldn't. If not for Zelia, they probably would have killed you anyway, on the pretext that you might – just might – have been working for me all along.*

You botched up, Luc said wearily. *You told me to speak to Ambassador Sachs, but he didn't seem interested in helping anyone, least of all me.*

You need to gain his trust, Antonov replied. *He saw me lurking inside you, but can't be sure yet of your motives, or who you might decide to report to if he tells you too much.*

Luc shook his head in disbelief. *Gain his trust? Do you even know where I am just now? Or what's happened to me?*

You're exactly where I wanted you to be.

Waiting to die in the snow?

You're not dead, Luc. In fact, you've already been rescued. Haven't you worked out yet that I'm the reason you came here in the first place?

Bullshit, Luc snapped. *I came out here looking for the Ambassador after he—*

Think back, said Antonov, *to when you were studying that map of Vanaheim.*

Luc recalled the globe Zelia had projected into the air. He had looked towards the range of mountains, and felt a twinge of pain behind his eyes . . .

Luc's fists tightened under his restraints. Something had drawn him towards those mountains, and to Maxwell's prison.

You did that to me? he demanded.

I needed you to come here, Antonov replied.

But why?

Because you need to hear the truth about Vasili, and about me – and Cheng, too.

You told me there'd be some terrible calamity without the Ambassador's help. Are you talking about war with the Coalition?

Antonov was growing visibly weaker. *Believe me,* he said, *there are far, far worse things out there than the Coalition.*

The cobalt blues and dark metallic greys surrounding them were beginning to lose definition, as if Luc's eyes were blurring. He sensed their encounter was coming to an end.

You need to tell me more, he insisted. *I know you're holding something back.*

But sometimes there's so much I can't remember myself, Antonov replied, his voice weak and pitiful. The air between them seemed to ripple. *There's only a fragment of me inside you, and it's not enough. Not nearly enough.*

The starship bridge faded, and was replaced by a different scene. Luc saw the streets of a biome on some airless world, unwinking stars fixed into the firmament beyond its precious pocket of atmosphere. Men and women, their flesh riddled with terrible pustules, lay scattered around. Other figures in contamination suits, their faces just visible behind wraparound visors, moved from body to body. They were taking measurements of some kind.

He found his attention drawn to one suited figure in particular, and after a moment he recognized the face behind the visor. Zelia.

Luc came awake with a start, to find himself in a room filled with books.

He had been laid out on a couch at the centre of a large hexagonal room, high walls of dark granite supporting recessed shelves crammed with hundreds of bound volumes much like those he had seen in Vasili's residence. The floor was tiled with dark slate, while soft, pearlescent light shone through translucent ceiling tiles. A single door led out of the room, while his cold-weather gear had been dumped in a pile in one corner.

He looked around, feeling wildly disoriented. From staggering through endless snowy wastes . . . to this.

Sitting up, he winced with pain. The muscles of both legs throbbed, and he massaged his calves with both hands until the cramp lessened. He stood carefully, stretching his legs before reaching out to pull a random volume down from a shelf close at hand.

The book turned out to be filled with what appeared to be proofs of mathematical equations. Before being summoned to Vasili's residence, Luc – in common with most citizens of the Tian Di – had only rarely encountered actual, physical volumes such as this. They were like the relic of a past and better age. The pages felt cool to the touch, even slightly metallic, indeed much like the one he had pulled out from under Vasili's half-burned corpse . . .

He froze, remembering what had happened when his fingers had brushed against the pages of that particular volume, and closed the book carefully before placing it back where it had come from.

Taking a step back, he regarded the shelves around him with new eyes. That other book – the one in Vasili's library, that had transported him into the mind of a dead man – might not officially exist, but if he was, as seemed likely, somewhere inside the prison that had held Javier Maxwell for all these centuries, then maybe that first book had originated from here.

If that was the case, then it might be best not to touch *any* of the books. That first experience had been traumatic enough.

He tried again to contact de Almeida, but had no more luck than before. It looked like he was still on his own.

The only thing left was to explore, so he pulled open the one door leading out of the room – and felt the breath catch in his throat at what he beheld.

The room he had been left to wake in proved to be little more than an antechamber to a vast, cathedral-like space. He saw an arched ceiling at least twenty metres overhead, from which hung chandeliers supported by heavy steel chains. And all around, rising up the walls and accessible by a multitude of narrow metal stairways and walkways, were tens of thousands more books. More physical, tactile volumes than he might ever have believed existed anywhere within the Tian Di, let alone Vanaheim.

If this really was Maxwell's prison, it was a hell of a luxurious one.

Luc turned to look down the other end of the hall and saw an elderly man regarding him from a few metres away. The old man's narrow skull was topped with a fringe of white hair. A long robe hung loose on his bony shoulders, while a faint nimbus of light around his head and upper shoulders indicated he was a data-ghost.

'You must be . . .'

'Javier Maxwell,' said the data-ghost in a reedy voice, the eyes bright blue and full of intelligence. 'You were close to dying out there in the snow, did you know that?'

'Thanks,' said Luc, 'for saving me.'

Maxwell cast his gaze up towards the ceiling and back down. 'You know where you are?'

'This is where they keep you locked up.'

'I fear you already know more about me than I know about you, Mr . . . ?'

'Archivist Luc Gabion.'

Maxwell nodded as if coming to a conclusion. 'You're clearly not a member of the Temur Council, are you?'

'I'm not, no.'

'An assassin, then?'

'*No*. I'm not here to kill you, or anyone else.'

'Really? I certainly *hope* that's not the case. I've had reason to become quite concerned about such things lately.'

Luc heard a slight hum as two mechants dropped down from the ceiling, taking station on either side of him. The mirror-smooth skin of one of the mechants parted, revealing intricate and deadly-looking weaponry mounted on tiny gimballed joints.

Glancing at the other mechant, Luc saw it had done the same, its weapons swivelling until they were directed at his skull.

'Now,' said Maxwell, 'I'll give you, hmm . . . let's say five seconds, to tell me why you're here, before I order them to kill you as a purely precautionary measure. And please,' he added, stepping slightly closer, 'be aware that I've been around for long enough to be able to tell when someone is lying to me.'

'I'm investigating Sevgeny Vasili's death,' Luc blurted, as the hum emanating from the mechants rapidly increased in pitch.

Maxwell stared at him with narrowed eyes for a period of time that felt much longer than five seconds. Then, just as the hum was about to reach a crescendo, Maxwell raised a hand, and the hum fell away into silence.

'I heard about Sevgeny,' said Maxwell, his voice grave. 'Joseph told me all about it on his last visit. A very unfortunate thing indeed, and something that has inspired me to greater than usual levels of paranoia. On whose authority, Mr Gabion, are you carrying out this investigation?'

'I'm here on Zelia de Almeida's authority,' Luc admitted.

Maxwell's brows furrowed together, and he sighed in consternation, pulling his robe tight around his shoulders.

'*Zelia*,' the old man muttered half to himself, then let out a soft laugh with a shake of the head. 'Now *there's* someone I haven't heard from in a long time. She didn't feel like paying me a visit in person?'

'She said she wasn't allowed to come here.'

Maxwell nodded. 'Of course, of course. Try, if you will, to see things from my point of view; I've so rarely encountered anyone outside of the Eighty-Five in such a very long time that I don't particularly care to recall just *how* long it's been.' His eyebrows, as white as the hair on his head, rose fractionally. 'And now I find an unexpected visitor struggling to reach my library and nearly dying in the attempt. And from what scant information I've been able to glean regarding what transpires in the outside world, I gather Zelia herself is a potential suspect in Sevgeny's murder. By all rights, I

229

should inform my gaolers of your presence. I can imagine they'd take a degree of pleasure in extracting considerably more information from you than you've provided me with so far.'

'You mean the Sandoz don't already know I'm here?'

'The Sandoz?' Maxwell chuckled under his breath. 'They know there's no way I could cross a thousand miles of ice and snow on my own. What need is there to watch me closely, given that knowledge? But perhaps I *should* let them know about you. What do you think?'

'I really don't think you want to do that.'

'Why not?' Maxwell demanded, his voice rising, and echoing from the high walls around them.

'Because then you might have to explain to them why the hell the Coalition Ambassador just paid you a visit.'

Maxwell gazed at him with an expression of utter stupefaction.

Luc waited, his hands clammy, all too aware of the gentle hum of the mechants on either side of him. His stomach growled audibly in the otherwise still silence of the library, and he realized it had been a good long while since he'd had anything to eat.

'May I say, this is turning out to be quite the novel day,' said Maxwell suddenly, as if coming unfrozen. 'You're hungry?'

'Yeah, very,' Luc admitted.

'My dining room is on the lowest level of the library,' Maxwell told him, gesturing towards the mechants. 'I'll see you there in a minute or two.'

Maxwell's data-ghost vanished, and Luc followed one of the mechants to an elevator platform that carried him swiftly downwards. He gazed along the length of the library in the moment before it disappeared out of sight, and wondered what it must be like to live in such a place, buried inside a mountain with no eyes to the outside world beyond the lenses of mechants.

The platform came to a halt, and he followed the mechant down a long gallery to another room lined with yet more books. A third mechant was busy placing serving dishes and bowls on a table, at one end of which sat the flesh-and-blood Javier Maxwell.

'Don't look so nervous,' said Maxwell, indicating an empty seat across the table from him. 'Take a seat. Please. It's nice to have the opportunity to eat with someone who isn't also my gaoler, even if he *is* intent on blackmailing me.'

Luc remained standing. The mechant that had guided him here floated up to hover in one corner of the ceiling. 'You still haven't told me why Ambassador Sachs was here. Or has he not departed yet?'

'No, the Ambassador is gone. He left just before one of my mechants found you. You know, I was just about to eat when you woke, and I don't know about you, but I *hate* long conversations on an empty stomach.'

'I need to get in touch with Zelia—'

His stomach rumbled again.

'Dear God,' said Maxwell, picking up a fork and stabbing it towards the empty chair. 'Sit down and eat first. *Then* we talk.'

Maxwell lifted the lid from a serving dish and the sweet, aromatic scent of grilled fish rose up. Luc sat and watched as Maxwell, pointedly ignoring him, focused all his attention on filling his plate.

Despite himself, and the terrible urgency that continued to dominate his every thought and action, Luc ate.

The food and wine helped chase some of his nerves away. He had the sense the meal was as much a delaying tactic for Maxwell as anything else, an opportunity for the imprisoned Councillor to try and work out what Luc's presence here meant. The mechants worked efficiently at clearing empty dishes away and replacing them with new ones.

He tried again to engage Maxwell in conversation, but the old man's only response was to tap the edge of a dish with a fork and shake his head.

When he was finished, Maxwell took a last sip of wine, regarding Luc from across the table. 'One of my mechants was observing you,' he said, 'when you woke up. I watched you picking through the books in that room I left you in.'

Luc hesitated, then carefully put down his knife and fork. 'What about it?'

Maxwell pushed his chair back and stood, then crossed over to a nearby shelf, trailing his fingers along a line of volumes before selecting one in particular and pulling it out.

'Perhaps you'd indulge me in a little experiment,' he said, bringing the book around the table and placing it next to Luc.

Luc cleared his throat nervously. 'What kind of experiment?'

Maxwell flipped the book open, then slid it closer to Luc's right hand. 'I want you to place your hand flat on these pages.'

'And if I don't?'

'Then my mechants will find a way to *make* you, Mr Gabion.'

'What is the book, exactly?'

'An account of the fall of Earth, by a man named Saul Dumont. Ever heard of him?'

Saul Dumont. 'Of course I have. He was the last man on Earth.'

'The last man to *escape* Earth, would be a more precise way of putting it.'

Luc shook his head. 'There's no such book. If there was, I'd have heard of it – we'd *all* have.'

Maxwell regarded him with an expression of tolerant pity. 'The book is called *Final Days*. He wrote it during his decades on Novaya Zvezda, back when it was still called Galileo. It's an eye-opener, let me tell you – it most certainly does *not* correlate with the sanctioned histories of the Tian Di, and is all the more fascinating because of that. Now,' Maxwell continued, 'do as I say: press your hand and fingers flat and firmly on the pages.'

Luc hesitated, and one of the mechants drifted towards him, weapons slithering from out of its belly.

'Just a minute,' said Luc, sweating now. 'How could this book possibly exist—'

'Unless it had been deliberately redacted on the orders of Cheng and his faithful Eighty-Five?' Maxwell chuckled. 'I could say much the same for many of the books I keep here. If this prison had a name, Mr Gabion, it would be called the Library of the Damned.'

Luc reached out hesitantly, his hand hovering over the pages. Maxwell made an impatient sound and pushed Luc's hand flat against the smooth, metallic paper.

He stood at the entrance to a room as small and undecorated as a monk's cell, the scent of ocean water mixed with the stink of rotting seaweed.

He stepped inside and past a heavy iron door to see a man seated by a desk, its surface bright with icons floating above it. Words formed in the air as the man murmured quietly to himself. The desk was an antique, manufactured on Earth prior to the Abandonment.

The man – Saul Dumont – had dark chocolate skin and close-cropped hair, and wore a heavy coat over a zipped-up jerkin to keep out the cold. He had undergone his second instantiation within the last several years, and so looked young despite being well into his second century.

Dumont glanced over his shoulder at him, favouring him with a weary smile.

'What took you so long, Javier?' he asked.

Javier glanced to the side as a woman in late middle-age entered the room beside him. She was similar enough in appearance to Dumont that one might easily assume them to be mother and son.

'Dad?' Her voice quavered slightly as she spoke to Dumont. 'We need to get going. Johnson's got the boat ready. We need to evacuate. Now.'

Dumont gripped the edge of the desk with one hand, then pushed so that his chair slid back from it.

'There's still time,' said Dumont, addressing his daughter. 'We can still negotiate with Hsiu-Chuan—'

'Cheng,' she replied. 'Please remember, Dad.'

Dumont waved a hand in irritation. 'Whatever the hell he calls himself these days, Hsiu-Chuan's no fool. He must know we'd blow the rigs before we'd let the Tian Di Hui install their puppet government here. We—'

'Warships set out from Ocean Harbour more than a day ago. Please,' she said, stepping closer to him. 'We know how hard you fought for autonomy. We all do, but you have to accept that the fight is over.'

'No, it's not.' Dumont's voice rose, and he slammed a fist against the desk, making the icons ripple. 'Ettrick and Litewski still have some say on Franklin,' he continued, a plaintive edge creeping into his voice. 'We can run our own damn affairs.'

'Ettrick and Litewski have already agreed to the transfer of power,' his daughter replied. 'They didn't have any choice. They've already arrived back through the transfer gate.'

Dumont stared back at her in horror.

'She's right,' said Javier. 'We need to retreat and regroup.'

'For God's sake, Javier,' said Dumont, 'I know Hsiu-Chuan – he's a monster. Whatever he's got in mind for us, he can't possibly—'

Luc gasped as his fingers slipped from the page. Maxwell stared down at him, tight-lipped.

'Impossible,' Maxwell muttered under his breath.

'How does it work?' Luc managed to croak. 'It's like I was actually there, out in the middle of the ocean somewhere. Saul Dumont was there—' He stared at Maxwell in shock. '*You* were there. I was seeing everything through *your* eyes.'

'The memories are encrypted,' said Maxwell, shaking his head. 'How could you possibly access them without an encryption key? In fact, how could you even have a *lattice*? No one outside of the Council or Sandoz has one, except . . .'

He stopped abruptly, his mouth trembling slightly.

Luc nodded at the shelves around them. 'Can all of these books do the same?'

Maxwell shrugged, looking defeated. 'A few, but not all.'

'And what I saw and heard . . . That was all real?'

Maxwell nodded. 'Quite real. You just experienced my own memories, from about a century after the Abandonment.'

'You were on Novaya Zvezda, with Dumont?'

Maxwell sighed as he sat back down. 'I grew up there, long ago enough that I can remember when the first transfer gate was destroyed, years before the Abandonment even took place. I remember the clamour when Dumont was first brought down from orbit.'

'What happened to Dumont? Didn't he disappear?'

'No, he simply decided he preferred life in the Coalition to the rule of the Council, some time before the Schism. If he's still alive, he's to be found there now.'

Luc recalled his history. Before escaping on board a starship carrying a new transfer gate to Galileo, Dumont had shut down the entire wormhole network to ensure the survival of the colonies. By the time the ship arrived at Galileo, the Earth had been sterilized by some unknown, alien force.

'Dumont said something about Cheng – that it wasn't always his name.'

Maxwell nodded. 'His name back in those days was Shih Hsiu-Chuan.'

'So why the change of identity?'

'Because he's a man with many secrets,' Maxwell muttered, taking his seat at the table once more and pouring himself a new glass of wine. 'Assuming a new identity makes it easier to ensure that those secrets stay secret; he picked Cheng because it's a common name, as is Joe.' He made a circle with one hand. 'A man of the people, you see. Father Cheng, because a father always takes care of his children.'

'But . . . why would Cheng allow you to keep those memories stored here, in this prison? Surely they'd be dangerous to him, if they were found out?'

Maxwell didn't reply, and Luc glanced at the book where it still lay on the floor, its pages half-folded.

He came to a realization. 'Cheng doesn't know these recordings exist, does he? Does anyone else know about them?'

Maxwell regarded him balefully. 'You know, I could still order these mechants to kill you. It might save me a lot of unnecessary bother.'

Luc glanced towards the mechants and saw that they had still not retracted their weapons. 'You could,' he replied slowly, 'but I think if you were going to, you already would have.'

'Please don't make the mistake of making too many assumptions about me,' Maxwell snapped. 'For all Zelia knows, you're lying dead out there in the snow. She might never know you were here.'

'Then why the hell did you even bother to rescue me at all?'

'I looked you up while the mechant was escorting you here,' Maxwell replied. 'You're the one who killed Winchell Antonov, my former colleague and, dare I say it, brother-in-arms.'

'So it's revenge you want?'

Maxwell laughed. 'I have no intention of harming you, Mr Gabion. Revenge is for the young, and killing you wouldn't bring Winchell back. If I'm guilty of anything, it's simple curiosity.'

'You said that apart from me, no one outside of the Council or Sandoz has a lattice,' said Luc, 'but then you said *except*. Except who?'

Maxwell didn't answer.

'You were going to say Ambassador Sachs, weren't you?' Luc hazarded. 'He's the only other one outside of either of them with an instantiation lattice.'

Maxwell sighed and took another sip of wine. 'Nobody should be able to access those memories without my permission,' he agreed. 'Not you, not Sachs, not anyone without the appropriate encryption key. And yet the Ambassador's lattice somehow unlocked the memories automatically, and without effort – as did yours.'

'Who else has a copy of that key?'

'Only me,' Maxwell replied.

Luc glanced around the ranks of books surrounding them, thinking about all those people, Cheng and the members of the Eighty-Five, coming here and browsing their pages, entirely unaware of the sophisticated circuitry contained within them. Surely they must handle these books all the time . . .

'You've been stealing their memories,' Luc guessed, regarding Maxwell with new eyes. 'Every time one of the Eighty-Five picks up one of your books, it sieves information out of their lattices without them ever knowing. Am I right?'

Maxwell's expression became strangely sad. 'The circuitry in the books is meant to push extra embedded information the other way – from the pages to the reader's lattice. It took me a while, but I worked out how to reverse the flow of data and keep it hidden.'

'Why do it?'

'Because one day, the people of the Tian Di will need to know the truth about their leaders, and they'll find all the evidence they need right here in this library. Tell me, just how much contact have you had with the members of the Temur Council, apart from Zelia?'

'More than enough, for this lifetime.'

'Dreadful people, aren't they?' Maxwell said dryly. 'If I had the means, I would destroy the Council, and Vanaheim along with them.'

Luc stared at him. 'Why?'

Maxwell put his glass back down, and Luc tried not to flinch when one of the mechants drifted forward to refill it. 'Because they're a travesty of what they once were, long sunk into the introspection of old age, and dark perversions you would scarcely believe.'

'What kind of perversions?'

Maxwell looked at him in disbelief. 'You're Zelia's puppet. Surely you've encountered the "experiments" I've been hearing so much about? Or has she grown bored with that now?'

Luc shifted uncomfortably, again seeing a hunched figure immolating itself in his mind's eye.

'So you *have* seen them,' said Maxwell with an expression of dour amusement. 'It's a shame you killed Winchell. He was one of the few men left from the old days still worth a damn.'

'Even knowing of all the atrocities he was responsible for? The assault on Benares, the Battle of Sunderland—'

'You've been taken in by Cheng's propaganda. I'm well acquainted with the details of the Benarean assault: Cheng came here on several occasions prior to that campaign, so he could describe to me his plan to discredit Black Lotus. He lied to you. All of them did.'

'Bullshit.'

Maxwell smiled enigmatically. 'You've already worked out, haven't you, that Vasili paid me a visit not long before his death?'

Luc stiffened. 'Why would you assume that?'

'Why else would you have been so afraid of that book you leafed through downstairs, unless you'd encountered a memory-enabled book before? And I can tell you for a fact that Vasili was the only person in possession of a book taken from here. Now tell me,' he said, leaning forward. 'That book I gave to him – do you have it with you?'

Luc licked his lips. 'I'm sorry, I don't.'

Maxwell sat back, looking deflated. 'Then tell me what you learned from it.'

'That he knew someone was coming to kill him,' Luc replied. 'He muttered something about how he'd been wrong, and Antonov had been right. But about what, I don't know.'

'It's such a shame you don't still have that book,' said Maxwell. 'It contained some very valuable information indeed.'

'What information?'

'The answer to that question,' Maxwell replied, 'lies in part inside *another* book, in another section of the library.' He pushed his chair back and stood. 'I'll take you there now.'

'Why not just tell me?'

'Encoded memories, Mr Gabion, offer more fundamental and easily assimilated truths than speech, which is so very vulnerable to interpretation in a way that direct experience is not. To experience the memories of a man is to know certain unassailable truths about him.'

'But how exactly does Ambassador Sachs tie into all this?'

'The Ambassador came here on several occasions in order to privately solicit my advice regarding Reunification,' Maxwell replied, both mechants trailing in his wake as he stepped towards the exit. 'But before I tell you anything more,' he said, pausing by the door,

'I'd like to ask you something. You couldn't have known the Ambassador was here unless you had already been watching him closely. Were you?'

'We were tracking him, yes. We discovered he wasn't where he'd claimed to be at the time of Vasili's death.'

Maxwell nodded. 'So that naturally made him a suspect in Sevgeny's murder, yes? Well, I suppose there's no harm in telling you that he was here, with me, when Sevgeny died. In that regard, you can rule the Ambassador out.'

Maxwell exited the room, Luc following behind, the sound of his boots echoing from the marble walls as he tried to absorb everything he had just learned.

'Just how many books are there in this place?' asked Luc, as Maxwell led him up a metal stairway in the main hall. The mechants kept pace at a discreet distance.

'At least half a million, if you mean the physical volumes,' Maxwell replied with a note of pride. 'There are many, many times that number in data-storage. A few of the physical volumes are particularly fragile, and have to be kept separate from the rest.'

'But why the hell do they let you keep them at all?'

'In what's meant to be a prison?' Maxwell queried over his shoulder. 'As a punishment. I have always been a firm opponent of censorship in any form, unlike dear Joe. Everything I keep here should be available to everyone, and not just those few Councillors foolish enough to think they have superior moral stamina to the common public. So even though Cheng allows me to keep these books, and read them if I choose, I can no more share their contents with anyone outside of his inner circle than I could walk out of here alive. Such things,' he said, waving to the vast ranks and rows of books, 'were meant for all of us, along with all the other privileges Cheng has only shared with the Temur Council.'

They arrived at a lounge-area that felt and looked different from anywhere else Luc had seen, and he guessed they were now in

Maxwell's private quarters. He watched as the Tian Di's second most famous renegade stepped over to a shelf and pulled out yet another book.

'Tell me,' asked Maxwell, 'is Ambassador Sachs the one who installed your lattice?'

'No. Antonov did, when he captured me on Aeschere.'

Maxwell's eyebrows shot up. 'So it wasn't voluntary?'

Luc described the worm-like mechant Antonov had sent scurrying inside his nostril.

'I had no idea such a thing was even possible,' said Maxwell with a shake of the head. 'But why on Earth would he have done that to you?'

'To save himself,' said Luc. 'He'd already uploaded a partial copy of his own mind to the lattice before he inflicted it on me, and now his memories are invading my own thoughts. Zelia told me it would probably kill me unless she could find some way to stop the lattice's growth. But now, for all I know, she's abandoned me altogether . . .'

He thought about how alone he was here on Vanaheim without her help, and how vulnerable, and fought back a black tide of despair.

'Please, continue,' said Maxwell, not without a hint of sympathy.

'Antonov told me to seek out Ambassador Sachs and ask for his help, but when I did talk to the Ambassador, he wasn't willing to do anything of the kind.'

'Then you told Sachs you had a lattice like his?'

'I didn't need to. He somehow knew as soon as he set eyes on me.'

'And your lattice already had Winchell's personality and memories encoded into it when he placed it inside your skull?' Maxwell nodded, half to himself. 'A desperate gamble on Winchell's part, certainly.'

'What's in the book that you wanted to show me?' asked Luc, nodding at the volume still gripped in the old man's hand.

Maxwell glanced down at it. 'If you're ever going to find out who killed Vasili, you need to better understand him, and what drove him in the last days of his life. On his last visit here – the same day I gave him that other book you unfortunately neglected to bring back to me – I persuaded him to let me capture some of his more recent memories for posterity.'

'Did he talk much about his suspicions over Ariadna Placet's death?'

'It would be unlike Sevgeny *not* to talk about it,' said Maxwell, settling into a chair across from Luc. He turned the book this way and that in his hands. 'Tell me, have you ever been to Thorne, where she died?'

'Only briefly,' Luc replied.

Maxwell nodded. 'I believe Zelia took over as Director of Policy after her death. The official verdict recorded that something went wrong with the navigational systems of Ariadna's flier while she was travelling between biomes. Vasili was heartbroken, hardly surprising given they'd been together longer than anyone else in the Council – literally centuries. He was never the same afterwards, always trying to have the circumstances around her death reinvestigated.' Maxwell smiled thinly. 'And, so I understand, making a terrible nuisance of himself in the process.'

During that one visit to Thorne, Luc had never once stepped outside of a biome. The tiny world orbited just far out enough from its star that temperatures at the equator rarely rose above freezing. There had been some plan to seed Thorne's wisp-thin atmosphere with CO_2-generating bacteria, to create a controlled greenhouse effect that might bump the global mean temperature up in another few decades.

'Did *you* ever suspect she had been murdered?' asked Luc.

'Look around you,' said Maxwell. 'There's a thousand times more information in just the physical books here than I could assimilate in a dozen lifetimes. I hate to think how many secrets might be hidden all around us, but that I'll never know about because I don't know to look for them.' He shook his head. 'No, Mr Gabion, I had no reason to have any such suspicion – but someone else did, someone who knew that the trail of evidence leading to the proof Vasili so desperately needed started right here, in this library.'

Winchell, Vasili had said. *I was wrong, so very wrong.*

The realization hit Luc like a soft punch to the belly.

'Winchell Antonov?' asked Luc.

'Indeed,' Maxwell confirmed. 'When Sevgeny first came to me, he told me how Winchell had approached him in secret and, despite their differences, convinced him he could find the answers he needed here. With my help, of course.'

'And Vasili admitted to you that he'd been dealing with a renegade like Antonov?'

'As I'm sure you can imagine, I was somewhat taken aback myself. But Sevgeny was deeply distraught when he came to me; so much so that he was willing to ignore the fact that Winchell was not only his polar opposite politically and philosophically, but also an enemy of the Council.'

'And you agreed to help Vasili, even though he was one of the people responsible for locking you up here for all these years?'

Maxwell regarded him wearily. 'That doesn't mean he wasn't an honourable man in his way, Mr Gabion. Perhaps you don't understand just how isolated Sevgeny had become following Ariadna's death. He had been Cheng's right-hand man at one time, with considerable influence on Tian Di policies, but he was a cold man, not given to emotions except when it came to Ariadna.'

Maxwell shook his head. 'Outside of her, there was no one in all of the Tian Di, except perhaps Cheng, he could even so much as call a friend. After her death, he demanded access to files and records that, when he was finally given permission to investigate them, proved to have vanished without explanation.' He gave Luc a crooked smile. 'Are you surprised to learn this only made him more paranoid? Of course, he came to believe he was the victim of a conspiracy, which led in turn to him being dismissed as a crank by his colleagues in the Eighty-Five.'

'But he wasn't a crank, was he? Or paranoid.'

'No, he wasn't,' Maxwell agreed. 'His gradual isolation from the centre of power had made him . . . receptive, you might say, to influences and ideas he never would have entertained before. Even if they came from someone like Antonov.'

'But how could the evidence he was looking for wind up here in this library,' asked Luc, 'without your knowledge?'

'Over the years, it came to my attention,' said Maxwell, 'that certain of the Eighty-Five were using this Library's databanks as a repository for what might be deemed highly sensitive or damaging information.'

'Seems careless. Why not just destroy it altogether?'

'Because knowledge is power, as they say, and such things can prove useful at a later date – perhaps as leverage, should those individuals ever find themselves suddenly out of Cheng's favour.' Maxwell favoured him with a thin smile. 'An insurance policy, of sorts.'

'So what did Antonov tell Vasili he could find here?'

Maxwell stood and stepped towards Luc, handing him the book. 'A set of communication protocols which, once I had helped Sevgeny to locate them, proved to allow access to information stored on a derelict orbital station, one of dozens in orbit around Vanaheim.'

'When I met him, Ambassador Sachs had taken up residence on a station called the *Sequoia*,' said Luc. 'Was it that one?'

Maxwell shook his head. 'No. Vanaheim's orbital space is littered with debris and abandoned habitats and follies. The station in question is unoccupied and, I suspect, serves as one of the Council's many secret hiding places for its instantiation backups. When Vasili returned to visit me a few days later, having visited the station in question, he was in a dreadful state, jumping at shadows. He told me he had uncovered something monstrous – something Cheng had kept hidden from us all.'

'Did he tell you what it was?'

'I wanted him to,' Maxwell sighed. 'Whatever he'd discovered clearly terrified him, and I knew he was desperate to talk about it. But he still couldn't quite bring himself to trust me with the information. He told me he was determined to force a general meeting of the Eighty-Five, so he could present the evidence to all of them. I told him he was being naive at best, at worst suicidal.' He shook his head. 'The next thing I heard, he was dead.'

'And you have no idea just what it was he found?'

'None.' Maxwell nodded at the book gripped, unopened, in Luc's hands. 'But I did manage to persuade Sevgeny to leave behind some last few memories – in case, I said, something happened to him. Once you've experienced what he—'

Maxwell paused mid-sentence, his eyes becoming fixed on some far-off point. Several seconds passed before he focused on Luc once more.

'What's wrong?'

'It seems there's been a failure of some of my perimeter mechants,' said Maxwell, looking noticeably paler. 'I'll have to leave you here for the moment while I go and find out what's happened.'

'Are we in danger?'

'I have no idea,' said Maxwell. 'But if we are, it's even more important you learn everything you can from that book while you have the chance.'

Luc watched as Maxwell headed back the way they'd come, the sound of his slippered feet echoing softly. Then he opened the book on his lap, and placed his fingers against a random page.

SIXTEEN

As soon as Jacob had dumped the old man's body into the well, he boarded the flier hidden by Sillars, its hatch hissing softly open. Data displays bloomed around him as he slid into the pilot's seat, while the upper part of the hull became transparent, giving him a fine view of the forest clearing and the ruins off to one side.

He had one more thing to do before departing. Taking a deep breath, he fetched Sillars' pin-sized transceiver from a pocket, holding it delicately between thumb and forefinger and letting more data flow out of it and into his lattice.

All the worry and tension he'd felt building up, ever since he'd discovered how badly his predecessors had screwed up, finally melted away. He had everything he needed to complete his mission and return to the Tian Di in triumph.

Tipping his head back, he gazed up through the hull at the band of light and silver arcing from horizon to horizon like a bridge of light spanning the world. Then the ground began to slip away and the flier rose above the forest clearing, before accelerating towards the world-wheel like an arrow shot straight up into the air.

The sky soon faded from a greenish-blue to black as the flier's AG drive pushed it out of Darwin's gravity well at a continuously accelerating rate. The curve of the horizon became increasingly pronounced until the forest merged into a coastline streaked with clouds, their shadows patterning the land below. Spindly arms that looked impossibly fragile, but each of which was in actuality some kilometres in breadth, reached up from Darwin's equator to support the world-wheel.

Jacob had time to review the information provided by Sillars and to make sure it matched mission expectations. Once he had recovered the Founder artefact that was his mission goal from a secure facility aboard the world-wheel, his next task would be to make his way through the recently activated Darwin–Temur gate. According to encrypted updates recently received by Sillars' transceiver, the only people as yet allowed to pass through it were special envoys from either culture, but subtle hacks on the Temur side of the gate would cause Jacob to be identified as one such envoy making a scheduled return trip to the Tian Di. The fact that he would be departing Darwin without having ever officially arrived there was unlikely to be discovered by the Coalition authorities until it was much, much too late.

He passed the time piecing together the modular beam-weapon Sillars had left behind for his use, fitting the last component into place and studying the resultant device with an enthusiast's eye. Next came the wave-scramblers, grenade-like things that would – if Sillars had done his homework – induce seizures in Darwin's global datanets, as well as disrupting communications up and down the world-wheel. He supplemented these with additional subterfuge devices and weapons from the case Kulic had been so curious about.

Lastly he checked his suit's integrated systems, making sure they were all fully functional. He'd already checked and rechecked those same systems many times since his arrival on Darwin, but he did it one more time anyway.

The world-wheel grew from a thin line of silver to a mottled band of grey and white, studded with countless brightly glowing lights. The flier soon merged into the local traffic, most of it unmanned and flying within a dozen kilometres of the wheel's inner surface as it moved from destination to destination. Jacob caught sight of zero-gee parks and urban centres embedded in the inner rim. His sense of anticipation grew, and he practised the breathing and meditation exercises he had been taught when young.

The minutes and seconds drew out interminably until the flier finally dropped its velocity almost to zero relative to the world-wheel. He waited until the local systems had accepted Jacob's faked authorization, then set the flier to dock automatically.

Activating his suit's defensive systems, he disembarked into a wide, deserted boulevard within the world-wheel's outer shell. Sillars' research had shown this part of the world-wheel to be deserted, and it appeared to still be so.

Abandoned or not, Jacob knew there was no way to predict just how long it might take the local security networks to reroute themselves around the aggressive countermeasures his suit was already broadcasting. After that, he would have to think on his feet.

As it turned out, the security networks recovered in less than a minute. Jacob had been hoping he might have rather more time than this, but his training had taught him the value of adaptability.

Within seconds, a mechant more astonishingly complex than any he had ever encountered before, even on the killing fields of Benares, appeared from an aperture in the ceiling and came rushing towards him. He took it out with a single shot from his beam weapon, and watched it shatter into a thousand white-hot fragments.

He walked briskly onwards, his suit informing him he was close to the physical location of a junction connecting together several local data-hubs. Pausing just long enough to break open a circuit-panel set into the wall of the boulevard and insert a wave-scrambler, he then continued along the boulevard. The scrambler rapidly integrated with the dedicated networks responsible for coordinating data traffic in this part of the world-wheel, spreading chaos.

Jacob had taken no more than a couple of paces before the lights lining the boulevard began to flicker spasmodically, then faded altogether. Another few seconds passed before aged emergency circuits kicked in. Vermilion emergency lights embedded in

the floor of the boulevard and integrated into the walls now illuminated the way, lending a claustrophobic quality to his surroundings.

Less than thirty seconds after Jacob had placed the scrambler,
emergency evacuation alerts began forming in the air up and down
the boulevard, rippling softly as he passed through them. AI systems
for a hundred kilometres in either direction proceeded to spontaneously reboot, only to be issued with new algorithms provided by
the scrambler.

The effect could only be temporary; according to Sillars,
Coalition technology was astonishingly flexible when faced with
the unexpected. He had nonetheless discovered that a very few
parts of the world-wheel, such as this one, had not been improved
or upgraded to any significant degree in centuries.

In truth, much of Darwin's world-wheel had become a relative
backwater, the majority of the action having long since moved into
the frozen depths of the outer system and the dark masses scattered
throughout the Oort cloud. The wheel had been reduced to the
status of a dusty attic, into which unwanted possessions could be
thrown against the day when they might – just might – be needed.

It was a vulnerability waiting to be exploited. And in order to
maximize that vulnerability, it was necessary to cause the greatest
damage possible.

After another minute, just as Jacob approached a door that
marked the end of the boulevard, gyroscopic motors designed to
coordinate and balance this segment of the world-wheel proceeded
to power down for the first time ever.

Jacob felt a faint but distinct tremor running through the floor
of the boulevard. His lattice informed him that within the hour,
oscillations normally dampened by the gyroscopic systems would
destabilize this part of the world-wheel, and ultimately tear it apart
if drastic countermeasures were not taken by Darwin's authorities.

The door slid shut at Jacob's approach, barring his way. He
stopped to contemplate his next step. Things had been going
almost too well up until this point.

He sensed, rather than saw, defensive mechants emerging from slots in the walls of the boulevard behind him.

He turned to face them. To call them mechants, he decided, was to do them slim justice. They constantly reshaped themselves with an organic fluidity he had never witnessed before as they bulleted towards him.

Jacob felt subjective time slowing down as his lattice took full control of his body. He swept his hands outward, causing microscopic darts tipped with infinitesimal quantities of antimatter to erupt from his gloves, fanning outwards and tearing the mechants apart in a blaze of destruction that would have blinded him if he hadn't immediately rolled into a ball and covered his eyes. His suit became as rigid as steel, protecting him as the force of the blasts picked him up and smashed him against the wall of the boulevard.

When he looked back up, the blasts had wrecked much of the boulevard and shattered the doorway that had previously been barred to him. There was little left of the mechants beyond some fragments of white-hot metal.

Jacob stood with care, testing his muscles and bones and finding he had suffered a few minor fractures. Under the circumstances, he could count himself lucky.

Flexing his hands, he continued on through the doorway, stepping around a corner – only to find himself face-to-face with something from his deepest nightmares. Its features flowed like mercury, jaws distending as it reached out for him with a thousand spiny fingers.

He recognized it as another defensive procedure, albeit immensely more sophisticated than any of those he had so far overcome: the monster wasn't real, but was instead a virtual rendition of deadly software countermeasures designed to burn the lattice in his skull and render him mindless in moments.

The passageway in which Jacob had been standing disappeared, and he plummeted down an abyssal well that reminded him uncomfortably of the fate to which he had assigned Kulic. The monster was there, swimming through the air towards him.

He reached out both hands, brightly glowing katanas emerging from his fists, and slashed out at the monster's throat. It died screaming, its corpse disintegrating into a jumble of subroutines and hopelessly scrambled cognitive algorithms.

As suddenly as it had vanished, Jacob found himself back in the passageway, hands clenching swords that were no longer there.

The emergency lights flickered, then momentarily brightened before fading altogether, leaving Jacob in pitch darkness. The artificial lenses in his eyes compensated immediately, rendering the corridor in pale and ghostly shades.

He stood straight and flexed his hands before advancing, his suit feeding him a message that it had fought off a counter-attack by the local security networks. There was no need to worry about any further countermeasures – at least, not for another few minutes.

A final door opened at his approach with a satisfying rumble. He stepped inside and found himself within a vault crammed full of Founder artefacts, either suspended within slow-time fields or flickering in and out of shadow-parallels; empty universes into which they could be permanently banished should they somehow be accidentally activated.

It took Jacob moments to locate the quantum disruptor he had been sent to retrieve: a dark, fan-shaped thing no more than a few inches in width, and somehow difficult to look at directly. The disruptor was held within its own slow-time field that, in turn, was contained within a kind of barred metal container, scarcely larger than one of Jacob's fists.

He picked the container up and placed it in a zipped pocket of his combat suit, before jogging back down the silent and devastated boulevard, every piece of sub-molecular circuitry for kilometres around by now scrambled beyond repair.

SEVENTEEN

Bottomless grief knotted every muscle in Vasili's body. Every night for the past several days had been long and sleepless, every thought wracked with remorse.

It was more than Luc could bear. He let go of the book Maxwell had left him with and fell back in his seat, the breath shuddering in his throat.

The library around him was silent and still. Maxwell hadn't returned yet, and Luc was starting to get the feeling he might not be back for a while.

He took a breath, and again pushed his fingers against the pages.

Bright sunlight illuminated the spines of the books all around Vasili where he stood in his library. Winchell Antonov stood with his back to the patio doors, his small, inquisitive eyes set above a thick black beard. Only the faint rainbow shimmer of light around his outline revealed the renegade to be a data-ghost. Some flaw in the projection made him appear to be hovering just a fraction above the floor.

'I've already proved to you that Ariadna was deliberately murdered,' said Antonov. 'That is what you wanted, isn't it? Proof.'

For so very long, Vasili had been convinced of a cover-up over Ariadna's death. The inquest had been filled with flawed and circumstantial evidence, while the final verdict implied she had been careless, ignoring and failing to take action on priority alerts issued by the very flier she had died in.

But the more he had learned, the more convinced he had become that the verdict was a crock of shit. There were too many unanswered questions over how the flier's navigational systems could possibly have failed without it alerting anyone else to the danger, and that led in turn to the suspicion that its programming had been deliberately altered – in other words, sabotaged. And on top of that, *an overseer responsible for the maintenance of many of Thorne's fliers had died under equally mysterious circumstances before he could provide vital expert witness testimony. Vasili's own private researches had uncovered yet further, damning evidence.*

But who would have the motive or reason to bring about her death?

Ariadna had been a Lost Russian like himself, part of that generation growing up on what had been the Russian Federation's Pacific coast, prior to the Chinese occupation. Much, much later, long after she had become estranged from Winchell, and on the very day the Coalition's occupation of Newton crumbled under the sustained assault of Cheng's guerrilla armies, they had become lovers. Until then they had been only comrades in arms, working on strategies to trigger shutdowns in enemy military networks, their relationship up to that point purely professional.

The first time they made love, by the light of burning furniture tossed from the windows of a Coalition barracks, it had been a spontaneous act brought about by their shared revolutionary fervour. He remembered the triumphant shouts of their compatriots filling the air, the sweet ecstasy of victory mixing with the pleasure of Ariadna's aroused flesh.

'Proof.' Vasili licked his lips, unable to keep a slight tremor out of his voice. 'This was all so much easier when everybody thought I was insane.'

'You weren't insane,' Antonov replied gently. 'For a long time I hated you for taking Ariadna from me, but then I realized it was I who had pushed her away.' He shook his head sadly. 'When I found out what had happened to her, I instigated my own investigation into the circumstances surrounding her death, but it took a very long time to bear fruit. For a while I foolishly believed that you yourself might be her murderer, but my jealousy for your long life with her had blinded me. For that, I ask forgiveness. By asking as many difficult

questions as you did, Sevgeny, you proved to me that you are an honourable man, and for that you have my respect, however much we might disagree on other matters.'

'They told me I had lost my senses,' muttered Vasili. 'That I was unable to . . . to accept there was no meaning to her death.'

'But you never stopped being suspicious, did you?'

'Of course not,' Vasili snapped, slamming one hand against a bookcase, taking a certain relish in the sudden burst of pain.

He could hardly believe he had consented to this meeting. Antonov represented everything he stood against – an enemy of order and sanity, a man who had proven himself more than willing to risk bringing the same destructive forces that had once destroyed the entire Earth raining down upon the colonies.

And yet here Antonov was, in his very home, offering answers to questions he had come to believe would never be answered. Ever since that terrible day when Ariadna had died, he had focused on his work as a way to avoid the despair of grief, fulfilling his duties both to the Council and to the Tian Di to the utmost. But it still had not been enough to prevent his slow abandonment by Cheng, a man he had once considered the closest thing to a friend.

'I've already given you a taste of what I know,' said Antonov, his voice calm and steady and infuriating in equal measures. 'Your wife was asking too many questions for the comfort of certain of your fellow Eighty-Fivers.'

Vasili's thoughts flashed back to a few days before, when an anonymous and heavily encrypted message had been delivered by a decrepit mechant, its hull pitted and rusted, its livery indicating it had belonged to Antonov prior to his fall from grace. God only knew where on Vanaheim Antonov had secreted it all these years.

Despite considerable misgivings, Vasili had loaded the message into his sensorium, curiosity overcoming his normal caution. He soon found himself watching shaky footage from the point of view of a Sandoz missile flying low across Thorne's rock- and boulder-strewn landscape, before homing in on a single flier as it passed over a range of crater-pocked mountains.

'You said Sandoz forces were ordered to kill her,' said Vasili. 'But who gave them their orders?'

'To find out the answer to that,' Antonov replied, 'you must first go somewhere I cannot.'

'You said she was asking too many questions. Questions about what?'

Antonov rolled his shoulders, as if one of them were slightly kinked. 'I need to get access to the information stored in a private data-cache maintained by Cheng – one that nobody else knows exists, and that contains, or so I believe, damning proof regarding Ariadna's death.'

Vasili stared at Antonov, his eyes burning. 'You're using me,' he rasped. 'You never gave a damn about me before now, and I'm not stupid enough to believe you're here solely for my benefit.'

Antonov laughed. 'Ever the pessimist, Sevgeny? Of course I'm using you. What kind of fool would I be, if it were any other way?'

'You're a devil,' rasped Vasili. 'When you go to hell, they should put you in charge. I swear you were made for the job.'

'I seek evidence of a different kind,' Antonov told him. 'Proof that your beloved Father Cheng has not only discovered a second entrance to the Founder Network, but is exploiting its discoveries just as recklessly as the idiots who brought about the Abandonment.'

Vasili stared open-mouthed at Antonov's data-ghost. 'Impossible!' he cried. 'I stood by Joe's side through almost every major policy decision the Council has made since its inception. He—'

'Used you,' Antonov finished, 'to get into power, then finally discarded you once you proved to be a liability. You know he always treated Ariadna with disdain; he allowed you to become part of his inner circle, but not her – and why? Because she asked the questions you refused to face. There's a reason, Sevgeny, that people called us the Thousand Emperors – because that's what we became, figureheads spouting the same old monopolistic bullshit to justify their grip on power.'

'And who would you prefer we emulated?' Vasili yelled. 'The Coalition? Their decisions nearly destroyed the human race!'

Antonov slammed a fist into the palm of his hand. 'When we fought them to a standstill all those years ago, Sevgeny, they were tyrants – no doubt about that. They used the chaos of the Abandonment to take *our colonies by force, and I fought them as hard as you or anyone else, but that was centuries ago.* Centuries.'

He stepped back slightly. *'They've evolved so much during the long separation of our two civilizations, while we've stood resolutely still. Their old guard are long gone, dissolved in the sweeping changes that overtook them. It's only us who call them the Coalition – they just call themselves the human race.'*

'Human?' Vasili laughed. *'Like that Ambassador of theirs? Have you or anyone else ever even seen behind that fucking mask of his?'*

'We could argue forever, Sevgeny, and we'd never see eye to eye, because we've become set in our ways, as impermeable to change as Joe, and that is precisely why none of us should be allowed to rule any longer.' He reached out a hand. *'Accept my offer or not. It's your choice, and one I cannot force upon you.'*

'Damn you,' Vasili hissed, his hands twisted into claws. *'Damn you to hell.'*

'No.' Antonov shook his head, eyes glistening. *'Damn them to hell, Sevgeny.'*

Something inside Vasili gave way, as if he were no longer able to contain so much anger. He collapsed into a chair in exhaustion, and stared out past the patio towards the courtyard and the ocean beyond.

'All right,' he said, too weary now even to be angry, *'where is this data-cache?'*

'That's where it gets complicated,' Antonov replied. *'You first need to go to Javier Maxwell. A set of communication protocols are hidden in that library of his; these will lead you straight to the location of the data-cache.'*

Javier Maxwell. Sevgeny shook his head and sighed. He should hardly be surprised Maxwell was involved in all of this somehow.

'Why do you need me to do your dirty work, Winchell?'

'You know I'd be risking detection if I data-ghosted into his prison, Sevgeny. You, however, have the right to enter his library at any time.'

It all suddenly became clear. *'So that's why you're here,'* said Vasili. *'Javier knows about these protocols?'*

Antonov shook his head. *'I'm far from sure he has any idea whatsoever that they exist. But remember, he acts as custodian to data-repositories to which you also have access. My researches show that the protocols are buried deep inside them, and I can tell you just how to locate them with his help.'*

'And what do you expect me to do, once I've uncovered this hidden goldmine of reputed scandal?' Sevgeny asked, feeling suddenly tired and old. 'Bring the curtains down on the Temur Council? Inspire a fiery revolution and watch the worlds burn?'

'I'll leave revolution to others younger than myself,' Antonov replied. 'I need solid, independently verifiable proof of Cheng's secret exploration of the Founder Network, which I believe this hidden data-cache will supply. All I'd been able to find until recently were hints – pieces of a puzzle that together implied a much greater picture. While you've been out in the rain – metaphorically speaking, of course – Cheng, Cripps and his fellow conspirators in the Sandoz Clans have been getting up to things that threaten the existence not only of the Tian Di, but of the human race as a whole.'

'What kind of things?' Vasili demanded.

'They have been searching for weapons,' Antonov replied, 'that Cheng believes will help him maintain his power and turn back the changes reunification with the Coalition would otherwise force upon the Tian Di. Or do you really believe Cheng is suited to survive those changes, Sevgeny?'

Vasili sighed and looked away. 'Perhaps not,' he admitted, feeling as if treason were spilling from his lips.

'I'll leave my mechant in your care for now,' said Antonov. 'Use it to get back in touch with me once you've spoken with Javier – and maybe you and I can work together again, the way we used to, back in the old days when we were young and burning with life.'

His data-ghost vanished, and Vasili sank deeper into his chair, staring at the cold stone walls surrounding him. More than ever, his home felt like a mausoleum, with him its premature guest.

He thought of Ariadna, and wept.

*

Luc found himself back in the library, the book in his lap, fingers aching from gripping its pages. He let out a shuddering breath, then pushed the book onto a table.

From the outside, Vasili had appeared an entirely cold and unlovable figure, his face bent into a permanent scowl; and yet his love for his deceased inamorata had burned with such intensity that Luc's own feelings for Eleanor seemed pale by comparison.

But that wasn't what made his hands shake as he lifted them from the book. In a few minutes his world had, almost literally, been turned upside down. A secret entrance to the Founder Network, one that was being recklessly exploited by the leaders of the Tian Di? It sounded absolutely preposterous. And yet it didn't explain the hammering of Luc's heart, or the sick feeling welling up in his chest.

He glanced towards the door, hearing hurried footsteps approaching. Javier Maxwell burst in a moment later, looking harried and wild-eyed.

'You have to leave,' Maxwell barked. '*Now.*'

Luc sat up, alarmed. 'Why?'

'Cripps is on his way here, with a detachment of Sandoz. It won't be long before they arrive.'

Shit.

'They must be looking for you,' Maxwell continued, twisting his hands together, 'or at least that's the logical conclusion.' He shook his head. 'The Sandoz have never come here in force like this before. Never.'

'Or maybe,' suggested Luc, 'they figured out that the Ambassador was here.'

Maxwell regarded him uneasily. 'Or that Zelia sent *you* here. I won't know one way or the other until they arrive – by which time, I suggest, you should be as far away from here as possible.'

'No,' said Luc, 'not yet.'

'There isn't the time—'

Luc held up the book. 'It was Father Cheng, wasn't it? He gave the order to kill Adriana Placet.'

'It seems you've been making good use of your time,' said Maxwell, nodding at the book.

'Antonov said that Cheng found a second entrance to the Founder Network. He also said Adriana Placet was killed because she was asking too many questions. Was it because she found out what Cheng was up to?'

'She knew *something* was going on, but not necessarily *what*.' Maxwell stepped closer, taking a grip on Luc's arm. 'You need to finish what Sevgeny started.'

Luc stood and pulled his arm away. 'What the hell are you talking about?'

'I may not know all the details, but I certainly know enough to understand that Father Cheng is doing something that is endangering us all. You need to go to that station Sevgeny visited and locate whatever data he found, and show the Tian Di what Cheng is doing. But that won't happen unless you get the hell away from here first.'

'But how can I possibly do that if I don't have the protocols Vasili—'

'You had the protocols in your hands,' Maxwell said softly. 'Hence my concern when you didn't bring them back.'

Luc stared at him for a moment, then cursed under his breath. 'The book I found on Vasili?'

Maxwell nodded. 'Which is why you must find it again.'

'Surely you must have copies of the protocols!'

'Whoever it was amongst the Eighty-Five who hid the protocols in the library's databases erased them remotely some time very recently, presumably once they realized Sevgeny was on their trail. That means, unfortunately, that the copy of them in Sevgeny's book is now the only one still in existence.'

'I don't even know if the book is still in Vasili's home. For one thing, it was damaged by the heat from the blast that killed him. For all I know, his house mechants threw the damn thing out.'

'That's a chance you're going to have to take. Without that book it would take you months to find the station.'

'But how can I possibly get away from here? I'm stranded since Zelia's flier disappeared.'

'There's a hangar below us, with a flier for emergency use by Cheng or anyone else in the Eighty-Five with an urgent need to make use of it,' explained Maxwell, stepping closer to the door. He gestured to the book still in Luc's hands. 'Take that with you and learn what you can once you're away from here.'

Luc hesitated for a moment, then stuffed the book into a large pocket on the inside of his jacket, taking care not to let his fingers brush against the pages.

'Why can't you use that flier to get out of here yourself?'

'It's programmed to refuse my orders under any circumstances,' Maxwell replied.

'But if I took you on board with me—'

Maxwell shook his head. 'Then it would never even take off.' He shrugged. 'Besides, where the hell could I go?'

Luc followed him along a short corridor, then down a winding stairwell, its walls bare and undecorated compared to the rest of the library complex.

'But where can *I* go from here?' he called after Maxwell's retreating back. 'I've got no idea what the hell's happened to Zelia, where she's gone or if she's in trouble of some kind. Without her, there's nowhere for me to go.'

They came to a single steel door at the bottom of the stairwell. The temperature had plummeted, the air frosting with their every breath.

'I knew Zelia well, back in the day,' said Maxwell, stopping for a moment, 'and she's more resourceful than you imagine. Whatever's happened to her, I wouldn't assume you've seen the last of her just yet.'

Luc followed him through this last door. Suddenly he was outside, a freezing wind sucking all the heat from his skin, as he found they had emerged into the cavernous hangar he had first sighted from the foothills. There was, he saw, enough space to park a fleet of fliers.

The storm that nearly killed him had passed, and the sun hung sharp and bright in a sky striped with narrow wisps of cirrus. He stepped forward, hugging himself against the cold, and realized belatedly that he'd left his cold-weather gear behind. *Idiot.*

Mechants dropped down from some point in the cavern's ceiling and moved towards them, weapons unfolding from their bellies. Luc turned to look at Maxwell, who had come to a halt just a short distance beyond the steel door.

'This is as far as I go, I think,' said Maxwell, retreating closer to the door.

Luc glanced between Maxwell and the approaching mechants. 'Are we in any danger?'

'*I* certainly am, if I try and go any farther than this. I don't see any reason why they would want to harm you, however.' He pointed towards a low-slung shape parked nearby and partly hidden beneath a heavy grey tarpaulin, AG field generators bulking out its sides.

'That's the flier you were talking about?'

Maxwell nodded. 'I don't see any others, do you?'

'How did you do it?' asked Luc, staring back at Maxwell in wonder. 'I came here looking for Ambassador Sachs, and somehow I wound up working for you.'

Maxwell smiled faintly. 'This is all Winchell's doing, remember? Vasili would never have sought out the protocols or Cheng's data-cache if not for that old renegade.' He nodded towards the flier. 'Go now, Mr Gabion, before the Sandoz arrive.'

'One last thing. You said the Ambassador came to you for advice. About what?'

Maxwell's shoulders rose and fell in a sigh. 'When I say there isn't much time, I mean—'

'Please,' Luc begged.

'He was trying to prevent a war, Mr Gabion. A war between the Tian Di and the Coalition.' Maxwell almost shouted the words in his agitation. 'I'd tell you more, but there simply isn't the time.'

Luc glanced towards the horizon beyond the foothills, and saw a tiny black dot moving across the sky towards them. 'If I take off now, they'll see me.'

Maxwell took a step forward, only for the mechants to drop down in front of him, blocking his path. 'This *really* isn't the time for debate,' he yelled. 'Stay here, and you're dead for sure.'

Luc ran towards the flier, and felt a flush of relief when the mechants guarding Maxwell made no move towards him. He quickly pulled the tarpaulin to one side, revealing a hatch in the side of the craft that hissed open automatically. Gazing into its darkened interior, he then turned back to Maxwell.

'Go back inside,' Luc yelled over to him, 'and wait there. I've got an idea.'

'What the hell are you doing, Mr Gabion?'

'You'll see.'

He climbed in through the open hatch, then turned, yanking the tarpaulin back down until it was draped back over the side of the craft. As he clambered into the cockpit, the hatch closed once more, sealing him inside.

Once there, he sat in the pilot's seat and waited for the Sandoz to arrive, wondering if what he was about to attempt wasn't in fact the stupidest thing he had ever done.

'This is insane,' Maxwell hissed.

'Just bear with me, okay?'

He stood side by side with Luc's data-ghost in the library's main hall, a real-time projection of the hangar floating before them. They could see that an armoured Sandoz heavy-lifter had just dropped down to a landing not far from the parked flier, still stationary beneath its grey tarpaulin. They watched as several figures emerged from the heavy-lifter, too far away to be immediately identified. All but two of the figures wore the heavy armoured suits of Sandoz warriors.

Maxwell made a gesture, and the view zoomed in towards the two in question. Luc saw with a spasm of shock that one of them was Eleanor; she wore her SecInt uniform, and was accompanied by Bailey Cripps.

They watched as Cripps, Eleanor and the soldiers made their way inside the library. Luc flexed his fingers by his sides, the breath catching in his throat.

Even though he had data-ghosted many times before, the depth of experience afforded by his lattice made it an effort of will to remember where he was, in reality, aboard Maxwell's flier, and not in fact standing next to Maxwell in the library. He'd tried to persuade Maxwell to do the same – hide elsewhere in the library and present only his data-ghost to Cripps – but, as Maxwell himself had pointed out, there were only so many places for him to hide. Something in the other man's manner gave Luc the sense that this was a confrontation the Councillor had been anticipating for a very, very long time.

'She shouldn't be here,' Luc muttered. Cripps must have followed up on his threat. He should have anticipated something like this.

'Is there a problem?' asked Maxwell.

'That's Eleanor Jaq. She's a SecInt officer. Cripps threatened to arrest her at one point, to try and force me to turn informant for him.'

'Ah.' Maxwell nodded. 'You believe she is his prisoner.'

The view changed, showing Cripps leading Eleanor and the Sandoz through the steel door connecting the hangar to the library, then up the steps leading to the main atrium. Eleanor walked side by side with Cripps, who leaned in towards her and said something inaudible into her ear. Eleanor smiled uncertainly in response.

'If I had to be honest,' said Maxwell, nodding towards Eleanor's image, 'she's not *acting* like a prisoner. And perhaps you haven't noticed, but she *is* armed.'

Luc started to say something, but the words died in his throat when he saw Maxwell was right. She had a holster on her hip.

'There's only one of her,' Luc managed to say, 'and several of them. If she tried to . . .'

'I think you know as well as I do they would have disarmed her immediately if she was under arrest,' Maxwell pointed out. 'What do you intend to do now?'

'Just what I was going to do anyway,' he said, feeling the first curdling threads of betrayal knot themselves around his stomach.

'Then you'd better start now,' said Maxwell, 'because they're going to be here any second.'

Luc nodded tightly. 'Good luck.'

'My luck ran out long ago, Mr Gabion,' Maxwell replied with a sigh. 'If I had any to spare, I'd let you have it. You're going to need it.'

Luc's data-ghost vanished from Maxwell's side, reappearing a moment later at the far end of the library's central atrium, and positioned slightly behind one of several pillars supporting a first-floor gallery. Local micro-relays fed him the sound of voices echoing from the high, vaulted ceiling, and he peered round the side of the pillar to see Cripps emerge from the stairwell, followed by Eleanor and the Sandoz. A library mechant came swooping down, falling into a stationary position to the one side of and slightly above Maxwell, its audio circuits open so Luc could hear everything that was said.

Cripps stepped up to Maxwell while the Sandoz hung back, their eyes scouring the library.

'It's been a long time, Bailey,' said Maxwell, stepping towards him. 'What brings you here?'

Luc saw Cripps unfasten the holster at his side. 'Master Rachid,' Cripps said over his shoulder, 'tell your men to search everywhere until you find Gabion.'

Luc pulled his data-ghost back into the shadows, not wanting it to be seen just yet, and watched as Rachid ordered four of the soldiers to the nearest elevator platforms. At the same time, he fired a command to Maxwell's flier. It lifted up from the frozen concrete, the tarpaulin that had been covering it falling away as it rose. Within seconds it was accelerating towards the clouds covering the nearby mountain peaks.

'To be honest, Javier,' said Cripps in that same moment, turning back to Maxwell, 'it's not been nearly long enough.' Eleanor remained silent by his side, her expression pale and nervous. 'Why don't you save us the time and trouble and tell us where Luc Gabion is?'

Maxwell affected mild confusion. 'Who?'

Cripps' face darkened. 'Don't waste my time. We both know Zelia de Almeida sent him here. Where is he?'

Maxwell affected a tone of distant curiosity. 'Why are you looking for this man?'

'Zelia has been conspiring to assassinate Father Cheng and destabilize the Tian Di – a conspiracy I have reason to believe *you* are part of. Gabion is a Benarean Black Lotus agent under her command. Now tell me where he is.'

'Or what? You'll kill me? Surely you can do better than that.'

'I know where every one of your backups are located,' Cripps barked. 'Don't think I would hesitate to wipe every damn one.'

'It makes no difference,' Maxwell replied with a shrug. 'I have no idea who or what you're talking about.'

'Fuck it,' said Cripps, sliding the pistol from its holster and shooting Maxwell at close enough range that the blast very nearly decapitated him. Blood hissed as it splashed against the floor and nearby furniture.

Cripps turned to the two remaining Sandoz and muttered something indistinct as Javier Maxwell's body crumpled to the floor. A moment later one of the Sandoz opened fire on the library mechant. It jerked backwards under the sudden assault, and Luc lost contact with it. He saw its blackened remains thud to the floor.

'Hey!'

Luc glanced up from behind the pillar to see a Sandoz staring down at him from the upper gallery. He darted backwards, moving fast, and a loud, hollow thud filled the air at the same moment that a crater appeared where his data-ghost had been standing only a moment before.

Maxwell had allowed Luc to upload a map of the library once

he had explained his intentions, and he now retreated towards a doorway leading out of the atrium and into a maze of reading rooms. He ran past low tables and couches and through several more doors connecting each room to the next, hearing muffled shouts and heavy footfalls following not far behind.

By now, Maxwell's flier had very nearly reached low orbit. Luc felt his weight begin to fall away. He squeezed his eyes shut, sweat trickling down his brow, and focused on what was happening in Maxwell's library, already some hundreds of kilometres behind him.

'Gabion!' Cripps' amplified voice boomed through the library as he ran. 'My men are seeding this place with explosives. You can either surrender, or go down with it. Your choice.'

Go to hell, thought Luc, guiding his data-ghost into a corridor lined with yet more doors. He checked Maxwell's map and saw that the corridor joined another up ahead to form a T-junction. That second passageway angled back at both ends to wrap around the reading rooms.

Another Sandoz appeared from around the corner of the T-junction, taking aim.

Luc dived through a door to one side, finding himself inside a reading room indistinguishable from any of the others, then ran through the door set into its opposite wall. He could hear the Sandoz stamping after him.

He passed through more doors and more rooms until he came out into a corridor, and saw an elevator platform tucked into an alcove to his left, right where he'd known it would be. Heavy, muffled footsteps came slamming through the reading rooms behind him, getting closer with every second.

In the blink of an eye, Luc was standing on the first floor gallery, looking down at Eleanor, who hadn't moved. There was no sign of Cripps.

'Eleanor?' he screamed down at her. 'What the hell is going on? Is Cripps holding you prisoner?'

She looked up at him, lips set in a thin line. 'None of this would have happened if you'd just listened to me and talked to Director Lethe, like I asked you to.'

'Eleanor, you have to listen—'

'No, Luc, you need to listen to me. I spoke to Lethe on your behalf and told him everything – about what really happened on Aeschere, about the lattice and Zelia de Almeida – all of it. I had to, don't you see?'

'I thought you understood,' he said. 'I trusted you more than anyone else. Or do you really believe what Cripps just said about me?'

She hesitated for a moment. 'No, of course I don't. But we need to find a way to fix you first. Then you can explain your side of things.'

Luc felt like she'd torn him open with claws of steel and left him to bleed to death. He stared down at her, suddenly lost for words.

Hearing a high-pitched beep to his right, he turned to see a Sandoz mechant accelerating towards him.

Instantly he ran, explosive rounds ripping chunks of wood and brick from the walls and shelves behind him, the mechant banging into walls as it came veering after him.

He was running blind now. Incredibly, Cripps still hadn't worked out he was already long gone.

Turning a corner, he came face to face with yet another Sandoz warrior. The suited figure lunged towards and then *through* him, and Luc heard the warrior grunt with surprise as he slammed into the balustrade overlooking the library floor.

Luc stood where he was and made no effort to escape. There was no point in running any more.

'Sir!' the Sandoz yelled, staring around at Luc. 'It's a data-ghost!'

Luc ignored him, stepping over to the balustrade. Cripps came darting out of a doorway, pistol in hand, and stared up at him.

'Very clever,' said Cripps, his voice echoing as he re-holstered his weapon. 'But wherever you're hiding, you must know you're only delaying the inevitable. You can't escape through the Hall of Gates now.'

'Why did you kill Maxwell?' Luc demanded.

'Because he'd become too dangerous for his own good,' Cripps snapped.

Another Sandoz came running over to Cripps and whispered something in his ear. Cripps whipped around to glare at Luc, his face full of hatred.

'Turn that goddamn flier back!' Cripps screamed up at him.

'And get my head blown off like Javier Maxwell did?' Luc shook his head. 'I don't think so. Sevgeny Vasili knew who was coming to kill him – and I'm pretty damn sure you're the one who pulled the trigger.'

Luc dropped the connection before either Cripps or Eleanor could say anything else.

He found himself back in his own body, staring up at the curved hull of the flier's cramped cockpit.

Eleanor's betrayal had shaken him to the core. He felt more alone than he had ever felt since he'd lost everything back on Benares as a child. The nearest thing he had left to a friend or ally was Zelia de Almeida, and he still wasn't sure if that was better than having her for an enemy.

<Zelia,> he sent, <if you're out there, for God's sake, answer.>

Still nothing. As he'd expected.

He had gained, at most, a few minutes head-start – and even then, he still didn't have an answer to the question he'd asked Maxwell: where the hell could he even *go*?

He was alone, on a hostile world, with no way home. All he could really do until he figured something better out was find somewhere to hide where Cripps might never find him.

Switching to the flier's external senses, he saw Vanaheim's sun burst over its horizon, making the oceans below looks like pools of golden fire, and remembered what Maxwell had said: if his lattice could bypass the encryption on the books in his prison, what else could it achieve?

<Zelia!>

Still no answer.

He had the flier dip back down into the upper atmosphere, soon feeling it shudder around him as it bit into denser air. Before long a steady rumble sounded through the tiny vessel's hull. He'd picked his next stop at random – an archipelago of islands dense with forest, just off the coast of a minor continent, black smoke trailing from one peak that was clearly volcanic.

Most importantly, the flier's records indicated the archipelago was entirely uninhabited, and rarely visited. He had no idea whether Cripps or anyone else would be able to track him there, but he was all out of any better ideas.

The flier made landing in a clearing about forty minutes later, dirt and leaves tumbling down after it as it broke through the forest canopy. The soil beneath the canopy was filled with a half-light that filtered down from above.

Sweat prickled his skin the moment he exited the flier. Luc stumbled over to a boulder thick with moss and sat there for a few minutes, trying to will his heart to slow down and his hands to stop shaking. The air was thick with small, buzzing things, and all he could do was hope that none of de Almeida's surveillance mechants were amongst them.

Thank God he'd taken the opportunity to eat something at Maxwell's library. If he was going to hide out here for any significant length of time, his first priority would have to be locating a source of fresh water, followed by trying to work out what, amongst Vanaheim's bio-engineered flora and fauna, might be edible.

And after *that* . . .

Maybe it was better not to think about *after* just yet.

He went exploring, making his way to the edge of a deep gorge that fell away to a river sluicing between dark granite walls on its long descent from the island's central peak. He worked his way deeper into the forest, keeping the gorge to one side, taking care not to stumble or fall in the permanent twilight beneath the canopy.

After a while he came across a shallow cave, and had an idea.

Making his way back to the flier, he guided the vehicle back above the canopy until it spread out below him like a sea of green, then flew low until he was hovering above the river gorge. He followed the river upstream, then carefully manoeuvred the flier back through the canopy; and before long, he had parked it just inside the mouth of the cave. Even with the canopy covering the flier over, it had still felt somehow exposed. There were no guarantees the Council didn't also have access to surveillance technology that could see through rock, but he'd take that chance.

He slept fitfully inside the flier, and found himself troubled by dreams in which he argued with Winchell Antonov. When he awoke, he could remember nothing of what they had said to each other. Staggering back outside, he worked his way downstream until the gorge flattened out sufficiently that he could cup the lukewarm water in both hands, drinking down as much of it as he could.

Upon his return to the flier, tired, grubby and still hungry, he failed at first to register that a light on one of the cockpit's virtual panels had begun to blink. He stared at it for several moments, fatigue making him unsure if it had been blinking the whole time and he'd only just noticed it.

Tentatively, he reached out and touched the panel with a finger.

<Shit, it really is you. I don't know how the hell you managed to stay alive, but you did.>

Luc let himself fall into the flier's crash couch, a fat grin spreading across his features. It was Zelia.

<What happened to you?> he demanded. <I managed to talk to Maxwell, but he didn't have any better idea where you were than I did. I thought maybe Cheng had finally ordered your arrest.>

<You actually *talked* to Javier? Where the hell *are* you?>

<Hiding on an island in the middle of nowhere. Maxwell rescued me and brought me into that weird library of his, but Cripps got

wind of it and turned up with some Sandoz in tow. I got away, but Cripps is looking for me now.>

<I don't want to talk like this too much,> she sent back. <It's better we meet face to face.>

<How the hell did you even manage to track me down?>

<There are back doors inside the security networks nobody else knows about. It took a while to get control of them back, but after that it was just a matter of time before I figured out how to find you. Now listen – I'm uploading coordinates to you. I need you to go to them and rendezvous with me there.>

<Maxwell's dead,> he told her. <I saw Cripps kill him. I learned a lot in that library, Zelia. I even have a pretty good idea just why Vasili was murdered.>

There was a brief pause before she replied. <Javier Maxwell is dead?>

<More than just dead. Cripps made a point of saying he was going to wipe Maxwell's backups. He was getting ready to blow the whole damn library to kingdom come when I got away.>

<God damn it, he can't . . .> She broke off for a moment, then came back. <Just get here, Gabion. I need you to brief me on everything that's been happening.>

Luc listened to the buzz of life from outside the flier's open hatch, the wind rattling the high branches of the trees shielding the mouth of the cave from view.

<You knew a lot more than you were letting on, Zelia. A *lot* more.>

<What?>

<That whole story about bringing me in to investigate Vasili's murder because of the work I'd done in the past. That was just bullshit, wasn't it?>

<You have no idea what you're talking about.>

<This all started after Antonov told me in a dream to alter a record in Archives as a message – to whom, he didn't specify. I felt like an idiot making those changes based on something in a Goddamn *dream*, but the next thing I knew Cripps had turned

up out of the blue and I was being hauled off to Vanaheim to take a look at charred corpses on *your* behalf. I'd have to be an idiot not to make the connection.>

<You think Antonov's message was meant for me?>

<A lot of things that happened on Thorne while you were still its administrator got swept under the carpet, Zelia.> He remembered the fleeting vision he'd had of her wearing a contamination suit, and walking through a biome filled with corpses. <But one of the worst was a containment breach involving unauthorized biotech research. Hundreds of research and development staff died and the whole thing stirred up a huge scandal. You resigned from your post as Director of Policy for Thorne after the investigation into the whole mess collapsed without ever working out who was responsible.>

<Luc, I sincerely hope you're not implying that *I* caused that breach.>

<Antonov said the message was for someone who'd done something they shouldn't have, a long time ago. The fact that he had me alter that particular record tells me that that *something* must have been the containment accident. And the first thing that happened after I'd altered that record was you first bringing me to Vanaheim, then sneaking me off to your own lab the instant I collapsed.>

<That's preposterous,> she scoffed. <How could I even know any such record was altered?>

<I figure my changing that record triggered a prearranged signal. It was a way for Antonov to contact you. So yes, I think you *were* the one responsible for that biotech accident, but after you covered it up, Antonov found out the truth and held you to ransom against the day he needed something from you. I also know there's no way I would have been able to alter that record without revealing my identity, and that's why you brought me into the investigation – not just because you were desperate to avoid being exposed, but so you could try and figure out how I fit into the scheme of things.>

<And what possible advantage could Antonov gain from all this?>

<Access to Vanaheim,> Luc replied, <through me, even after his physical death.>

<I should leave you there in that jungle to rot,> she hissed. <You have no real understanding of what took place on Thorne – it *was* an accident, but one that involved secret research carried out on behalf of an internal committee of the Eighty-Five. They made me take a bullet when they removed me from my post, not that it would have made a difference to Antonov. He thought I was little better than a butcher, same as you clearly do.>

<What I think about you doesn't matter. And I don't need to come to you to tell you what I know – Vasili found out the location of a secret data-cache belonging to Cheng, one containing the proof of Ariadna Placet's death – and Cripps murdered him for his efforts. And he would never have found that cache without Antonov's help.>

<You're not seriously suggesting Vasili and Antonov were *working* together?>

<Why not? *You* were collaborating with Antonov, whether you liked it or not. But Vasili found much more than he'd anticipated in that data-cache, enough to exonerate you and get me out of Vanaheim alive if I can find it. Which brings me to my next question – I need you to tell me how to find Vasili's island.>

Luc's fingers reached out and touched the edge of the book he'd taken from Maxwell's prison, still tucked inside his jacket. He'd save the revelations about the Founder Network for the moment.

<Vasili's island? Why?>

<There's something there I need to try and find.>

<Tell me what.>

<No, Zelia. I'm not sure if I trust you well enough to hand you all my cards.>

<Then that leaves us at an impasse,> she replied, <because as I think I already made clear, trust does not come easily to me.>

<Then think of this as a new and life-enhancing experience,> he responded, feeling his temper slip, <unless you really think you can dig your way out of this mess without my help.>

He waited a long time before her response came. So long, in fact, he was starting to think she had cut the connection.

<You're only going to get yourself killed if you go anywhere near Vasili's on your own, you understand that, don't you?> she said, when she finally came back.

Luc let out a breath he hadn't even realized he'd been holding. <I'll take that chance.>

<His house mechants will have been set to guard against intrusion. You can't fight them on your own.>

He waited in silence.

<Damn you, I . . .> She paused. <Fine, Gabion. You win. I'll give you the coordinates to his island. But I want you to wait at least an hour before you leave for there.>

<What are you up to, Zelia?>

<I'm not trying to stop you, Luc. But I meant it when I said you can't do this on your own. Just wait an hour before you leave for there – agreed?>

<One hour> he said, and cut the connection. Despite his misgivings, he knew she was almost certainly right.

Luc reached Vasili's island a little under two hours later, having travelled more than a third of the way around Vanaheim's circumference. The flier dipped back down through the cloud cover and dropped towards storm-tossed cliffs he had first set his eyes on just days before.

Words materialized in the air before him, floating against the dim light of the cockpit. UNAUTHORIZED APPROACH. PLEASE TURN BACK OR SEEK CLEARANCE.

Ignoring the warning, he guided the flier to a landing on a rocky beach by a cliff on one side of Vasili's island before disembarking. He squinted into bright sunlight, then looked around until he saw the steps cut into the cliff that he'd spotted on the way down.

Just before Luc reached the top of the cliff, something dark passed overhead. Immediately he froze, afraid he might have triggered the house security systems.

The dark shape resolved into a large craft, nearly twenty metres in length. It came to a halt over the roof of one of the buildings comprising Vasili's home, turning through one-third of its circumference before drifting a few metres to one side and settling down on a flat grassy area at the top of the cliff. The craft, he saw, had Zelia's livery painted on its hull.

Luc pulled himself up the last of the steps and found himself standing at one end of a gentle, boulder-strewn slope, leading upwards from the cliff towards the nearest of the buildings. As he watched, the rear of Zelia's ship slid open, and over a dozen of her walking dead experiments emerged unblinking into the sunlight, shambling down a ramp.

Luc's skin crawled at the sight of so many of them. He found he could make out subtle differences between each of them, although they all followed the same basic pattern: most of their primary sense organs had been replaced; all had pin-studded structures where their eyes should have been; all wore loose, filthy clothing little better than rags. But they were also, Luc noted with a mixture of alarm and relief, heavily armed.

He turned towards Vasili's home in time to see one of the house mechants come rocketing over a rooftop. Before he could so much as react, one of Zelia's monsters had fired off a shot. The mechant wobbled in the air, then span hard as a second shot hit home.

Zelia was creating a diversion.

He ran upslope towards a narrow alleyway separating two buildings and ducked down it, emerging a moment later into a smaller version of the courtyard Zelia's flier had brought him to on his first visit. He glanced behind himself to see Zelia's creations were now following him down the alleyway.

Two more mechants hovered into view above the courtyard,

their weapons swivelling in different directions. Luc saw an open door to his left and threw himself through it, into a gloomy, unlit hallway thick with dust, its walls damp and streaked with mould.

Explosive fire flared through the doorway behind him, and he made his way deeper into the building with considerable haste. He passed through room after room, each more desolate and ruined than the last, making it obvious that outside of the library and perhaps a few other rooms, Vasili had let most of the island's buildings fall into a state of considerable disrepair.

Luc came to a dirt-streaked window and peered out. A narrow strip of beach to his left was partly obscured by wild-growing bushes, but almost directly below his vantage point was a walled garden in far better condition than anything else he had seen so far, and a set of patio doors that were immediately familiar. By the look of it, the drop to the ground was no more than a couple of metres.

He looked around, then jogged into the next room to the left, finding a chair lying on its side. Carrying it back through, he slammed it against the window. The glass fractured and bowed outwards, but it took several more attempts before it finally shattered.

Salty air flowed in through the window, stirring up dust and dirt. Something hummed from one of the other rooms, sounding like it was coming nearer. Luc used his elbow to knock out a couple of shards of broken glass still sticking out of the frame, then scrambled over the window ledge, dropping down to land in the walled garden.

The landing knocked the wind out of him. Shots echoed over the rooftops, followed by the hum of another kind of weapon; light flashed in the air above a rooftop, and a thin trail of greasy dark smoke rose up, only to be rapidly dispersed by the wind. He pushed himself to his feet and staggered towards the patio doors leading into Vasili's library.

Vasili's body was long gone, as was the carpet his body had lain on, but the floor where he had fallen was still charred. Luc stared around the towering bookcases receding into the library's dim recesses with a feeling of hopelessness. The bookcases were arranged in orderly ranks, a dozen or so on each side of the library, with couches and low tables arranged in the empty space between.

There must have been thousands of books there – even more than Luc remembered from his previous visit. It hit him how little time he really had to try and find the book Maxwell had given to Vasili, assuming it hadn't simply been thrown out by the mechants charged with removing his corpse.

He heard the hum of an AG field through the closed door, beyond which lay the hall where he'd first met Zelia. Something then bumped against the door, and Luc instinctively ducked between two bookcases, making his way to a corner of the library that was hidden in deep shadow. His fingers itched for lack of a weapon of some kind.

The door swung open, and one of the house mechants drifted into the library. It came to a halt after a few metres, rotating on its axis until it faced Luc's hiding place.

Something silvery slid out of a recess in its belly.

Luc grabbed the nearest, heaviest volume he could get his hands on and threw it towards the mechant. He scored a direct hit, and the machine wobbled slightly in the air. Before the machine could recover, he ran past it, diving into the shadowy recesses of the bookcases on the opposite side of the library.

The mechant corrected itself and turned to follow. It fired as Luc dived into the narrow space between one end of a bookcase and the wall of the library, feeling heat sear the back of his neck.

He kept moving, running back towards the light streaming in through the patio doors, the wall to his left and ranks of book-cases to his right. Glancing behind himself, he saw through gaps in the open shelves that the mechant had passed between two of the tall bookcases. It had come to a halt, as if suffering a moment of indecision.

Luc dashed in between two bookcases, turning until he could see the mechant through more gaps between books. It didn't appear to have spotted him yet. Pressing his shoulders up against the bookcase behind him, he then kicked at the one before him, feeling it rock slightly on its base.

The bookcases were heavy, and therefore given to considerable inertia, but the one he'd just kicked was top-heavy, its lower shelves almost entirely empty.

Kicking at it again, he lifted both feet up, pressing them against the top-heavy bookcase, pushing hard, and then tried again, grunting with the effort.

The bookcase rocked away from him once more and tipped back towards him, before finally settling back into place with a thump. A few volumes slid noisily to the floor.

The mechant hummed and ticked as it swivelled this way and that, apparently waiting to see whether he might come out of hiding. He guessed Vasili had programmed it to protect the books, placing the machine at an impasse.

Luc drew on whatever reserves of energy he still had left and again kicked and pushed at the bookcase, yelling and cursing. It rocked away from him, and then back, yet more volumes crashing to the floor.

He kept pushing. This time, the bookcase kept going the other way, finally overbalancing and sending a torrent of books falling to the floor as it toppled against its nearest neighbour. That one, in turn, crashed into the next, and so on, until the mechant was caught in an avalanche of paper and wood.

Clouds of dust rose into the air. Luc pulled himself up from where he'd slid to the floor and heard the mechant buzzing as it tried to fight its way out. It was, however, clearly trapped.

He turned towards the patio doors in time to see another mechant come crashing through them, sending splinters of glass flying everywhere. It aimed its weapons at him and Luc froze, expecting to die at any moment.

There was a sound like a muffled grunt and the mechant spun, apparently out of control. A second grunt slammed the mechant against the ceiling. It fired wildly, a beam of energy cutting a burning swathe across one wall, nearly blinding Luc with its intensity. He dropped to the floor, heard a third grunt, and when he looked back up, bright spots obscured his vision.

By the time he could see again, he found that the mechant had fallen to the floor, smoke trailing from several holes in its shell. One of Zelia's monstrosities stood at the entrance to the hall, the weapon it had used to down the mechant gripped in both hands.

The creature looked over at him, its head twitching from side to side as if it had difficulty focusing on him. A brief burst of static issued from its mouth-grille, and it returned its attention to the fallen mechant.

Luc staggered to his feet, only slightly less afraid of Zelia's machine-man than he had been of the mechant. He could hear the asthmatic rattle of its breath.

The library was a wreck, half of its bookcases collapsed and innumerable volumes scattered everywhere. Luc stared around himself, again feeling a fool for thinking he stood any chance of finding Maxwell's missing book. Surely the house mechants would have alerted someone that Vasili's home had been invaded?

But he still had to try.

Think. Heading for the couches close by the patio doors, he tried hard to picture Vasili's body just as it had been when he had first encountered it. The scorch marks on the floor of the library made that act of visualization a great deal easier than it might otherwise have been.

He squatted down where Vasili's body had been, staring around himself until his gaze alighted on a still-upright bookcase within easy reach. When he had suffered the seizure that had seen him spirited away by Zelia, he had leaned against it for support. He noticed for the first time that the bookcase, like all the rest of them, stood on legs, meaning a narrow gap of a few centimetres separated the lowest of its shelves from the floor.

It couldn't be that easy. Could it?

Dropping down until his cheek was pressed against the cold

flagstones, Luc peered into the darkened space beneath the book-case.

He could see something, wedged underneath. A book.

His fingers soon worked their way into the gap beneath the bookcase, seeking out the nearest edge of the trapped volume, but in his desperation to get hold of it, he wound up pushing it slightly further out of reach.

Pausing, he took a deep breath and tried again, working much more carefully this time. Teasing the book around until he could just about grasp the edge of the book's cover between two fingers, it took him another minute or so to gradually slide it back out from where it had become wedged.

Clutching the book to his chest, he was almost giddy with joy. Despite the scorch marks blackening the spine, he could still read the title: *A History of the Tian Di*, by Javier Maxwell. It must have slid out of sight, or been accidentally pushed beneath the book-case when Vasili's mechants had removed his body.

A shadow loomed over Luc; he rolled onto his back in a panic, thinking he was about to come under attack from another mechant. But instead he saw Zelia's creature standing over him, its rifle gripped in both hands like a club and held high over its head.

Luc rolled out of the way just as the creature swung the rifle down in a long arc, the breath rattling from its grille mingled with static that almost sounded like words.

Scrambling to his feet, he tried to rip the rifle from the crea-ture's grip before it could either take another swing or, worse, try and shoot him. They struggled, rapid bursts of static emerging from the creature's throat. But its movements were slow and ponderous, and it took relatively little effort to tear the rifle from its grasp.

Luc staggered back and fell onto one of the couches, then aimed the rifle at the machine-man, pulling the trigger. The creature clat-tered back against a bookcase before sliding to the floor, half its head sheared away, the buzzing from its mouth-grille diminishing into silence.

For a few seconds all he could do was lie there on the couch, panting. Zelia had tried to double-cross him, letting him find what he was looking for so she could then steal it from him.

The rifle's readout told him it still had several slugs remaining. Standing back up, he slung it over his shoulder by a strap before making his way through the hall adjoining the library to the court-yard. There he found several more of Zelia's monstrosities waiting, and they moved towards him as soon as they saw him.

He ducked back inside the hall and slammed the door shut, then glanced to one side and saw a heavy-looking table nearby. Grabbing hold of one edge of the table, he tried to drag it across the door but it proved too heavy, so he went around its far end and managed, not without considerable effort, to finally push it into place.

For a moment he reeled, sweat burning his forehead, and listened to the muffled bursts of static from the other side of the door as Zelia's minions tried to force their way through. They'd manage it soon enough, but not, he hoped, before he had himself a good head-start.

Looking around, he spotted another way out of the hall, and a few seconds later found himself back outside, in another narrow alleyway running between two buildings. He headed left until he came to a low wall running along the top of the cliff, below which lay the beach.

Following the wall back around to where Zelia's heavy-lifter was still parked on a slope, he found she had left only one of her monstrosities behind to guard it. It grunted static as it saw him, and came shuffling forward.

Luc made for the steps leading back down to the beach, the rifle still slung over his shoulder, and sprinted for the waiting flier. The hatch hissed shut behind him as he boarded, and he took off immediately, driving hard towards the clouds lying low over the water.

EIGHTEEN

Jacob had seen such wonders in the past few days. Following his theft of the Founder artefact, he had hidden his flier in a kind of space-borne favela, populated by creatures that constituted a strange hybrid of the organic and inorganic. He had seen swarms of insect-like mechants moving at will through this orbital slum, engaged in what might have been warfare, or some intricate mating ritual.

Despite the traumatic damage Jacob had done to Darwin's world-wheel, it remained intact. His intent, after all, had not been to destroy the world-wheel, but to create a sufficient distraction that he could make his escape undetected. Even so, the aftermath of his actions had proved to be spectacular; Jacob had seen vast chunks of machinery and the shattered ruins of living-spaces burning as they tumbled down from orbit, sending up great clouds of dust and rock when they impacted on Darwin's surface, thereby generating a second crisis for the Coalition authorities.

He did not have long to wait before a Special Envoy from the Tian Di, only recently arrived from Temur, made his way up to orbit via a prearranged signal and allowed Jacob to board his flier. There, Jacob took from the Envoy a case designed to be entirely opaque to deep scans, and placed the stolen artefact inside it.

The Envoy did not struggle as Jacob cut his throat. He held the man as he died, then dumped his body into the vacuum.

After that, it was a simple matter of piloting the flier down to one of Darwin's largest conurbations, a rippling tide of silver and grey spreading out from one of the world-wheel's spokes. He touched down next to a residential building neighbouring a Gate Array serving half a dozen Coalition worlds. By the time he rendezvoused with the other Special Envoys waiting there, his face had undergone a series of subtle alterations that included changes in his skin tone and eye colour, in order to more closely resemble the man whom he had replaced.

A few of the Tian Di Envoys greeted him with uncomfortable or even hostile glances. All of them were aware in advance that their new companion would be required to make a necessary sacrifice, even if they were not permitted to know the exact details of that sacrifice. It was clear to Jacob, however, that a few of them did not approve of his presence. He made a mental note of which ones appeared particularly disturbed by the circumstances of his arrival for future reference. It might prove necessary to terminate some or all of the Envoys at some later date, to reduce the risk of his mission being compromised.

A few hours passed before they all departed for the nearby Gate Array, now equipped with a new transfer gate connecting to a station in orbit around Temur. On their way there Jacob saw squid-like creatures swarming down a tunnel apparently formed from the air, broad wing-like fronds wafting around their massive bodies. Their enormous dark eyes swept across the huddled crowd of Envoys, and as they passed out of sight and into the Array, Jacob found himself wondering how easy it might be for some truly alien species to hide undetected amongst the Coalition's citizens. The thought was enough to make him shudder with horror.

Jacob understood then that the pale, drawn faces of the Envoys accompanying him were not entirely due to his sudden appearance amongst them. Their time here in the Coalition had been enough to reduce the majority of them to a state of numb shock.

They boarded a train that would carry them through the transfer gate and back to Temur, a journey of light-years in less than a moment. After that would come a short trip down from orbit, and then Jacob would journey to Vanaheim, in order to present his prize to Father Cheng in person.

And after *that*, a new age would dawn for the Tian Di. Jacob knew only a very few would ever know the nature of his mission or even his name, but he bore the burden of anonymity gladly. He would happily die unknown and unloved, so long as it was in the service of his beloved Father Cheng.

NINETEEN

The flier juddered as it accelerated upwards, soon rising above a sea of clouds that dwindled beneath it. Luc closed his eyes and let his head sink back against his seat before letting out a rush of shaky breath.

I should have realized Zelia might turn on me.

But then again, Zelia had been right about one thing: he would never have got past Vasili's house mechants without her help, even if the only reason she had done so was in order to betray him.

Pulling Vasili's book out of the netting where he had secured it, he weighed it in his hands before opening it, placing his fingers against its cool, faintly metallic pages.

He sat still for several seconds, his breath gradually evening out. Navigating the memories and other information encoded within the book was far from intuitive. He had flashes once more of Vasili's last moments before his death, including, he noted with grim satisfaction, a glimpse of Cripps' own face as he entered Vasili's home. But he could sense other information buried in the pages, in essence almost indistinguishable from his own half-remembered thoughts . . .

He let go of the book with a gasp, blinking and shaking his head, and then laughed. He had them: the coordinates of Father Cheng's secret data-cache, hidden in orbit above Vanaheim.

All he had to do now was feed them into the navigational systems via his lattice, and the flier would take him there immediately.

The cache might as easily have been hidden somewhere far more inaccessible, such as the Red Palace back in Liebenau. In that case, Luc would have been forced to admit defeat. But to keep it so close to home would, he suspected, have invited a greater risk of discovery. Whereas if Vanaheim's orbital space was as clogged with junk as Maxwell had claimed, there probably wasn't a better place for Eighty-Fivers to hide their dirty laundry.

The same light that Zelia had used to make contact with him following his escape from Maxwell's prison began flashing once more. Luc stared at it for a few moments, then ignored it, setting the flier on a new course.

Before long, he was on his way to high orbit.

An hour or so later, the flier's external sensors gave Luc a view of what at first appeared to be a zero-gee junkyard. Much of what he could see had been jury-rigged from discarded fuel tanks and temporary accommodations, and looked it. But a query to the station's datanet – unexpectedly still functioning – reassured him that although it was entirely abandoned, having apparently served for some decades as a kind of orbital storage depot, it was still pressurized. At least he wouldn't have to suit up.

The flier thumped gently against the station's one airlock, followed by a rumbling hiss on the other side of the hatch. The hatch unfolded a moment later, revealing a claustrophobically narrow metal passageway. Long-dormant emergency lights flickered into life, tinting the interior of the station with a soft red glow.

Luc made his way along the passageway, propelling himself along with his fingertips in the zero gravity, until he found himself inside something that looked like it had started life as a cargo flier. The interior of the flier had been stripped and converted into a makeshift storage depot; he could see a few dozen plastic crates still lashed to a bulkhead to prevent them from floating away, while an ancient-looking fabricant was mounted on a wall, printed machine-parts still stacked on a plastic pallet beside it. Three more passageways radiated outwards from this central point, giving access to the pressurized fuel tanks that constituted much of the station's bulk.

Luc carefully picked his way over to the lashed-together crates and pulled himself into a sitting position next to one. Unzipping his jacket, he again withdrew the book Maxwell had given Vasili, slipped one arm through a cable securing one of the crates, and then shook the book open, placing it on his lap before opening it carefully and touching the revealed page.

Vasili hit the auto-mechanism for the airlock and listened to the distant hiss of air as the ancient satellite re-pressurized for the first time in years. He made his way down a narrow passageway, before emerging into a makeshift bay.

Here, he studied his surroundings with an engineer's eyes. The station had been designed to be nothing more than a temporary structure, a pressurized orbital dock where mechants could store materials for later use. After that, the station should have been disassembled and destroyed.

But in this case, the station had remained intact. It had even been carefully maintained, though you couldn't tell from the outside. If it had been truly abandoned, Vasili knew, it would long since have fallen out of orbit and plunged into Vanaheim's atmosphere.

He moved deeper into the station until he came to a maintenance port, a cramped alcove tucked away at the far end of a branching passageway, where an interface panel newer and considerably more up to date than anything else aboard the station could be accessed. Pulling himself into a narrow seat, he touched a hand to a virtual panel.

Verification took just a moment, and he was in.

Luc opened his eyes and pulled himself loose from the cable. It took him just a minute or so to make his way down the same branching passageway and pull himself into the same alcove Vasili had found.

A virtual panel shimmered into existence the moment he sat down. It didn't look like anything much out of the ordinary, little more than a standard interface for the station's AI systems. But then, Cheng would hardly have gone out of his way to advertise the presence of his secret data-cache.

Screw it.

Luc reached out and touched the panel. In response, something slid out from the alcove next to his right hand, a metal bar that had also appeared when Vasili had been here before him.

Luc next reached out and gripped the bar. The metal was cold to the touch. His fingers tingled slightly with the contact, and he guessed the bar operated on the same principles as the lattice-enabled circuitry embedded in Maxwell's books.

A sudden burst of data washed over him, and it didn't take much navigating to realize the station was, indeed, one of the many secret repositories in which the Temur Council maintained copies of their backups. There were undoubtedly other such repositories scattered all across Vanaheim and in orbit.

He was only peripherally aware of the station around him, its bulkheads creaking softly, as he navigated further through a blizzard of data, centuries-worth of instantiation backups and dirty little secrets.

Wait. There was something there, tugging at his awareness. He focused on it, and . . .

All of a sudden, something enormous landed inside Luc's skull.

It started as a feeling of pressure building inside his head, then a flurry of names and places and experiences. His body began to shake, his teeth clattering together, but he couldn't prise his hand away from the metal bar.

Lines of fire criss-crossed his skull, forming a cage around the tender flesh of his brain. The cage grew rapidly smaller, sending him into paroxysms of pain.

Cheng booby-trapped the cache.

Luc convulsed, his head banging off one wall of the alcove, and yet his hand remained locked to the metal bar.

Some part of him dimly realized then that it wasn't a booby-trap, but another seizure, triggered by the thunderous tide of information now flowing into his overwhelmed mind.

The pain became overwhelming, unbearable. He tried to scream, the sound dying in his throat and emerging instead as a thin rattle. The station's bulkheads continued to creak around him like an old man laughing asthmatically.

Fire raged through his skull. His back arched and he convulsed with sufficient force that his hand was finally twisted free of the metal bar, sending him tumbling in the zero gravity like a discarded rag doll.

The pain gradually began to recede. Luc curled into a ball, pale and shivering, and waited until the worst was over. After that he dragged himself back through to the central hub, where he collapsed, too weak to move any further.

Losing all sense of time, he swam in and out of consciousness, and only barely registered a dull clang, followed by the hiss of an airlock.

A figure loomed into sight over Luc as he lay shivering by the pallet of crates. 'Lucky I came looking for you,' said Zelia, kneeling down so he could see her face.

A while later, Luc sat on a stool bolted to the floor of a utilitarian-looking living space in another part of the station, nursing what felt like the mother of all hangovers. A desk, sink, and a small cubby-hole for personal possessions were arranged around him with the easy disregard for conventional notions of up or down typical of every space habitat Luc had ever been in. The mechant Zelia had used to carry him from the hub waited by the entrance.

'I don't understand you,' said Luc, his voice still weak. 'First you try to kill me, then you come here and save my life.'

She shook her head. 'I wasn't trying to kill you, Luc. I just wanted to know what it was you were trying to find that was so important.'

'And having that thing take a swing at my head wasn't trying to kill me?'

She looked genuinely embarrassed. 'I just wanted it to take that book from you.' She glanced down at it, now tucked under one of her arms. 'I don't like having things kept from me, Luc. You were breaking the terms of our arrangement.'

Luc wanted to laugh, but it still hurt too much. 'Believe me,' he said, 'it isn't going to be much use to you. You couldn't possibly access the data hidden inside it without Maxwell's decryption key, and that died with him.'

Her face coloured slightly. 'Then what the hell use was it to *you?*'

He tapped the side of his head. 'Apparently I have an unfair advantage in that regard. I don't need a key.'

'I know what you've got lodged inside your skull gives you an edge, but don't make the mistake of underestimating *me*.'

'At least promise me you're not going to try to beat me to death a second time.'

'Look – maybe I overreacted, back there.'

This time, he did manage to laugh.

'It's just that when you flew off like that,' she said, 'headed for Vasili's, I felt like I was losing control of the situation.'

Losing control of me, you mean. 'You've managed to hang on to Vanaheim's security networks?' he asked.

She smiled triumphantly. 'Of course. Otherwise I would never have been able to track you here.'

'What about Cheng or Cripps or any of the rest of them? Will they know we've been here?'

'Only if they manage to grab control of the networks from me again. Things are moving fast, Luc. Javier Maxwell's murder was only the beginning. Now Cheng's claiming Black Lotus have penetrated the Council itself, starting with me. People are starting to take sides.'

'Sounds like a war's going on down there.'

'A war is pretty much what it is,' she agreed. 'But if I lose control of the networks again, we'll also lose most of our advantage.' She flipped the half-burned book open and flicked through its pages. 'What exactly was in here that turned out to be so important?'

He realized, having found what he'd come looking for, there was little point in hiding things from her any more. 'Coordinates,' he explained, 'for this station.' He glanced around. 'And Vasili's last memories from just before he died.'

She stared at him. 'How . . . ?'

He told her what he had learned so far from Maxwell's books. She listened, hand over her mouth, eyes wide.

Nausea gripped him as he finished. Trying to push himself up from the stool, he saw the cabin tumble around him.

'Easy,' said Zelia, grabbing hold of him.

He let her guide him towards a wall-recess by the sink that contained a thin plastic mattress, which she pushed him down onto.

'Your nervous system must have suffered one hell of a shock,' she said, looking down at him.

'It's not safe here,' he mumbled.

'If anyone's on the way to this station,' she assured him, 'I'll know a long time before they arrive, don't you worry. Right now this is probably safer than a lot of places on Vanaheim.'

He lay back against the mattress, pulling an elbow over his face. 'The data-cache hidden on this station. Have you accessed it yet?'

'Not yet, no. You?'

'Yes, just in the last moments before the seizure hit.'

'Where is it?'

He told her where she could find the access terminal. She disappeared, her mechant trailing after her, then came back several minutes later, her expression troubled.

'I don't know just what happened after you got here,' she said, 'but if there was ever any data there, it's gone.'

'Gone?' he asked, looking up at her. 'How is that possible?'

'The backups were probably set to self-delete if they were accessed by anyone the systems didn't recognize. Anything else would have been deleted right along with them.'

'And that's why it didn't wipe itself when Vasili was here?'

She nodded. 'He had all the access privileges of an Eighty-Fiver, and you didn't, protocols or not.'

Luc nodded, and realized he was feeling better than he had just moments before. Moving cautiously, he pulled himself upright, and found that most of the dizziness and nausea had now been replaced by a deep thirst and hunger.

Zelia watched as he pulled himself out of the alcove, hunting through several drawers until he found some protein bars that were probably long, long past the point where they were still edible. He ate them anyway.

'So tell me then,' Zelia asked as he tore the bars apart and shovelled them into his mouth, 'did you manage to get anything at all from the cache?'

He nodded wearily. 'I did. Why, what's the plan? I tell you everything I know, and then you kill me?'

To his surprise, she looked hurt. 'You talk about me like I'm a monster. Part of a man I once loved is still alive inside you.'

He stared at her. 'You and Antonov? But you were never . . .'

But then he realized how wrong he was. She was there, in Antonov's memories, rising to the surface of his own thoughts as if he had always known. It felt like walking into a house he'd always lived in, and finding a room he never knew existed.

She stared at him, her eyes becoming round. 'But you *must* have known,' she said. 'You have his memories. You must . . .' her voice trailed off.

He remembered he had dreamt of making love to her, that night she had data-ghosted into his home. Everything about it had felt real, far more like an actual memory than a mere dream, and now the reason was obvious: it *was* a memory - but Antonov's, rather than his own.

'I think maybe I suspected,' he said.

'It was a long time ago,' she said, close enough to him in the cramped quarters that he could smell her skin. 'A very long time ago, even before he met Ariadna. But we . . . saw things differently. There were things we left unsaid, things I wanted to say to him but never could.'

'I had no idea.'

She drew back slightly, peering at him with curiosity. 'How much is there left of him inside you, would you say?'

He shook his head. 'I'm not sure. Maybe just a little.'

'But I saw the way you looked just now, when I told you we had once been lovers. You looked like you remembered something.'

'I did,' he admitted. 'Just not my *own* memories.'

'And he still . . . speaks to you?'

'Sometimes.'

'But does he hear things?' she asked haltingly. 'Does he understand what's going on around you – around him?'

Luc thought about it. 'I think he does, yeah.'

Just for a second the mask slipped, and Luc saw a part of de Almeida he never had before, vulnerable and soft and yielding. Despite his fear of her, the sight and smell of her commingled with Antonov's own memories until they were very nearly impossible to distinguish.

Some instinct made him reach out to her. He half-expected her to react with anger, but instead she responded with unexpected hunger. Their mouths mashed together, Luc's hands curling around the back of her neck to grip her by the hair, pulling her close enough that he could feel her heartbeat thrumming through her chest.

She stood, first pulling off her jacket, and then her thin blouse, revealing small, high breasts, before sliding into the narrow alcove containing the mattress. He followed, sliding one hand under her back, but then she locked her ankles around his waist and flipped him around in the zero gravity until she was straddling him.

He reached up to cup her breasts with his hands, eliciting a soft moan from her, while she reached down to his waist, tugging at his belt.

Soon he was struggling out of his clothes with some difficulty, unsurprising given the exceedingly cramped nature of the alcove. Zelia lifted herself up and out of the way, taking the opportunity to wriggle out of the rest of her clothes before again straddling him, her breath coming in small, nervous gasps.

Luc could feel his erection pulsing against her belly. Taking hold of her hips, he lifted her slightly, as she reached down between her legs and manoeuvred him inside her.

He started to move. Zelia gripped him hard with her knees, grinding herself against him, the fingernails of one hand digging into his chest while she kept the other pressed flat against the ceiling of the alcove. Luc held off as long as he could, holding her tight with both hands, her gasps becoming shorter and higher-pitched.

Somewhere in the back of his thoughts, he could hear Antonov laughing.

'Now,' she gasped, her voice ragged. 'Please.'

He looked up at her naked form with fascination. Her skin glistened with perspiration, while her long dark hair had come undone from the loose knot she'd had it in behind her head. It floated around her face like something alive. Her back arched in tangent with his own, increasingly urgent movements until, finally, he came.

'Wait,' she hissed. 'Don't move.'

Holding still, he watched as she rocked her hips back and forth with a gentle, barely detectable motion. Then her mouth opened wide and she let out a tiny, bird-like cry before pulling herself down and forward, letting her head rest against his chest. He felt himself slide back out of her.

They lay there together for what felt like a long time. Almost without realizing, Luc pictured Eleanor as she had been in Maxwell's prison, side by side with Bailey Cripps, but found he felt nothing whatsoever.

'The question,' he finally managed to say after an indeterminate amount of time had passed, 'is whether you were fucking me, or him.'

He felt her fingernails stroke against one shoulder as she brought her head back up to regard him. 'Both, I think,' she said with a faint smile.

'You said that there were things you'd wanted to say to him, but never did.'

She was silent for a minute before answering. 'I wanted to tell him that I'm sorry.'

He twisted his head up slightly to look down at her. 'Sorry for what?'

'Betraying him,' she said quietly, then dropped her head back down against his chest.

Luc frowned. 'Zelia . . . what exactly happened between you two?'

He felt her move into a slightly different position. 'Does it matter? We saw things differently, and I was stupid and foolish and inexperienced enough to let that matter to me more than it should have. And you know what the worst thing was?'

'What?'

'He forgave me.'

He felt her tears dampen his chest.

'But you still wanted to tell him you were sorry.'

'Once I realized what he'd done to you, I knew there'd never be another chance.'

For the next few minutes, Luc was content to remain where he was.

'When I was in Maxwell's prison,' he said at last, 'he showed me things that made me re-evaluate what I thought I knew about Antonov. But what I saw when I opened the data-cache here on this station made me realize my whole life isn't worth a damn unless I do everything I can to finish what Antonov started.'

She sat up and regarded him with eyes wide. 'Did you even *hear* what you just said?'

'Everything's different now, Zelia.'

'Different how?'

'Because of what I learned from that data-cache.'

'So you *did* get something from it.'

'Father Cheng,' said Luc, 'is planning to destroy Benares.'

She blinked as if she hadn't quite heard him right. 'What?'

'I saw it all, through his own eyes.' He let out a small, soft laugh at the thought of just how much of his life had been wasted chasing the wrong people. 'Do you know Cheng sent agents all the way to Coalition space, on ships that took decades to get there? He wanted them to find some artefact the Coalition had recovered from the Founder Network, so he could use it to wipe out every living thing on Benares.'

Zelia stared at him. 'But . . . why Benares? What possible benefit is there to doing any such thing?'

'Apart from it being a hotbed of anti-Council sentiment? Once he's dealt with Benares, he's going to blame Black Lotus for its destruction. He'll say the Coalition supplied them with advanced weapons technology, but they screwed up, destroying Benares by accident instead of Temur.'

Her expression now shifted from indignant disbelief to outright horror. 'Please tell me you're lying,' she said.

'After that,' said Luc, 'he'll close down the Darwin gate forever, declare martial law throughout the Tian Di, and use the Sandoz to assume total power prior to dissolving the Council. And then there won't be a Thousand Emperors of the Tian Di – just one.'

Zelia stared past him as she worked through the implications. 'He's trying to turn the clock back, to the days of the Schism.'

'That's not even all of it,' Luc continued. 'Cheng's been playing a very, *very* long-term strategy ever since the idea of Reunification was first mooted. Once he realized he had no choice but to go along with it, he started laying the groundwork for a plan that wouldn't just wipe out Benares, but would have the whole of the Tian Di *begging* him to stay in power.'

'What else did you find?'

'More than you ever wanted to know.' No wonder Vasili had been so frightened. 'Back at that funeral service, Ruy Borges came up to you, and mentioned a rumour about Cheng being in negotiations with the Coalition. Remember?'

Zelia nodded. 'Well, they weren't just rumours,' he continued. 'Before Cripps murdered him, Javier Maxwell told me the reason the Coalition Ambassador had been to see him was to prevent a war with the Coalition – and it has to do with a second entrance to the Founder Network, discovered decades ago, here in the Tian Di.'

'No.' Zelia shook her head. 'I don't believe it.'

'Ever since, Cheng's been sending teams of Sandoz in through that entrance, to carry out secret explorations of the Network.' He shrugged. 'We always knew there were gates leading inside the Network scattered all over time and space. It's hardly surprising that Cheng, or exploration teams working on his behalf, stumbled across another in one of our own systems.'

'I would have . . .' her words drifted off.

'You'd have known about it?' he guessed. 'Are you absolutely sure about that?'

She didn't meet his eyes.

'Cheng even kept it secret from most of the Eighty-Five,' Luc continued, 'restricting the knowledge to a very few members of his inner circle. Vasili was as in the dark about all of this as you or anyone else, at least until Antonov persuaded him to come here and open that data-cache. And that's where Ariadna Placet comes into it.'

'In what way?'

'She found out about the secret entrance to the Network, and Cheng had her murdered before she could tell anyone else what she knew.'

She shook her head in dismay. 'Poor Sevgeny. So the crazy son of a bitch wasn't really that crazy after all.'

Luc sighed and slid out from under her, and began to pull his clothes back on. He turned to look at her, still naked, and felt a touch of amazement at what had just taken place between them.

'But where is this Founder Network gate?'

'It's in the Thorne system, Zelia. Cheng found it while you were still its Director of Policy.'

Her face grew fractionally paler. 'Go on.'

'After you were replaced by Ariadna Placet, she figured out there was a cover-up, and was murdered on Cheng's direct orders to stop her telling anyone else.'

Zelia stared at him, clearly outraged. Luc finished dressing, then heard a thump as she picked up one of her boots and threw it towards a wall. It bounced back, somersaulting through the air before rebounding from the ceiling.

Luc reached out and managed to catch it, handing it back to her.

'I hope you weren't throwing that at me,' he said, 'because if you were, you're a lousy shot.'

'All right,' she said at last, her voice flat, 'I believe you. I don't *want* to, but I do. Except there's one thing that doesn't make much sense to me – if Cheng really had access to the Founder Network for all this time, why bother sending agents to the Coalition to recover Founder artefacts, if he can just go and get them at the source? And after going all that way, how's he going to bring them back to . . .'

She halted and looked at him, then closed her eyes. 'The new transfer gate.'

'That's just about the only reason he agreed to let the Coalition bring the transfer gate here,' Luc confirmed. 'As for why he's sending agents to Darwin, the part of the Network he's been able to access was cleared out long ago by some other long-gone race. He hasn't been able to find anything he could use as a weapon.'

'Dear God,' said Zelia. 'Cheng's data-cache told you all *this*?'

'Yes,' he said triumphantly. 'But Cheng didn't place it here – Cripps did.'

'What?'

'Maxwell told me before he died that some of the Eighty-Five sometimes hid sensitive or incriminating information in his library, against the day that Cheng might turn against them. Cripps is Cheng's right-hand man, but I think he knew the day might come when he knew too much for Cheng to want to keep him alive.

He placed the data-cache here, without Cheng's knowledge, against the day he could use it for a bargaining chip. But he wasn't quite clever enough.'

'Meaning, Antonov found out about it?'

Luc nodded. 'The cache might have self-deleted once I'd accessed it, but the evidence is still around, even if it is locked up inside my head. When Cheng first sent those agents to Darwin, it was only intended to be a backup plan in case his reconnaissance teams failed to find an appropriate weapon inside the Founder Network.'

'But he never did find anything, so now the backup plan is the *main* plan.'

'Which works out better for Cheng, since this way he can lay the blame for Benares on the Coalition as well as Black Lotus.'

'We need to talk to Ambassador Sachs,' she said, suddenly decisive, 'and tell him everything you just told me. Maybe his own people can find some way to stop this from their side of the gate.'

Luc recalled childhood nightmares, of witnessing Benares consumed by flames. He had decided not to tell her what else he had discovered; that everything Antonov and, later, Maxwell had told him was true – Cheng really had ordered the Benares raid that changed his life, in order to discredit Black Lotus.

And now, with Antonov out of the way, there was nothing to stop Cheng from delivering the final coup de grâce to a world that had offered nothing but resistance since the beginning of his rule.

'The only problem,' he said, 'is that we don't know whether one of Cheng's agents hasn't already brought an artefact back from Darwin.'

Zelia nodded, as if to herself. 'Perhaps I should go and find Cripps and ask him that question myself.'

'What? How could you—'

'Just leave it to me,' she snapped, a wild look in her eyes. 'That man's had a reckoning coming to him for a long, long time, and I want to be the one who finally gets to deliver it to him.'

She got up and started to pull on her own clothes.

'Listen,' said Luc, suddenly feeling awkward. 'I . . .'

'I know what you're going to say,' she replied without meeting his eyes. 'It was just something that happened. Besides . . . it wasn't really about you.'

'It was about Antonov.'

'I'm sorry.'

He shrugged. 'Don't be.'

'Look,' she said, 'maybe you should stay up here on this station until it's all over. There's air, and even if there's not enough food, I can send another flier with supplies up to you. At least until all the fighting is over.'

'No, Zelia. I'm not going to let you cut me out of the picture again.'

Her face coloured. 'Damn it, Luc, don't you understand? This isn't your war any more. Whatever Cheng or Cripps have done, you still serve the Council, and that includes me. Wait here until it's safe for you to pass through the Hall of Gates, then let me and the rest of the Council take care of this.'

'And once I'm home, what do I do?' he asked her, 'wait until I die from another seizure?'

'I told you already I'd help you—'

'No,' he reminded her, 'you said you'd *try* and help me, but I don't think you have any idea what you're doing. Antonov told me Ambassador Sachs has some way to save both of us. I'm going to find the Ambassador and tell him everything I just told you, and maybe this time he *will* help me.'

De Almeida looked more tired than angry when she next spoke. 'Damn you, Gabion—'

He stared at her adamantly. Her nostrils flared, and for a moment he thought she might do something, perhaps attack him or hit him or, worse, order her mechant to do it for her. But in the next moment something changed in her demeanour, as if all the fight had gone out of her. For a moment, she looked all of her many, many years.

'Then go find Sachs, if you must,' she said, her tone weary. 'Do you even know where to look?'

Luc checked. 'If things are as bad as you say they are down there, I'm going to guess he's probably back on the *Sequoia*. And you?'

'I'll take a look at the list of Tian Di envoys who've travelled back through the transfer gate from Darwin. It's possible one of them could have brought something back they weren't supposed to.'

'What happened to you, Zelia?' Luc asked her. 'You, and the rest of the Council. What went wrong?'

'Hang around a couple more centuries,' she said, 'and you can answer the question yourself.'

Luc turned away from her then, making his way back through the station to the flier that had brought him there.

TWENTY

Any nagging doubts Luc had about the Coalition Ambassador's location slipped away once he arrived in the vicinity of the *Sequoia*, and found it under attack from Sandoz forces.

An image of the *Sequoia* floated before him in the cockpit of his flier, rendered in real-time. One of its several domed arboretums dotted around its exterior had been torn open and exposed to vacuum, and as a result a glittering halo of debris and frozen atmosphere now surrounded the station, while here and there attack-pods of Sandoz design had locked onto the hull like so many fat metal leeches.

Something shot out of the darkness as Luc watched, striking the station's primary hub and sending more glittering fragments spinning outwards. A dark shape silhouetted against the planet below proved, upon magnification, to be a Sandoz orbital platform, emitting a steady stream of heavily armed mechants making their way across the intervening gap.

Luc watched all of this with a terrible sinking feeling, debating whether it might be wiser to turn back. But if he could see the Sandoz forces attacking the *Sequoia*, then they undoubtedly could see his flier decelerating towards the station on an approach vector. Even if he chose to turn back, by the time he managed to accelerate away they would already be on his tail, and the chase would be as good as over.

That left him with only one choice: to go forward. He maintained his course, despite the awful tightness in his throat, and the growing conviction that at any moment kinetic slugs would rip his little craft to shreds.

In the last moments before the flier finally docked with the *Sequoia*, Luc allowed himself to believe he might actually escape the assault unharmed. He was rewarded with a stream of fire that scored the flier's hull, shattering most of its external sensors.

For several seconds more than was good for his mental health, Luc found himself cut off from the outside world, unable to verify if the craft had even made it to the relative safety of the station's dock. Then the emergency systems activated, and the flier informed him in cool machine tones that the external air pressure had equalized, and he could now disembark.

On exiting the flier, he briefly surveyed its cracked and burned hull with dismay. He didn't need an expert to tell him it would very likely disintegrate if he tried using it to escape back down to Vanaheim's surface. If he was ever going to get back off the *Sequoia* again, he'd have to find some other mode of transport.

On the other hand, if the Ambassador was hiding somewhere on the *Sequoia*, there must be a second flier somewhere. He made haste, exiting the dock and moving down the station's long, central hub as fast as he was able.

Luc didn't get far before a low, rattling boom travelled the length of the hub. After a moment, he found himself drifting slowly to one wall. Whatever had just hit the *Sequoia* had pushed it into a slow spin that he suspected was outside of its design limitations.

His bowels turned to water when the walls and bulkheads around him screamed in protest, and he felt the irrational yet nearly overwhelming urge to turn back. But after another minute the station's gyroscopic systems appeared to reassert themselves, halting the spin. He pushed on, travelling along the length of the hub with the help of rungs embedded into its cylindrical walls.

A thin wail echoed down the hub, and a breeze tugged at him. Grabbing onto a rung, he realized it was getting harder to breathe. Up ahead, he saw an emergency pressure-field pop into existence.

And flicker out again.

And back again.

Clearly, the station was in bad need of maintenance.

In that same moment, several mechants, all with Sandoz livery, came rocketing out of a side passageway. Luc froze for a moment, then looked around for some kind of hiding place.

More mechants came hurtling after the first group, these ones lacking markings of any kind. They engaged the Sandoz mechants in a blur of clashing steel and directed-energy fire.

Luc scrambled for the meagre shelter of a flange that joined two sections of the hub, then cautiously peered over the top of the flange, watching through splayed fingers as the carapace of a Sandoz mechant turned first orange, then white, before exploding messily and sending molten steel and plastic spraying in all directions. He ducked back down, squeezing his eyes shut.

The next time he looked, Ambassador Sachs had appeared from the side passageway. Most of the Sandoz mechants had been destroyed, but the remainder appeared to sight Luc when he popped his head up, accelerating towards him.

Then something very remarkable happened.

One of the Sandoz mechants aiming straight towards Luc halted abruptly, its limbs weaving spastically for a moment before it began to drift, out of control, striking the flange behind which Luc hid before rebounding and drifting back towards the centre of the hub.

The same thing happened within moments to each of the two other surviving Sandoz mechants. They span out of control, apparently lifeless.

Luc stared over at the Ambassador, who gestured to him to come out of hiding. His unmarked mechants set about finishing off the enemy machines with their energy weapons.

Somehow, Luc knew Sachs had stopped the mechants with his lattice. He wondered if anyone in the Tian Di realized just how powerful the Ambassador apparently was.

'Over here, Mr Gabion,' Sachs called to him, his voice sounding thin and far away, as if he was shouting to Luc across mountaintops. The malfunctioning pressure-field continued to flicker on and off further down the hub.

Luc didn't need any more encouragement and kicked himself across the hub, black dots swimming at the edges of his vision as he struggled for breath. He grabbed onto a handhold and pulled himself inside the passageway, following the Ambassador as he turned, passing through yet another pressure-field.

Suddenly Luc's lungs were filled with moist, scented air. The Ambassador's mechants followed them through the pressure-field moments before heavy doors swung into place behind them, blocking access to the hub.

Luc slumped against the side of the passageway, almost drunk on oxygen, while Ambassador Sachs regarded him from nearby, one gloved hand casually slung through a wall-rung.

'Mr Gabion,' the Ambassador said with wry humour, 'we hope this wasn't just a social call, because your timing is terrible.'

Luc followed Sachs along the passageway and into one of the arboretums with feelings of deep trepidation. These feelings only increased when he saw through its streaked and filthy transparent panes the battle that still raged beyond the fragile dome. He followed the Ambassador over to a low stone bench near the centre of the dome, where tall ferns spread broad leaves above their heads.

'Why the hell do you want to talk *here*?' Luc yelled after him. 'One of the other domes is already cracked open and you're losing atmosphere all over the station. If the Sandoz target this dome, we're dead!'

At first, instead of responding, Sachs turned to face him, pushing back his hood to reveal a close-shaven skull. Then he pinched the front of his mask with two fingers, deftly peeling it away to reveal a mouth that was little more than a lipless line below a pair of indents where a nose should have been. His eyes were wide, and entirely black. Luc stared back at him in shock.

'Contrary to appearances,' said Sachs, 'we are quite human. This body is optimized for survival, and can function in vacuum for short periods if required. In answer to your question, it is our belief the Sandoz forces are intent on capture rather than execution. That is why they are being so cautious.'

Luc laughed weakly. 'You call what happened back there *cautious?*'

'They could have destroyed this station in seconds,' the Ambassador pointed out, 'something they have manifestly *not* chosen to do. And that other arboretum was accidentally destroyed by one of our own mechants during an exchange of fire.'

This is crazy, Luc wanted to yell, but managed to hold it back.

'All right,' he said instead, 'then you should be aware that I know you visited Javier Maxwell in his prison, because I visited him there myself not long after. I learned more about what's been going on than I ever wanted to.'

The Ambassador regarded him with surprise. 'How did you know we were there?'

'By keeping a close eye on you after my previous visit here. When you disappeared from Zelia's surveillance networks, we realized the nearest thing to your last known location was Maxwell's prison.'

'Very impressive,' the Ambassador conceded. 'We assume you want to know what we were doing there.'

'I already have a pretty good idea what. I know Vasili was killed because he'd found out about Cheng's secret entrance into the Founder Network.'

'And how did you come by this information?'

Reaching inside his jacket, Luc withdrew one of the two books, holding it up before the Ambassador.

'Ah,' the Ambassador replied. 'We should have guessed. But why bother coming all this way, just to tell us things we already know?'

'Because there's still something I don't understand. Whether or not Cheng was exploring the Founder Network, that in itself still isn't sufficient reason for the Coalition to threaten war against the Tian Di. So what *is* the reason?'

A dull boom directly overhead made them both look up at the same time. Luc could just make out something with multiple arms pressed up against the dome's exterior, twisting around as it engaged at close quarters with a second mechant. The two machines suddenly pulled apart, and for a moment Luc almost imagined they were caught in some complicated dance.

A moment later one of the mechants darted away, disappearing from view in a flash. The second mechant launched itself away from the dome in the next moment, presumably giving chase.

The Ambassador brought his gaze back down to Luc. 'We see no reason why we should discuss confidential affairs of state with a member of what is, as you yourself pointed out on your last visit, an enemy civilization.'

'I can give you something in return,' said Luc. 'Something you *don't* know.'

'A moment,' said the Ambassador, who then gazed blankly over Luc's shoulder. He sat like this, unblinking, for several seconds, then returned his gaze to Luc. 'We agree to your proposal, but request that you share your information first.'

'And then you'll answer my question?'

'That depends on the usefulness of your information.'

'All right,' said Luc. 'Cheng sent agents to the Coalition, to retrieve some kind of artefact your people recovered from your part of the Founder Network, and they're going to try and bring that artefact back through the Darwin–Temur gate, assuming they haven't done so already. I can't tell you anyone's name, or anything like that, but whatever it is Cheng sent them to look for is a planet-killer, the same kind of thing that brought about the Abandonment.'

'And you learned this from where?'

'Your turn,' said Luc.

He waited, and the Ambassador's shoulders rose and fell with a sigh.

'Well?' Luc demanded. 'Or did you already know everything we just told you?'

'No, we didn't, Mr Gabion. Although it makes sense of certain recent events back on Darwin.'

'Then you must know that your top priority is to stop whoever Cheng sent to Darwin from completing their mission, because literally billions of lives are at stake, as well as the future of the Tian Di. Is there any way you can get in touch with your people back home to warn them?'

'They have already been warned,' the Ambassador replied, 'since you just told them.'

Luc frowned. 'We're being listened to? Right now?'

'Every word you say is being transmitted via a secure link running through the Hall of Gates back to Temur, and then through the Darwin–Temur gate. We wish to know, for what purpose would Cheng want to acquire such an artefact?'

Luc imagined shadowy figures listening in to their conversation from untold light-years away. 'My understanding is that Cheng is going to use the artefact to wipe out Benares, then blame the whole catastrophe on Black Lotus.'

'*Destroy* one of the Tian Di's own worlds?' The Ambassador shook his head. 'What could he possibly gain from that?'

'He intends to use it as a pretext for staying in power indefinitely. He'll also claim that the Coalition supplied the weapon to Black Lotus. Ambassador, you *must* take immediate action.'

'While we agree that your intent is genuine, it may already be too late for the particular solution you seek.'

Luc shook his head, confused. 'Too late? How?'

'There are still certain details that you are not aware of. As you already know, I visited Maxwell with regard to preventing a war between our civilizations. I am sorry to tell you that war has already begun.'

Luc struggled to formulate a coherent answer. 'It has?'

'And has been under way, for some hours – not that this will be evident for some time yet.'

'I don't understand.'

'As you are now clearly aware, Tian Di exploration teams did indeed discover another gate leading into the Founder Network, following which Cheng authorized his own, secret assessment of any artefacts that might be found there, despite his stated reasons for bringing about the Schism.

'However,' the Ambassador continued, 'as our ancestors once discovered for themselves, the Founder Network is an *enormously* dangerous place. The human race was lucky to avoid total extinction following the Abandonment, and so when we became aware that Tian Di expeditions had entered the Network, we were concerned not only for their safety, but that of our entire species, whether here or in the Coalition.'

'So how exactly did you know Cheng had entered the Network?'

The Ambassador studied his gloved hands. 'The point about a network is that it is interconnected. Given that, it was inevitable we would eventually become aware of Cheng's presence within it. But what they were doing was placing us all in terrible danger.'

'What kind of danger?'

At that point, the assault on the *Sequoia* grew more vicious. Luc heard a loud crash from the far side of the arboretum, and within moments a ferocious gale began to tear at the trees and bushes around them, filling the air with a terrible, deafening howl.

<This way, Mr Gabion,> the Ambassador scripted.

Luc grabbed at the branches of the surrounding trees as the sudden expulsion of air dragged him backwards along the path. He yelled, then threw his hands over his face as a mechant came hurtling towards him. It gripped him in its manipulators, and fought to make headway against the outrushing air.

A moment later Luc felt his ears pop, and the arboretum grew eerily quiet. The air had already been sucked out of the dome. He felt like he was drowning, and caught sight of the Ambassador held in the grip of a second mechant. Perhaps the Sandoz had decided it wasn't necessary to take them alive after all.

The two mechants hurtled back through the passageway by

which Luc had entered the arboretum. The heavy doors that had isolated the dome from the rest of the station had already swung half-open again by the time they passed between them.

Luc struggled to stay conscious. The mechants carrying both him and the Ambassador took a sharp turn sideways into another tunnel, and through another pressure-field.

For the second time that day, Luc gasped and floundered like a fish as the mechant released him. He collapsed onto hard steel decking, coughing and gasping as his lungs again found purchase in breathable air.

'We need to get off this station,' Luc gasped, seeing the Ambassador climbing to his feet a few paces away, his robe now rumpled and stained. 'You must have *some* way off of here, right?'

'We have a flier,' the Ambassador agreed, 'but it only has room for one. You may use it if you wish.'

Luc gaped at him. 'But . . . what about you? Why would you give a damn about saving *my* life?'

'You think I'm sacrificing myself, but you'll soon understand that that's far from being the case. Besides, we have come to the conclusion that you may have it within your means to bring current events to a more peaceful conclusion than they might otherwise. If we may?'

The Ambassador peeled off a glove, revealing an entirely ordinary-looking hand, with long and tapering fingers, and carefully trimmed nails.

He stepped towards Luc, reaching out to him with his ungloved hand. Luc jerked back in alarm.

'What the hell are you trying to do?'

'A touch is all it takes, Mr Gabion,' said the Ambassador. 'You offered a trade. Let us then fulfil our side of the bargain. This way, you'll see and understand everything in an instant.'

Luc felt his eyes widen. 'Like Javier Maxwell's books. Is that the kind of thing you mean?'

'Encoding memories into all manner of physical substrates is an art in itself,' the Ambassador replied, briefly drawing his hand back and showing his palm to Luc. 'There are almost no limits to the possible substrates that can be used, since the information is stored on the deep quantum level. It is possible, in the Coalition, to ingest or even drink memories and data – even to breathe them in. Living flesh, allied with a lattice of the type Antonov gifted you with, can become a conduit for sensory data of all kinds.'

Irrational fear gripped Luc. 'The last time I was here,' he said tightly, 'I mentioned that Antonov told me in what I thought was a dream that you could prevent a calamity, and save both our lives.'

Something rocked the station around them. 'Perhaps it's safest to keep moving for the moment,' said the Ambassador. 'We can reach the flier in just a few more minutes.'

They passed into another part of the station, walking quickly through what appeared to be a series of laboratories linked one to another by a common passageway. Luc observed a number of sealed compartments with glass walls, within which lay samples of mosses and lichens.

'I have another question for you,' Luc called after the Ambassador as he strode ahead. 'The lattice in my head. Did Antonov get it from you?'

The Ambassador turned to regard him as they came to a door at the end of the passageway. 'He did, yes, but I had no part in what Antonov did to you. You must understand that.'

Ambassador Sachs next led him through a dusty reception area filled with mouldering couches. Sachs moved through the zero-gee environment with a fluid grace like he'd been born to it – and then Luc remembered that he had.

Luc also remembered the anger written across Antonov's face, reflected in the Ambassador's mirrored mask. 'He wasn't very happy with you, for some reason. I saw part of one of his memories. He was arguing with you, clearly extremely upset. Why?'

'He believed we in the Coalition had dangerously underestimated Father Cheng's determination to remain in power at all costs. Given what you've told us since your arrival here, it appears we entirely misjudged the situation. Once it became evident Cheng had no intention of bringing his explorations of the Founder Network to a halt, we began conducting private negotiations with both Javier Maxwell and Winchell Antonov. In return for Antonov's help, and as a gesture of goodwill, we supplied him with certain technologies he might need if either he or Maxwell were to have any chance at deposing Cheng.'

'Such as my lattice?'

'Such as your lattice, yes.'

Despite everything he'd learned, a part of Luc was scandalized. 'All this time, and the Coalition really has been working against the Tian Di?'

'No, Mr Gabion, against Father Cheng and the Eighty-Five, specifically, and out of a desperation to avoid the war Cheng has forced us to initiate. If Cheng should remain in power and continue his exploration of the Founder Network, he risks driving the human race into extinction.'

'You keep telling me that, but you haven't explained what you mean.'

'We offered to show you, but you refused.'

'Tell me first.'

'The Network is vast, Mr Gabion, a billion open doors scattered all across space and time and leading who knows where. Some of Cheng's reconnaissance teams encountered something quite terrifying during one of their forays into it.'

'What?'

'Intelligent life,' Sachs replied, and turned back to the door.

Sachs cycled the mechants through the airlock first, the door sealing behind them. The docking bay where his flier waited had, he explained, suffered a breach during the initial stages of the assault. The mechants would venture ahead in order to seal the breach, following which he and Luc would be able to continue on their way.

'As vast as the Founder Network is,' the Ambassador explained as they waited, 'it's difficult to imagine a universe in which such a thing did *not* exist, given what we know of the mutability of space and time. It seems to be a historical inevitability that any race advanced enough to discover the means to generate wormholes would then use them as a fast way to access their nearest star systems. And, over time, these scattered networks inevitably fused together, becoming what we call the Founder Network.'

'And that's who the Sandoz encountered?' asked Luc, unable to keep a note of awe out of his voice. 'The Founders?'

'Remember there is no evidence of there ever being any one race of Founders,' the Ambassador cautioned. 'The name is merely a collective term for an unknown number of intelligent species who independently created their own wormhole networks, but ultimately used them to access the networks of other species, over vast epochs of time. As you know, the Coalition have continued to explore the Network, despite the Schism, but always with the greatest caution imaginable. By our standards, Cheng's expeditionary forces have been behaving in a manner almost suicidally reckless.'

'For all your caution,' Luc growled, 'you still didn't prevent someone travelling to one of your worlds to steal something that could be used to murder billions.'

'Which is extremely unfortunate, if it does prove to be the case,' the Ambassador agreed, 'and it reveals a serious lapse on our part. But to get back to the point, Mr Gabion, Cheng's Sandoz teams were not the first to encounter alien life. We first made contact with the very same alien species a few decades after the Schism. At first, our discovery was a cause of celebration: first contact with another species, via the Network. But our joy didn't last for long. If the creatures we encountered ever had a name for themselves, we never learned it, but it wasn't long before we started calling them the Inimicals. Communication with them proved difficult from the start, indeed more or less impossible. There are many ways to build some kind of common language – by building mathematical and physical constants, for instance. At first we thought we might succeed in learning to communicate with them, and they with us; but every time we tried to advance beyond those initial building blocks towards anything remotely abstract, we ran into trouble.'

'You mean you couldn't understand them?'

The Ambassador shook his head. 'Or they, us. They showed us images of one of their worlds, dotted with what we at first took to be cities, but then later proved to be graveyards, or perhaps some mixture of both. Every time we thought we had a grasp on how their minds worked or what they were trying to say to us, we'd find ourselves having to throw away all our carefully constructed strategies as new data came in.' He shrugged. 'Then things turned nasty.'

'In what way?'

'You must understand the extraordinary lengths we had gone to, from the very beginning, to prevent the Inimicals from uncovering the route back to our own time and space until we could be certain we would be safe. At the time we first encountered them, the Inimicals had already colonized an entire hub of the Network – thousands upon thousands of transfer gates placed in close orbit around a black hole with the mass of a million stars, located at the heart of a dying galaxy. We never knew just what triggered the hostilities – whether we somehow brought it on ourselves, or if they'd intended to attack us all along – but those of us who survived the attack in our physical forms managed to retreat and warn the rest. We destroyed transfer gates behind us as we went, hoping to block off their pursuit and prevent them from finding their way back to our own worlds, but had only limited success. The Inimicals had already spent millennia inside the Network, and knew routes through it we hardly knew existed. Our exploratory teams came under attack several more times over the next few decades, as the Inimicals attempted to find some way around our hastily erected defences. In response, we initiated research programmes that constructed weapons from certain artefacts we had recovered throughout the post-Abandonment period.

Using these, we managed to halt the Inimicals' progress – but only at a dreadful cost.'

The Ambassador came to a halt as something thudded and clanged on the far side of the airlock door.

'And that's what the Sandoz encountered inside the Network? The Inimicals?'

'Several Sandoz Clans engaged in routine explorations of the deep future via the Network disappeared without trace. We know with great certainty that the Inimicals were responsible. Should they manage to trace the route of Cheng's expeditions back to the Thorne system, we will all have a great deal more to worry about than just the destruction of Benares – such as the survival of our species.'

'But you must have told Cheng all this!'

'Oh, we have, Mr Gabion,' the Ambassador replied, a trace of wistfulness in his voice. 'Despite the abundance of evidence, he and his advisors have consistently ignored all of our warnings.'

'And that's why you threatened war?'

'We have no objections to the Tian Di exploring the Founder Network,' said the Ambassador, 'so long as it is conducted with an appreciation of the considerable dangers involved. Cheng initially agreed to halt any further explorations for the duration of our negotiations with him, but he constantly reneges or ignores every agreement we have made. We now believe he has no intention of honouring any of our demands.'

'But why would he do that? Why take such a huge risk with all our lives?'

'A question that has been on our minds from the beginning, Mr Gabion, but the information you have brought us may answer that question. If Tian Di agents truly have attempted to retrieve artefacts from Darwin – and there is strong circumstantial evidence to support that conjecture – it may be that Cheng has simply been stalling for time until he can acquire those artefacts. It adds fuel to our growing conviction that neither Cheng nor his closest advisors are wholly sane.'

'So what will you do now?'

'Since he is apparently unprepared or unwilling to deal with the threat, we will have to deal with it for him, and either seal or destroy the Thorne gate. It is likely this will provoke violent action from the Sandoz, and become a full-fledged conflict throughout the Tian Di. We are extremely well prepared, however, for the coming conflict. Now, Mr Gabion,' he said, again reaching out with his ungloved hand. 'Time is running short.'

Luc hesitated for a moment, then reached out and gripped the Ambassador's hand.

In a moment, the *Sequoia* slipped away.

He saw ships like shards of black ice tear the underlying structure of space apart, triggering the death of a star in a burst of blazing energy. He realized he was witnessing a battle between evenly balanced Inimical and Coalition forces, each side equipped with weapons the nature of which neither truly comprehended.

You see? said the Ambassador, from somewhere far away.

He remembered that once his name had been only Luc Gabion, but now he had a billion names and faces, scattered across multiple worlds, and in the cold, dark depths between stars.

Simultaneous with witnessing this battle, he stood in a busy street and watched figures – some more or less human in appearance, some multi-limbed and bizarrely alien – engage in what might have been a dance, or a ritual, or something else entirely, their emotions and thoughts tumbling around and through him.

He stood on the bottom of an ocean in a body constructed of plastic and metal, leaning in close to observe tiny, finger-like polyps that populated the edges of a volcanic fissure.

There were other eyes and other faces, some on the surfaces of worlds, and others floating above the roiling surfaces of stars, naked to the vacuum.

He was anyone and anything he chose to be.

It was, he thought, like being God.

But it was too much. Luc's senses reeled under the assault of so many crowded perspectives and tumbling, chaotic thoughts.

Then, finally, he was all alone once more, and back in his own skull – all except for Antonov, somewhere in the depths of his thoughts, grinning toothily through a bushy black beard.

He opened his eyes to find he had folded his body into a ball next to the now open airlock door, his skin bright with sweat. Ambassador Sachs knelt on one knee by his side.

'Now do you see?' said Sachs. 'Some of those weapons you saw being used were first developed so that we might defend ourselves against the Inimicals. We fought battles that destroyed entire star systems, but we did what we had to do because it was a choice between survival and extinction. But when it comes to a fight between the Tian Di and the Coalition, believe us when we say it is not a war we could possibly lose. Long ago, we seeded weapons fabricants in the outer reaches of several Tian Di systems, including this one, against the possibility that a day such as this might come.'

'You're not human,' Luc gasped, the words rasping in his throat. 'Not any more.'

'We in the Coalition prefer to think we are *more* human,' the Ambassador observed. 'But perhaps you now more clearly understand the threat we all face, and the reason for our actions.'

'I could be talking to anyone right now,' said Luc. 'There *is* no one, single Ambassador, is there?'

He'd seen how the Coalition's citizens leapt from body to body at will, instantaneously, across continents and even light-years, using instantaneous communications technology, a constant shunting of encoded consciousnesses in and out of the lattices filling their skulls. Notions of privacy, as they were understood within the Tian Di, simply did not, could not exist for them. Bodies were there to be shared, rather than owned. A single mind might find itself in a dozen different bodies in the space of a week, a day, or an hour; a constant flow of conscious, living data across a civilization that now itself encompassed dozens of star systems.

In that brief moment of contact with the Ambassador, Luc had seen how a single mind could split itself into a dozen copies, each occupying a separate body simultaneously, before later reintegrating itself into a single consciousness. It was wonderful and terrifying in equal measure, and Luc wasn't sure he could experience it all again without going insane.

'We understand how all this must frighten you,' said the Ambassador. 'You think you would lose your individuality if you came to live amongst us. That's not the case: the Coalition embraces change, since to become static is to stagnate and die. By contrast, very little in the Tian Di has changed in centuries. Your ruling Council live artificially extended lives, but they do not live *well*. You've seen how they have sunk into a mire of depredation and excess, down on that miserable sandpit of a world they call home. They keep life- and intelligence-boosting technology from the rest of you and have the audacity to claim it's for your own good. Tell us honestly,' Sachs continued, 'after everything you've seen, who, may we ask, is more human? Men and women like Cripps and de Almeida, or what you've seen of the Coalition?'

Luc blinked sweat out of his eyes. 'Was it you I spoke to when I last came here? Or was there someone else using that body?'

'There are up to thirty agents using this body at different times,' the Ambassador replied. 'But the individual mind you are addressing just now is the same one that you spoke with then.'

'So who exactly am I talking to right now? Is your name really Horst Sachs?'

'That is the name of the individual occupying this body *at this moment*, yes,' Sachs replied. 'Of all of us, we – or rather, *I* – spend the most time in this body, but whatever you and I say to each other is heard by all.'

'And where are you the rest of the time?'

The Ambassador shrugged. 'In other places, other bodies – even other times, if duty calls me into the Founder Network. Now do you understand why Antonov did to you what he did? He was saving your life – and his own.'

'No.' Luc shook his head. 'That's not what you said to me before. You said I was just one life measured against billions.'

'Much has changed since then, Mr Gabion. We did not yet fully understand your role in current events. Look.'

The Ambassador reached into a pocket and pulled out something metallic that squirmed in the open palm of his hand. Luc stared at the writhing thing with horrible fascination.

'So why did Antonov put one of those things in me, instead of using it on himself?'

'Because he was already equipped with the more primitive form of lattice still used by the Council,' the Ambassador explained. 'It cannot be removed, even by surgery. The only way to ensure his survival, or that of any member of the Temur Council, would be to acquire a clone body pre-equipped with its own lattice, then place backups of his preserved mind-state into that new body. Since such means were not available to him while he was trapped on Aeschere, the only option left to him under the circumstances was to imprint a number of his memories and some fragment of his personality onto a device such as this one, and implant it within you.'

'Except that it's killing me.'

'Killing the body you *currently* occupy, yes,' the Ambassador agreed, 'but the same cannot be said for your *mind*. With the aid of your lattice, everything that defines you – every thought, memory, and learned skill, along with the manifold and near-infinite inter-relationships between those thoughts and memories – can be stored, shuffled, or copied indefinitely, so long as there is Coalition instantiation technology to receive it all.'

Luc stared at the Ambassador's single gloved hand. 'That's why you wear those gloves, isn't it? Even shaking someone's hand . . .'

'Has considerably deeper meaning in our culture than in yours, yes,' the Ambassador agreed. 'It can allow the sharing of the most intimate gestures and thoughts, or it can reveal the very essence of one's soul. When everything and everyone around you is capable of either imbuing you with its own thoughts and memories, or of absorbing your own, one must be careful in the extreme. Come.'

The Ambassador stood and pulled his glove back on, then reached down, helping Luc upright. Luc found himself wondering what kind of pronoun you used for more than one person taking turns sharing a single body – or was it safer just to refer to Ambassador Sachs as 'they'?

The airlock door finally opened, letting them pass through into the now re-pressurized dock. The air inside was filled with the stink of burning plastic, and a pile of half-melted metal in one corner, still radiating heat, was only just recognizable as the remains of a Sandoz mechant. Luc saw that a lone flier sat in a launching cradle at the centre of the bay, watched over by one of the Ambassador's own mechants. The flier's hatch hissed open as they approached.

'It's best you leave immediately,' said the Ambassador. 'But first I have some more information for you. Within the past few days, an attack took place on an orbital facility above Darwin. The raid was both unexpected and unexpectedly sophisticated, and it appears an artefact originating from the Founder Network, in storage aboard that orbital facility, may indeed have been removed from it. Our consensus, given what you've already told us, is that the raid must have been carried out by agents working on behalf of Father Cheng.'

'But can you stop them from bringing the artefact, whatever it is, back to Temur?'

'Unfortunately, it may already be too late,' the Ambassador replied with a pained expression. 'Not long after the raid, there was an unexpected breach of security at the Darwin–Temur gate.'

Luc felt his insides turn hollow. 'What kind of breach?'

'Special Envoys originating from the Tian Di passed back through the Darwin–Temur gate less than half a day ago. On further investigation, it seems one of the Envoys did not precisely match our records. Our conclusion is that one of the Envoys was replaced, presumably by whichever agent acquired the artefact for Cheng.'

'The last time I spoke to Zelia, she said the Council's effectively gone to war with itself.'

'We can corroborate that,' said the Ambassador. 'We have

observed fighting in the vicinity of Liebenau and the Red Palace.'

'Can't you hold off your invading forces for a little while longer?' Luc pleaded. 'I have all the proof I need to discredit Cheng in the eyes of all but his most loyal supporters. I just need an opportunity to show it to them.'

'We can perhaps delay for a few hours,' the Ambassador admitted. 'But Cheng appears to be winning the battle for control of Vanaheim. That will leave us no choice but to subjugate his forces, and Vanaheim, with utmost prejudice.'

'I'll talk to Zelia de Almeida, tell her everything you've told me. She can take it to the rest of the Council and make them understand just how bad things have become.'

The Ambassador thought for a moment. 'Twelve hours,' he said. 'Is that enough?'

'Not nearly enough.'

Sachs smiled gently. 'But enough for now.'

The station emitted a series of howling, metallic shrieks, and Luc reached out to grab hold of the flier's hatch as the station shuddered around them. An automated voice sounded, announcing in calm tones that anyone remaining on board the *Sequoia* should evacuate immediately.

'What about you?' Luc shouted over the din. 'Why the hell won't you come with me?'

'We told you, the flier only has room for one. Besides, your chances are considerably improved if we *don't* join you.'

'Why?'

'We intend to destroy the *Sequoia* immediately following your departure.'

'*What?*'

'At the very least, the detonation should disguise your departure, otherwise you would likely be blown out of the sky long before you reached the surface. And please remember, Mr Gabion, this is hardly an act of sacrifice. In fact, I – or rather, Horst Sachs – fully intend to speak to you again, regardless of what happens to either this body or yours.'

The station shook again. 'Then I should go,' said Luc, his throat tight.

'You should be aware,' the Ambassador added, 'that we took the opportunity to make some necessary adjustments to your lattice when we made physical contact.'

Luc's eyes narrowed. 'What kind of adjustments?'

'Your lattice required optimization. The crude surgery performed on you was insufficient to allow the full use of its potential.'

'What potential?'

'The ability to control mechants in the way you saw us do, to subvert attack-systems, or even boost physical response times. We have also given you the means to track down the stolen artefact, which we strongly urge you to do.'

Luc nodded wordlessly as the hatch hissed into place before him. He pulled himself into his seat restraints, then watched as the doors at the far end of the dock swung open to reveal a vista of stars.

With any luck, his departure wouldn't be anywhere near as bad as his arrival.

TWENTY-ONE

Almost as soon as the flier lifted up from its cradle, something slammed into the station with tremendous force. Clearly the Ambassador wasn't wasting time following through on his promise. The stars wheeled past the open bay doors, and the flier was sent crashing into a bulkhead.

Luc's head snapped sideways, his teeth clicking together. Blood began to fill his mouth and he swallowed hard, grimacing at the taste. Emergency alerts flowered in the air all around him.

Tubes dropped down from immediately overhead, reaching towards him and forming a seal over his nose and mouth at the same time that a thick, glutinous liquid began pouring out from hidden nozzles, filling the interior of the flier in seconds.

Luc breathed in the high-oxygen mix coming through the tubes and felt suddenly calmer, so much so that he found himself wondering if there might be some form of narcotic in the air mix. The flier meanwhile pumped visual data to him directly, via his lattice, and he saw a Sandoz mechant had entered through the open bay doors, its carapace bristling with weaponry.

The mechant launched itself immediately towards the flier. Luc flinched, hearing it land on the hull, a soft thud that reverberated through the impact gel surrounding and cushioning him. He watched with horror as the mechant extended manipulators, using them to secure itself to the flier's hull. It then applied a tightly focused blue flame to a spot on the hull, which brightened to a dull orange almost immediately.

Go away, thought Luc.

The mechant jerked suddenly, and the flame switched off. It let go of the flier, its manipulators undulating around it, as if in confusion. Drifting across the bay, it rebounded from a bulkhead, now apparently lifeless.

Luc stared at it in stupefaction as the stars wheeled by beyond the bay doors.

The flier carefully manoeuvred its way out through the bay doors before quickly boosting far away enough from the *Sequoia* that Luc could see the station's long hub had been shattered in several places. Pieces of the *Sequioa* were drifting apart from each other, some spinning as they went.

What came next happened so fast that Luc only had time to think about it clearly a few minutes after the fact.

First, his flier flashed a warning that it was being targeted by multiple energy and kinetic weapon systems. Then it accelerated hard enough to break every bone in his body, if not for the impact gel surrounding and supporting him.

He blacked out. The next time he became aware of his surroundings, the *Sequoia* was twenty kilometres distant and receding fast. The flier's onboard AI outlined each and every one of the thousands of pieces of spinning and flying wreckage with bright green circles and associated impact probability estimates.

Luc called up a view of the Sandoz platform, and saw a heavily shielded framework supporting multiple weapons systems. Red circles marked dart-sized missiles hurtling across the intervening space towards him. Clearly Ambassador Sachs' pre-emptive tactic of destroying the *Sequoia*, however drastic, hadn't worked as well as he'd hoped.

Luc imagined the missiles detonating, and then watched as incandescent points of light suddenly bloomed amongst the stars.

I did that, Luc realized with a thrill of shock that ran up his spine like electricity.

He glanced towards the Sandoz platform. Light bloomed at half a dozen points across its framework, as its remaining stocks of missiles also spontaneously detonated.

The resulting explosions tore the platform apart like soft candy under a blowtorch.

Luc found himself wondering just how much chaos and death one man could bring about with that much power. He felt numb, as if he were no more substantial than a ghost drifting high above Vanaheim's upper atmosphere.

The flier informed him it was receiving a transmission coded for the *Sequoia*. On investigation, it proved to be from Zelia.

<Zelia.>

<You're alive? I saw the attack on the station. Didn't you go there?>

<I did. Ambassador Sachs destroyed the station himself.>

<You mean he's dead?>

He thought for a moment about everything Sachs had shown to him. <Not in the way you mean, no.>

<I want you to rendezvous with the rest of us at my home,> she sent, then added: <I found Cripps, Luc – and now I know just who it was Cheng sent to Darwin.>

<What do you mean, 'the rest of us'?> asked Luc, but by then the flier was re-entering Vanaheim's atmosphere, rendering any further communications impossible for at least the next few minutes.

Luc gasped as rough hands yanked the breathing mask from his face. The impact gel had congealed into a thick translucent sludge around his feet shortly after the flier had landed safely by Zelia's domed laboratory.

Harsh sunlight cut through the flier's open hatch. He felt hands take hold of him, pulling him out from his seat restraints. He collapsed onto grass, half-blinded by the light, and heard the distant hiss of the sea.

Looking up, he discovered he was surrounded by several of Zelia's machine-men. For one terrible moment he thought perhaps

Zelia had sent them to kill him, but they kept their distance as he staggered to his feet, gel still dripping from his clothes.

One of the creatures gestured towards Zelia's laboratory, a short walk away, a faint buzzing emerging from the grille where its mouth should have been. Luc nodded warily, then watched the creatures shuffle out of his way as he stepped forward.

Part of the building housing Zelia's laboratory had caved in, while the twisted wreckage of a Sandoz mechant lay nearby. Burned, ragged shapes scattered around the surrounding land were recognizable as fallen soldiers in Zelia's army of machine-men. Dark smoke rose from the mansion next door, the wind carrying an acrid smell of ashes down to the sea.

He found Zelia inside the laboratory, wearing a bloodied smock and perched on the edge of a chunk of masonry that had smashed a work table, having fallen from the ceiling, wrecking the room's carefully-wrought astronomical mural.

She was not alone. At least a dozen other men and women stood or sat where they could amidst the scattered laboratory equipment, all turning to stare at Luc with varying degrees of suspicion as he entered from the greenhouse. A few of them looked as if they had been through their own trials: one had a heavily bandaged arm, while another appeared to have suffered serious burns to one side of her face. He ignored them all, focusing his attention on Zelia as he stepped over to her.

'Who is he?' one of the others shouted. 'He's not a member of the Council!'

'Mr Gabion is working for me,' said Zelia, without looking around. 'He found the evidence that Cheng is responsible not only for Sevgeny Vasili's assassination, but that of Ariadna Placet before him.'

'That doesn't mean he should be here,' said another voice. 'Send him away, Zelia.'

She glanced around them all with an irritated expression. 'I brought you all here so we'd have some chance at salvaging something from this mess,' Zelia shouted, 'not so you could dictate terms to me. Gabion being here is my choice, not yours.'

'Who are all these people?' Luc asked her quietly.

She slid down from the chunk of masonry. 'Members of the Council who've made the mistake of opposing Cheng in any number of ways. He's accused us all of being Black Lotus sympathizers and ordered our arrests.'

'But why bring them *here*?' he demanded. 'Surely you're making it easy for Cheng to kill or capture you all at once?'

'There is strength in numbers, Mr Gabion.' She nodded towards the steps leading down to the basement. 'There's something I need you to see.'

'What you did to Cripps was wrong, Zelia,' said another voice from the crowd. 'You should have waited to speak to the rest of us before electing yourself judge and jury.'

Luc gazed around until he saw who had spoken: a dignified-looking man wearing a dark suit, his steely-grey hair cut close to the scalp. A few other heads nodded or muttered their agreement.

'I made a necessary decision,' Zelia snapped, her voice full of wounded anger, 'while the rest of you sat around with your thumbs up your fucking asses. Where the hell were *you*, Ben,' she said to the man in the dark suit, 'when Cripps was trying to hunt me down like a dog?'

Luc grabbed hold of Zelia's arm. 'How much else have you told them?'

'Told us what?' asked Ben.

'That Cheng's been sending Sandoz reconnaissance teams through a secret gate leading into the Founder Network,' Luc replied.

'I already told them,' Zelia grated. 'They know what Cheng had planned for Benares as well.'

'But do they know that the Coalition are about to start a war with us because Cheng refused to pull his teams back out from the Network?'

That shut them up, he thought with satisfaction, as they all stared at him in stunned silence.

'How do you know this?' demanded Ben. 'And why would the Coalition want to start a war?'

'I know because I just got back from a meeting with Ambassador Sachs,' Luc explained. 'He told me the whole story. It seems the Coalition came under attack from an alien race they encountered inside the Founder Network not long after the Schism, and they only barely survived the encounter. Several of Cheng's reconnaissance teams have disappeared without trace inside the part of the network they've been exploring, and Sachs believes the same creatures that attacked the Coalition are responsible. It's my understanding that if those aliens found their way back here through Cheng's secret transfer gate in the Thorne system, they could spread through this part of the Milky Way and kill everything they encounter.'

Their expressions ranged from frankly disbelieving to utterly terrified. 'Once the Coalition realized there were Sandoz exploring the Network,' he continued, 'they entered into secret negotiations to try and persuade Father Cheng to stop. But the talks broke down, and unless you can find some way in the next twelve hours to persuade Cheng to stand down, or else pull his Sandoz teams back out of the Network, we're going to come under attack from Coalition forces far in advance of anything we could possibly throw back at them.'

Somebody laughed, the sound low and derisive, and Luc turned to see it came from a dark-skinned woman, her hair cropped close to her skull, sitting with her back to a wall. 'That's quite some story,' she said, 'and you honestly *believed* one word of this?'

'You heard what Cripps confessed to Zelia!' someone else yelled. 'What Gabion says fits in with everything else he said.'

Within moments the air was filled with a hubbub of conflicting voices.

'Come on,' said Zelia, stepping up beside Luc and leading him by the arm towards the stairwell. 'I told you there's something you need to see.'

'Don't let her take you down *there*,' someone called after them with a mocking tone, 'or you might never come back!'

Luc followed her down into the same stone corridor he had since revisited only in his nightmares. The passageway was as dark and dank as he remembered, the same rusting junk still piled in alcoves, the same thudding of distant machinery reverberating through walls and sending faint tremors through the floor. Zelia led him towards the steel trestle tables lined up neatly in a row where the corridor widened. As before, a few mechants and one of her machine-men stood around a single, supine form laid out on one of the tables.

Luc knew immediately it was Cripps, despite what had been done to him. In the few short hours since he'd last seen her, Zelia had found some way not only to capture Cheng's right-hand man, but also begin the process of butchering his living body. Parts of his skull had been cut away, exposing the living brain matter beneath, while a nest of wires and sensors were now plugged into the raw flesh. Cripps' lower jaw had been removed, the mechants hovering over him engaged in the process of securing machinery in its place.

The worst thing of all was when his eyes glanced towards Luc. Cripps was not only conscious, but also clearly aware of everything that was happening to him. He stared at Luc with maddened, pleading eyes.

Luc turned away from the sight, sick to his stomach. 'What the hell have you done to him?' he gasped.

Zelia regarded him with an expression of faint amusement. 'You don't actually feel *sorry* for him, do you?' she asked. 'He's the one who caused all this, or carried out the orders, at the very least.'

Luc shook his head. 'How . . . ?'

'*How* did I find him?' She let out a bark of laughter. 'I know Cripps well enough to know just where to look, after all these years.'

'Does he know what's happening to him?'

'Of course he does. There's no point punishing someone unless they know they're being punished, and what for,' she remarked, her voice edging towards shrill. '*Please* don't feel pity for him, Luc: he's a miserable, sadistic little shit, and there's a long queue of people who'd be very envious to know I'm the one who got to him first.'

'Including the people upstairs?' Luc asked. 'How do *they* feel about . . . about this?'

Her nostrils flared. 'They care about what's important, such as Cripps' full and frank confession to his part in Father Cheng's crimes. This is no time for half-measures, don't you understand that?'

Luc glanced back at Cripps just as the eyeless creature attending to him carefully snipped off one of his fingers, just above the knuckle. Cripps' eyes grew wide with pain and shock, and a rattling sound emerged from the grille that had now been secured over the lower half of his face. The creature next to him then fitted some form of needle-tipped device over the raw stump where the finger had been.

Luc turned away and just about managed to resist the urge to throw up again.

'Maybe you're not as strong as I thought,' mused Zelia, watching the surgery with keen attention.

'There's something seriously wrong with you,' Luc gasped.

'Let's just stick for now to what's important,' she muttered darkly. 'You were right. Cripps hid that data-cache on board that orbital station himself, without Cheng's knowledge. I also persuaded our friend here to give me the name of the agent responsible for transporting a weaponized Founder artefact back through the Darwin–Temur gate.'

'And?'

'His name is Jacob Moreland.' She turned her gaze back to Luc. 'Unfortunately, he's already returned to the Tian Di.'

'And Cripps told you all this?'

'Once he understood what I'd do to him if he *didn't* tell me, yes.'

Luc glanced back at Cripps, then just as quickly turned away when one of the hovering mechants reached towards his eyes with sharp-looking instruments. 'God in hell, Zelia – you're telling me what you're doing to him now is *better* than what you might have done to him otherwise?'

'Oh no,' she said. 'What I'm doing to him is exactly what I threatened to do.'

Luc felt the blood freeze in his veins. Just a few hours before, he and Zelia had broached some kind of barrier, and he'd caught a glimpse of someone beneath the mask – a living, feeling human being. Now he understood just how badly she had fooled him.

'So you did it to him anyway, even after he confessed,' Luc spat. 'Is that how much anyone should trust you at your word?'

'He deserves no better. Now listen, so you understand the important facts. Moreland made his way back down from orbit to Temur in just the last few hours.'

'Do we know exactly what it is he brought back?'

She nodded. 'Something called a "quantum disruptor".'

'A *what?*'

She glanced back at Cripps with a thoughtful look. 'Apparently the device can pull time and space apart like moist tissue paper.'

Luc recalled the war he had witnessed when Sachs had taken his hand, and felt his blood chill.

'So far as I understand it,' Zelia continued, 'Moreland is on his way here, to Vanaheim, to present the artefact in person to Cheng – assuming he didn't get here already. After that, the plan was to pass it on to Cripps so he could take charge of transporting it to Benares. Obviously *that* isn't going to happen, but we still have only a short window of opportunity while the artefact is here before Cheng finds someone else to finish Cripps' job for him. That's another reason I gathered everyone here – I figured there was at least some chance one of them might turn out to have information that could help us pinpoint either Moreland or the artefact.' She shook her head. 'Unfortunately, we've had no luck so far.'

'I can find the artefact,' said Luc. 'Sachs gave me the means to track it. It's in Liebenau, somewhere inside Cheng's Red Palace.'

Zelia stared at him in surprise, then faltered. 'That's great, Luc – and I guess there's nowhere it'd be more likely to be. But it does mean it's going to be surrounded by Sandoz security.'

'Those people upstairs – do they have the resources to take Cheng on and win? Do *you*?'

She regarded him uncertainly. 'As far as my own resources go, the Red Palace security have their own, dedicated communications network, which means I can't tie them up in knots the way I can the Sandoz elsewhere on Vanaheim. As for the rest, it depends. Some of them, I think, have been stockpiling weapons against a day like this, but as far as the rest go, all they have are their personal mechants – not nearly enough to take on anyone's army.'

'You make it sound hopeless. Is it?'

She hesitated for a moment. 'I watched your departure from the *Sequoia* remotely. I saw what happened to that Sandoz platform – was Ambassador Sachs responsible for that?'

'I did that,' Luc said quietly. 'You told me yourself that the lattice in my skull is like no other you've seen before, and you were right. Antonov got it from the Coalition.'

'So the Coalition really *have* been supplying technology to Black Lotus?'

Luc nodded, and reached a hand towards one of the mechants hovering above Cripps, concentrating. After a moment the machine wobbled in the air, then moved towards the centre of the passageway.

Luc brought his hand sweeping down, and the mechant landed on the dusty flagstones with a thump, becoming dark and silent.

'How could you do that?' Zelia rasped, staring at the mechant with wide, frightened eyes.

'To be honest with you,' he said, turning back to her, 'I don't really know. But I'm pretty sure I can do a lot more than just that.' He nodded back towards the stairwell. 'We need to figure out our next move before Cheng has a chance to get that artefact anywhere near Benares.'

The lights dotting the ceiling above them flickered, and they both felt a tremor run through the floor and walls around them, one that had nothing to do with the machinery lurking beneath Zelia's home. A commotion of voices and screams flooded down from the upper floor.

'What the hell happened?' Luc demanded.

Zelia ran towards the stairwell. 'The networks are down,' she shouted back at him. 'I've lost control of them again. My guess is that the Sandoz have found us.'

They ascended the steps into chaos. Luc glanced up towards the sky, visible through the ruined ceiling, and caught sight of a couple of fliers rocketing upwards. Zelia's co-conspirators were making a run for it.

Something huge drifted between the escaping fliers and the clouds, blocking out the sky. A Sandoz cruiser, its underside studded with sensors and defensive systems.

Luc followed Zelia through the greenhouse and outside in time to see several more fliers erupting upwards. One disappeared in a blaze of heat and light before it had ascended more than a few hundred metres. He glanced back up at the belly of the vast ship overhead, seeing a stream of tiny dots descending towards them. Mechants.

Zelia grabbed hold of his arm. 'What you just did to that mechant – can you do it again?'

The dots had by now resolved into multi-armed silhouettes, approaching rapidly. A burst of incandescent light indicated the destruction of yet another flier.

Stop, thought Luc, focusing on the approaching mechants.

As he watched, the mechants broke formation, spinning off in different directions. Several hit the dirt close by the mansion house, sending up clods of soil. Others span out of control, their limbs flailing spasmodically.

'Come on,' said Zelia, tugging him by the arm. 'Let's get out of here.'

Luc stumbled after her and inside her own flier, which had barely enough room for the both of them. Luc's insides lurched as he saw the ground dropping away from them with terrifying speed. The flier veered wildly, and Luc gasped as he was slammed against the curved upper hull. Several seconds of free-fall followed, then another sudden wrenching burst of acceleration. The ground rushed towards them at gut-wrenching speed before suddenly spinning away once more.

'Sorry,' Zelia muttered. 'Had to take evasive action. We were being targeted.'

'Can we get away from them?'

'Possibly,' she replied. 'Not that there's that many places left to run to.'

'Your friends,' Luc gasped, 'did the rest of them get away? Can they help us?'

'I don't know, Luc,' she said, sounding hopeless. 'It's not looking good now. There's fighting around the Red Palace now, but I don't think we're winning.'

'What about the Hall of Gates? Is there any way we could get through it and escape?'

She shook her head. 'The last I heard, the Hall of Gates was in lockdown, and guarded by a heavy contingent of Sandoz on either side.' She turned and glanced at him. 'You do understand, don't you, just how bad things are? Cheng has all the cards on his side. What about Sachs? Would the Coalition be willing to help us?'

'Sachs is gone,' he told her. 'He was on board the *Sequoia* when it was destroyed.'

'But . . . you said he was still alive?'

'You asked me if he was dead, and I said not in the way you meant.'

'I don't understand.'

'People in the Coalition maintain multiple iterations of themselves, Zelia – they jump in and out of bodies like we do fliers.

Even if the particular instantiation of Sachs I met is gone, I have no doubt there's another one somewhere back on Darwin right now reporting on everything that happened here.'

'Shit.' Zelia slammed the console before her. 'Then that's it, isn't it? The Coalition's invading forces are on their way, and Cheng's got all the firepower on his side.'

'No, that's not it,' said Luc, with a determination that surprised even himself. 'We have to try, because if we don't, all that's left is to see who kills us first – Cheng, or the Coalition.'

And I still have one more card up my sleeve, he thought. One it might be best not to tell Zelia about.

TWENTY-TWO

The landscape below them curved in on itself as the flier carrying Luc and Zelia boosted upwards and into low orbit, the sky darkening and becoming filled with stars. They saw brief flashes of light, like lightning, from somewhere over the horizon.

'I'm guessing the fighting turned nuclear,' Zelia said quietly from beside him when he turned to look at her. She studied the console. 'No direct hits on any major targets yet, but only because there are still enough functioning countermeasures to take out the missiles before they reach their targets.'

'How many dead?'

'Hard to say,' said Zelia, pressed up close beside him in the tiny cramped cockpit. 'A hundred, maybe more. The majority of the dead were on our side, I'm afraid to say.'

A hundred, maybe more. More deaths within a few hours than had occurred amongst the Temur Council in centuries.

'You're planning something, aren't you?' she asked quietly.

He regarded her. 'What makes you say that?'

'Centuries of observational politics,' she replied. 'That, and the fact of what you did to that mechant in my laboratory, not to mention an entire Sandoz weapons platform.'

'Just before I left the *Sequoia*,' Luc explained, 'Sachs did something remotely to my lattice. He said he'd optimized it.'

'"Optimized"?'

'He said I wasn't using its full potential.' He glanced at her. 'It's also how I know where the stolen artefact is.'

She turned away from him, looking unsettled. 'I just hope whatever it is you're planning is good, because we're going to need nothing short of a miracle if we're going to get out of this alive.'

A sombre silence settled over them, and Luc distracted himself by keeping an eye on the flier's screens. He didn't want to tell her that survival wasn't part of his plan; he'd given up any hope of surviving Antonov's lattice some time ago.

'I'll tell you what, though,' said Zelia, suddenly. 'If, by some fucking miracle, I actually get out of this alive, I'm going to go a long, long way away and never come back.'

He glanced at her. 'Where would you go?'

She waved a hand towards the cockpit's ceiling. 'Out there, somewhere. With the right instantiation equipment and a growth-tank for clone bodies, I could extend my lifespan to thousands of years, maybe even longer. I'd travel out into the galaxy and see what I could find.'

'You mean you'd travel through the Founder Network?'

She gave him a bemused look. 'No, I'd build a ship, one that could take me out amongst the stars as close to the speed of light as I could push it. The Founder Network is a trap.'

'How do you mean?'

'I'm not saying it was intentionally built for that purpose, but I have a theory that once a species finds its way inside the Network, they either stumble across something that wipes them out, or they . . . they lose themselves inside it.'

'How?'

'Think about it. How big is the Network, really? Some of the earliest expeditions into it travelled as far as a *hundred trillion years* into the future. That's an unimaginable length of time. Think of what might happen to a civilization with access to the Founder Network over thousands of years, and not just centuries, like the Coalition. I wouldn't give it more than a couple of millennia at the outside before civilizations become sufficiently fragmented as they spread through the Network that they wind up forgetting where they came from. Plus, it explains the Fermi Paradox.'

'Excuse me?'

'It's a question that used to get posed before they discovered how to build transfer gates,' she explained. 'If you make the assumption that there must be intelligent life somewhere out there in the universe, and if you also assume it's inclined to spread out through space as we have, then why didn't our ancestors on Earth ever encounter them?'

'If there are aliens, then why aren't they here?'

'That's it exactly. But what we know now is that the Founder Network's been in existence for billions of years, apparently vacuuming up every intelligent race that comes across an entrance to it. That's why we never encountered living aliens before – because they discovered the Network first.'

'What does that have to do with not wanting to take a shortcut through the Network?'

'There are a hundred billion stars in our galaxy alone, Luc, with God knows how many intelligent civilizations out there who never had either the luck or the misfortune to stumble across the Network. None of us have any idea just what's out there, because as soon as we discovered a way inside the Network' – and here, she put a hand out in front of her chest, palm forward – 'we more or less came to a dead stop as far as the rest of the universe was concerned.'

'I guess it makes sense when you put it that way.' The flier was already tilting nose-up as it dropped out of orbit, shaking as it hit the upper reaches of the atmosphere.

Luc glanced at a screen and saw it would not be long before they reached Liebenau. The stars were fading from sight once more, and before long they were racing towards the rising sun, the terrain beneath them becoming increasingly mountainous the lower they dropped. Vast swathes of green and blue to the south marked the confluence of several rivers on their long journey to the coast.

In less than half an hour, they'd be at the Red Palace.

'Is there still fighting going on?' he asked Zelia.

'Some,' she replied. 'But most of the strikes I know about came from Sandoz ships in orbit, aimed at fabricant complexes.'

'Why them?'

'The fabrication systems here on Vanaheim are built for large-scale industrial construction. It's how we build our homes, but it's not that hard, if you know how, to retool them to manufacture weapons.'

'And that's what your friends have been doing?'

She nodded. 'The Sandoz are attacking fabrication plants fairly indiscriminately. Pretty much anything, really, that could be used to resist them.'

Another bright flare of light erupted from just over the horizon and the flier began to drop, losing altitude fast. The light grew in intensity, the flier responding by darkening the transparent sections of the hull until they were entirely opaque.

Screens and virtual panels flashed red all around them. One screen showed a swathe of green jungle rushing up towards them at a furious rate, and Luc swore under his breath when the flier suddenly levelled out, flying low over the treetops. The flier's AI announced critical damage to its hull.

'That was bad,' said Zelia, her voice high and tight. 'We got broadsided by an A-M missile. It was six kilometres from us when it detonated. Any closer, and neither of us would be here.'

Luc checked the view to their rear and saw a column of smoke rising up into a mushroom high above the landscape. He pulled his eyes away from the screen, heart palpitating.

The jungle gave way to level grasslands, and the flier dropped lower until it was barely skimming above the ground, rushing over shimmering oxbow lakes and gaining height only when it encountered patches of forest.

Luc saw they were headed for a series of rounded hills to the north, stretching across the horizon. The upper parts of several pale and shimmering towers could be seen rising from beyond the hills: Liebenau.

Zelia half-mumbled a series of commands, the fingers of her

right hand twitching as she focused on a screen immediately to one side of her. The hull began to de-opaque, making it easier to see their surroundings.

The flier banked hard, following the course of a river. Incandescent beams of light split the sky a moment before a ball of light, as bright as the midday sun, bloomed far overhead. The flier's skin opaqued immediately in response.

'That was a strike in near-orbit,' Zelia announced tersely. 'Doesn't matter. We're here.'

The flier rose again, barely skimming over the crest of a hill before suddenly dipping down again as it entered a valley on the far side. Luc saw Liebenau, via the flier's external sensors, stretched out before them in all its glistening diversity. A forest fire raged in woodlands lying east of the settlement, sending up a colossal column of smoke that curled in on itself as it rose.

The majority of the settlement appeared to have escaped the fighting unscathed, although a few buildings on the outskirts of the settlement appeared to be burning. A long section of the wall surrounding the Red Palace looked like it had been partly demolished, judging by what he could see, and the thick haze of dust in the air around it.

A haze of fast-moving dots swarmed around the rooftops within the Palace's walls, like bees around a hive. Mechants, apparently still locked in battle. Clearly the fight wasn't quite over yet.

The external feeds cut off, blocking their view of the settlement for several seconds before they returned. Luc felt his gorge rise as the flier span, like a ballerina performing a pirouette.

'That was a direct hit,' shouted Zelia. 'I'm putting us down before we get shot down. So whatever it is you've got in mind, now would be a really fucking good time to tell me!'

'First, we need to find the artefact,' Luc replied, pulling up an aerial map of the Red Palace and displaying it where Zelia could also see it. 'There,' he said, pointing to an L-shaped building not far from a gate set into the west-facing outer wall.

She glanced at him. 'You're sure that's where it is?'

'I could find my way to it blindfolded, believe me. It's right there. Is there any way someone can target that building, and take it out from a distance?'

'If I can figure out just who's leading the assault on Liebenau,' she replied, 'maybe I can get them to—'

A sledgehammer came crashing into Luc's skull.

He blinked, seeing a sky stained with smoke trails. Somehow, he was outside.

He realized Zelia was hauling on his arm, swearing and shouting at him. Smelling something burning, he took a breath, and choked on something clogging his throat.

Pulling free of her grasp, he rolled onto all fours as he hacked and coughed. His lungs felt like they were filled with burning embers.

'Come *on*,' Zelia screamed at him, reaching down and grabbing hold of his shoulder.

Luc stared up at her through watery eyes, seeing smudges of dirt streaking her face.

He looked around. She had dragged him into the shelter of a seating area overhung by tall, mossy ferns that partially hid them from sight. The nearest wall of the Palace was only about fifty metres away. Stone bridges arched over a wide moat surrounding the palace, leading towards tall archways piercing stone walls that had to be close on nine metres tall.

Looking back the other way, he saw the remains of their flier not too distant. The craft had ploughed a hole into the carefully maintained lawns surrounding the palace. It was clearly a write-off, a smoking ruin hard up against the trunk of an enormously ancient-looking gnarled tree, its branches dotted with autumn leaves.

'I tried to get hold of Ben,' said Zelia, her voice ragged, 'but I think he might be dead. He was the one coordinating the strike on the Red Palace. No one else is responding either.' She shook her head and laughed weakly. 'We're so fucking screwed, it's actually funny.'

Luc coughed again, the world swaying gently around him. He let Zelia lower him onto a seat, and squeezed his eyes shut until the worst of the dizziness had passed.

'The artefact,' he said, when he looked back up at her. 'We're close to it, Zelia. Very close.'

She sank to her knees on the grass before him. 'Luc, listen to me,' she said, looking more scared in that moment than he recalled ever seeing her before. 'I really think we might be the only ones left alive. Maybe we should try and get away from here, make a run for it while we still can—'

'No.' Luc shook his head irritably and forced himself to think. 'Not after everything I've been through.'

It was like the nightmare he'd suffered for so many years had finally come true, except he wasn't a child any more. Instead of Razorback Mountain looming in the distance, he saw the broad wall of Cheng's Red Palace – and instead of a ball of incandescent light and heat evaporating everyone and everything he had ever known and loved, he saw only smoke rising from a burning forest, and the flashing silver of mechants engaged in high-speed battles.

'Listen to me, Zelia,' he said, leaning forward and taking hold of her by the shoulders. 'What Cheng did to Benares made me into an orphan. I lost everything. *Everything*. I dedicated my life to hunting Antonov, except now I discover it should have been Cheng. I'll be damned if I'm going to stand by and let him deliver the final coup de grâce to Benares.' He shook his head violently. 'Not if I have any chance of doing something about it.'

Zelia stared at him like he was crazy. 'He has an army of mechants, Luc, and God knows how many Sandoz either already here or on their way through the Hall of Gates. We've *lost*, can't you see that? But if we can find another flier, we can—'

He got up and walked away from her without another word, heading for the nearest of the stone bridges passing over the moat around the Red Palace. He passed cultivated lawns and artfully arranged groves and, although there were several more flashes of light and the sound of distant detonations, he had a sense the battle was winding down. More than likely, Cheng was consolidating his victory.

Even so, the artefact was like a magnet, drawing Luc towards it. He felt like he could almost reach out and grasp it.

Hearing feet running down the gravel path behind him, he turned to see Zelia catch up with him.

'Are you sure?' he asked her.

She shrugged, dirty and exhausted. 'Fuck it,' she said, 'even if I get killed, I have a backup. Right?'

Luc knew Cheng would never allow her re-instantiation after everything that had happened, but also knew better than to say. He nodded and continued across the bridge without another word, surprised to find he was glad she had chosen to stay by his side.

They passed over the bridge and came to a tall arched gate giving access to the interior of the Red Palace. He saw that the wall tapered slightly as it rose towards grey stone battlements.

Thin trails of smoke rose from different points within the palace walls. Before them lay a cobbled street, and brick buildings with a carefully crafted appearance of great age.

He heard Zelia come up behind his shoulder. 'If we can't find a way to get hold of the artefact,' he said, 'our next option is to find some way to destroy it.'

'Can we do that?' she asked.

He shook his head. 'I don't know until we try. Have you been here before?'

'I know my way around the palace grounds a little,' she said. 'You think the artefact's somewhere around here?'

'It's just up ahead,' he told her, moving forward at a slow jog. He hadn't seen anyone – neither men, nor machines. 'Do we know what's happening in the rest of the Tian Di?'

'Last I heard, things aren't much better on Temur.' She followed him down the cobbled street. 'There were reports of fighting inside the White Palace with the Sandoz guarding the Hall of Gates.'

The buildings within the palace walls were closely packed together.

He glanced up, seeing mechants flying high above the cobbled street.

They made for the shadows cast by the overhanging roof of a pagoda-like building to their right, pressing themselves up against the wall. The mechants appeared not to have spotted them, and soon disappeared from sight.

They kept moving along the side of the building until they came to the next corner. Luc saw the building they were headed for and sensed the artefact's presence on the other side of a door, straight ahead.

'It's in there somewhere,' he said, pointing.

Something struck the cobblestones immediately before them and rolled closer.

It felt as if a giant hand had reached down, picking Luc up and throwing him several feet into the air. He landed hard next to the entrance to an alleyway, his entire body wracked with pain. For a few moments, the world was suffused with an eerie silence. Something in his shoulder and arm didn't feel quite right.

His hearing came back only slowly, but all he could hear at first was his own ragged breathing. He saw Zelia struggling to push herself upright against a nearby wall, one of her legs twisted at an odd angle. She had her hand to her chest, the fingers stained red.

A shadow passed overhead. Luc looked up to see another Sandoz heavy-lifter dropping to a landing a few streets away. As it descended, a shape swooped down from the heavy-lifter – a mechant, making straight for him.

'Stop,' he muttered.

Drifting suddenly to one side, the mechant crashed into a tiled roof, finally tumbling to the cobbles below like an oversized discarded toy.

More mechants appeared overhead. He sent them all scattering across the sky like storm-tossed leaves, but already he felt tired, enormously so, and struggled to stay awake.

Luc looked back over at Zelia, who stared back at him with a blank expression. The red stain on her chest had grown larger. He managed to crawl over to her, despite one of his arms being useless.

'Zelia,' he said, collapsing against the wall beside her. 'How bad?'

Her face was paler than he'd ever seen it, lips thin and translucent.

'It's not deep, I don't think,' she said. 'But I'm losing too much blood.'

'Can you get up?'

'No, Luc. Leave me be.'

'If you stay here, you'll die!'

She laughed weakly. 'I can't die, you fucking idiot. I have backups, remember?'

'Cheng would never let you come back.'

She stared at him with loathing. 'Fuck you,' she said. 'You think I don't know that?'

Nevertheless, she managed to struggle back onto her feet, and he draped his good arm around her, grabbing under one shoulder, holding her upright.

'We're nearly there,' he said, glancing up and seeing more mechants descending towards them. The taste of gritty ash was on his tongue, carried on the wind.

With a burst of effort, he dragged her towards the doorway. The artefact was just on the other side.

Voices, calling from somewhere nearby. He glanced to one side, but couldn't see where they were coming from.

The ground again came rushing towards him, hard enough this time to break several of his teeth. He could feel their ragged edges with the tip of his tongue. Another grenade, he guessed.

Rolling over, he saw Zelia lying motionless nearby, and that the door had opened from the inside, a darkened vestibule lying beyond.

The voices he'd heard came closer. A shadow fell across his face; a mechant, hovering less than a metre above him.

More shadows gathered around him, some people-shaped. Hands reached down and took a grip on him, lifting him up with the minimum of care.

But it wasn't over. Not yet.

TWENTY-THREE

'Is he awake?'

'One moment, Father Cheng,' said a voice in reply.

Light dazzled Luc's eyes. He tried to squeeze his eyelids shut, but found he couldn't, no matter how hard he tried. His eyeballs itched and burned furiously.

There was a faint hiss from close by his face, and cool vapour dampened his skin, dripping down his cheeks like tears. The itching and burning faded a little.

He twisted away from a beam of light bright enough that it felt like it could burn its way through the back of his head. Barely visible in the light were the silhouettes of figures standing around him in an otherwise darkened room. When he tried to move, he discovered his wrists had been secured to the arms of a high-backed chair with heavy straps. Other straps secured his feet to the chair's legs.

Leaning forward, he could see that he had been stripped naked. He swallowed, pain pulsing around his broken teeth. His mouth was still full of the taste of his own blood.

For some reason, he could neither blink nor close his eyes. The urge to block out the light was maddening, but there was nothing whatsoever he could do to avoid it.

'Yes, he does appear to be conscious,' said the second voice.

Luc twisted his head from side to side to try and see who had just spoken.

'If you don't mind me asking,' asked the voice of a third man, 'is what you've done to him *entirely* necessary?'

'I would say it was *absolutely* necessary, my dear Meinhard,' Cheng replied. 'Didn't you see what this creature and his accomplice did to poor Bailey? Or are you really suggesting someone guilty of such a crime deserves *better*?'

Meinhard Carter, Luc realized with a shock: the man Cheng had put in charge of the Tian Di's deep-space exploration. And the same man with whom Ambassador Sachs had attempted last-minute negotiations over the Founder Network.

'Of course not, Father Cheng,' Carter replied with nervous haste.

The pain in Luc's eyes was becoming extraordinary, maddening. An instant later he felt another burst of cool moisture on his face, reducing the pain and discomfort – but no more than marginally.

'Reduce that light,' said Cheng. 'I want our guest to be able to see himself quite clearly.'

The light dimmed a little, and someone sprayed more moisture into Luc's eyes. It tasted cool and damp and fresh on his tongue. He swallowed a few drops, filled with a sudden, raging thirst.

'I think he's thirsty,' said another, unidentifiable voice.

'Maybe we should give him something to drink,' chuckled yet another. 'Maybe I should . . . ?'

Luc heard a faint rustle, followed by a stifled giggle.

'Very droll,' he heard Cheng reply, with what sounded like faint humour. 'As you please – but *not*, I beg you, in his eyes. I don't want him to end up in so much pain that he can't talk.'

Something warm and sticky splashed onto Luc's torso and ran down between his thighs. One of the shadowy figures, he realized, was pissing on him.

He jerked at his restraints and tried to scream, but all that came out of his throat was a hoarse rattle.

'Enough of this,' Cheng snapped irritably, and the stream of urine ceased. 'Let him see.'

Someone turned the spotlight away from Luc's face, instead focusing it on the ceiling so that he could see his surroundings more clearly.

The room in which they had him was long and low and entirely bare of decoration. The floor had a drain at its centre, while large and unpleasantly sharp-looking hooks hung from the ceiling. A heavily muscled Sandoz warrior stood to one side of Luc, while Cheng, Carter and four others he did not recognize stood facing him. He guessed they were members of the Eighty-Five.

Glancing to his other side, he saw another, unfamiliar man standing immediately next to him. This man's apparent physical age was much younger, and he wore a plain black tunic, fluted at the waist, that reached very nearly to the ground. His face was gaunt, and devoid of emotion. Lifting a small bulb to Luc's face, the man quickly squirted moisture into his eyes, one after the other, before stepping back once more.

'Turn him so he can see her,' Cheng commanded.

The Sandoz warrior stepped around behind Luc's chair and, with a grunt, turned it through ninety degrees, the metal legs scraping noisily against the bare concrete floor. Luc found himself facing an identical steel chair, the body of a naked woman secured to it at the wrists and ankles.

Zelia had been so badly beaten he almost couldn't recognize her. Her face had swollen up, severely distorting her features, her whole body a patchwork of bruises and welts. Although fresh bandages had been placed over her chest wound, there were burn marks all across her breasts and thighs.

But that wasn't the worst thing.

Her eyelids had been cut away, along with her nose. Luc slowly understood that the same had been done to him, that this was the reason he could neither blink nor close his eyes. A second Sandoz warrior stood by Zelia, occasionally squirting moisture onto her exposed eyeballs, to prevent them from drying.

'Zelia has been most helpful,' said Cheng, stepping up beside Luc and nodding towards her, 'if initially uncooperative. But thanks to her wise decision to work with us, we now understand the full extent of your involvement in Winchell Antonov's revolution, as well as the nature of the Coalition technology inside your head.'

Cheng turned to the man in the dark tunic beside Luc. 'Jacob,' he said with a gesture, 'if you please.'

Jacob squirted more moisture onto Luc's face, regarding him with pitiless eyes.

'Jacob Moreland,' Luc managed to rasp.

'I understand,' said Moreland, 'that you came here hoping to prevent me from completing my mission. Don't you understand that everything Father Cheng does, he does out of love?'

It took an effort for Luc to say anything more, his tongue sliding across the ragged ruins of his teeth. 'Ambassador Sachs told me everything,' he said, spitting the words at Cheng and ignoring Moreland. 'You'd kill a whole world, rather than risk falling out of power.'

Cheng smiled sadly. 'It's a terrible price for so many people to pay, I agree entirely. But do you think I would do any such thing, if I really believed there could be any possible alternative?'

'Alternative to *what*?' Luc rasped. 'The Coalition are going to wipe you out. Don't you understand that?'

'Regardless of whatever offensive action the Coalition are planning, our Sandoz forces are well equipped to engage them.'

'You're insane. The Inimicals—'

'—are a product of Ambassador Sachs' imagination,' Cheng snapped. 'They do not *exist*. Jacob, please tell Mr Gabion what we're going to be doing here today.'

'The plan,' said Jacob, squirting more moisture onto Luc's naked eyeballs, 'is to perform a live dissection, starting with the lattice inside your skull. You'll be kept awake and conscious throughout, in order that your responses may be measured and assessed.'

A door slid open, and a mechant floated into the centre of the room. Razor-tipped instruments glinted from its underbelly.

'The artefact,' Luc rasped. 'I know it's close to here.'

'Now do you see how badly we've let things slip over the years?' Cheng declared, turning angry eyes on those of his advisors who were present. 'Do you *see* how much this man knows?'

They all glanced away, as if the walls around them were of sudden and unexpected interest.

'Father—' one of the men tried to say.

'Shut up!' Cheng shouted, his face twisted in fury. 'You've failed me. You've *all* failed me. I should send you all to the same hell as these two. Do you understand?'

'The artefact is here, yes,' Moreland told Luc with a smirk. 'But not, I assure you, for much longer.'

Luc laughed, the sound descending into violent, hacking coughs. His eyes were becoming painfully dry once more, but Moreland made no move to squirt more moisture onto them.

He looked back over at Zelia. He tried to script to her, but got no answer. She gazed dully back at him.

'I'm sorry, Zelia,' Luc whispered. 'I wanted to tell you, but I was afraid you might stop me.'

Her lips moved fractionally, and a faint mumble emerged from the bruised wreckage of her mouth.

'What was that?' Cheng demanded sharply.

Luc licked dry, cracked lips, and shuddered with relief when Moreland finally stepped forward and sprayed moisture onto his eyeballs.

'When I met Ambassador Sachs that last time on the *Sequoia*,' Luc said to Cheng, 'he gave me the means to track the artefact Moreland brought back here. But on the way here, I realized he'd given me much more than just that.'

'I am not in the mood for speeches, Mr Gabion,' said Cheng, sounding irritable. 'Please get to the point, and all this unpleasantness will be over that much sooner.'

'At first I wondered, *why me?* But then I realized he didn't see it as being a decision he could make. The choice had to be made by someone from the Tian Di – someone like me.'

'What the hell are you talking about?' demanded Cheng, his tone suspicious.

'I realized the Ambassador had given me a way to control the artefact, not just track it down.' Luc smiled through cracked and broken teeth. 'Even activate it, should it happen to be within sufficient proximity.'

Cheng gaped at him. They all did.

'Kill him,' Cheng barked. '*Now.*'

'Too late,' Luc whispered, and triggered the artefact.

EPILOGUE

He sat on a bench and watched an entire world die.

First, the atmosphere rippled outwards from a central point, as if an object the size of a moon had struck it. A haze spread up and out from that same central point like dark smoke, spiralling upwards with sufficient velocity to escape the gravitational tug of the planet itself.

Seen from a distance of some tens of thousands of kilometres, it made for a startlingly beautiful sight, until he remembered that hurricanes of a ferocity unseen since the planet's formation were tearing the soil from its bedrock, and sending vast, towering tsunami sweeping across its continents, scouring it clean of any evidence that men had ever been there.

He kept watching, as the crust was stripped away from the hot molten core. By now, much of Vanaheim had been reduced to a smear of dust and gravel spread along the path of its orbit.

The laws of physics, briefly interrupted by the activation of the quantum disruptor, began reasserting themselves. He saw trillion-ton chunks of debris collide with each other, obscured by that same dense haze, still spreading out into a circle around the nearby sun.

I made this happen.

No matter how many times Luc said it to himself, he couldn't quite take it in. Perhaps he never would.

Finally, he dismissed the recording. No matter how often he watched it, it always had the same effect, like being punched in the gut at the same time as having his head submerged in a bucket of ice-water.

He looked around the communal lounge, one wall of which displayed an entirely different view – that of a supermassive black hole orbited by blue-shifted stars, caught in slowly decaying orbits that would eventually send them spiralling to their doom. The lounge itself was vast, filled with dozens of couches and tables, all of them currently unoccupied. He was quite alone, but not, he knew, for very much longer.

He passed the time in silent contemplation, unsure of what he would say or do when his visitors finally arrived.

When he grew bored enough, he ran the recording a second time.

He stiffened on hearing a door open at the far end of the lounge, somewhere behind him. Footsteps echoed as they crossed the floor, growing closer. He felt a tightness in his chest, suddenly afraid to turn around.

'A magnificent sight, is it not?' asked Antonov, coming to stand by him and nodding towards the footage. 'Zelia would have had much to say about this, I think.'

Luc looked up at him. Antonov's lips were curled in a wistful smile, only half-visible through his bushy black beard.

Horst Sachs stood just behind and to one side of Antonov, shorn of his mirror mask, and dressed in colourful robes entirely unlike those he had worn in the course of his duties as Coalition Ambassador.

'Zelia once told me that she wanted to journey across the galaxy,' Luc managed to say.

'She once told me the same thing too,' said Antonov, nodding, regarding Luc with a merry smile. 'And here we are, enjoying those same sights for her. A touch of irony that it should be us two dead men, rather than her.'

The lounge they occupied was not real, of course – or not real in the way Luc had understood such things by the measure of his former existence. The starship whose lounge they occupied, here so very close to the heart of the Milky Way, was in reality barely any larger than a dandelion seed. The lounge had only a virtual existence. And yet Luc's subjective experience of the vessel was of a vast and luxurious liner, measuring perhaps fifty kilometres from bow to stern.

There were thousands of other passengers, in an astonishing variety of forms. And yet, by a simple trick of focus, Luc could make them effectively disappear from his sight, giving him the illusion of solitude. They were still there, of course – or as *there* as he, Antonov or indeed the lounge were – and every one of them shared the same ability. They could all, if they so chose, occupy precisely the same spot without ever being aware of one another's presence.

Winchell Antonov looked much the same as Luc remembered him from the deep tunnels beneath Aeschere. Luc understood that this was now really a kind of affectation, since both he and Antonov were in a position to choose any form they desired. But, given their proximity to their former lives, they had each made the same, unspoken decision to maintain outward forms that closely matched those they had been born with.

Perhaps, give or take a few thousand years of subjective lifetime, they might come to see things differently. But not yet.

'So our friends in the Coalition put you back together again,' said Luc.

'That, and more,' Antonov agreed.

'But *how*?' asked Luc. 'There was only a fragment of you inside me. Nothing more.'

'I must apologize,' said the Ambassador from beside Antonov. 'That brief moment of physical contact between you and I aboard the *Sequoia* was all that was necessary to allow me to make a complete copy not only of your mind-state, stored within your lattice, but also of Antonov's. Under the circumstances, there was no time to explain as much as I wanted to.'

'You essentially tricked me by getting me to take your hand,' said Luc. 'Is that it?'

'I regret the deception,' said the Ambassador, a touch disingenuously.

'Good old Coalition super-science, eh?' Antonov said brightly.

'I am sorry for being unable to meet with either of you before now,' Sachs continued. 'But I've been very busy these past few weeks, negotiating with the interim government on Temur. They're still fighting renegade Sandoz forces refusing to accept their authority, but they expect to overcome these sooner rather than later.'

'So are you here, or there?' asked Luc.

'Both,' Sachs responded.

Luc sighed. 'None of this has been easy for me. It's . . .' he waved a hand.

'Too much to take in, so soon?' Antonov chuckled. 'Entirely understandable. But allow me to thank you for saving my life.'

Luc shook his head. 'I was too busy worrying over my own to worry about yours too much.'

'Even so, you did what had to be done.'

'I *destroyed a world*,' said Luc.

'In order to save the rest of the human race, yes,' agreed Sachs.

'Cheng had endless opportunities to change things for the better,' said Antonov. 'And few of the Council were willing to challenge his rule. They were seduced by the same things that always seduce human beings; power, and privilege. A few amongst them will be missed, but not, I think, so many.'

'But what about the threat of the Inimicals?' asked Luc. 'Nobody's been able to tell me anything about that.'

'I have news on that front,' said Sachs. 'Coalition forces have successfully wrested control of the Thorne transfer gate from the Sandoz forces guarding it. We will more than likely seal it, hopefully forever.'

'Destroy it, you mean.'

'Better that, Mr Gabion, than risk the alternative.'

'You still haven't told me how you managed to build a whole new Antonov out of just that fragment I was carrying around in my head.'

'You are not the only one the Ambassador tricked,' Antonov explained. 'He did the same to me on one of our last meetings, taking the opportunity to copy my mind-state to his own lattice and then transmit it all the way to the Coalition. Then they combined my old memories with newer ones, some shared with you, following my placing a lattice inside your skull.'

'Indeed,' said the Ambassador. 'Our lattice technology takes advantage of certain properties of the ultimately granular structure of reality at its most base level. Further, when combined firstly with certain properties of superluminal communications, such as the ability to maintain constant contact between two points regardless of distance, and secondly with a memory substrate that can . . .'

Luc groaned, unable to take it all in.

Antonov chuckled and clapped the Ambassador hard on the shoulder. 'Yes, all very dry and dull. Much more fun to call Sachs a wizard, and say that he has stolen our spirits away to some magical realm. But what he is trying to describe is the means by which we are able to witness Vanaheim's destruction.'

'All right,' said Luc, 'you've answered pretty much everything I wanted to know, except for one thing – why did you both want to meet me here, on this ship, so very far from home?'

'As Winchell pointed out, we do have a magnificent view of the Milky Way,' said Sachs. 'And besides, it feels appropriate to our purpose in bringing you here.'

'Appropriate in what way?'

Antonov turned to the Ambassador, punching him lightly on the upper arm. 'Go on, tell him, Horst.'

Sachs cleared his throat, regarding Antonov with a mixture of amusement and befuddlement. 'There was, it turns out, some information of genuine value that Father Cheng recovered via the Thorne gate,' he explained, stepping closer to Luc. 'Here.'

Sachs opened one hand, to reveal something very like a firefly, glowing with inner radiance, nestled on his palm.

'What is it?'

'Please,' said Sachs. 'Take it.'

Luc opened his hand, and the firefly hopped from Sach's open hand and into Luc's.

Luc closed his fingers, the light of the firefly fading away at the same moment that a torrent of information spilled into his conscious mind. A second later he regarded his two companions with an expression of astonishment.

'You discovered yet *another* race in the Milky Way?' he gasped.

'So it seems,' Sachs agreed. 'Naturally, we intend to be vastly more cautious in meeting with them than we were even throughout our initial encounters with the Inimicals. We have, however, even in the brief period since making contact, experienced a level of communication with them that has proven to be far more than merely satisfying.'

'And that's why you're here?'

'That's why *we're* here, Luc,' said Sachs. 'All three of us.'

'But – another race? Are you sure that's wise? I mean, after everything that happened with the Inimicals?'

'We have learned from our past mistakes,' Sachs explained, 'and have learned much about this new species already. Enough to be convinced that they offer no possible threat to us. More than that, each has much to gain from the other.'

'But . . . why bring *me* here?'

'Our reward,' said Antonov, 'for services rendered.'

'Few in history have had the opportunity to observe or indeed engage in a genuine first-contact scenario,' added Sachs.

'And that's where you come in,' said Antonov, his grin growing wide. 'You *are* an information specialist, are you not?'

'We have been given an opportunity to study this civilization's history,' said Sachs. 'It's an incredible opportunity, and one we hope to share with the citizens of the Tian Di as our two societies become more fully reintegrated. But you have to tell me first whether you want to be involved.'

Luc gazed again at the sight of the Milky Way, a wreath of stars circling a stormy void.

'Yes,' he said.

THE END.

Acknowledgements

This time, particular thanks go out to my agent, Dorothy Lumley, who was the first to believe there was potential in my ratty first-novel manuscript way back in the Nineties. I should also take time to mention the sterling work done not only by beta reader *numero uno*, Jim Campbell, in helping get this manuscript into shape, but also by those hard-working people at Tor who keep me from putting my foot in my mouth more often than might be the case otherwise. Thanks, guys.